The Best AMERICAN SHORT STORIES 1993

GUEST EDITORS OF
THE BEST AMERICAN SHORT STORIES

1978 TED SOLOTAROFF
1979 JOYCE CAROL OATES
1980 STANLEY ELKIN
1981 HORTENSE CALISHER
1982 JOHN GARDNER
1983 ANNE TYLER
1984 JOHN UPDIKE
1985 GAIL GODWIN
1986 RAYMOND CARVER
1987 ANN BEATTIE
1988 MARK HELPRIN
1989 MARGARET ATWOOD
1990 RICHARD FORD
1991 ALICE ADAMS
1992 ROBERT STONE
1993 LOUISE ERDRICH

The Best AMERICAN SHORT STORIES 1993

Selected from
U.S. and Canadian Magazines
by LOUISE ERDRICH
with KATRINA KENISON

With an Introduction by Louise Erdrich

HOUGHTON MIFFLIN COMPANY
BOSTON • NEW YORK 1993

ISSN 0067-6233
ISBN 0-395-63628-0
ISBN 0-395-63627-2 (PBK.)

Printed in the United States of America

AGM 10 9 8 7 6 5 4 3 2 1

Contents

Foreword

WHEN I BECAME the annual editor of *The Best American Short Stories* in 1990, I was conscious of the fact that the three editors who nurtured the collection through its first seventy-five years approached their task with no small degree of commitment. Edward O'Brien edited the series for twenty-six years, from its inception in 1915 until 1941. Martha Foley carried on for the next thirty-five years and was surrounded by stacks of short stories when she died at age eighty. Shannon Ravenel produced thirteen collections while raising her two children.

What had their lives been like, I wondered, swept along as they were on a never-ending current of stories? How had they coped, once the novelty of receiving fifty or sixty magazines a week had worn off? Two of those three editors are long gone; only Shannon Ravenel could offer advice. Even though she already had her hands full with new projects, she had lost none of her zeal for this one. "Read everything," she advised. "Stay open-minded. Never write someone off just because you've read twenty-five of his stories and none of them has worked; the twenty-sixth might be wonderful."

It did not take long for me to begin to sense what it was that had fostered such enduring devotion in my predecessors. Editing this anthology is not just a job, it is a vocation — rewarding, challenging, sometimes all-consuming, but above all great fun. There is the challenge of staying abreast of the current — I suspect every editor has grappled with the feeling of always being behind when confronted with the task of reading more than

2500 stories a year — and there is also the suspense borne of knowing that each magazine, no matter how large or small, may harbor a marvelous discovery.

What joyful work, to bear good news each spring to the twenty writers whose stories are chosen, and to the astute magazine editors who first published them. Perhaps this annual task is the one I look forward to most of all, for every writer, young or old, emerging or well established, seems pleased to have a particular work singled out for recognition. "The thrill hasn't gone away yet," admitted an author making her debut in the series this year, "and neither is the bruise I got when, in my glee at receiving your letter, I fell down in my wallpapering water. It's a mark I'll bear gladly."

The appearance of a new volume of *The Best American Short Stories* each fall gives rise to strong feelings and spirited dialogue. One newspaper critic, dismayed by the paucity of humor in recent editions, declared that she would not review the anthology again until she could say something more positive — but promised that she would continue to read it. (I am happy to report that this year those who seek humor here will find it.) Another critic, also writing about last year's volume, proclaimed, "The mere act of choosing the best from the rest has produced a lasting work," resulting in "the best collection since Carver's in 1986 and John Gardner's in 1982." The stories in any given year are judged not only on their own merit, but also by how well they stack up against fondly remembered volumes from decades past.

Readers, too, contribute to the dialogue. A schoolteacher who uses the series in her classroom wrote that one of her students had become fascinated by an author whose first published story appeared in the anthology — how could they learn more about the writer? A man in Israel, his appetite for stories whetted by last year's volume, offered to pay for copies of the hundred notable stories of the year listed at the back. Usually people write simply to alert me to a story they have read which has moved them deeply.

This year, we were fortunate to have Louise Erdrich as the guest editor. She approached her task with the best possible combination of integrity and delight. Each exceptional story was occasion for celebration; the borderline cases were given long contemplation. The care she lavished on this volume is evident both in the selections themselves and in the order in which she has chosen to present them, and the book she assembled is much more than the sum of its parts.

The Contributors' Notes at the back of the book are, in a sense, a continuation of the ongoing dialogue between those who write short stories and those who read them. It is a dialogue that the authors themselves take seriously and in which they participate with generosity. As one contributor confessed, "Enclosed is my commentary, which of course was harder to write than the story itself."

The stories chosen for this year's anthology were originally published in magazines issued between January 1992 and January 1993.

The qualifications for selection are: 1. original publication in nationally distributed American or Canadian periodicals; 2. publication in English by writers who are American or Canadian, or who have made the United States or Canada their home; 3. publication as short stories (novel excerpts are not knowingly considered). A list of magazines consulted for this volume appears at the back of the book. Publications that want to make sure that their fiction will be considered each year should include the series editor on their subscriptions list (Katrina Kenison, *The Best American Short Stories,* Houghton Mifflin Company, 222 Berkeley Street, Boston, Massachusetts 02116-3764).

K.K.

Introduction

DOWN THE HILL and around the lake, in the center of this western town, there is a market-restaurant-butchershop-pharmacy-cafe where coffee is ten cents a cup and you can buy dog food, Hudderite-raised chickens, lefse, and huckleberry pie in season. Large yellow-and-white-striped cellophane bags of Vernell's Licorice Twisters are stacked on the lowest reaches of this store's candy section. In preparation for a long, hard season of snow, and for reading short stories deep into the night, I bought many packages. The snow came, the manuscripts deepened, and I settled in to the reading. Now I report to you, heavier, head full of telling images, that this was an unusually good year for short stories.

Perhaps it's weather, the dearth or timing of the snow, the rain, the simple flow of human events — no one can actually assess what makes some years better than others for writing. This collection is at least twice as good as it appears. For every story included, there was one almost as extraordinary. Katrina Kenison, the series editor, laboriously culled thousands to choose 120, and I pared them down to about 25, and finally to 20, but both of us agreed that, in this bumper crop year, we had gathered enough fine work to make two volumes.

There are readers-in-bed, bathtub readers, stand-up readers, noshing readers, and probably even readers who sit in the approved fashion, in an easy chair, pillow at the small of the back, under a good glare-free reading lamp. In an attempt to be fair, I always sat in the same spot, on the floor, propped with pillows. I can't help but wonder where all of the writers who edited this collection before me read their stories. I do know that Katrina Kenison did so with her infant son in her arms. I read sometimes with our daughters sprawled alongside me on the floor, picture books splayed brilliantly open, but our agreement was that they not distract while my head was lowered.

I ate licorice only, drank water, no wine, and attempted to replicate the exact lighting, time of evening, degree of peace, for each session. To clear my mind, I sometimes did sit in a hot bath — stories at hand on a safe, dry shelf — but I hasten to add that I always calibrated the water's temperature precisely, so as not to give one story or another an advantage. I did sit-ups to keep alert, mulled and chewed and worried over text. I read these pieces without knowing who wrote them, and work by those I knew, the work of loved ones, I did not choose even if it meant omitting my sister Lise Erdrich's, and my other very favorite stories, Michael Dorris's, from consideration. Still, I can claim only to have done the best that can be done by one woman and a case of black licorice.

The best short stories contain novels. Either they are densely plotted, with each line an insight, or they distill emotions that could easily spread on for pages, chapters. I have heard that one's downfalls are often also one's greatest strengths, and am by that thought encouraged to admit that I have no particular definition of what a short story *should* be. Therefore, this group is various in tone, outlook, tenor, and form.

My most basic criterion for selection was that the work provide pleasure. For the edification of short story puritans, intellectual pleasure was my aim here, the singed gulp of mental satisfaction and emotional rue with which a truly good short story is consumed. And for you short story sensualists, let me also add that I went for texture, place, aroma, succulence, and stiff particularity. These stories can be read once, twice, many times, slowly. I found that the best ones haunted me for days after the reading, and that lingering also became part of the selection process. If the story was strong enough to hold on to me, then I did not let go of it.

Usually these collections are structured alphabetically, according to author. I wanted to play with the order so that I could set off the strengths of each piece. The collection begins with the most evocative first paragraph, which I think belongs to John Updike's "Playing with Dynamite," an unostentatious, painful, faultless story about a crack in the ice, a marriage, and a man's entry into the uneven reality of old age. I'm also pleased that Mr. Updike should for once appear first, since he is usually last by alphabet in this collection. The story that appears next, Mary Gaitskill's "The Girl on the Plane," was the only piece that came in from a women's magazine and did not seem edited to patronize its readership. Gaitskill writes a grimy portrait of a man who has undergone personal corrosion because he has raped a young woman who very deeply loved him. He seems bound, like Coleridge's wedding guest, to continually tell his tale to women in the slim hope of redemption. This piece is powerful, macabre, and eerily ordinary, full of undertone and twist. The editors at *Mirabella* must have decided that their readers have acute brains beneath their hairstyles. I'm grateful for this story and hope the trend continues.

To my mind, Alice Munro has attained short story sainthood and can practically do no wrong. "A Wilderness Station," one of the hundred notables listed at the back of this volume, is as strong as "A Real Life," but, like Mr. Wilkinson Speirs in the story, I could not resist Dorrie Beck. Larry Woiwode's flowing "Silent Passengers" is one of the most moving short pieces of fiction I have ever read. Its impact is so personal, its lessons so deep, that I believe I will always keep this story near in heart. "Queen Wintergreen," by Alice Fulton, follows. This is a densely woven, abstractly textured, fierce and feminine tale about pride, entrapment, the personal-political complications of Catholicism, and social expectation.

A strange feast, a fit of brilliance, "The Man Who Rowed Christopher Columbus Ashore" is one of Harlan Ellison's wittiest visionary explosions. There is nothing to say about this story but that it just *is,* somehow, and it works with and against all expectations on a bewildering level.

Anyone who ever was a teenager, or has raised a teenager, or knows a teenager will read "Poltergeists" nodding and sighing and wishing that Jane Shapiro simply had a vivid imagination.

She does, and yet everything she writes about is also unbearably real. This story could be included in a time capsule about American life in this last decade of the twentieth century.

Katrina Kenison tells me that she was continually handed Thom Jones's "I Want to Live!" by readers who knew what she was up to, and indeed, this is a piece of such humor, force, and agony that I felt it should be centered in this book. "I Want to Live!" needs counterweights, because it is, at once, impossible to read and impossible not to read, and so vivid that I went out and got a CA 125 blood test the next week. This story needs Susan Power's "Red Moccasins" on one side and Tony Earley's "Charlotte," on the other, not to prop it in any way, but to deflect its head-on force.

Coming across the best short stories out of the boxes of stories that were sent to me was a little like having a perfect blackjack turn up in a game — a natural, a bit of grace. I felt that way about "Red Moccasins." This story strikes at every level. It is, simultaneously, a love tale, a mother-child heart-wrencher, traditionally Lakota, and, as well, a Hans Christian Andersen dream recast with a powerful dislocated energy. Power is an intensely intellectual and emotional writer whose gifts are equal to the rage and sympathy that one feels for her characters. Her story "Moonwalk" is among those mentioned at the end of this collection.

Tony Earley, who wrote "Charlotte," also wrote "My Father's Heart," a far different, more serious, many-layered story that I hope readers will seek in their local libraries or in his forthcoming collection. Stories run in types, and the only reason "Charlotte" appears here instead of "My Father's Heart" is that Earley does the practically impossible with "Charlotte." This story is incredibly funny, effortlessly convincing, and concerns professional wrestling. His use of heightened slapstick is even uplifting.

In contrast, "What the Thunder Said," by Janet Peery, is a cloud so low it becomes a richly mudded clump of earth, a piece so vital and brutal that it is nothing short of believable. The setting and tone couldn't be more different from "Naked Ladies," Antonya Nelson's rich, familial tale. I approached "Man, Woman and Boy," a story by Stephen Dixon from the *Western Humanities Review,* with some skepticism because of its surprising form; but I ended up feeling as though I'd been seen through, spared, assisted, and in some deep way understood. Dixon's inspired chunk of complexity forms the image of a marriage and its attendant ambivalences, fears, and pleasures like nothing else I've ever read. There is no way to tell a moment's truth more simply than to make it this involuted.

Some stories have a distinct sensuousness attached to their first readings. For instance, Andrea Lee's "Winter Barley" has the odor to me of very old and well-oiled Moroccan leather and the texture of cracked gold leaf. Ancient lusts, narrated by a coolly decadent young woman in white cotton underwear, make this perhaps the most politically incorrect and humanly satisfying of erotic tales. Joanna Scott's "Concerning Mold upon the Skin, Etc." is next, an exquisite, tantalizing piece that leaves one in a choice state of frustration, grateful for this writer's existence yet wanting more, more, more. For that reason, "Pray Without Ceasing," by Wendell Berry, directly follows. His is such a different sort of story — a full-course, long-stretch, generational reminiscence. Beautifully knit, pitch-perfect in design, this story is a meal after which you don't want coffee or brandy or even a cigar, but simply to walk outside and gaze up into dark space.

Although these are stories by American writers, the settings and characters are like our hodgepodge cross-fertilized culture — anybody, anywhere. I'm glad to have found Kim Edwards's "Gold," not just for its unexpected locale but for its classic rendition of madness, greed, poverty, and an agonizing dream of possibility. Salt ocean blows through Diane Johnson's "Great Barrier Reef." Her portrait of an unwilling traveler is a picture of us all, so often displeased, and yet seduced gradually by the details of our own lives and natures. The penultimate scene is such a transcendent moment of destructive oneness that I will permanently harbor the unseen picture.

Although I read each of these stories with the name of the author emphatically blacked out, I did search in the anonymous piles for telltale evidence of my favorite authors. I always feel that when starting one of Lorrie Moore's stories I've lit an exploding cigar and don't know when my hair will start burning. Sure enough. "Terrific Mother" is ten-licorice-twister funny. It is a firecracker-studded fruitcake, and it is, as well, immensely sad and savage in its unsparing personal gaze.

This book ends with the story that is best read at a lingering pace, and has, as well, the most devastating last line in the collection. Mary Gordon's eidetic and detailed "The Important Houses" builds itself around the reader. The description here is so meticulous and compelling that it verges on memoir, and yet the line blurs, for Gordon's powers to recreate are so profound. "The Important Houses" has the gift of deeply imagined conjuring and presents the presiding genius of a place or person in every sentence.

Because I am not, after all, free of subjective whims no matter how hard I try to be impartial, I hope that after finishing the last story in this collection the reader will turn to the back pages listing the other best stories. W. D. Wetherell's energetic and yet elusive "The Road to the City" is one story I would have included, for instance, if we had had more pages, as is Denis Johnson's "Rescuing Ed," Jack Cady's "Tinker," "Nurses," by Ellen Cooney, "Cutter," by C. E. Poverman, and "Not for Sale," by Judith Ortiz Cofer. There are terrific stories by Alice Adams, John Edgar Wideman, and Robert Olen Butler.

Previous guest editors of this series have felt compelled to say something of this sort: "I took pains to be fair but found that many of the best stories were published in *The New Yorker*." I did too. However, since I'm writing this essay in an unusual week in which a work of fiction does *not* appear in that magazine, this may be the last time that one has to cavil or apologize. I dearly hope not. Each year there are fewer paying venues for short fiction, and since we all need to make a living, that means fewer writers concentrate on stories, fewer people put their best moments into tense, shorter works, saving them up instead for longer and more salable book manuscripts. In the end, fewer readers will seek and find.

Harper's Magazine, The Atlantic Monthly, The Paris Review, Story, The Georgia Review, New England Review, GlimmerTrain, Ploughshares, Antaeus, TriQuarterly, and the other magazines included in the list at the end of this collection, have continued to fiercely nourish the short story form. Who can ever know what jobs and passions and theories collide in editorial or advertising offices each day over such decisions? This collection exists because within magazines and book companies and schools and universities, there are people committed to celebrating fine writing.

Along with Houghton Mifflin and the dedication of Katrina Kenison, I'd like to thank them. Most of all, since magazines pay, but the human heart invents, thanks to all writers who work tenaciously and for uncertain recompense, who remind us that stories matter, stories have meaning, all human stories address the mystery.

LOUISE ERDRICH

JOHN UPDIKE

Playing with Dynamite

FROM THE NEW YORKER

ONE ASPECT OF CHILDHOOD Fanshawe had not expected to return in old age was the mutability of things — the willingness of a chair, say, to become a leggy animal in the corner of his vision, or the sensation that the solid darkness of an unlit room is teeming with inimical presences. Headlights floated on the skin of Fanshawe's windshield like cherry blossoms on black water, whether signifying four motorcycles or two trucks he had no idea, and he drove braced, every second, to crash into an invisible obstacle.

It had taken him over fifty years to internalize the physical laws that overruled a ten-year-old's sense of nightmare possibilities — to overcome irrational fear and to make himself at home in the linear starkness of a universe without a supernatural. As he felt the ineluctable logic of decay tightening its grip on his body, these laws seemed dispensable; he had used them, and now was bored with them. Perhaps an object *could* travel faster than the speed of light, and we each have an immortal soul. It didn't, terribly, matter. The headlines in the paper, with their campaigns and pestilences, seemed directed at somebody else, like the new movies and television specials and pennant races and beer commercials — somebody younger and more easily excited, somebody for whom the world still had weight. Living now in death's immediate neighborhood, he was developing a soldier's jaunty indifference; if the bathtub in the corner of his eye as he shaved were to take on the form of a polar bear and start mauling him, it wouldn't be the end of the world. Even the end of the world, strange to say, wouldn't be the end of the world.

His wife was younger than he, and spryer. Frequently, she impatiently passed him on the stairs. One Sunday afternoon, when they were going downstairs to greet some guests, he felt her at his side like a little gust of wind, and then saw her, amazingly reduced in size, kneeling on the stairs, which were thickly carpeted, several steps below him. He called her name, and thought of reaching down to restrain her, but she, having groped for a baluster and missed, rapidly continued on her way, sledding on her shins all the way to the bottom, where she reclined at the feet of their astonished visitors, who had knocked and entered. "She's all right," Fanshawe assured them, descending at his more stately pace, for he knew, watching her surprising descent, that she had met no bone-breaking snag in her progress.

And, indeed, she did rise up as resiliently as a cartoon cat, brimming with girlish embarrassment, though secretly pleased, he could tell, with having so spontaneously provided their little party a lively initial topic of discussion. Their guests, who included a young doctor, set her up on the sofa, with a bag of ice on the more bruised and abraded of her shins, and conducted a conversational investigation that concluded she had caught her heel in the hem of her dress, unusually long, in the new fashion. A little rip in the stitching of the hem seemed to confirm the analysis and to remove all mystery from the event.

Yet later, after she had limped into bed beside her husband, she asked, "Wasn't I good, not to tell everybody how you pushed me?"

"I never touched you," Fanshawe protested, but without much passion, because he was not entirely sure. He remembered only her appearance, oddly shrunk by perspective on the stairs in their downward linear recession, and the flash of his synapses that pictured his reaching out and restraining her, and his dreamlike inability to do so. She blamed him, he knew, for not having caught her, for not having done the impossible, and this was as good as his pushing her. She was, in their old age, a late-blooming feminist, and he accepted his role in her mind as the murderous man with whom she happened to be stuck, in a world of murderous men. The forces that had once driven them together now seemed to her all the product of a male conspiracy. If he had not literally pushed her on the stairs, he had compelled her to live in a house with a grandiose stairway and had dictated, in collusion with male fashion designers, the dangerous length of her skirt and height of her heels; and this was as good as a push. He tried to recall his emotions as he watched her body cascade out of his reach, and came up with a cool pang of what might be called polite astonishment, underneath a high hum of constant grief, like the cosmic background radiation. He recalled a view of a town's rooftops covered in snow, beneath a dome of utterly emptied blue sky.

His wife relented, seeing him so docilely ready to internalize her proposition. "Sweetie, you didn't push me," she said. "But I did think you might have caught me."

"It was all too quick," he said, unconvinced by his own self-defense. With the reality of natural law had receded any conviction of his own virtue. Their guests that afternoon had included his wife's daughter, by an old and almost mythical marriage. He could scarcely distinguish his stepchildren from his children by his own former marriage, or tell kin from spouses. He was polite to all these tan, bouncy, smooth-skinned, sure-footed, well-dressed young adults — darlings of the advertisers, the now generation — who claimed to be related to him, and he was flattered by their mannerly attentions, but he secretly doubted the reality of the connection. His own mother, some years ago, had lain dead for two days at the bottom of the cellar stairs of a house where he had allowed her to live alone, feeble and senile. He was an unnatural son and father both, why not a murderous husband? He knew that the incident would live in his wife's head as if he had in fact pushed her, and thus he might as well remember it also, for the sake of marital harmony.

At the Central Park Zoo, the yellow-white polar bears eerily float in the cold water behind the plate glass, water the blue-green color on a pack of Kool cigarettes (the last cigarettes Fanshawe had smoked, thinking the menthol possibly medicinal), and if a polar bear, dripping wet, were to surface up through his bathtub tomorrow morning while he shaved, the fatal swat of the big clawed paw would feel like a cloud of pollen.

Things used to be more substantial. In those middle years, as Fanshawe gropingly recalled them, you are hammering out your destiny on bodies still molten and glowing. One day, he had taken his children ice-skating on a frozen river — its winding course miraculously become a road, hard as steel, hissing beneath their steel edges. As he stood talking to the mother of some other young children, his six-year-old son had fallen at his feet, without a cry or thump, simply melting out of the lower edge of Fanshawe's vision, which was fastened on the reddened cheeks and shining eyes, the perfect teeth and flirtatiously curved lips of Lorna Kramer, his fellow-parent. A noise softly bubbled up through the cracks in their conversation; the little body on the ice was whimpering, and when Fanshawe impatiently directed his son to shut up and to get up, the muffled words "I can't" rose as if from beneath the ice.

It developed that the boy's leg was broken. Just standing there complaining about the cold, he had lost his balance with his skate caught in a crack, and twisted his shinbone to the point of fracture. How soft and slender our growing skeletons are! Fanshawe, once his wife and the other woman and their clustering children had made the problem clear to him, carried the boy in his arms up the steep and snowy riverbank. He felt magnificent, doing so. This was real life, he remembered feeling — the idyllic Sunday afternoon suddenly crossed by disaster's shadow, the gentle and strenuous rescue, the ride to the hospital, the emergency-room formalities, the arrival of the jolly orthopedic surgeon in his parka and Ski-Doo boots, the laying on of the cast in warm plaster strips, the drying tears, the imminent healing. Children offer access to the tragic, to the great dark that stands outside our windows, and in the urgency of their needs bestow significance; their fragile lives veer toward the dangerous margins and measure the breadth beyond the narrow path we have learned to tread.

"It wouldn't have happened, of course," his first wife said, "if you had been paying attention to him instead of to Lorna."

"What does Lorna have to do with it? She was the first one to realize that the poor kid wasn't kidding."

"Lorna has everything to do with it, as you perfectly well know."

"This is paranoid talk," he said. "This is Nixon-era paranoid talk."

"I've gotten used to your hurting me, but I'm not going to have you hurting our children, Geoff."

"Now we're getting really crazy."

"Don't you think I know why you decided to take us all ice-skating, when poor Timmy and Rose don't even have skates that fit? It was so unlike you — you usually just want to laze around reading the *Times* and complaining about your hangover and watching 'Wide World of Golf.' It was to see her. Her or somebody else. That whole party crowd, you don't get enough of them Saturday nights anymore. Why don't you go live with them? Live with somebody else, anybody except me! Go. Go!"

She didn't mean it, but it was thrilling to see her so energized, such a fury, her eyes flashing, her hair crackling, her slicing gestures carving large doomed territories out of the air. At that age, Fanshawe saw now, we are creating selves, potent and plastic, making and unmaking homes, the world in our hands. We are playing with dynamite. All around them, as he and his wife stood hip-deep in children, marriages blew up. Marriage counselors, child psychiatrists, lawyers, real-estate agents prospered in the ruins. Now, in old age, it remained only to generate a little business for the mortician, and an hour's pleasant work for the local clergyman. Just as insurance salesmen had at last stopped approaching him, and the moviemakers had written him out of audience demographics, so the armies of natural law, needed all over the globe to detonate dynamite where it counted, left him to wander in a twilight of inconsequence.

In early August, a pair of birds decided they had to build a nest on the Fanshawes' porch. They were warblers too far north, if he could trust his eyes and the battered old bird book. Something must have gone wrong with their biological clocks. It was too late in the season for nesting, but, even more willful than children, they persisted, while warbling back and forth furiously, in piling up twigs and wands of hay on the small shelves created by the capitals of his porch pillars. The twiggy accumulations blew off, or Mrs. Fanshawe briskly knocked them off with a broom. She had always been less sentimental than he. It was her clean white porch and her porch boards that would be spattered with bird shit. But the warblers kept coming back, as children keep demanding to go to an amusement park or to buy a certain kind of heavily advertised candy, until finally, the adult world wearying, they have their way. A pillar next to the house afforded shelter enough from the wind; the twigs and grass accumulated, and from its precarious pile the stone-colored head of the female bird haughtily stared down one afternoon when the Fanshawes returned from a day in town shopping. The warbling ceased. The male had vanished. Then, after two weeks, the female, it dawned on the Fanshawes, had vanished. Vanished without a warble of goodbye. All the time she had been in the nest, her profile had radiated anger.

Getting out the stepladder, Fanshawe fetched down an empty, eggless nest, its rim tidily circled round with guano, its rough materials worked in the center to a perfect expectant cavity. A nest in vain. What ever had those birds been thinking of? His impulse was to save the nest — his mother had always been saving bird's nests, setting them in bookshelves, or on top of the piano — but his wife held out an open garbage bag, as though the innocent wild artifact were teeming with germs. Bird's nests shouldn't go in garbage bags, he thought, but dropped it in. We're in this together, he aimlessly thought, as in the shade of the porch his wife stared up at him, with shining dark eyes, trying to control her impatience as he wrestled with his sentimental scruple.

At his fifth (at a guess) birthday party, a piece of cake mysteriously vanished from the plate in front of him and reappeared a few seconds later in his lap. He had never touched it, so it must have been a miracle, there in the candlelight and childish babble. He could still see it lying on his corduroy lap, the cake peeping out from its inverted dish — a chocolate cake with caramel icing of a type only his mother had ever made for him, its sugary stiffness most delicious where the icing between the layers met the outside layer in a thick, sweet T. A few years later, lying in bed with a fever, he had seen a black stick, at a slight angle, hop along beyond the edge of the bed, like one of the abstract sections of *Fantasia*. In those years, the knit of the physical world was stretched thin, and held a number of holes. When he was in the fourth grade, his new glasses vanished from his pocket, in their round-ended case with its murderous metallic *snap,* and a week later, cutting across a weedy vacant lot thinking of them and of how hard his father would have to work to buy him another pair, he looked down, and there the case was, like a long egg in the tangled damp grass. Inside it, the glasses had become steamy, as if worn by an overexcited, myopic ghost. Perhaps this was less a miracle than the transposed birthday cake, but the fact that he had been thinking of them *at that very moment* made it the strangest of all. Could it be that our mind does, secretly, control the atoms? On that possibility, Fanshawe had never quite broken his childish habit of prayer. Yet, staring at a model airplane that had unaccountably disintegrated during the night, or confronting the bulging shadows at the head of the stairs, it was hard to think of God and Jesus; one seemed to be down among frivolous demons, in a supernatural no more elevated in its aims than a Disney animated feature.

That curious cartoon lightness and jumpiness had returned. Fanshawe would find himself in a room with no knowledge of how he got there — as if the film had been broken and spliced. As he lay in bed, the house throbbed with footsteps, heard through the pillow, that fell silent when he lifted his head. Perhaps it had been his heartbeat.

In the sedate neighborhood where he now lived, everyone was old, more or less. For years he had watched the neighbor to his right, a widower, slowly deteriorate, his stride becoming a shuffle, his house and yard gradually growing shabbier and shaggier, inch by inch, season by season, in increments so small that only a speeded-up film would show the process. The two men would converse across the fence from time to time; Fanshawe once or twice offered to do some pruning for his neighbor. "No, thanks," would be the answer. "I'll get to it, when I'm feeling a little more lively." We look ahead and see random rises and falls; the linear diminishment so plain to others is invisible to us.

One Saturday morning, a fire engine appeared along his neighbor's curb, though there was no sign of smoke. The fireman, who had moved up the front walk with some haste, stayed inside so long that Fanshawe grew tired of spying. An hour later, with the fire engine still parked there, its great throbbing motor wastefully running, a small foreign convertible appeared, and a fashionably dressed young woman — all things are relative, perhaps she was forty — uncoiled rapidly out of the low-slung interior, flashing her long smooth shins, and clicked up the flagstone walk. This was his neighbor's daughter, who explained to Fanshawe later, at the party after the funeral, that her father had been found by the cleaning lady, sitting up in his favorite chair, shaved and dressed in a coat and tie as if expecting a caller. So that was death, Fanshawe realized — a jerky comedy of unusual comings and goings on a Saturday morning, followed in a few days by a funeral and a "For Sale" sign on the house.

"Thank you for being such a good neighbor to my father," the daughter said. "He often mentioned it."

"But I wasn't," Fanshawe protested. "I never did a thing for him."

Why had the dead man benignly lied? Why had the cleaning lady called the fire department and not the police? And why had the fireman never shut off his engine, discharging carbon monoxide and consuming fossil fuel at taxpayer expense? Fanshawe didn't ask.

He often felt now, going through the motions of living — shaving, dressing, responding to questions, measuring up to small emergencies — that he was enacting a part in a play at the end of its run, while mentally rehearsing his lines in the next play to be put on. It was repertory theater, evidently. When he remembered how death had once loomed at him, so vivid and large that it had a distinct smell, like the scent of chalk up close to the schoolroom blackboard, he marveled, rather patronizingly. When had he ceased to fear death — or, so to say, to grasp it? The moment was as clear in his mind as a black-and-white-striped gate at a border crossing: the moment when he first slept with Lorna Kramer.

How inky black her eyes seemed, amid the snowy whiteness of the sheets! There was snow outside, too, hushing the world in sunstruck brilliance. Melt-water tapped in the aluminum gutters. There had been a feeling of coolness, of freshly laundered sheets, of contacts never before achieved, by fingertips icy with nervousness. He had peeled off her black lace bra — her back arched up from the mattress to give him access to the catches — almost reluctantly, knowing there would be a white flash that would obliterate everything that had existed of his life before. She had smiled encouragingly, timorously. They were in it together. Her teeth were, after all, less than perfect, with protuberant canines that made the bicuspids next to them seem shadowy. Her pupils were contracted to the size of pencil leads by the relentless light; he had never seen anything so clearly as he saw her now, the fine mechanism of her, the specialized flesh of her lips, the trip wires of her hair; he got out of the bed to lower the shade, the sight of her was such a blinding assault.

A dull reddish bird, a female cardinal, was hopping about on the delicately tracked-up snow beneath the bird feeder a story below, pecking at scattered seed. A whole blameless town of roofs and smoking chimneys and snow-drenched trees stretched beyond, under an overturned bowl of blue light that made Fanshawe's vision wince. He drew the curtain on it and in merciful twilight returned to where Lorna lay still as a stick. He heard his blood striding in his skull, he felt so full of life. Sex or death, you pick your poison. That had been forever ago. She was still younger and spryer than he, but all things were relative. He did not envy those forever-ago people, for whom the world had such a weight of consequence. Like the Titans, they seemed beautiful but sad in their brief heyday, transition figures between chaos and an airier pantheon.

MARY GAITSKILL

The Girl on the Plane

FROM MIRABELLA

JOHN MORTON came down the aisle of the plane, banging his luggage into people's knees and sweating angrily under his suit. He had just run through the corridors of the airport, cursing and struggling with his luggage, slipping and flailing in front of the vapid brat at the seat assignment desk. Too winded to speak, he thrust his ticket at the boy and readjusted his luggage in his sticky hands. "You're a little late for a seat assignment," said the kid snottily. "I hope you can get on board before it pulls away."

He took his boarding pass and said, "Thanks, you little prick." The boy's discomfiture was heightened by his pretense of hauteur; it both soothed and fed John's anger.

At least he was able to stuff his bags into the compartment above the first seat he found. He sat down, grunting territorially, and his body slowly eased into a normal dull pulse and ebb. He looked at his watch; desk attendant to the contrary, the plane was sitting stupidly still, twenty minutes after takeoff time. He had the pleasing fantasy of punching the little bastard's face.

He was always just barely making his flight. His wife had read in one of her magazines that habitual lateness meant lack of interest in life, or depression or something. Well, who could blame him for lack of interest in the crap he was dealing with?

He glanced at the guy a seat away from him on the left, an alcoholic-looking old shark in an expensive suit, who sat staring fixedly at a magazine photograph of a grinning blonde in a white jumpsuit. The plane continued to sit there while stewardesses fiddled with compartments and women rolled up and down the aisles on trips to the bathroom. They were even boarding a passenger; a woman had just entered, flushed and vigorously banging along the aisle with her luggage. She was very pretty and he watched her, his body still feebly sending off alarm signals in response to its forced run.

"Hi," she said. "Can I sit here?"

"Of course." The force of his anger entered his magnanimity and swelled it hugely; he pinched his ankles together to let her by. She put her bag under the seat in front of her, sat down and rested her booted feet on its pale leather. The old shark next to her, with an appraising glance at her breasts through her open coat, made smile movements. The stewardess did her parody of a suffocating person reaching for an air mask, the pilot mumbled, the plane prepared to assert its unnatural presence in nature.

"They said I'd missed my flight by fifteen minutes," she said. "But I knew I'd make it. They're never on time." Her voice was unexpectedly small, with a rough, gravelly undertone that was seedy and schoolgirlish at once.

"It's bullshit," he said. "Well, what can you do?" She had large hazel eyes.

She smiled a tight, rueful smile that he associated with women who'd been fucked too many times, and which he found sexy. She cuddled more deeply into her seat, produced a *People* magazine and intently read it. He liked her profile — which was an interesting combination of soft (forehead, chin) and sharp (nose, cheekbones) — her shoulder-length, pale brown hair and her soft Mediterranean skin. He liked the coarse quality in the subtle downturn of her lips, and the heavy way her lids sat on her eyes. She was older than he'd originally thought, probably in her early thirties.

Who did she remind him of? A girl from a long time ago, an older version of some date or crush or screw. Or love, he thought gamely.

The pilot said they would be leaving the ground shortly. She was now reading something titled "AIDS Wedding — One Last Chance." He thought of his wife at home in Minneapolis, at the stove poking at something, in the living room reading, the fuzzy pink of her favorite sweater. The plane charged and tore a hole in the air.

The woman next to him was hurriedly flipping the pages of *People,* presumably looking for something as engrossing as "AIDS Wedding." When she didn't find it, she closed the magazine and turned to him in a way that invited conversation.

She said she'd lived in L.A. for eight years and that she liked it, even though it was "gross."

"I've never been to L.A.," he said. "I picture it being like *L.A. Law.* Is it like that?"

"I don't know. I've never seen *L.A. Law.* I don't watch TV. I don't own one."

He had never known a person who didn't own a TV, not even an old high school friend who lived in a slum and got food stamps. "You must read the newspapers a lot."

"No. I don't read them much at all."

He was incredulous. "How do you connect with the rest of the world? How do you know anything?"

"I'm part of the world. I know a lot of things."

He expelled a snort of laughter. "That's an awfully small perspective you've got there."

She shrugged and turned her head, and he was sorry he'd been rude. He glanced at her profile to read her expression and — of course; she reminded him of Patty LaForge, poor Patty.

He had met Patty at Meadow Community College in Coate, Minnesota. He was in his last semester; she had just entered. They worked in the student union cafeteria, preparing, serving and snacking on denatured food. She was a slim, curvy person with dark blond hair, hazel eyes and remarkable legs and hips. Her beauty was spoiled by the aggressive resignation that held her features in a fixed position and made all her expressions stiff. Her full mouth had a bitter downturn and her voice was quick, low, self-deprecating and sarcastic. She presented her beautiful body statically, as if it were a shield, and the effort of this presentation seemed to be the source of her animation.

Most of the people he knew at Meadow were kids he'd gone to high school and even junior high with. They still lived at home and still drove their cars around together at night, drank in the small bars of Coate, adventured in Minneapolis and made love to each other. This late-adolescent camaraderie gave their time at Meadow a fraught emotional quality that was like the shimmering fullness of a bead of water before it falls. They were all about to scatter and become different from one another and this made them exult in their closeness and alikeness.

The woman on the plane was flying to Kentucky to visit her parents and stopping over in Cincinnati.

"Did you grow up in Kentucky?" he asked. He imagined her as a big-eyed child in a cotton shift playing in some dusty, sunny alley, some rural Kentucky-like place. Funny she had grown up to be this wan little bun with too much makeup in black creases under her eyes.

"No, I was born there, but I grew up mostly in Minnesota near Minneapolis."

He turned away, registered the little shock of coincidence and turned back. The situation compounded: she had gone to Redford Community College in Thorold, a suburb much like Coate. She had grown up in Thorold, like Patty. The only reason Patty had gone to Meadow was that Redford didn't exist yet.

He felt a surge of commonality. He imagined that she had experienced his adolescence and this made him experience it for a moment. He had loved walking the small neat walkways of the campus through the stiffly banked hedges of snow and harsh morning austerity, entering the close food-smelling student union with the hard winter air popping off his skin. He would see his friends standing in a conspiratorial huddle, warming their hands on cheap cups of coffee; he always remembered the face of a particular girl, Layla, turning to greet him, looking over her frail sloped shoulder, her hair a bunched dark tangle, her round eyes ringed with green pencil, her perfectly ordinary face compelling in its configurations of girlish curiosity, maternal license, sexual knowledge, forgiveness and femininity. A familiar mystery he had meant to explore sometime and never did except when he grabbed her ass at a Halloween party and she smiled like a mother of four who worked as a porn model on the side. He loved driving with his friends to the Red Owl to buy alcohol and bagged salty snacks which they consumed as they drove around Coate playing the tape deck and yelling at each other, the beautiful ordinary landscape unpeeling before them, revealing the essential strangeness of its shadows and night movements. He loved driving with girls to the deserted housing development they called "the Spot," loved the blurred memories of the girls in the back seat with their naked legs curled up to their chests, their shirts bunched about their necks, their eyes wide with ardor and alcohol, beer and potato chips spilled on the floor of the car, the tape deck singing of love and triumph. He getting out of the car for a triumphant piss while the girl daintily replaced her pants. In the morning his mother would make him "cowboy eggs," eggs fried on top of bacon, and he would go through the cold to Meadow to sit in a fluorescent classroom and dream.

"Did you like growing up in that area?" she asked.

"Like it? It was the greatest time of my life." Some extremity in his voice made her look away, and as she did, he looked more fully at her profile. She didn't look that much like Patty, she wasn't even blond. But the small physical resemblance was augmented by a less tangible affinity, a telling similarity of speech and movement.

Patty belonged to a different crowd at Meadow. They were rougher than the Coate people, but the two groups were friendly. Patty was a strange, still presence within her group, with her hip thrust out and a cigarette always bleeding smoke from her hand. She was loose even by seventies standards, she had a dirty sense of humor and she wore pants so tight you could see the swollen outline of her genitals. She was also shy. When she talked she pawed the ground with her foot and pulled her hair over her mouth, she looked away from you and then snuck a look back to see what you thought of her. She was accepted by the Thorold people the way you accept what you've always known. The stiffness of her face and body contradicting her loose reputation, her coarse language expressed in her timid voice and shy manners, her beauty and her ordinariness all gave her a disconnected sexiness that was aggravating.

But he liked her. They were often a team at work and he enjoyed having her next to him, her golden-haired arms plunged in greasy black dishwater, or flecked with garbage as she plucked silverware from vile plates on their way to the dishwasher. She spooned out quivering red Jell-O or drew long bland snakes of soft ice cream from the stainless steel machine, she smoked, wiped her nose and muttered about a fight with her mother or a bad date. Her movements were resigned and bitter, yet her eyes and her nasty humor peeked impishly from under this weight. There was something pleasing in this combination, something congruent with her spoiled beauty.

It was a long time before he realized she had a crush on him. All her conversation was braided together with a fly strip of different boys she'd been with or was involved with, and she talked of all of them with the same tone of fondness and resentment. He thought nothing of it when she followed him outside to the field behind the union where they would walk along the narrow wet ditch, smoking pot and talking. It was early spring: dark, naked trees pressed intensely against the horizon, wet weeds clung to their jeans and her small voice bobbed assertively on the vibrant air. The cold wind gave her lips a swollen raw look and made her young skin grainy and bleached. "So why do you let him treat you like that?" "Ah, I get back at him. It's not really him, you know, I'm just fixated on him. I'm working out something through him. Besides, he's a great lay." He never noticed how often she came up behind him to walk him to class or sat on the edge of his chair as he lounged in the union. Then one day she missed work and a buddy of his said, "Hey, where's your little puppy dog today?" and he knew.

"Did you like Thorold?" he asked the girl next to him.

"No, I didn't." She turned toward him, her face a staccato burst of candor. "I didn't know what I was doing and I was a practicing alcoholic. I kept trying to fit in and I couldn't."

"That doesn't sound good." He smiled. How like Patty to answer a polite question from a stranger with this emotional nakedness, this urgent excess of information. She was always doing that, especially after the job at the cafeteria ended. He'd see her in a hallway, or the union lounge, where normal life was happening all around them, and she'd swoop into a compressed communication, intently twining her hair around her finger as she quickly muttered that she'd had the strangest dream about this guy David, in which a nuclear war was going on, and he, John, was in it too and —

"What did you do after Meadow?" he asked the girl next to him.

"Screwed around, basically. I went to New York pretty soon after that and did the same things I was doing in Thorold. Except I was trying to be a singer."

"Yeah?" He felt buoyed by her ambition. He pictured her in a tight black dress, lips parted, eyes closed, bathed in cheap, sexy stagelight. "Didja ever do anything with it?"

"Not much." She abruptly changed expression, as though she'd just remembered not to put herself down. "Well, some stuff. I had a good band once, we played the club circuit in L.A. for a while six years ago." She paused. "But I'm mostly a paralegal now."

"Well, that's not bad either. Do you ever sing now?"

"I haven't for a long time. But I was thinking of trying again." Just like Patty she looked away and quickly looked back as if to check his reaction. "I've been auditioning. Even though — I don't know."

"It sounds great to me," he said. "At least you're trying. It sounds better than what I do." His self-deprecation annoyed him and he bulled his way through an explanation of what he did, making it sound more interesting than selling software.

A stewardess with a small pink face asked if they'd like anything to drink, and he ordered two little bottles of Jack Daniel's. Patty's shadow had a compressed can of orange juice and an unsavory packet of nuts; their silent companion by the window had vodka straight. He thought of asking her if she were married, but he bet the answer was no and he didn't want to make her admit her loneliness. Of course, not every single person was lonely, but he guessed that she was. She seemed in need of comfort and care, like a stray animal that gets fed by various kindly people but never held.

He thought of telling her that she reminded him of someone he'd known in Coate, but he didn't. He sat silently knocking back his whiskey and watching her roll a greasy peanut between her two fingers.

Out in the field they were sitting on a fallen branch, sharing a wet stub of pot. "I don't usually say stuff like this," said Patty. "I know you think I do because of the way I talk but I don't. But I'm really attracted to you, John." The wind blew a piece of hair across her cheek and its texture contrasted acutely with her cold-bleached skin.

"Yeah, I was beginning to notice."

"I guess it was kind of obvious, huh?" She looked down and drew her curtain of hair. "And I've been getting these mixed signals from you. I can't tell if you're attracted to me or not." She paused. "But I guess you're not, huh?"

Her humility embarrassed and touched him. "Well, I am attracted to you. Sort of. I mean, you're beautiful and everything. I'm just not attracted enough to do anything. Besides, there's Susan."

"Oh, I thought you didn't like her that much." She sniffed and dropped the roach on the raw grass; her lipstick had congealed into little chapped bumps on her lower lip. "Well, I'm really disappointed. I thought you liked me."

"I do like you, Patty."

"You know what I meant." Pause. "I'm more attracted to you than I've been to anybody for two years. Since Paul."

A flattered giggle escaped him.

"Well, I hope we can be friends," she said. "We can still talk and stuff, can't we?"

"Patty LaForge? I wouldn't touch her, man, the smell alone."

He was driving around with a carload of drunk boys who were filled with a tangle of goodwill and aggression.

"Ah, LaForge is okay."

He was indignant for Patty but he laughed anyway.

"Were you really an alcoholic when you lived in Thorold?" he asked.

"I still am, I just don't drink now. But then I did. Yeah."

He had stepped into a conversation that had looked nice and

solid and his foot had gone through the floor and into the basement. But he couldn't stop. "I guess I drank too much then, too. But it wasn't a problem. We just had a lot of fun."

She smiled with tight terse mystery.

"How come you told me that about yourself? It seems kind of personal." He attached his gaze to hers as he said this; sometimes women said personal things to you as a way of coming on.

But instead of becoming soft and encouraging, her expression turned proper and institutional, like a kid about to recite. "It's part of the twelve-step program to admit it. If I'm going to admit it to other alcoholics in the program, I think I should talk about it in regular life too. It humbles you, sort of."

What a bunch of shit, he thought.

He was drinking with some guys at the Winner's Circle, a rough pick-up bar, when suddenly Patty walked up to him, really drunk.

"John," she gasped. "John, John, John." She lurched at him and attached her nail-bitten little claws to his jacket. "John, this guy over there really wants to fuck me, and I was going to go with him, but I don't want him, I want you, I want you." Her voice wrinkled into a squeak, her face looked like you could smear it with your hand.

"Patty," he mumbled, "you're drunk."

"That's not why, I always feel like this." Her nose and eyelashes and lips touched his cheek in an alcoholic caress. "Just let me kiss you. Just hold me."

He put his hands on her shoulders. "C'mon, stop it."

"It doesn't have to mean anything. You don't have to love me. I love you enough for both of us."

He felt the presence of his smirking friends. "Patty, these guys are laughing at you. I'll see you later." He tried to push her away.

"I don't care. I love you, John. I mean it." She pressed her taut body against his, one sweaty hand under his shirt, and arched her neck until he could see the small veins and bones. "Please. Just be with me. Please." Her hand stroked him, groped between his legs. He took her shoulders and shoved her harder than he meant to. She staggered back, fell against a table, knocked down a chair and almost fell again. She straightened and looked at him like she'd known him and hated him all her life.

He leaned back in his seat and closed his eyes, an overweight, prematurely balding salesman getting drunk on an airplane.

"Look at the clouds," said the girl next to him. "Aren't they beautiful?"

"What's your name?" he asked.

"Lorraine."

"I'm John." He extended his hand and she took it, her eyes unreadable, her hand exuding sweet feminine sweat.

"Why do you want to talk about your alcoholism publicly? I mean, if nobody asks or anything?"

Her eyes were steadfast, but her body was hesitant. "Well, I didn't have to just now. It's just the first thing I thought of when you asked me about Thorold. In general, it's to remind me. It's easy to bullshit yourself that you don't have a problem."

He thought of the rows and rows of people in swivel chairs on talk-show stages, admitting their problems. Wife beaters, child abusers, dominatrixes, porn stars. In the past it probably was a humbling experience to stand up and tell people you were an alcoholic. Now it was just something else to talk about. He remembered Patty tottering through a crowded party on smudged red high heels, bragging about what great blow jobs she gave. Some girl rolled her eyes and said, "Oh no, not again." Patty disappeared into a bedroom with a bottle of vodka and Jack Spannos.

He remembered a conversation with his wife before he married her, a conversation about his bachelor party. "It was no women allowed," he'd told her. "Unless they wanted to give blow jobs."

"Couldn't they just jump naked out of a cake?" she asked.

"Nope. Blow jobs for everybody."

They were at a festive restaurant drinking margaritas. Nervously, she touched her tiny straws. "Wouldn't that be embarrassing? In front of each other? I can't imagine Henry doing that in front of you all."

He smiled at the mention of his shy friend in this context.

"Yeah," he said. "It probably would be embarrassing. Group sex is for teenagers."

Her face rose away from her glass in a kind of excited alarm, her lips parted. "You had group sex when you were a teenager?"

"Oh. Not really. Just a gangbang once."

She looked like an antelope testing the wind with its nose in the air, ready to fly. "It wasn't rape," she said.

"Oh, no, no." Her body relaxed and released a warm, sensual curiosity, like a cat against his leg. "The girl liked it."

"Are you sure?"

"Yeah. She liked having sex with a lot of guys. We all knew her, she knew us."

He felt her shiver inwardly, shocked and fascinated by this dangerous pack-animal aspect of his masculinity.

"What was it like?" she asked.

He shrugged. "It was a good time with the guys. It was a bunch of guys standing around in their socks and underwear."

Some kid he didn't know walked up and put his arm around him while he was talking to a girl named Chrissie. The kid's eyes were boyish and drunkenly enthusiastic, his face heavy and porous. He whispered something about Patty in John's ear and said, "C'mon."

The girl's expression subtly withdrew.

"What?" said John.

"Come on," said the kid.

"Bye bye," said Chrissie, with a gingerly wag of her fingers.

He followed the guy through the room, seizing glimpses of hips and tits sheathed in bright, cheap cloth, girls doing wiggly dances with guys who jogged helplessly from foot to foot, holding their chests proudly aloof from their lower bodies. The music made his organs want to leap in and out of his body in time. His friends were all around him.

A door opened and closed behind him, muffling the music. The kid who'd brought him in sat in an armchair, smiling. Patty lay on a bed with her skirt pulled up to her waist and a guy with his pants down straddling her face. Without knowing why, he laughed. Patty twisted her legs about and bucked slightly. For a moment he felt frightened that this was against her will — but no, she would have screamed. He recognized the boy on her as Pete Kopiekin, who was thrusting his flat hairy butt in the same dogged, earnest, woeful manner with which he played football.

Kopiekin got off her and the other guy got on; between them he saw her chin sticking up from her sprawled body, pivoting to and fro on her neck while she muttered and groped blindly up and down her body. Kopiekin opened the door to leave and a fist of music punched the room. His body jumped in shocked response and the door shut. The guy on top of Patty was talking to her; to John's amazement he seemed to be using love words. "You're so beautiful, baby." He saw Patty's hips moving. She wasn't being raped, he thought. When the guy finished he stood and poured the rest of his beer in her face.

"Hey," said John lamely, "hey."

"Oh man, don't tell me that, I've known her a long time."

When the guy left, he thought of wiping her face, but he didn't. His thoughts spiraled inward and he let them be chopped up by muffled guitar chords. He sat awhile, watching guys swarm over Patty and talking to the ones waiting. Music sliced in and out of the room. Then some guy wanted to pour maple syrup on her and he said, "No, I didn't go yet." He sat on the bed and, for the first time, looked at her, expecting to see the sheepish bitter look he knew. He didn't recognize her. Her rigid face was weirdly slack, her eyes fluttered open, rolled and closed, a strange mix of half-formed expressions flew across her face like swarming ghosts. "Patty," he said, "hey." He shook her shoulder. Her eyes opened, her gaze raked his face. He saw tenderness, he thought. He lay on her and tried to embrace her. Her body was leaden and floppy. She muttered and moved, but in ways he didn't understand. He massaged her breasts; they felt like they could come off and she wouldn't notice.

He lay there, supporting himself on his elbows, and felt the deep breath in her lower body meeting his own breath. Subtly, he felt her come to life. She lifted her head and said something; he heard his name. He kissed her on the lips. Her tongue touched his, gently, her sleeping hands woke. He held her and stroked her pale, beautiful face.

He got up in such a good mood that he slapped the guy coming in with the maple syrup a high five, something he thought was stupid and usually never did.

The next time he saw Patty was at a Foreigner concert in Minneapolis; he saw her holding hands with Pete Kopiekin.

Well, now she could probably be on a talk show about date rape. It was a confusing thing. She may have wanted to kiss him or to give Jack Spannos a blow job, but she probably didn't want maple syrup poured on her. Really though, if you were going to get blind drunk and let everybody fuck you, you had to expect some nasty stuff. On the talk shows they always said it was low self-esteem that made them do it. His eyes rested on Lorraine's hands; she was wadding the empty nut package and stuffing it in her empty plastic cup.

"Hey," he said, "what did you mean when you said you kept trying to fit in and you couldn't? When you were in Thorold?"

"Oh you know." She seemed impatient. "Acting the part of the pretty, sexy girl."

"When in fact you were not a pretty, sexy girl?"

She started to smile, then gestured dismissively. "It was complicated."

It was seductive, the way she drew him in and then shut him out. She picked up her magazine again. Her slight arm movement released a tiny cloud of sweat and deodorant which evaporated as soon as he inhaled it. He breathed in deeply, hoping to smell her again. Sunlight pressed in with viral intensity and exaggerated the lovely contours of her face, the fine lines, the stray cosmetic flecks, the marvelous profusion of her pores. He thought of the stories he'd read in sex magazines about strangers on airplanes having sex in the bathroom or masturbating each other under blankets.

The stewardess made a sweep with a gaping white garbage bag and cleared their trays of bottles and cups.

She put down the magazine. "You've probably had the same experience yourself," she said. Her face was curiously determined, as if it were very important that she make herself understood.

"I mean doing stuff for other people's expectations or just to feel you have a social identity because you're so convinced who you are isn't right."

"You mean low self-esteem?"

"Well, yeah, but more than that." He sensed her inner tension and felt an empathic twitch.

"It's just that you get so many projections onto yourself of who and what you're supposed to be that if you don't have a strong support system it's hard to process it."

"Yeah," he said. "I know what you mean. I've had that experience. I don't know how you can't have it when you're young. There's so much crap in the world." He felt embarrassed, but he kept talking, wanting to tell her something about himself, to return her candor. "I've done lots of things I wish I hadn't done, I've made mistakes. But you can't let it rule your life."

She smiled again, with her mouth only. "Once, a few years ago, my father asked me what I believed to be the worst mistakes in my life. This is how he thinks, this is his favorite kind of question. Anyway, it was really hard to say because I don't know from this vantage point what would've happened if I'd done otherwise in most situations. Finally, I came up with two things, my relationship with this guy named Jerry and the time I turned down an offer to work with this really awful band that became famous. He was totally bewildered. He was expecting me to say 'dropping out of college.' "

"You didn't make a mistake dropping out of college." The vehemence in his voice almost made him blush; then nameless urgency swelled forth and quelled embarrassment. "That wasn't a mistake," he repeated.

"Well, yeah, I know."

"Excuse me." The silent business shark to their left rose in majestic self-containment and moved awkwardly past their knees, looking at John with pointed irony as he did so. Fuck you, thought John.

"And about that relationship," he went on. "That wasn't your loss. It was his." He had meant these words to sound light and playfully gallant, but they had the awful intensity of a maudlin personal confession. He reached out to gently pat her hand to reassure her that he wasn't a nut, but instead he grabbed it and held it. "If you want to talk about mistakes — shit, I raped somebody. Somebody I liked."

Their gaze met in a conflagration of reaction. She was so close he could smell her sweating, but at the speed of light she was falling away, deep into herself where he couldn't follow. She was struggling to free her hand.

"No," he said, "it wasn't a real rape, it was what you were talking about, it was complicated."

She wrenched free her hand and held it protectively close to her chest. "Don't touch me again." She turned tautly forward. He imagined her heart beating in alarm. His body felt so stiff he could barely feel his own heart. Furiously, he wondered if the people around them had heard any of this. Staring ahead of him he hissed, "Do you think I was dying to hear about your alcoholism? You were the one who started this crazy conversation."

He felt her consider this. "It's not the same thing," she hissed back.

"You don't understand," he said ineptly.

She was silent. He thought he dimly felt her body relax, emitting some possibility of forgiveness. But he couldn't tell. He closed his eyes. He thought of Patty's splayed body, her half-conscious kiss. He thought of his wife, her compact scrappy body, her tough-looking flat nose and chipped nail polish, her smile, her smell, her embrace which was both soft and fierce. He imagined the hotel room he would sleep in tonight, its stifling grid of rectangles, oblongs and windows that wouldn't open. He dozed.

The pilot woke him with a command to fasten his seat belt. He sat up and blinked. Nothing had changed. The girl at his side was sitting slightly hunched with her hands resolutely clasped.

"God, I'll be glad when we're on the ground," he said.

She sniffed in reply.

They descended, ears popping. They landed with a flurry of baggage-grabbing. He stood, bumped his head and tried to get into the aisle to escape, but it was too crowded. He sat back down.

"Excuse me." She butted her way past him and into the aisle. He watched a round vulnerable piece of her head move between the obstruction of shoulders and arms. She glanced backward, possibly to see if he was going to try to follow her. The sideways movement of her hazel iris prickled him. They burst from the plane and scattered, people picking up speed as they bore down on their destination. He caught up with her as they entered the terminal. "I'm sorry," he said to the back of her head. She moved farther away, into memory and beyond.

ALICE MUNRO

A Real Life

FROM THE NEW YORKER

A MAN came along and fell in love with Dorrie Beck. At least, he wanted to marry her. It was true.

"If her brother were alive she would never have needed to get married," Millicent said. What did she mean? Not something shameful. And she didn't mean money, either. She meant that love had existed, kindness had created comfort, and in the poor, somewhat feckless life Dorrie and Albert Beck had lived together, loneliness had not been a threat. Millicent, who was shrewd and practical in some ways, was stubbornly sentimental in others. She believed always in the sweetness of affection that was untainted by sex.

She thought it was the way Dorrie used her knife and fork that had captivated the man. Indeed, it was the same way he used his. Dorrie kept her fork in her left hand and used the right only for cutting. That was because she had been to Whitby Ladies' College when she was young. A last spurt of the Becks' money. Another thing she had learned there was a beautiful handwriting, and that might have been a factor as well, because after the first meeting the entire courtship appeared to have been conducted by letter. Millicent loved the sound of Whitby Ladies' College, and it was her plan — not shared with anybody — that her own daughter would go there someday.

Millicent was not an uneducated person herself. She had taught school, she hadn't married early. She had rejected two serious boyfriends — one because she couldn't stand his mother, one because he tried putting his tongue in her mouth — before she agreed to marry Porter, who was nineteen years older than she was. He owned three farms, and he promised her a bathroom within a year, and a dining-room suite and a chesterfield and chairs. On their wedding night he said, "Now you've got to take what's coming to you," but she knew it was not unkindly meant.

That was in 1933.

She had three children, fairly quickly, and after the third baby she developed some problems. Porter was decent — mostly, after that, he let her alone.

The Beck house was on Porter's land, but he wasn't the one who had bought them out. He bought Albert and Dorrie's place from the man who had bought it from them. So, technically, they were renting their old house back from Porter. But money did not enter the picture. When Albert was alive he would show up and work for a day when important jobs were undertaken — when they were pouring the cement floor in the barn or putting the hay in the mow. Dorrie had come along on those occasions, and also when Millicent had a new baby or was housecleaning. Dorrie had remarkable strength for lugging furniture about, and could do a man's work, like putting up the storm windows. At the start of a hard job — such as ripping the wallpaper off a whole room — she would settle back her shoulders and draw a deep, happy breath. She glowed with resolution. She was a big, firm woman with heavy legs, chestnut-brown hair, a broad, bashful face and dark freckles like dots of velvet. A man in the area had named a horse after her.

In spite of her enjoyment of housecleaning, she did not do a lot of it at home. The house that she and Albert had lived in — that she lived in alone after his death — was large and handsomely laid out but practically without furniture. Furniture would come up in Dorrie's conversation — the oak sideboard, Mother's wardrobe, the spool bed — but tacked on to this mention was always the phrase "that went at the Auction." The Auction sounded like a natural disaster, something like a flood and windstorm together, about which it would be pointless to complain. No carpets remained, either, and no pictures. There was just the calendar from Nunn's Grocery, which Albert used to work for. Absences of customary things — and the presence of others, such as Dorrie's traps and guns and the boards for stretching rabbit and muskrat skins — had made the rooms lose their designations, made the notion of cleaning them seem frivolous. Once, in the summer, Millicent saw a pile of dog dirt at the head of the stairs. She didn't see it while it was fresh, but it was fresh enough to seem an offense. Through the summer it changed, from brown to gray. It became stony, dignified, and stable, and, strangely, Millicent herself found less and less need to see it as anything but something that had a right to be there.

Delilah was the dog responsible. She was black, part Labrador. She chased cars, and eventually this was how she got herself killed. After Albert's death, both she and Dorrie may have come a little unhinged. But this was not something anybody could spot right away. At first, it was just that there was no man coming home, and so no set time to get supper. There were no men's clothes to wash — cutting out the idea of regular washing. Nobody to talk to, so Dorrie talked more to Millicent or to both Millicent and Porter. She talked about Albert and his job, which had been driving Nunn's Grocery Wagon, and later their truck, all over the countryside. He had gone to college, he was no dunce, but when he came home from the Great War he was not very well, and he thought it best to be out-of-doors, so he got the job driving for Nunn's and kept it until he died. He was a man of inexhaustible sociability and did more than simply deliver groceries. He gave people a lift to town. He brought patients home from the hospital. He had a crazy woman on his route, and once when he was getting her groceries out of the truck he had a compulsion to look around. There she stood with a hatchet, about to brain him. In fact, her swing had already begun, and when he slipped out of range she had to continue, chopping neatly into the box of groceries and cleaving a pound of butter. He kept on making deliveries to her, not having the heart to turn her over to the authorities, who would take her to the asylum. She never took up the hatchet again but gave him cupcakes sprinkled with evil-looking seeds, which he threw into the grass at the end of the lane. Other women, more than one, had shown themselves to him naked. One of them arose out of a tub of bath water in the middle of the kitchen floor, and Albert bowed low and set the groceries at her feet. "Aren't some people amazing?" said Dorrie.

And she also told about a bachelor whose house was overrun by rats, so that he had to keep his food slung in a sack from the kitchen beams. But the rats ran out along the beams and leaped upon the sack and clawed it apart, and eventually the fellow was obliged to take all his food into bed with him.

"Albert always said people living alone are to be pitied," said Dorrie — as if she did not understand that she was now one of them. Albert's heart had given out — he had only had time to pull to the side of the road and stop the truck. He died in a lovely spot, where black oaks grew in a bottomland, and a sweet, clear creek ran beside the road.

Dorrie mentioned other things Albert had told her, concerning the Becks in the early days. How they came up the river in a raft, two brothers, and started a mill at the Big Bend, where there was nothing but the wildwoods. And nothing now, either, but the ruins of their mill and dam. The farm was never a livelihood but a hobby, when they built the big house and brought out the furniture from Edinburgh. The bedsteads, the chairs, the carved chests that went in the Auction. They brought it round the Horn, Dorrie said, and up Lake Huron and so up the river. Oh, Dorrie, said Millicent, that is not possible, and she brought a school geography book she had kept, to point out the error. It must have been a canal, then, said Dorrie. I recall a canal. The Panama Canal? More likely it was the Erie Canal, said Millicent.

"Yes," said Dorrie. "Round the Horn and into the Erie Canal."

"Dorrie is a true lady, no matter what anybody says," said Millicent to Porter, who did not argue. He was used to her absolute, personal judgments. "She is a hundred times more a lady than Muriel Snow," said Millicent, naming the person who might be called her best friend. "I say that, and I love Muriel Snow dearly."

Porter was used to hearing that, too: "I love Muriel Snow dearly, and I would stick up for her no matter what." "I love Muriel Snow, but that does not mean I approve of everything she does."

The smoking. And saying hot damn, Chrissakes, poop. *I nearly pooped my pants.*

Muriel Snow had not been Millicent's first choice for best friend. In the early days of her marriage she had set her sights high. Mrs. Lawyer Nesbitt. Mrs. Doctor Finnegan. Mrs. Doud.

They let her take on a donkey's load of work in the Women's Auxiliary at the church, but they never asked her to their tea parties. She was never inside their houses, unless it was to a meeting. Porter was a farmer. No matter how many farms. She should have known.

She met Muriel when she decided that her daughter, Betty Jean, would take piano lessons. Muriel was the music teacher. She taught in the schools as well as privately. Times being what they were, she charged only twenty cents a lesson. She played the organ at the church and directed various choirs, but some of that was for nothing. She and Millicent got on so well that soon she was in Millicent's house as often as Dorrie was, though on a rather different footing.

Muriel was over thirty and had never been married. Getting married was something she talked about openly, jokingly, and plaintively, particularly when Porter was around. "Don't you know any men, Porter?" she would say. "Can't you dig up just one decent man for me?" Porter would say maybe he could, but maybe she wouldn't think they were so decent. In the summers Muriel went to visit a sister in Montreal, and once she went to stay with some cousins she had never met, only written to, in Philadelphia. The first thing she reported on, when she got back, was the man situation.

"Terrible. They all get married young, they're Catholics, and the wives never die — they're too busy having babies."

"Oh, they had somebody lined up for me, but I saw right away he would never pan out. He was one of those ones with the mothers."

"I did meet one, but he had an awful failing. He didn't cut his toenails. Big yellow toenails. Well? Aren't you going to ask me how I found out?"

Muriel was always dressed in some shade of blue. A woman should pick a color that really suits her and wear it all the time, she said. Like your perfume. It should be your signature. Blue was widely thought to be a color for blondes, but that was incorrect. Blue often made a blonde look more washed-out than she was to start with. It suited best a warm-looking skin, like Muriel's — skin that took a good tan and never entirely lost it. It suited brown hair and brown eyes, which were hers as well. She never skimped on her clothes — it was a mistake to. Her fingernails were always painted — a rich and distracting color, apricot or blood ruby or even gold. She was small and round; she did exercises to keep her tidy waistline. She had a dark mole on the front of her neck, like a jewel on an invisible chain, and another, like a tear, at the corner of one eye.

"The word for you is not 'pretty,' " Millicent said one day, surprising herself. "It's '*bewitching*.' " Then she flushed at her own tribute, knowing she sounded childish and excessive.

Muriel flushed a little too, but with pleasure. She drank in admiration, frankly courted it. Once she dropped in on her way to a concert in Walley, which she hoped would yield rewards. She had on an ice blue dress that shimmered.

"And that isn't all," she said. "Everything I have on is new, and everything is *silk*."

It wasn't true that she never found a man. She found one fairly often but hardly ever one that she could bring to supper. She found them in other towns, where she took her choirs to massed concerts, in Toronto at piano recitals to which she might take a promising student. Sometimes she found them in the students' own homes. They were the uncles, the fathers, the grandfathers, and the reason that they would not come into Millicent's house but only wave — sometimes curtly, sometimes with bravado — from a waiting car was that they were married. A bedridden wife, a drinking wife, a vicious shrew of a wife? Perhaps. Sometimes no mention at all — a ghost of a wife. They escorted Muriel to musical events, an interest in music being the ready excuse. Sometimes there was even a performing child, to act as chaperon. They took her to dinners in restaurants in distant towns. They were referred to as friends. Millicent defended her. How could there be any harm when it was all so out in the open? But it wasn't, quite, and it would all end in misunderstandings, harsh words, unkindness. A wife on the phone. Miss Snow, I am sorry we are canceling — Or simply silence. A date not kept, a note not answered, a name never to be mentioned again.

"I don't expect so much," Muriel said. "I expect a friend to be a friend. Then they hightail it off at the first whiff of trouble, after saying they would always stand up for me. Why is that?"

"Well, you know, Muriel," Millicent said once, "a wife is a wife. It's all well and good to have friends, but a marriage is a marriage."

Muriel blew up at that — she said that Millicent thought the worst of her, like everybody else, and was she never to be permitted to have a good time, an innocent good time? She banged the door and ran her car over the calla lilies, surely on purpose. For a day Millicent's face was blotchy from weeping. But enmity did not last and Muriel was back, tearful as well, and taking blame on herself.

"I was a fool from the start," she said, and went into the front room to play the piano. Millicent got to know the pattern. When Muriel was happy and had a new friend she played mournful, tender songs, like "The Flowers of the Forest." Or:

She dressed herself in male attire,
And gaily she was dressed —

Then, when she was disappointed, she came down hard and fast on the keys, and she sang scornfully some such song as "Bonnie Dundee."

To the Lords of Convention
'Twas Claverhouse spoke,
Ere the King's head go down
There are heads to be broke!

Sometimes Millicent asked people to supper (though not the Finnegans or the Nesbitts or the Douds), and then she liked to ask Dorrie and Muriel as well. Dorrie was a help in washing up the pots and pans afterward, and Muriel could entertain on the piano.

A couple of years after Albert died, Millicent asked the Anglican minister to come on Sunday, after Evensong, and bring the friend she had heard was staying with him. The Anglican minister was a bachelor, but Muriel had given up on him early. Neither fish nor fowl, she said. Too bad. Millicent liked him, chiefly for his voice. She had been brought up an Anglican, and though she'd switched to United, which was what Porter said he was (so was everybody else, so were all the important and substantial people in the town), she still favored Anglican customs. Evensong, the church bell, the choir coming up the aisle in meager state, singing — instead of just all clumping in together and sitting down. Best of all, the words. *But thou, O Lord, have mercy upon us, miserable offenders. Spare thou them, O God, which confess their faults. Restore thou them that are penitent; According to thy promises. . . .*

Porter went with her once and hated it.

Preparations for this evening's supper were considerable. The damask was brought out, the silver serving spoon, the black dessert plates painted by hand with pansies. The cloth had to be pressed and all the silverware polished, and then there was the apprehension that a tiny smear of polish might remain, a gray gum on the tines of a fork or among the grapes round the rim of the wedding teapot. All day Sunday Millicent was torn between pleasure and agony, hope and suspense. The things that could go wrong multiplied. The Bavarian cream might not set (they had no refrigerator yet and had to chill things in summer by setting them on the cellar floor). The angel food cake might not rise to its full glory. If it did rise, it might be dry. The biscuits might taste of tainted flour or a beetle might crawl out of the salad. By five o'clock she was in such a state of tension and misgiving that nobody could stay in the kitchen with her. Muriel had arrived early, to help out, but she had not chopped the potatoes finely enough, and had managed to scrape her knuckles while grating carrots, so she was told off for being useless and sent to play the piano.

Muriel was dressed up in turquoise crêpe and smelled of her Spanish perfume. She might have written off the minister but she had not seen his visitor yet. A bachelor, perhaps, or a widower, since he was traveling alone. Rich, or he would not be traveling at all, not so far. He came from England, people said. Someone said no, Australia.

She was trying to get up the "Polovtsian Dances."

Dorrie was late. It threw a crimp in things. The jellied salad had to be taken down cellar again, lest it should soften. The biscuits put to warm in the oven had to be taken out, for fear of their getting too hard. The three men sat on the veranda — the meal was to be eaten there, buffet style — and drank fizzy lemonade. Millicent had seen what drink did in her own family — her father had died of it when she was ten — and she had required a promise from Porter, before they married, that he would never touch it again. Of course he did — he kept a bottle in the granary — but when he drank he kept his distance, and she truly believed the promise had been kept. This was a fairly common pattern, at that time, at least among farmers — drinking in the barn, abstinence in the house. Most men would have felt there was something the matter with a woman who didn't lay down such a law.

But Muriel, when she came out on the veranda in her high heels and slinky crêpe, cried out at once, "Oh, my favorite drink! Gin and lemon!" She took a sip and pouted at Porter. "You did it again. You forgot the gin again!" Then she teased the minister, asking if he didn't have a flask in his pocket. The minister was gallant, or perhaps made reckless by boredom. He said he wished he had.

The visitor who rose to be introduced was tall and thin and sallow, with a face that seemed to hang in pleats, precise and melancholy. Muriel did not give way to disappointment. She sat down beside him and tried in a most spirited way to get him into conversation. She told him about her music teaching and was scathing about the local choirs and musicians. She did not spare the Anglicans, telling about the Sunday school concert when the master of ceremonies announced that she would play a piece by Chopin, pronouncing it "Choppin."

Porter had done the chores early and washed and changed into his suit, but he kept looking uneasily toward the barnyard, as if recalling something that was left undone. One of the cows was bawling loudly in the field, and at last he excused himself to go and see what was wrong with her. He found that her calf had got caught in the wire fence and managed to strangle itself. He did not speak of this loss when he came back with newly washed hands. "Calf caught up in the fence" was all he said. But he connected the mishap somehow with this entertainment, with dressing up and having to eat off your knees. It was not natural.

"Those cows are as bad as children," Millicent said. "Always wanting your attention at the wrong time!" Her own children, fed earlier, peered from between the bannisters to watch the food being carried to the veranda. "I think we will have to commence without Dorrie. You men must be starving. This is just a simple little buffet. We sometimes enjoy eating outside on a Sunday evening."

"Commence, commence!" cried Muriel, who had helped to

carry out the various dishes — the potato salad, carrot salad, jellied salad, cabbage salad, the deviled eggs and cold roast chicken, the salmon loaf and warm biscuits, and the relishes. Just when they had everything set out, Dorrie came around the side of the house, looking warm from her walk across the field, or from excitement. She was wearing her good summer dress, a navy blue organdie with white dots and white collar, suitable for a little girl or an old lady. Threads showed where she had pulled the torn lace off the collar instead of mending it, and in spite of the hot day a rim of undershirt was hanging out of one sleeve. Her shoes had been so recently and sloppily cleaned that they left traces of whitener on the grass.

"I would have been on time," Dorrie said, "but I had to shoot a feral cat. She was prowling around my house and carrying on so, I was convinced she was rabid."

Dorrie had wet her hair and crimped it into place with bobby pins. With that, and her pink, shiny face, she looked like a doll with a china head and limbs attached to a cloth body firmly stuffed with straw.

"I thought at first she might have been in heat, but she didn't really behave that way. She didn't do any of the rubbing along on her stomach such as I'm used to seeing. And I noticed some spitting. So I thought the only thing to do was to shoot her. Then I put her in a sack and called up Fred Nunn to see if he would run her over to Walley, to the vet. I want to know if she really was rabid, and Fred always likes the excuse to get out in his car. I told him to leave the sack on the step if the vet wasn't home on a Sunday night."

"I wonder what he'll think it is?" said Muriel. "A present?"

"No. I pinned on a note, in case. There was definite spitting and dribbling." Dorrie touched her own face to show where the dribbling had been. "Are you enjoying your visit here?" she said to the minister, who had been in town for three years and had been the one to bury her brother.

"It is Mr. Speirs who is the visitor, Dorrie," said Millicent. Dorrie acknowledged the introduction and seemed unembarrassed by her mistake. She said that the reason she took the animal for a feral cat was that its coat was all matted and hideous, and she thought that a feral cat would never come near the house unless it was rabid.

"But I will put an explanation in the paper, just in case. I will be sorry if it is anybody's pet. I lost my own pet three months ago — my dog, Delilah. She was struck down by a car."

It was strange to hear that dog called a pet, that big black Delilah who used to lollop along with Dorrie all over the countryside, who tore across the fields in such savage glee to attack cars. Dorrie had not been distraught at the death; indeed, she had said she had expected it someday. But now, to hear her say "pet," Millicent thought there might have been grief she didn't show.

"Come and fill up your plate or we'll all have to starve," Muriel said to Mr. Speirs. "You're the guest, you have to go first. If the egg yolks look dark, it's just what the hens have been eating — they won't poison you. I grated the carrots for that salad myself, so if you notice some blood it's just where I got a little too enthusiastic and grated in some skin off my knuckles. I had better shut up now or Millicent will kill me."

And Millicent was laughing angrily, saying, "Oh, they are not! Oh, you did *not!*"

Mr. Speirs had paid close attention to everything Dorrie said. Maybe that was what had made Muriel so saucy. Millicent thought that perhaps he saw Dorrie as a novelty, a Canadian wild woman who went around shooting things. He might be studying her so that he could go home and describe her to his friends in England.

Dorrie kept quiet while eating, and she ate quite a lot. Mr. Speirs ate a lot, too — Millicent was happy to see that — and he appeared to be a silent person at all times. The minister kept the conversation going by describing a book he was reading. It was called *The Oregon Trail.*

"Terrible, the hardships," he said.

Millicent said she had heard of it. "I have some cousins living out in Oregon, but I cannot remember the name of the town," she said. "I wonder if they went on that trail."

The minister said that if they went out a hundred years ago it was most probable.

"Oh, I wouldn't think it was that long," Millicent said. "Their name was Rafferty."

"Man the name of Rafferty used to race pigeons," said Porter, with sudden energy. "This was way back, when there was more of that kind of thing. There was money going on it, too. Well, he said the problem with the pigeons' house, they don't go in right away, and that means they don't trip the wire and don't get counted in. So he took an egg one of his pigeons was on, and he blew it clear, and he put a beetle inside. And the beetle inside made such a racket the pigeon naturally thought she had an egg getting ready to hatch. And she flew a beeline home and tripped the wire, and all the ones that bet on her made a lot of money. Him, too, of course. In fact, this was over in Ireland, and this man that told the story, that was how he got the money to come out to Canada."

Millicent didn't believe that the man's name had been Rafferty at all. That had just been an excuse.

"So you keep a gun in the house?" said the minister to Dorrie. "Does that mean you are worried about tramps and suchlike?"

Dorrie put down her knife and fork, chewed something up carefully, and swallowed. "I keep it for shooting," she said.

After a pause she said that she shot groundhogs and rabbits. She took the groundhogs over to the other side of town and sold them to the mink farm. She skinned the rabbits and stretched the skins, then sold them to a place in Walley which did a big trade with the tourists. She enjoyed fried or boiled rabbit meat but could not possibly eat it all herself, so she often took a rabbit carcass, cleaned and skinned, around to some family that was on relief. Many times her offering was refused. People thought it was as bad as eating a dog or a cat. Though even that, she believed, was not considered out of the way in China.

"That is true," said Mr. Speirs. "I have eaten them both."

"Well, then, you know," said Dorrie. "People are prejudiced."

He asked about the skins, saying they must have to be removed very carefully, and Dorrie said that was true, and you needed a knife you could trust. She described with pleasure the first clean slit down the belly. "Even more difficult with the muskrats, because you have to be more careful with the fur, it is more valuable," she said. "It is a denser fur. Waterproof."

"You do not shoot the muskrats?" said Mr. Speirs.

No, no, said Dorrie. She trapped them. Trapped them, yes, said Mr. Speirs, and Dorrie described her favorite trap, on which she had made little improvements of her own. She had thought of taking out a patent but had never gotten around to it. She spoke about the spring watercourses, the system of creeks she followed, tramping for miles day after day, after the snow was mostly melted but before the leaves came out, when the musk-rats' fur was prime. Millicent knew that Dorrie did these things, but she had thought she did them to get a little money. To hear her talk now, it would seem she loved that life. The blackflies out already, the cold water over her boot tops, the drowned rats. And Mr. Speirs listened like an old dog, perhaps a hunting dog, that has been sitting with his eyes half shut, just prevented, by his own good opinion of himself, from falling into an unmannerly stupor. Now he has got a whiff of something — his eyes open all the way and his nose quivers as he remembers some day of reck-lessness and dedication. How many miles did she cover in a day, Mr. Speirs asked, and how high is the water, how much do the muskrats weigh and how many could you count on in a day and for muskrats is it still the same sort of knife?

Muriel asked the minister for a cigarette and got one, smoked for a few moments, and stubbed it out in the middle of her dish of the Bavarian cream. "So I won't eat it and get fat," she said. She got up and started to help clear the dishes, but soon ended up at the piano, back at the "Polovtsian Dances."

Millicent was pleased that there was conversation with the guest, though its attraction mystified her. Also, the food had been good and there had not been any humiliation — no queer taste or sticky cup handle.

"I had thought the trappers were all up north," said Mr. Speirs. "I thought that they were beyond the Arctic Circle or at least on the Precambrian shield."

"I used to have an idea of going there," Dorrie said. Her voice thickened for the first time, with embarrassment — or excite-ment. "I thought I could live in a cabin and trap all winter. But I had my brother. I couldn't leave my brother. And I know it here."

Late in the winter Dorrie arrived at Millicent's house with a large piece of white satin. She said that she intended to make a wed-ding dress. That was the first anybody had heard of a wedding — she said it would be in May — or learned the first name of Mr. Speirs. It was Wilkinson. Wilkie.

When and where had Dorrie seen him, since that supper on the veranda?

Nowhere. He had gone off to Australia, where he had property. Letters had gone back and forth between them.

Millicent's questions drew out a little more information. Wilkie had been born in England but was now an Australian. He had traveled all over the world, climbed mountains, and gone up a river into the jungle. In Africa, or South America — Dorrie was not sure which.

"He thinks I am adventurous," said Dorrie, as if to answer an unspoken question about what he saw in her.

"And is he in love with you?" said Millicent. It was she who blushed then, not Dorrie. But Dorrie, unblushing, unfidgeting, was like a column of heat, bare and concentrated. Millicent had an awful thought of her naked, so that she hardly heard what Dorrie said. She amended the question to what she believed she had meant: "Will he be good to you?"

"Oh — yes," said Dorrie, rather carelessly.

Sheets were laid down on the dining room floor, with the dining table pushed against the wall. The satin was spread out over them. Its broad, bright extent, its shining vulnerability, cast a hush over the whole house. The children came, only to stare at it, and Millicent shouted to them to clear off. She was afraid to cut into it. And Dorrie, who could so easily slit the skin of an animal, laid the scissors down. She confessed to shaking hands.

A call was put in to Muriel, to drop by after school. She clapped her hand to her heart when she heard the news, and called Dorrie a slyboots, a Cleopatra who had fascinated a millionaire.

"I bet he's a millionaire," Muriel said. "Property in Australia — what does that mean? I bet it's not a pig farm! All I can hope is maybe he'll have a brother. Oh, Dorrie, am I so mean I didn't even say congratulations?"

She gave Dorrie lavish, loud kisses — Dorrie standing still for them, as if she were five years old.

Dorrie said that she and Mr. Speirs planned to go through "a form of marriage." What do you mean, said Millicent, do you mean a marriage ceremony, is that what you mean? — and Dorrie said yes.

Muriel made the first cut into the satin, saying that somebody had to do it, though maybe if she were doing it again it wouldn't be in quite that place.

Soon they got used to mistakes. Mistakes and rectifications. Late every afternoon, when Muriel got there, they tackled a new stage — the cutting, the pinning, the basting, the sewing — with clenched teeth and grim rallying cries. They had to alter the pattern as they went along, to allow for problems unforeseen, such as the tight set of a sleeve, the bunching of the heavy satin at the waist, the eccentricities of Dorrie's figure. Dorrie was a menace at the job, so they set her to sweeping up scraps and filling the bobbin. Whenever she sat at the sewing machine she clamped her tongue between her teeth. Sometimes she had nothing to do, and she walked from room to room in Millicent's house, stopping to stare out the windows at the snow and sleet, the long-drawn-out end of winter. Or she stood like a docile beast in her woolen underwear, which smelled quite frankly of her flesh, while they pulled and tugged the material around her.

Muriel had taken charge of the clothes. She knew what there had to be. There had to be more than a wedding dress. There had to be a going-away outfit, and a wedding nightgown and a matching dressing gown, and of course an entire new supply of underwear. Silk stockings, and a brassiere — the first that Dorrie had ever worn.

Dorrie had not known about any of that. "I considered the wedding dress as the major hurdle," she said. "I could not think beyond it."

The snow melted, the creeks filled up, the muskrats would be swimming in the cold water, sleek and sporty, with their treasure on their backs. If Dorrie thought of her traps she did not say so. The only walk she took these days was across the field from her house to Millicent's.

Made bold by experience, Muriel cut out a dressmaker suit of fine russet wool, and a lining. She was letting her choir rehearsals go all to pot.

Millicent had to think about the wedding luncheon. It was to be held in the Brunswick Hotel. But who was there to invite, except the minister? Lots of people knew Dorrie, but they knew her as the lady who left skinned rabbits on doorsteps, who went through the fields and the woods with her dog and gun and waded along the flooded creeks in her high rubber boots. Few people knew anything about the old Becks, though all remembered Albert and had liked him. Dorrie was not quite a joke — something protected her from that, either Albert's popularity or her own gruffness and dignity — but the news of her wedding had roused a lot of interest, not exactly of a sympathetic nature. Her marriage was being spoken of as a freakish event, mildly scandalous, possibly a hoax. Porter said that bets were being laid on whether the man would show up.

Finally, Millicent recalled some cousins, who had come to Albert's funeral. Ordinary, respectable people. Dorrie had their addresses, invitations were sent. Then the Nunn brothers from the grocery, whom Albert had worked for, and their wives. A couple of Albert's lawn-bowling friends and their wives. The people who owned the mink farm where Dorrie sold her groundhogs? The woman from the bakeshop who was going to ice the cake?

The cake was being made at home, then taken to the shop to be iced by the woman who had got a diploma in cake decorating from a place in Chicago. It would be covered with white roses, lacy scallops, hearts and garlands and silver leaves and those tiny silver candies you can break your tooth on. Meanwhile it had to be mixed and baked, and this was where Dorrie's strong arms could come into play, stirring and stirring a mixture so stiff it appeared to be all candied fruit and raisins and currants with a little gingery batter holding everything together like glue. When Dorrie got the big bowl against her stomach and took up the beating spoon, Millicent heard the first satisfied sigh to come out of her in a long while.

Muriel decided that there had to be a maid of honor. Or a matron of honor. It could not be her, because she would be playing the organ. "O Perfect Love." And the Mendelssohn.

It would have to be Millicent. Muriel would not take no for an answer. She brought over an evening dress of her own, a long sky blue dress, which she ripped open at the waist — how confident and cavalier she was by now, about dressmaking! — and she proposed a lace midriff, of darker blue, with a matching lace bolero. It will look like new and suit you to a T, she said.

Millicent laughed when she first tried it on, and she said, "There's a sight to scare the pigeons!" But she was pleased. She and Porter had not had much of a wedding — they had just gone to the rectory, deciding to put the money saved into furniture. "I suppose I'll need some kind of thingamajig," she said. "Something on my head."

"Her veil!" cried Muriel. "What about Dorrie's veil? We've been concentrating so much on wedding dresses, we've forgotten all about a veil!"

Dorrie spoke up unexpectedly and said that she would never wear a veil. She could not stand to have one draped over her, it would feel like cobwebs. Her use of the word "cobwebs" gave Muriel and Millicent a start, because there were jokes being made about cobwebs in other places.

"She's right," said Muriel. "A veil would be too much." She considered what else. A wreath of flowers? No, too much again. A picture hat? Yes, get an old summer hat and cover it with white satin. Then get another and cover it with the dark blue lace.

"Here is the menu," said Millicent dubiously. "Creamed chicken in pastry shells, little round biscuits, molded jellies, that salad with the apples and the walnuts, pink and white ice cream with the cake —"

Thinking of the cake, Muriel said, "Does he by any chance have a sword, Dorrie?"

Dorrie said, "Who?"

"Wilkie. Your Wilkie. Does he have a sword?"

"What would he have a sword for?" Millicent said.

"I just thought he might," said Muriel.

"I cannot enlighten you," said Dorrie.

Then there was a moment in which they all fell silent, because they had to think of the bridegroom. They had to admit him to the room and set him down in the midst of all this. Picture hats. Creamed chicken. Silver leaves. They were stricken with doubts. At least Millicent was, and Muriel. They hardly dared to look at each other.

"I just thought since he was English, or whatever he is," said Muriel.

Millicent said, "He is a fine man, anyway."

*

The wedding was set for the second Saturday in May. Mr. Speirs was to arrive on the Wednesday and stay with the minister. The Sunday before, Dorrie was supposed to come over to have supper with Millicent and Porter. Muriel was there, too. Dorrie didn't arrive, and they went ahead and started without her.

Millicent stood up in the middle of the meal. "I'm going over there," she said. "She'd better be sharper than this getting to her wedding."

"I can keep you company," said Muriel.

Millicent said no thanks. Two might make it worse.

Make what worse?

She didn't know.

She went across the field by herself. It was a warm evening, and the back door of Dorrie's house was standing open. Between the house and where the barn used to be there was a grove of walnut trees, whose branches were still bare, since walnut trees are among the very latest to get their leaves. The hot sunlight pouring through bare branches seemed unnatural. Her feet did not make any sound on the grass.

And there on the back platform was Albert's old armchair, never taken in all winter.

What was in her mind was that Dorrie might have had an accident. Something to do with a gun. Maybe while cleaning her gun. That happened to people. Or she might be lying out in a field somewhere, lying in the woods among the old, dead leaves and the new leeks and bloodroot. Tripped while getting over a fence. Had to go out one last time. And then, after all the safe times, the gun had gone off. Millicent had never had any such fears for Dorrie before, and she knew that in some ways Dorrie was very careful and competent. It must be that what had happened this year made anything seem possible. The proposed marriage, such wild luck, could make you believe in calamity also.

But it was not an accident that was on Millicent's mind. Not really. Under this busy, fearful imagining of accidents, she hid what she really feared.

She called Dorrie's name at the open door. And so prepared was she for an answering silence, the evil silence and indifference of a house lately vacated by somebody who had met with disaster (or not vacated, yet, by the body of the person who had met with, who had *brought about,* that disaster) — so prepared was she for the worst that she was shocked, she went watery in the knees, at the sight of Dorrie herself in her old field pants and shirt.

"We were waiting for you," Millicent said. "We were waiting for you to come to supper."

Dorrie said, "I must've lost track of the time."

"Oh, have all your clocks stopped?" said Millicent, recovering her nerve as she was led through the back hall with its familiar, mysterious debris. She could smell cooking.

The kitchen was dark because of the big, unruly lilac pressing against the window. Dorrie used the house's original wood-burning cookstove, and she had one of those old kitchen tables with drawers for the knives and forks. It was a relief to see that the calendar on the wall was for this year.

Yes — Dorrie was cooking some supper. She was in the middle of chopping up a purple onion, to add to the bits of bacon and sliced potatoes she had frying up in the pan. So much for losing track of the time.

"You go ahead," said Millicent. "Go ahead and make your meal. I did get something to eat before I took it into my head to go and look for you."

"I made tea," said Dorrie. It was keeping warm on the back of the stove, and when she poured it out it was like ink.

"I can't leave," she said, prying up some of the bacon that was sputtering in the pan. "I can't leave here."

Millicent decided to treat this as she would a child's announcement that she could not go to school.

"Well, that'll be a nice piece of news for Mr. Speirs," she said. "When he has come all this way."

Dorrie leaned back as the grease became fractious.

"Better move that off the heat a bit," Millicent said.

"I can't leave."

"I heard that before."

Dorrie finished her cooking and scooped the results onto a plate. She added ketchup and a couple of thick slices of bread soaked in the grease that was left in the pan. She sat down to eat, and did not speak.

Millicent was sitting, too, waiting her out. Finally she said, "Give a reason."

Dorrie shrugged and chewed.

"Maybe you know something I don't," Millicent said. "What have you found out? Is he poor?"

Dorrie shook her head. "Rich," she said.

So, Muriel was right.

"A lot of women would give their eyeteeth."

"I don't care about that," Dorrie said. She chewed and swallowed and repeated, "I don't care."

Millicent had to take a chance, though it embarrassed her. "If you are thinking about what I think you may be thinking about, then it could be that you are worried over nothing. A lot of the time when they get older they don't even want to bother."

"Oh, it isn't that! I know all about that."

Oh, do you, thought Millicent, and if so, how? Dorrie might imagine she knew, from animals. Millicent had sometimes thought that no woman would get married, if she really knew.

Nevertheless, she said, "Marriage takes you out of yourself and gives you a real life."

"I have a life," Dorrie said. "Perhaps I am not adventurous," she added.

"All right, then," said Millicent, as if she had given up arguing. She sat and drank her poison tea. She was getting an inspiration. She let time pass and then she said, "It's up to you, it certainly is. But there is a problem about where you will live. You can't live here. When Porter and I found out you were getting married we put this place on the market, and we sold it."

Dorrie said instantly, "You're lying."

"We didn't want it standing empty to make a haven for tramps. We went ahead and sold it."

"You would never do such a trick on me."

"What kind of a trick would it be when you were getting married?"

Millicent was already believing what she said. Soon it could come true. They could offer the place at a low enough price, and somebody would buy it. It could still be fixed up. Or it could be torn down, for the bricks and the woodwork. Porter would be glad to be rid of it.

Dorrie said, "You would not put me out of my house."

Millicent kept quiet.

"You are lying, aren't you?" said Dorrie.

"Give me your Bible," Millicent said. "I will swear on it."

Dorrie actually looked around. She said, "I don't know where it is."

"Dorrie, listen. All of this is for your own good. It may seem like I am pushing you out, but all it is is making you do what you are not quite up to doing on your own."

"Oh," said Dorrie. "Why?"

Because the wedding cake is made, thought Millicent, and the satin dress is made, and the luncheon has been ordered and the invitations have been sent. All this trouble that has been gone to. People might say that was a silly reason, but those who said that would not be the people who had gone to the trouble. It was not fair, to have your best efforts squandered.

But it was more than that, for she believed what she had said, telling Dorrie that this was how she could have a life. And what did Dorrie mean by "here"? If she meant that she would be homesick, let her be! Homesickness was never anything you couldn't get over. Millicent was not going to pay any attention to that "here." Nobody had any business living a life out "here" if she had been offered what Dorrie had. It was a kind of sin, to refuse such an offer. Out of stubbornness, out of fearfulness, and idiocy.

She had begun to get the feeling that Dorrie was cornered. Dorrie might be giving up, or letting the idea of giving up seep through her. Perhaps. She sat as still as a stump, but there was a chance such a stump might be pulpy within.

But it was Millicent who began suddenly to weep. "Oh, Dorrie," she said. "Don't be stupid!" They both got up and grabbed hold of each other, and then Dorrie had to do the comforting, patting and soothing in a magisterial way, while Millicent wept, and repeated some words that did not hang together. *Happy. Help. Ridiculous.*

"I will look after Albert," she said, when she had calmed down somewhat. "I'll put flowers. And I won't mention this to Muriel Snow. Or to Porter. Nobody needs to know."

Dorrie said nothing. She seemed a little lost, absent-minded, as if she was busy turning something over and over, resigning herself to the weight and strangeness of it.

"That tea is awful," said Millicent. "Can't we make some that's fit to drink?" She went to throw the contents of her cup into the slop pail.

There stood Dorrie in the dim window light — mulish, obedient, childish, female — a most mysterious and maddening person, whom Millicent seemed now to have conquered, to be sending away. At greater cost to herself, Millicent was thinking — greater cost than she had understood. She tried to engage Dorrie in a somber but encouraging look, canceling her fit of tears. She said, "The die is cast."

Dorrie walked to her wedding. Nobody had known that she intended to do that. When Porter and Millicent stopped the car in front of her house, to pick her up, Millicent was still anxious. "Honk the horn," she said. "She better be ready now."

Porter said, "Isn't that her down ahead?"

It was. She was wearing a light gray coat of Albert's over her satin dress and was carrying her picture hat in one hand, a bunch of lilacs in the other. They stopped the car and she said, "No. I want the exercise. It will clear out my head."

They had no choice but to drive on and wait at the church and see her approaching down the street, people coming out of shops to look, a few cars honking sportively, people waving and calling out, "Here comes the bride!" As she got closer to the church she stopped and removed Albert's coat, and then she was gleaming, miraculous, like the pillar of salt in the Bible.

Muriel was inside the church, playing the organ, so she did not have to realize, at this last moment, that they had forgotten all about gloves and that Dorrie clutched the woody stems of the lilac in her bare hands. Mr. Speirs had been in the church, too, but he had come out, breaking all rules, leaving the minister to stand there on his own. He was as lean and yellow and wolfish as Millicent remembered, but when he saw Dorrie fling the old coat into the back of Porter's car and settle the hat on her head — Millicent had to run up and fix it right — he appeared nobly satisfied. Millicent had a picture of him and Dorrie mounted high, mounted on elephants, panoplied, borne cumbrously forward, adventuring. A vision. She was filled with optimism and relief and she whispered to Dorrie, "He'll take you everywhere! He'll make you a queen!"

"I have grown as fat as the Queen of Tonga," wrote Dorrie from Australia, some years on. A photograph showed that she was not exaggerating. Her hair was white, her skin brown, as if all her freckles had got loose and run together. She wore a vast garment, colored like tropical flowers. The war had come and put an end to any idea of traveling, and then when it was over Wilkie was dying. Dorrie stayed on, in Queensland, on a great property where she grew sugarcane and pineapples, cotton, peanuts, tobacco. She rode horses, in spite of her size, and had learned to fly an airplane. She took up some travels of her own in that part of the world. She had shot crocodiles. She died in the fifties, in New Zealand, climbing up to look at a volcano.

Millicent told everybody what she had said she would not mention. She took credit, naturally. She recalled her inspiration, her stratagem, with no apologies. "Somebody had to take the bull by the horns," she said. She felt that she was the creator of a life — more effectively, in Dorrie's case, than in the case of her own children. She had created happiness, or something close. She forgot the way she had wept without knowing why.

The wedding had its effect on Muriel. She handed in her resignation, she went off to Alberta. "I'll give it a year," she said. And within a year she had found a husband — not the sort of man she had ever had anything to do with in the past. A widower with two small children. A Christian minister. Millicent wondered at Muriel's describing him that way. Weren't all ministers Christian? When they came back for a visit — by this time there were two more children, their own — she saw the point of the description. Smoking and drinking and swearing were out, and so was wearing makeup, and the kind of music that Muriel used to play. She played hymns now — the sort she had once made fun of. She wore any color at all and had a bad permanent — her hair, going gray, stood up from her forehead in frizzy bunches. "A lot of my former life turns my stomach — just to think about it," she said, and Millicent got the impression that she and Porter were seen mostly as belonging to those stomach-turning times.

The house was not sold or rented. It was not torn down, either, and its construction was so sound that it did not readily give way. It was capable of standing for years and years and presenting a plausible appearance. A tree of cracks can branch out among the bricks, but the wall does not fall down. Window sashes settle, at an angle, but the window does not fall out. The doors were locked, but it was probable that children got in and wrote things on the walls and broke up the crockery that Dorrie had left behind. Millicent never went in to see.

There was a thing that Dorrie and Albert used to do, and then Dorrie did alone. It must have started when they were children. Every year, in the fall, they — and then, she — collected up all the walnuts that had fallen off the trees. They kept going, collecting fewer and fewer walnuts every day, until they were fairly sure that they had got the last, or the next-to-last, one. Then they counted them, and they wrote the total on the cellar wall. The date, the year, the total. The walnuts were not used for anything once they were collected. They were just dumped along the edge of the field and allowed to rot.

Millicent did not continue this useless chore. She had plenty of other chores to do, and plenty for her children to do. But at the time of year when the walnuts were lying in the long grass she would think of that custom, and how Dorrie must have expected to keep it up until she died. A life of customs, of seasons. The walnuts drop, the muskrats swim in the creek. Dorrie must have believed that she was meant to live so, in her reasonable eccentricity, her manageable loneliness. Probably she would have got another dog.

But I would not allow that, thinks Millicent. She would not allow it, and surely she was right. She has lived to be an old lady, she is living yet, though Porter has been dead for decades. She doesn't often notice the house. It is just there. But once in a while she does see its cracked face and the blank, slanted windows. The walnut trees behind, losing again, again, their delicate canopy of leaves.

I ought to knock that down and sell the bricks, she says, and seems puzzled that she has not already done so.

LARRY WOIWODE

Silent Passengers

FROM THE NEW YORKER

SHUT IT OFF, Steiner told himself, and the station wagon was silent. He had pulled into the drive and up to the Chinese elm at the house without the reality of any of it registering, and now he turned to his nine-year-old, James, in the seat beside him, and saw the boy's face take on the expression of sly imbalance that Steiner had noticed in it for the first time this afternoon.

Steiner got out and James bucked against his seat belt, holding up a hand, so Steiner eased back in, shoving his unruly hair off his forehead, and took hold of the wheel. He was so used to James being out of the car and headed across the yard the second after they stopped that he felt dazed. His white-blond twin daughters, seven, who were in the rear with his wife, Jen, were whispering, and Steiner turned to them with a look that meant *Silence!* He got out again, with a heaviness that made him feel that his age, forty-five, was the beginning of old age, and that the remorse he'd recently been saturated with had a focus: it was a remorse that he and Jen hadn't had more children.

As he was driving home, a twin had pulled herself forward from the back seat and whispered that James had reached over and honked the horn while Steiner was in the department store, where he had gone to look for a shatterproof, full-length mirror and an exercise mat of the kind the physical therapist had recommended. And since James hadn't spoken for two weeks, the incident had set the twins to whispering about James, in speculative and hopeful terms (with James sitting right there!), for most of the long trip home.

"I'm sorry," Steiner said, seeing that he was still the only one outside the car, as if he had to apologize for being on his feet. He slid back in, brushing aside his hair again, and began to unbuckle James's seat belt. The boy stared out the windshield with an intensity Steiner couldn't translate, and, once free, tried to scoot over to the passenger door by bending his torso forward and back.

"Take it easy, honey," Steiner said, and then added for the boy and the others, in the phrase that he'd used since James was an infant, "Here we are home." Silence. Steiner turned to Jen, who was leaning close, her pretty lips set, and said, "Do you have his other belt?" She gave a nod.

Steiner got out and looked across the top of the station wagon, through the leaves of the four-trunked elm, at their aging farmhouse. He hadn't seen it in two weeks. He'd spent that time at the hospital with James, first in intensive care, then in a private room, where physical therapists came and went, and at the sight of the white siding that he and James and Jen had scraped and repainted at the beginning of summer, he had to swallow down the loss that he'd started to feel when he realized he was grieving for a son he might never see again.

He looked up at a second-story window and remembered waking, sweaty, from a nap on the day that this began, on the floor of the twins' upstairs room, where he'd gone to be alone, and hearing James say, "Dad, do you still need me to help, or can I go to Allen's with Mom and the girls and go riding?"

"They're going now?" Steiner had asked, feeling dislocated at finding himself on the floor of a room he usually visited only at the twins' bedtime. He had climbed up there after downing two beers in the August heat, and since he drank so seldom lately he had all but passed out. He and the family were back at their high-plains ranch for the summer, to get away from the silicon-chip firm on the Coast which Steiner partly owned, and he and James and a neighbor had been trying to start a tractor that Steiner wanted to use to cultivate trees — "to play farmer," as the neighbor said. Steiner and the neighbor had spent most of that hot August morning pulling the diesel tractor in ovals around the drive with a second tractor, getting it going for a while and then listening to it die, with James hooking and unhooking the drawbar chain and having to jump aside once in his nimble way when the neighbor missed the clutch and struck Steiner's big rear tires and merely bounced backward as the tractor stalled again.

Now Steiner strained to hear James's voice from that afternoon — the last time he'd heard him speak — and sensed that James had been at a distance, perhaps already heading downstairs, aware that Steiner was angry at the tractor, and might be short-tempered after the beer. James would sometimes come up to Steiner, take his hand, and say, "Dad, I forgive you," before Steiner realized he'd been harsh or unfair, but James wasn't a do-gooder or tattletale: more a conscience.

Steiner had hoped to establish their home on this ranch and run his business from here, in order to spend more time with the children, as Jen had said he should. This last year he had been out of the office every month, traveling on consulting trips to Europe, and at the thought of all those jet-fuel-smelling 747s, Steiner was back on the floor of the twins' bedroom that August afternoon, reeking of the tractor fuel on his hands and clothes, and the beer on his breath. He felt caught off guard, laid low by the beer, and then he heard, as if James were standing above the spot where he lay, "I'll stay and help with the tractor if you want, Dad."

The memory of his response went through Steiner so wildly that he felt even more dislocated. What was it he'd said? "I don't care."

He realized Jen had spoken, and saw James rubbing the window on his side, impatient to get out. Steiner hurried over and opened the door, and James grabbed at the dash and the seat, trying to propel himself from the car. Steiner squatted at the boy's level and took his hands in his. "Be patient a minute, honey," he said. "Remember your belt?"

The boy's hair was as unruly as his, and the sandy-colored curl at its edges needed trimming. James's eyes were nearly covered by it, Steiner saw, and then they rested on him in a dull love. Steiner coughed and felt a hand on his shoulder. Jen was standing above him, smiling — wisps of hair lifting from her forehead in a wind Steiner hadn't noticed until now — and the sight of her somehow enabled him to understand that he could endure handling James in his helpless condition on home ground. The boy loved the ranch so much that his usual good health always appeared to get even better, once they were here; he seemed to grow an inch his first week back, each time. Careful of the boy's ribs, Steiner lifted James from the seat, turning him so his back rested on Steiner's stomach, and the heated weight of James against him had the effect of blocking the blood to his brain. His mind went blank.

James started pedaling his feet in a spinning run in place, and Jen laughed and shook her head. Then she glanced around the yard and off to a blue-shaded butte, as if to make the landscape hers again, and looked buoyant with the breath she took, then wiped at the corner of an eye. "You're so dear," she said to James, smiling down at him.

Steiner had spent the last week or so trying to decide if James's sense of humor was returning, as when a therapist had helped the boy down a ramp into the hospital pool for the first attempt at one of the forms of therapy a pediatrician had prescribed, and James, a natural swimmer, had become so excited at the sensation of water that he tried to run and fell with a splash. When the therapist and Jen, who got her skirt soaked, pulled him from the pool, James mimicked a hangdog look, and then, for the first time since the accident, he contrived a smile, wry and lopsided, that caused Steiner to laugh. James produced the same smile when he was on his next instrument of therapy — a stainless-steel tricycle — every time the therapist relaxed her control over the handlebars and he rammed it into a wall, reminding Steiner of the time a colleague from the East, a designer whose chips were as intricate as a gridwork of Manhattan, with each cornice and window in place in each building, was scheduled to arrive at the ranch and Steiner wanted to impress him with the comfort of the place. Steiner had been on the phone, trying to deal with a local plumber who had promised to check their failing sewage system but now was pretending he hadn't promised *when* he would, and Steiner tried to say, "But we must have a bathroom," and was only able to get out "But . . . but . . ." And when he hung up, James came hurrying past — nearly impossible now to recapture this dancing half run the boy performed with such agility — and said from the side of his mouth, "Is your butt broke, Dad?"

Once Steiner had begun to grieve for the James he had known, the grief grew worse when he realized that in the last year or so it had been James, more than anyone, who had had the ability to cheer him.

Now Jen slid an arm between Steiner's stomach and James, passing the padded canvas belt around the boy's waist. She drew it snug, and then buckled him in. James's closed-head injury, as the doctors called it, was in the rear-left quadrant, so his right limbs weren't responding well, and the physical therapist had demonstrated to Steiner and Jen how to grip the belt from behind, in order to support James in his walking, which kept improving with his visits to the pool.

"Do you want to —" Steiner began, but Jen already had the belt, and James went teetering off, with her in tow, past the front of the car, as if on a beeline toward the last moment he might have remembered — the tractor. Steiner's daughters went past with their hair streaming back, laughing at the speed of James's walk and at Jen's attempts to keep up. James was enamored of farm equipment, and the connection he might make to the person he'd been before, Steiner had thought through the hospital stay, was the tractor. Their neighbor had finally fixed it — a plugged fuel filter, he discovered — and had driven to the hospital to tell them this when James was still in the state the doctors called comatose, and Steiner was positive he had seen James respond.

So all through the hospital stay, Steiner kept telling James they would get the tractor going as soon as they got home. He was grateful to Jen now, though, that she had taken him away. Steiner tried again to hear James's voice asking to go to Allen's that afternoon, and then remembered waking a second time, after the family was gone from the house, to somebody calling his name — the neighbor who had been helping with the tractor. "Billy Allen's on the line," the man had said, and Steiner's first thought was *Something's happened to James.* The neighbor was in the kitchen, staring out at the tractor, Steiner saw as he went by, noticing the broken-open six-pack on the table.

"Yes?" he said into the receiver.

"Steiner," Billy Allen said. "Bad news. The kids was back from riding, unsaddling the horses — your wife was there, I wasn't — when my gelding, Apache, spooked, I guess, and went over the top of James. He's hurt. I don't know how bad, Steiner, but he ain't conscious yet." Allen's voice parted with fear at this. "I called the ambulance. We'll meet you at the hospital."

Steiner called right back, but the phone kept ringing. Billy Allen lived on a river-bottom ranch thirty miles off, and all summer had been asking the twins to come and ride, and Steiner's response had been "What's wrong with our horses?" until Jen said, "Surely you know that poor lonely old bachelor dotes on girls." So why did James go? Steiner almost yelled into the phone, which kept on ringing.

He drove to the hospital at a speed his pickup probably wouldn't recover from, trying not to picture the ways James might be injured. He had bought the six-pack on an errand in town — for his neighbor to enjoy in the heat, he told himself — but back home he cracked a can for himself, irritated at the damn tractor that had already cost him enough, and then looked down to see James staring up in sadness, prepared to forgive him. Then he recalled that he had told James on the trip to the ranch that he wasn't going to drink this summer, not even a beer — since lately drinking made him unpredictable. The image of James staring up — with Jen's beauty in his features — stayed in Steiner's mind throughout the twenty-some miles to the hospital, while he kept saying, "Please, please," meaning, Don't let his face be disfigured.

He beat the ambulance in. The nurse at the emergency desk, wearing an orange stopwatch on a cord around her neck, seemed the bulky focus of the world that was still stable. She said the ambulance had called in, and from somewhere under the counter between them a radio crackled on and an amplified voice said something Steiner couldn't catch. Before he was able to ask the nurse anything, she picked up a microphone from under the counter, and said, "How is he?" A wash of static went through Steiner like a further form of anxiety, and again he couldn't make out a word.

The nurse studied him with set lips, appraising him, and said, "There are no marks on him, they say" — as if she knew what he needed to hear — "but he isn't conscious."

Now Steiner saw James swerve toward the granary near the drive, with Jen keeping up and with one daughter holding

James's hand and the other grabbing at her mother's skirt. The tractor sat in the unmowed grass ahead. Steiner turned from them into a flash like a press camera's — the mirror in the rear of the station wagon reflecting sun into his eyes. He leaned against the automobile, unable to stop this sequence that kept returning: the stretcher tilting from the ambulance, James's blue face against sheets, Jen squalling up in the station wagon and running over in riding denims, the girls running after her, and then the glass doors to the hospital springing open with a hiss; hearing this and the clattering of all the footsteps but no sound of a voice. Then the stretcher rolled close, and he could hear James going, "Ohhh, ohh," in shallow sighs. Jen embraced Steiner with an impact that set him off balance, and cried, "It's my fault!"

"No," Steiner said, holding her so hard that the snaps of her jacket dug into his chest. The stretcher paused, as if the ambulance attendants were waiting for a command, and Steiner turned, one arm still around Jen, and tried to locate James's hand under the blanket and discovered that James was strapped to some sort of hard-plastic carrier. Two swelling, padded curves gripped his jaw on each side, and straps were buckled across his forehead and near his neck.

"It's Dad, I'm here," Steiner said, and thought he heard a catch in James's breathing. *Good God,* he thought, and closed his eyes and understood that each "oh" from James was an attempt to cry out in pain, and felt that if he could enter James and bear this moment for him the boy would rise from the stretcher and walk away. Then the doctor, a French-Vietnamese who had taken over a local quarter-horse ranch, was in the midst of them, looking like a jockey in a torn red T-shirt, saying to an ambulance attendant, "You thought a spinal injury?"

He quickly undid the buckle near James's neck to help him breathe more freely, and the attendant said, "In case."

"Here," the doctor said, and grabbed the head of the stretcher and pulled it into a side room himself — as if to be free of the attendants — and over to an examining table. "Dad and Mom, here," he said, and when an attendant with a full beard attempted to block the door, he called, "No! I want them in here to help, answer questions! What's his name?"

"James."

"James! Can you hear me?"

James lay inert, expressionless, ivory, and beneath the overhead lights Steiner saw the boy's lips tugging with inner pain. The nurse helped the doctor slide James and the board onto the examining table, and the doctor probed his neck and skull and took a flashlight from the nurse and looked into James's eyes, drawing his lids high with a thumb, and then, with a tool, scraped the soles of both feet, hammered at James's knees and elbows, drew the tool up his sternum, and said, "Get upper X-rays, quick."

To Steiner he said, "I'm going to give him some oxygen through a nasal cannula here," already tearing open a sack. A coil of blue-tinted plastic fell from it over the boy's bare legs, pale and dirt-smeared. Why was he wearing shorts to ride? Steiner almost shouted, and felt a hand on his back. Billy Allen stood with a hat over his chest, chin trembling, and said, "I should have been there to help. Call my insurance company. Sue me." The elderly man looked almost in tears, and one of the ambulance attendants led him into the hall.

"That's all I can do," the doctor said. "I see head injury but no sign of it. He's not posing or putting on displays of extensive damage, but is comatose, you see. I'm running quick X-rays" — the machine above them clicked on, humming, and the doctor glanced at it and shrugged. "I'm sending him to the city hospital. You'll want all the attention he can —"

Steiner swooped for James, who had grabbed the side of the table to pull himself over, about to fall as Steiner got to him, and then, in a spasm that drew his knees near his chest, he gagged up watery stuff, then groaned and gagged up a dark spoonful the nurse caught in a stainless-steel bowl.

"Last meal?" the doctor asked.

"Lunch," Jen whispered, hoarse, and Steiner saw her on the other side, ducking the X-ray machine a technician was running on an overhead track, holding James's hand.

"Goodness," the doctor said. "Look at him empty his stomach — good response. We'll have to keep his lungs clear. I'm putting in a stomach tube. Catheter, too," he said to the nurse. He was already through a leg of James's shorts with glittering shears and clipping off his stained T-shirt.

"Test that," he said, to the nurse, nodding at the bowl. "Could be bloody-tinged. Maybe internal injuries," he whispered to Steiner. "I'm telling you straight. You see he doesn't respond in any normal way. Oh — a hoof got him." A curved ridge of torn skin lay under the stained T-shirt, and James's high arch of ribs was dented in. "Ribs," the doctor said to the technician. "Poor kid." Then to Steiner, "He'll be prepped for the ambulance."

"Let's call a helicopter," Steiner said, and everybody looked up, as if the shout he'd held back had emerged. He'd heard that helicopters were being used in this sparsely populated countryside to ferry people to city hospitals, and the thought of this had arrived in a jolt: *critical accident victim.*

"The ambulance is as fast, I bet," the doctor said. "And about as smooth a ride. I don't want him jarred too much till we get a CAT scan. His spine's O.K., I think. I'll get him ready and can just about guarantee he'll get to the hospital fine."

A silence came, and as Steiner waited for further reassurance he looked across at Jen and saw her head bowed over James's hand, which she held to her lips. "James!" she cried. "I know you can hear me!" The boy writhed; tubes were in his nostrils and one was in his mouth — hurriedly taped to his sleepstruck face — and this writhing seemed to be in resistance to the catheter the nurse was trying to insert; his hand swung at her.

"Good!" the doctor said, and took the tube from the nurse and tried himself, sweat running beneath his glasses until he whispered, "This is so hard with little boys," nearly in tears. "It's just that we got to have access to his functions. Oh, little guy. His heart is steady, good." A black-and-gray negative clopped into a white-lighted frame. "Oh," the doctor said, "four ribs, at least, in this first X-ray, but no lung puncture that I see. I can say for sure they'll get him there without a change."

"I'll ride in the ambulance!" Jen declared.

There were looks all around, and the doctor said, "I'm sorry — they have regulations. Is the driver here?"

"Me." A young fellow at the door in a baseball cap.

"Follow right behind," the doctor told Steiner, tucking a blanket around James. To an elderly nurse who was looking in from the hall, he said, "Ride along and keep him warm. And you," he said to the ambulance driver, "take it slow, easy over bumps, no use exceeding — play it safe."

It was the longest trip Steiner had ever endured, he felt, following at the ambulance's back, separated from James. But during it he heard the story from Jen. Billy Allen had been busy moving irrigation pipes, so he got the horses saddled and went back to work, and when they were done and had started to unsaddle, the horse James was riding, Apache, went wild, Jen said — all of this happening so fast she hardly had a chance to get the girls out of the way as Apache charged. She had been sure James was safe, because he'd been standing farther back, and then the horse spun, its saddle swinging to one side, and she heard a sound like a post struck and came around the corner where she'd taken cover and saw James, a ways from Apache, hit down.

"I knew right away he was terribly hurt. The horse went off to a fence, kicking at the saddle, and the worst part of it, I mean now, is that James was on his back trying to push himself up. He's that strong. His head came up, he tried to open his eyes, and then he sank back and I caught his head. I didn't think he'd breathe, I waited so long, I don't know how long, rubbing him and asking him to breathe — I felt I had to support his head — and finally he gasped."

Steiner saw that James had traveled past the tractor with his mother and was heading toward the pasture at the edge of the yard. The twins were going ahead through shaggy grass that hadn't been mowed in weeks and reached to their hips, toward a garage that stood alone at a corner of the two-acre farmyard, the peak of its roof like a parody of the tepee buttes that rose above it — so hazy in the late-summer heat they seemed to simmer on the horizon like a mirage. Then Steiner saw where James was headed. At the end of the garage, on the other side of the pasture fence that from Steiner's distance was invisible, three of their quarter horses — a stately bay the size of a cavalry mount and a buckskin mare who seemed on a constant nervous search for the colt nudging up behind her — came ambling forward, all of them at attention, their heads and ears up. Then the bay whinnied in acknowledgment of the family he knew.

James was heading toward him.

He remembers, Steiner thought, his hair going back in the wind, and sat down in the seat where James had been sitting.

Steiner had imagined taking a .30-30 to Allen's and dropping the rogue Apache. I still might, he thought, once James is — The second night at the hospital, while he stood watch in the intensive care ward as Jen slept, he heard the beeps of James's heart monitor start to slow, and when he checked the digital display that printed out every half minute, he saw it read forty-six. At forty an alarm went off, and the nurse on duty, who was at a desk behind glass, looked up. It was a large ward, but James's bed was the only one in it, and the nurse glanced at the monitor on her desk and then shook her head as if to clear it. She was Steiner's age, responsible for supervising the student nurses, besides her I.C.U. duties, and Steiner understood by her response that she was overworked.

She came through the door into the ward, which was dimly lit by baseboard lights, and stood at the other side of James's bed. "Is our boy tired?" she whispered, and with the second sense Steiner was developing he realized that her concern for James exceeded medical limits; she had become personally involved. She was wearing slacks and a turtleneck — the informality on pediatrics disturbed Steiner; nobody wore white — and he could see her standing like this with her husband, the baseboard lights projecting their shadows on the ceiling above a son's bed. "Should his heartbeat be so slow?" he whispered, imagining James heard every word.

"Oh, he's a child," she said, recovering from whatever state she had slipped into. "It's surprising how low it can go in a kid. Did he used to run a lot?"

"Yes."

"If it was you or me, I'd be worried."

But when she went back to her desk he saw her turn aside to make a phone call. The next digital printout read thirty-five. At thirty Steiner saw her go to a refrigerator and prepare a syringe, and then he had to blink against the overhead lights she suddenly switched on. She walked in and looked down at James, her hands on her hips, detached and half angry, a nurse again, then strode back to her station.

Steiner put a hand on the far side of James and leaned over him. "James," he said, and couldn't say any more. Without any sign of injury, James looked more beautiful than ever, and all

Steiner could do was stare down at him and take in every feature and inch of skin in case he never saw him alive again. He felt that he could see into James to the place he had retreated to, where his real self rested, hidden, and that he should call to him there. Then this seemed presumptuous, grandiose — as if it were in his power to call James back! His lips felt sealed. But if he, the boy's father, wouldn't make this effort, who would? "James," he said firmly, more severely than he'd intended, and with a skip the boy's heart rate on the monitor picked up again.

The neurologist was noncommittal, one neurosurgeon was hopeful, many of the physical therapists were hopeful, but the pediatrician overseeing James was pessimistic, given to scowling, and when James didn't fully wake from the coma after forty-eight hours, and seventy-two, and then four days, his scowl deepened. Wriggling a toothbrush mustache as he pursed and compressed his lips, he asked Steiner and Jen to "step with" him from James's bed, where they were sharing a shift. He sat them down in a lounge and said that since they hadn't seen any of the signs in James they were looking for, all of them had to face the worst: that James might not recover, or, if he did, he would have to undergo the most comprehensive therapy merely to restore his basic functions, which did not include — his mustache wriggled — vocal speech.

They tried to convince him that they had seen a change, that James's eyes were open more often, that he seemed to respond to his name, that the head nurse had said she was sure he was following along when she read from a children's book she held in front of him, and Jen brought up a theory she'd mentioned to Steiner — that James was such a perfectionist he wouldn't speak until he could speak as he used to. No, the doctor insisted, they must not get their hopes up, that was why they were having this "counseling session."

So Steiner got up and took Jen's hand and walked off with her to a room the head nurse was letting them use for naps, and in a rawness of intimacy he wanted to have her on the spot but knew they must do something as parents. Then Jen said, "I want to hold him."

They went into the hall hand-in-hand and hurried to the boy's bed, like youngsters, escaping the pediatrician. Steiner helped

Jen draw James from the bed, moving tubes and an I.V. stand, and into a rocker with her. James's head dropped back, his lips apart and his eyes open, and he stared up at her with the distant look Steiner had seen in him when he rested in the crook of her arm as a nursing infant. Then James struggled to rise and put his arms around his mother's neck.

The next morning as the pediatrician was doing his daily tests and called, "James, squeeze my finger!" he glanced at Steiner and Jen, eyes wide, and said, "Some grip!" Later that day James opened his mouth to speak and looked puzzled, then tried again, shifting his lips, and finally gave up. But from then his progress was fast. The next day he was transferred from intensive care and put on the course of therapy, and then Jen said it was time to go home. The pediatrician, who by now was less pessimistic, went so far as to say that Jen was doing more for James than most of the — his mustache bobbed — "care professionals."

And now, away from that institution and under this expanse of sky, Steiner understood that though he may have thought the worst at times, and didn't always know how to handle what was happening, there was a part of him that never doubted that James would recover. Which was what had helped him stay sane enough to be available to the boy. James's recovery seemed an internal process, nearly separate from him and Jen, and they had been carried along by it, silent passengers, until it had brought them home.

So now Steiner drew himself from the seat and walked around the station wagon to watch James and Jen and his daughters at the fence. The horses were arching their necks down to them, and James leaned forward from the belt, his left hand up, and stroked the nose of the bay, then the skittish buckskin, who jerked back at his touch, checked for her colt, then came forward and nodded her head at him. His hand traveled over her face and muzzle, unsteadily at first, and then he assumed a courtly stance that he used to favor, and Steiner had a glimpse of the son who had always had a way with pardon, and thought, That's enough. He had always wondered how parents with injured or diminished children were able to bear it. He pitied their patience and calm, but now he understood; it was enough to have the child with them, alive.

James turned, sensing Steiner's eyes on him, and brought Jen swinging around as she held to his belt, and the horses wheeled away, heading down the hill toward the pasture. *Get back,* Steiner cried to himself. He could feel the battering of hooves from where he stood and imagined the weighty charge of Apache toward James, and then a gust of wind took his hair straight up and he saw James's and Jen's and the twins' hair climb the air also, the girls' high above their heads. And over the days and months afterward, when James had started talking, and traveling everywhere on a run, the sensation of that moment kept returning to Steiner — all of them suspended for a second against the horizon, silent in the wind.

ALICE FULTON

Queen Wintergreen

FROM TRIQUARTERLY

MARGARET MERNS was on her knees in the front yard, picking dandelions for wine, when she spotted a snowy mystery on the ground. Jarvis Fitzgerald's sight was surer than her own. Yet she had to call his attention to the crumpled whiteness. Jarvis picked it up and settled spectacles on his face. Although the temperature was over eighty at seven A.M., he wore his best heavy coat with no tatters at the cuffs and a vest smooth as a new sail. There must be some high fussing on him to send him into his holiday clothes, she thought. I suppose he thinks we're keeping company. But it must be a brother and sister state of affairs at our age. He curled the wire spectacles like tiny ram's horns around his ears and read the white circular aloud: "Americans who believe in the demands of Ireland that they be allowed to govern themselves will hold a meeting the night of July 1, 1919, at St. Comin's Hall."

Peg Merns didn't listen. He is here again, as he is every morning, she thought. He is here, reading to me with the vast gaze in his granite blue eyes. Since the girls in her hamlet weren't sent to school, she'd never learned to read. Was it just three years since her husband Michael had read to her the accounts of the Irish and the Strangers? Although she was tired of the Troubles, she would have liked to read on her own about the girls of the city fighting shoulder to shoulder with the boys.

Jarvis braced his feet apart like a horse in rough country as he concluded, ". . . so cognizant of their rights, and so determined to remain what God made them — a distinct and independent nation." He folded the flier and put down the sack he'd been holding for her. "Except for the shoes on your feet, you could be a pilgrim circling the stone beds of St. Patrick's Purgatory," he said. "Get yourself up from the dirt, and we'll have a word."

Her straightening was hampered by the arthritis, the shingles and the bee buzz in her head. These days she had no pluck in her limbs to walk without a hard blackthorn stick. The heat weighed like a basket of wet seaweed on her back. Peg Merns had never lived far from water. First the sea, so full of itself; now the state waterway calm and contained as a pint of bitter behind their house. Addled, she'd lately mistaken this canal for Irish water.

"Dandelion wine, is it?" Jarvis said, steadying her elbow.

"I'll hold in big esteem the man that gets a great country to take the pledge."

She knew the tale of the king who had another head darned with blond wool inside his skull. All her life she'd felt there was another, arguing head sewn within her own. And lately she'd begun to see glowing stitches on the outside of things. There was a wreath of rubbery shimmer around each yellow flower, and Port Schuyler, New York, had taken on the cloud colors of Ireland. America, once so brashly bright, was getting dim as a chapel.

They sat on the stoop. Peg separated the roots from the greens in her apron, and Jarvis began to fill his pipe. "On my soul, if it's not good to yourself you are," she said. He hesitated. "The appearance of desire is on your face. Go on, put fire to your pipe." But he planked it down on the step. At this hour the kitchen was full of her son's family launching themselves on another day of dust. It hadn't rained in over a month. With so many bodies inside, the house would be close and hot. And her son's wife, Dolly, had nerves. Still, Peg felt sorry for Jarvis, who had no people. She could well imagine his rented room with its cracked shaving mug and yellowed brush, the pictures of Thomas Ashe and the heroes of 1916 on the walls.

"I'd say come in, but the children would be in a hundred pieces around us," she told him.

"How are you this Saturday morning, Peg Merns?" he said, and he wasn't one for pleasantries. She had sized him up as a direct man with no mischief in him. Straight as the hands on a clock.

"Ailing I am, and wasting. It's a grief to be old."

"And a sorrow." He glanced at her. "But you've still got a fine physique. Will you be at the freedom meeting tonight?" He gestured with the circular.

"Oh, it's the Cause you've come for, is it?" There's little taste of Gaelic in his language, she thought. If I said some, he wouldn't know but it was Latin I spoke.

Jarvis hooked a thumb in each lapel. "I have more than the one Cause today. But every Irishman wants her to remain a distinct and independent nation. This notice is signed by the men and the Fathers. I know you'll take an interest in their manly and dignified stand."

She secretly believed that Ireland was a bad-luck country, where people were sent to dine on rocks and hope. As a girl she'd looked at the messy stone fences full of voids and thought they should turn the place into a tombstone quarry. She'd stood on the point to watch the ships coming home in a lather, the ghost of a mountain in every wave.

"I wish them well, indeed I do. But a woman isn't welcome when the talk is of the Troubles. A woman has no vote nor did she ever."

She watched a rivulet of sweat run down his neck, which was long and clean as a gander's. He laced his fingers together over his vest. "Now, Peg, if women got the vote the Blessed Mother would blush."

"It's only a man who'd think that Mary Mother of Sorrows would care at all about such a thing after losing the idol of her heart." There was a spark on his small finger. A diamond pinkie ring. Holiday clothes! Isn't that the spit for the venison and the deer not yet killed, thought the head inside her own.

"If Irish freedom don't interest you, there's another wonder in town you'll want to see. The flying boat is coming. It gave an exhibition and raced with a train, and tonight it stops in the water." He fiddled with his watch chain. "Will you come along with me to see it?"

A flying boat! exclaimed the royal voice inside. What would such a thing resemble at the departing of day for night? Would it have the two sails set and a nice following wind? Would it have wings? " 'Come along,' he says to a woman with the gait of a three-legged horse, the third leg being a cane," she said.

"Then let me be the fourth," Jarvis said. There was a small gap in his smile so you could tell it was not store-bought. She was reminded of the spaces her son Tom, a train conductor, punched in tickets. Jarvis took the flat cap off his head and revolved it in his hands. She'd wondered whether he had hair underneath, but there it was, calm as carded wool. "Peg, we understand each other. You're a bold woman, and I like that. As for myself, I don't spit or wipe my mouth on my sleeve. It would be an honor and a pleasure —"

"Not to come before you in your speech, but can I fetch you a cup of cold milk? I'm sure that's what you're after asking."

Jarvis paused. His collar had dug a ring into his neck, and he touched the red brand. "Like I said, you're a woman full of sport, and I get a fit on my heart when I think of you." He tapped his toe on each word. "It would be an honor and a pleasure if you'd consider this an offer of matrimony. I've been meaning this while back to ask you."

Thank the Lord for faces to cover what you felt, though it caper behind the smile or frown, she thought. A vain bit of her warmed to think of Jarvis's words. It was a triumph to be proposed to at the age of sixty-five by a man not given to drinking or fisticuffs, neither God-beset nor from a family of soupers — those who'd turned in their religion for broth during the famine years — a man, what's more, without the ringworm or the twitch, neither a brute nor a murderer. A fine physique, he'd said. He must be touched in the head to want me, she thought and thought, I'll not have him anyway. Don't be a gloat, she told her triumphant self and felt shamed in advance at the scandal. The scorn of the world her wedding would bring upon her family! And she wasn't about to give up her pleasures. She had a clay pipe to smoke on the sly and no wish to serve a husband like a Christ on earth. A wife must sit to the side of the fire and let her husband warm his vamps in front. She could still hear her children cry "Oh, Ma, Daddy is coming and Katey has taken his newspaper!" In the pinch times, she'd said she'd already eaten so Michael could have his plenty. He had passed away a year ago.

"I'm not the one to hold a man to a rash word. To think of a wedding at our age! Wouldn't that be the grand occasion — with none to hand me over but my own son and the neighbors lined up to laugh on either side. No, I had the one good man, and one is all I'll have. I'll lay it down flat. Even if I were an airy girl again I'd not be the one for you who wants a female mild as turnip water. Have sense," she told him.

He knocked the fresh tobacco from his pipe. "You misjudge me, Peg. A man alone is a great pity, but a wife is company. I'll pray you change your mind."

In a pig's rump I will, said the voice in her skull's vault. "Then pray to Saint Jude who loves a lost cause," she said aloud. A long straying on you, said the voice, as Jarvis Fitzgerald, a fine, well-standing figure of a man got smaller in her sight.

She stood toiling with her hair before the little mirror in her room, sick to her soul of the body: the constant caring for it and its constant complaints. The shingles illness stung like a bodice of briars. Soon she'd get soft in the head, and they'd have to lead her on a leash to the state home. A fine physique. Well, what did he know. In the long ago she'd stood tall as a guarding goat. She'd had hair the yellow of Indian meal. Now it is as the psalm says, she thought, "My moisture is turned into the drought of summer." She'd pulled down the shades to make a cool night season. Her room was a welter of feathery doilies, china figurines, and patterned fabrics. She had three clocks, counting her lavaliere watch, and each told a different hour. There was a small fireplace of marble, its hearth blocked by a piece of green tin. Scapulars hung from the lamp, and you had to walk a slim path around the iron bed to get somewhere. On the dresser she kept an altar to the Virgin, a jar of pennies for the Missions, and a heap of bone jewelry. She stood toiling with her hair, remembering the long-ago when the sea bashed the cliffs by the cottage where they'd lived.

She was born in 1854, six years after the famine. She'd heard tales of that time — the people living on barnacles and nettles, the coffin ships sent out with sacred medals and holy water fastened to their prows. Her father swore he'd never trust Ireland to feed them again. She'd gone into service under an English gentlewoman when she was fourteen. Behind the diamond windows of the rich she'd learned there was nothing worse than being under the hand of other people. And she'd learned about the secret yearnings of men. She attributed the worse vices to the

English. As a domestic she'd learned that the jerky walk and glandular madness of certain old men stemmed from their wild ways as boys. Some of them believed that if they sinned with a virgin they'd be cured. Her employer's second cousin had come into her room one night, and she'd poured the washbowl's water over his head. The next morning she gave her notice. By that time she was sixteen, and her father had saved enough money for the trip to America. They piled their belongings behind them in the wagon, and Peg turned to fix the West country in her head. She saw a woman walking with a load of brushwood on her back like a pair of raveling wings. In the distance, the ashen water and a figure sitting on the sea wall with her head in her hands.

In her day, girls were raised to be pure and not transgress. Then, my sorrow! she thought, some learned all the mortifications of the saints at their husband's hands. Not that Jarvis would expect wifely duties of that kind. He was as godly as De Valera. She knew he'd not tamper with her. Like herself, he'd believe the act was for procreation — or sin. Still she didn't want his flannel breeches on her bedside chair, his skin next to her sleeping skin, a crescent of hair oil on her pillows, a bedful of tobacco sweat. Her own smell of camphor and wintergreen was a place to live. Not once had Michael told her to belt up or had a rod onto her. He was a gent. On their wedding night he had dropped to his knees and prayed before entering the high iron frame and coarse sheets. That first time she was reminded of a visit from the dentist: the screech along the nerves and the duty to open against your deepest instinct. She had no good words but the Irish for the body and what happened in the marriage bed. Gaelic was more direct, less soiled than English. A month before a niece gave birth, the young woman had asked Peg where the baby would come out, and Peg hadn't the words to make her much the wiser.

And the things she knew how to tell in English wouldn't have comforted the girl. Many a strong tough woman I've seen laid low in the anguish, bellowing to Mary, and some never came to themselves again, she thought. Wasn't God far from the words of their roaring! In some houses, the men sat round the fire nice and chatty wondering why didn't the woman stir herself and pass the babe in a mad rush, getting the release from her task. Or a husband would run in and cry, Oh, God be with us stop, his blood shaking from the sound. Her Michael had always gone to his brother's house when her time came, which suited Peg nicely. She'd put a tea towel between her teeth, so her courage might be firm as Queen Maeve's of long ago. It wasn't the pain down in the bowels but the fiery needle of no heed sewing through your spine that put the amazement on you. Each time was different except for her thinking this time I'm at the end of my soul! This time I'll be cliff grass when it's over! Now some women were more nicely formed. But for her the family way meant the toothache, the leg cramps, the vomiting, the dropsy and the jaundice. One infant was born yellow, and Peg's hands swelled fat as cream crocks, so she could hardly haul water from the well to wash the baby's clothes. She'd had three girls and three boys. Once the doctor had used instruments to pull from her a dead child, black and blue, her skin peeling off in places. Only the baby's fingers had their natural color. They said that once you touched a dead person you wouldn't have any loneliness in you. But stroking that sweet and goodly girl had put the solitude of the world in her. And then Joseph had died at two — of empyema, the doctor said.

Well, she had always feared God and done her duty. Now she had four grandchildren, each more afraid of her than the other, all of them too shy to give sharp ear to her marvels. And that is a shame, she thought, for it is as the psalm says, "My tongue is the pen of a ready writer." A woman didn't tell hero stories, after all, only ghost stories. Hers were so potent the children ran when they saw her coming, though she gave them Mary Janes and more at Christmas.

"I hear you had a visitor this morning," her son Tom said from the doorway. He was in his suspenders and rolled-up shirtsleeves. Peg stopped sorting her baubles into groups on the bed and began knitting to put the appearance of work upon her. "A gentleman caller."

"You wouldn't mean Jarvis Fitzgerald." Tom's Dolly must have been listening from the kitchen. Peg could imagine her picking with her ears by the window, her hair in rags around her Temperance Lady face, to hear what Jarvis had to say. Dolly has the spite in her nose for me; she'd give me the ropes side of the house if she had her way, thought the head inside Peg's head.

"Is that who it was?" Tom sat himself down on the spread. He was her pet son, a boy of fun and tricks. It was years since she had seen him clearly. She remembered him dressed finely on his days off, his hat at an angle. And there were spokes of blue and gray in his glance, which she had memorized. His eyes had rays in them like a dartboard's. Even as a child he wouldn't flinch when things hit him. No matter how hot the day, Tom Merns would assure you the breeze would soon be in from the river, people said. People said he'd stake his last dollar against the sun's setting. And she couldn't deny his liking for a wager. But those people hadn't heard his fine wide laugh. She thought he looked always as if he should have an accordion strapped to his chest, so ready for happiness he was. It wasn't true either that he was bone-lazy. He worked as a train conductor five days a week, but she'd seen his Dolly place a quarter of a pound of butter out for tea, squandering his pay. And didn't she, his mother, eat out of his pocket, pushing him to the poorhouse with every bite?

"What did you and Mr. Fitzgerald discuss, might I ask?" Tom said. He toyed with a coral necklace, staring idly into nothing. Then he removed a small pad of paper from his pocket.

"Home rule." Her eyes fell on a garnet ring given her by Michael.

"Ah. And I heard he touched on matters of the heart. I heard he asked you to be his lady wife." Tom scribbled on the pad. Toting up his bill with the turf accountant, she thought.

"At his great age he'll be wanting a lady nurse. You'd have to buy a pair of wheelbarrows to roll us to the altar. That would be a sweet sight for the parish, indeed. But I'll not shame your father's memory with such talk."

He smiled. "What's wrong with old Fitz? The man has no vices that I know of. And he's here every morning, so don't say you don't like his company."

"Would you have your own mother marry a stranger? You get the award."

"He couldn't be more of a stranger than Dad was when you married. You'd only known him a day, remember?"

"God rest him." She kissed the crucifix she wore on a chain, thinking we were a made match. When I die, will the dust praise him? "And what are you composing as we speak?" she asked.

"Young Michael has a touch of the croup. I'm just reminding myself to buy mustard for a plaster. But to return to our subject, Mr. Fitzgerald is a decent, God-fearing citizen. Well-spoken, too." Tom grinned, and put the pad away. Jarvis was famous for his earnest sermons on political matters.

"His talk is like a peat fire. Lovely at first, but it chokes you after a while. Your father and I were as close as the Shannon and the Suck."

"Jarvis is a widower himself, isn't he?"

"So he's not of a queer nature," she conceded. "Oh, he's a good enough creature. But I'd sooner walk naked through the streets than take a husband at my age." Here she'd been thinking how ashamed they'd be to have her marry, yet it seemed the very thing Tom wanted. And why wouldn't he? Didn't he have the full of the house of croupy children, and she and Dolly in each other's haircombs all day?

"Wasn't he married to Mary Hurlehey?" Tom asked. His hands flew over the tobacco he was rolling. He didn't once look down.

"Now there was a ramblin' rose. He might as well have put a roof of stone on a house of thatch." If she left, they'd have room for the children, and she wouldn't be pushing in on them. But she'd be on the shift for shelter, living like a tink in the weather unless she married. And if she stayed, she'd have to hide in her room or have on her conscience the spoiling of a home.

"I just wanted to point out that a man has his pride." He picked up the garnet ring and studied it. "If you offend him he'll be without a wife forever before he'll have you. You're a stubborn woman, but don't be too hasty in saying no to a fair offer."

"Your father said, 'Peg, I might as well argue with the wind that strokes the water as with yourself.' A rare man he was!"

Tom sighed and rose to leave. Then he hesitated. "What's that noise? Hear it? In the chimney?"

"The chirping and scratching? I heard it but was afraid to say aught in case it was the imagination of the ears."

"It sounds as if some animal's caught there. I don't see how it got in with the flue sealed."

"The flue sealed, is it! This morning after Jarvis left I was down to the canal with a sack like a picaroon. Didn't I trap a seagull and put it up the chimney because yourself said it needed cleaning and so we couldn't use it. Last winter I wished for a good blaze." There hadn't been a fire in the hearth since she and Michael were young.

Tom's broad face furrowed in a scowl. "Oh, Ma, you didn't! Jesus, Mary and Joseph! Have you taken leave of your senses? How did you ever sneak the bird past Dolly?" He continued, greatly stirred, saying he would buy her a stove if she felt chilly. And how could she remember winter on a ninety-degree day? At last he left to get the long-handled broom. She would put her hair in a snood, take her shawl and go to Edward McWilliams's wake. Then Tom's family could have the house to themselves for a while. How wearisome it must be to live with an old woman who brought livestock in the building. She was shaking with humiliation. Hadn't she raised Tom from a tiny mite only to find the back of his hand given her now? He had said Jarvis was proud. She knew the Fitzgeralds had been the most spoken-of family in Western Ireland. Even during the famine they'd had a budgetful of yellow gold and sauce with their potatoes. "Well, he's cold poor now," she said aloud. Though he thought he'd be a mouthful in this country, he'd never advanced beyond foreman at the mill. As for those who whispered of a fortune hidden in his house, let them try to live on whispers. His lady wife! As if she'd be rich and wear white stockings. She'd planned on having safe moorings here for the rest of her life. But when a person thinks it's nice 'tis how it's a mocking trick, she thought, overcome with self-pity.

Tom hurried in with his stern face on. "A seagull! You'd sell your shawl rather than do anything the normal way." He opened the flue and pushed the straw end of the broom up the chimney. The beating stopped, and his face cleared. "I think it's gone. Are you going to see the hydroairplane? I hear it's docked in the canal."

"I am not." She selected an earring from the trinkets on the spread and held it out to him. "Would you be giving this to your Dolly from myself? It's lost its mate, but it'll make a lovely brooch."

Edward McWilliams was stretched in the front parlor with eleven lit candles at his head and feet. The twelfth candle went unlit to stand for Judas. A lamp glowed red in the corner of the room, and the air hung thick as a blanket of flowers. People stood around chatting or sat in rows before the casket, waiting for the lovely young priest to say a prayer. None of the women could do enough for the young Father. They at least would stay until he spoke. Jarvis was there, looking ill at ease since the afternoon mourners were mostly female. Peg waited until he stood alone, then went over.

"Did you know Edward McWilliams well?" he asked.

"Not at all," she admitted.

"Then why are you here to pay respects?"

"They say death makes your praying more sincere," she said with a flick of her shawl. Putting her hand to her mouth she added, "I heard it was the cancer killed him. But whisper! I have a recipe for that." She had to get someone to write down her cancer cure before she cleared off.

"I heard his last words were 'Show me the mercy you'd show a beast and shoot me,' " Jarvis whispered back.

"He was a great dramatist then, was he?"

"The despair runs in that family," he told her. "They're from the West Country, you know. His father died after leaping in a holy well, may they be safe where it's told."

"They say a holy death is a happy death," she noted piously.

"But to die without penance, or anointing rites, without the Host!" Jarvis sighed. "And didn't he change his mind after the leap and come up with the moss in his hair. And Jim Boyle, staggering home on a toot, shot him for the anti-Christ."

"It is short until we join him on high," she said sweetly.

"There's nothing but a while in this life for anyone," Jarvis agreed. After a bit he added, "I've heard that heaven's a yard and a half above the height of a man."

"Wouldn't that be the way of it," she said. "To be just out of reach." The subqueen in her mind wondered why people feared death if death meant entering forever to bright welcomes from your darling dear ones. But she held her tongue.

"I was after coming to inquire for you tonight. I don't suppose you've considered the story I opened this morning?"

So he'd still want her, though she poured a hundred discouragements on his head! "I have," she said.

"Well, let it to me, woman. Has your answer changed?"

"It has." She wouldn't dig her heels in any longer.

Jarvis brightened. "Then the matter is right. God never failed the patient heart."

"Patient, is it? It's been all of the eight hours since you honored me with your attentions, my good gentleman."

"You're right, Peg," he said. "It's well late for us to be patient." She would have to do for him for the rest of his life. The thought made her want to flee the fuzzy, red-lit room. Talking with Jarvis was like trying to sit still on a prickly horsehair couch, she thought.

She went home and told them right before supper. Then, entering the little room off the kitchen where they ate, she saw that Tom's Dolly had set out enough cutlery for courses. And a fruitcake left from Christmas, jeweled with candied fruit like a dark crown, sat on the sideboard. They had to eat in shifts or suffer bruised elbows at the table. Usually she took a tray of tea to her room, but tonight Tom insisted she join them. The babies would eat in the parlor. But when Tom's Dolly placed a chop before her she found she had no edge on her teeth. "I thought you were partial to lamb," Dolly chided.

"I'll have a tomato with a whiff of sugar on it. I have the liking of the world for that," she said.

"Why didn't you invite Jarvis over to see his new home?" Tom asked.

"When a woman marries she goes to her husband," Peg said. She thought of Jarvis's rented room, the hunks of sun falling through its windows and herself perishing with the heat. What wouldn't she give for a hole of her own! A steady hut on a stump of land out of the water, an old boat turned upside down as hens would live in.

"Nonsense!" said Tom. "You have to stay here with your family, with all of your things."

"You really must live with us, Mother," Dolly added. "This was your house before we moved in."

Why is it my nose would bleed if I met her without warning in the dark, Peg thought. You can't hate a woman because she has no complexion on her. Isn't it that when I sit with her for thirty minutes I feel I've been dead and buried that full half hour? How it must distress Tom, the two women raking each other! But what if she'd been wrong, and her son had no grudge against her living here? There was still no going against the promise she'd made Jarvis. And she'd never bring a husband into their crowded lot, another someone to bump into on the back-stairs.

Later, as her room grew dark, Tom came up with a bottle he'd stashed before Prohibition became law. "What if herself finds out you've been drinking?" Peg asked. "She'll Carry Nation you for a week."

"A man has a right to celebrate his mother's wedding."

They had a glass and laid into talk with each other. Peg said a psalm that went, "The king's daughter is all glorious within: her clothing is of wrought gold," having learned it by heart from her mother. And Tom told her of the great events he'd read in the evening's paper. Does it not seem Tom would like me to stay, she thought.

"It's much I admire those people whose lives would make books you'd need two hands to lift," she told him. It would be grand to do one bold, soul-gambling deed before she died. But a wedding! The ancient bride and groom hobnobbing with the gossiping guests . . . that was never it. Who would dance on the table to "The Hard Summer"? Then to live with Jarvis Fitzgerald's worryings until the end day of her life. And wouldn't he seem the wisp in place of the brush whenever she thought of Michael? "It's close in here. I'm thinking I need a breath of air. I won't be long," she said.

It was a dusky nine o'clock by then, and the evening was made dimmer by her fading eyes. She walked along the towpath near the canal until she saw a new shape near the opposite shore. Was this the flying thing? She moved closer to the water to get a better look. It was moored next to a grove of gas lamps and hallowed by their churchly yellow glow. The canal was tall and dark as a priest's gown; the Northern locks must be open wide, she thought. It was a perfect night: calm and desolate. Since there was no one to see, she sat down on the bank, dangling her feet over the darkness like a girl. She let one foot, then the other, dip into the water, brogues and all. It was the first cool she'd felt in weeks. She set down her cane, and slid forward a bit so that the waves reached up her shins, wetting the dense black lisle of her stockings. She'd never understood why a person was urged to pray for the souls of the faithful departed. The subqueen inside said to pray for the unfaithful: tinker, hawker, gypsy, Protestant and Jew. Oh my God, I am heartfully sorry, she said, easing herself into the state waterway, which at first felt coldly foreign, then as her skirts turned to fetters, warmer, more familiar.

HARLAN ELLISON

This is a story titled

The Man Who Rowed Christopher Columbus Ashore

FROM OMNI

LEVENDIS: On Tuesday the 1st of October, improbably dressed as an Explorer Scout, with his great hairy legs protruding from his knee-pants, and his heavily festooned merit badge sash slantwise across his chest, he helped an old, arthritic black woman across the street at the jammed corner of Wilshire and Western. In fact, she didn't *want* to cross the street, but he half-pulled, half-dragged her, the old woman screaming at him, calling him a khaki-colored motherfucker every step of the way.

LEVENDIS: On Wednesday the 2nd of October, he crossed his legs carefully as he sat in the Boston psychiatrist's office, making certain the creases of his pants — he was wearing the traditional morning coat and ambassadorially-striped pants — remained sharp, and he said to George Aspen Davenport, M.D., Ph.D., FAPA (who had studied with Ernst Kris *and* Anna Freud), "Yes, that's it, now you've got it." And Dr. Davenport made a note on his pad, lightly cleared his throat and phrased it differently: "Your mouth is . . . vanishing? That is to say, your mouth, the facial feature below your nose, it's uh disappearing?" The prospective patient nodded quickly, with a bright smile. "Exactly." Dr. Davenport made another note, continued to ulcerate the inside of his cheek, then tried a third time: "We're speaking now — heh heh, to maintain the idiom — we're speaking of your lips, or your tongue, or your palate, or your gums, or your teeth, or —" The other man sat forward, looking very serious, and replied, "We're talking *all* of it, Doctor. The whole, entire, complete aperture and everything around, over, under, and within. My *mouth,* the allness of my mouth. It's disappearing. What part of that is giving you a problem?" Davenport hmmm'd for a moment, said, "Let me check something," and he rose, went to the teak and glass bookcase against the far wall, beside the window that looked out on crowded, lively Boston Common, and he drew down a capacious volume. He flipped through it for a few minutes, and finally paused at a page on which he poked a finger. He turned to the elegant, gray-haired gentleman in the consultation chair, and he said, "Lipostomy." His prospective patient tilted his head to the side, like a dog listening for a clue, and arched his eyebrows expectantly, as if to ask *yes, and lipostomy is what?* The psychiatrist brought the book to him, leaned down and pointed to the definition. "Atrophy of the mouth." The gray-haired gentleman, who looked to be in his early sixties, but remarkably well-tended and handsomely turned-out, shook his head slowly as Dr. Davenport walked back around to sit behind his desk. "No, I don't think so. It doesn't seem to be withering, it's just, well, simply, I can't put it any other way, it's very simply disappearing. Like the Cheshire cat's grin. Fading away." Davenport closed the book and laid it on the desktop, folded his hands atop the volume, and smiled condescendingly. "Don't you think this might be a delusion on your part? I'm looking at your mouth right now, and it's right there, just as it was when you came into the office." His prospective patient rose, retrieved his homburg from the sofa, and started toward the door. "It's a good thing I can read lips," he said, placing the hat on his head, "because I certainly don't need to pay your sort of exorbitant fee to be ridiculed." And he moved to the office door, and opened it to leave, pausing for only a moment to readjust his homburg, which had slipped down, due to the absence of ears on his head.

LEVENDIS: On Thursday the 3rd of October, he overloaded his grocery cart with okra and eggplant, giant bags of Kibbles 'n Bits 'n Bits 'n Bits, and jumbo boxes of Huggies. And as he wildly careened through the aisles of the Sentry Market in La Crosse,

Wisconsin, he purposely engineered a collision between the carts of Kenneth Kulwin, a 47-year-old homosexual who had lived alone since the passing of his father thirteen years earlier, and Anne Gillen, a 35-year-old legal secretary who had been unable to find an escort to take her to her senior prom and whose social life had not improved in the decades since that death of hope. He began screaming at them, as if it had been *their* fault, thereby making allies of them. He was extremely rude, breathing muscatel breath on them, and finally stormed away, leaving them to sort out their groceries, leaving them to comment on his behavior, leaving them to take notice of each other. He went outside, smelling the Mississippi River, and he let the air out of Anne Gillen's tires. She would need a lift to the gas station. Kenneth Kulwin would tell her to call him "Kenny," and they would discover that their favorite movie was the 1945 romance, *The Enchanted Cottage,* starring Dorothy McGuire and Robert Young.

LEVENDIS: On Friday the 4th of October, he found an interstate trucker dumping badly sealed cannisters of phenazine in an isolated picnic area outside Phillipsburg, Kansas; and he shot him three times in the head; and wedged the body into one of the large, nearly empty trash barrels near the picnic benches.

LEVENDIS: On Saturday the 5th of October, he addressed two hundred and forty-four representatives of the country & western music industry in the Chattanooga Room just off the Tennessee Ballroom of the Opryland Hotel in Nashville. He said to them, "What's astonishing is not that there is so much ineptitude, slovenliness, mediocrity and downright bad taste in the world . . . what *is* unbelievable is that there is so much *good* art in the world. Everywhere." One of the attendees raised her hand and asked, "Are you good, or evil?" He thought about it for less than twenty seconds, smiled, and replied, "Good, of course! There's only one real evil in the world: mediocrity." They applauded sparsely, but politely. Nonetheless, later at the reception, *no one* touched the Swedish meatballs, or the rumaki.

LEVENDIS: On Sunday the 6th of October, he placed the exhumed remains of Noah's ark near the eastern summit of a nameless mountain in Kurdistan, where the next infrared surveillance of a random satellite flyby would reveal them. He was careful to seed the area with a plethora of bones, here and there around the site, as well as within the identifiable hull of the vessel. He made sure to place them two-by-two: every beast after his kind, and all the cattle after their kind, and every creeping thing that creepeth upon the earth after his kind, and every fowl after his kind, and every bird of every sort. Two-by-two. Also the bones of pairs of gryphons, unicorns, stegosaurs, tengus, dragons, orthodontists, and the carbon-dateable 50,000-year-old bones of a relief pitcher for the Boston Red Sox.

LEVENDIS: On Monday the 7th of October, he kicked a cat. He kicked it a far distance. To the passersby who watched, there on Galena Street in Aurora, Colorado, he said: "I am an unlimited person, sadly living in a limited world." When the housewife who planned to call the police yelled at him from her kitchen window, "Who are you? What is your name!?!" he cupped his hands around his mouth so she would hear him, and he yelled back, "Levendis! It's a Greek word." They found the cat imbarked halfway through a tree. The tree was cut down, and the section with the cat was cut in two, the animal tended by a talented taxidermist who tried to quell the poor beast's terrified mewling and vomiting. The cat was later sold as bookends.

LEVENDIS: On Tuesday the 8th of October, he called the office of the District Attorney in Cadillac, Michigan, and reported that the blue 1988 Mercedes that had struck and killed two children playing in a residential street in Hamtramck just after sundown the night before, belonged to a pastry chef whose sole client was a Cosa Nostra *pezzonovante*. He gave detailed information as to the location of the chop shop where the Mercedes had been taken to be banged out, bondo'd, and repainted. He gave the license number. He indicated where, in the left front wheel-well, could be found a piece of the skull of the younger of the two little girls. Not only did the piece fit, like the missing section of a modular woodblock puzzle, but pathologists were able to conduct an accurate test that provided irrefutable evidence that would hold up under any attack in court: the medical examiner got past the basic ABO groups, narrowed the scope of identification with the five Rh tests, the M and N tests (also cap-S and small-s variations), the Duffy blood groups, and the Kidd types, both A and B; and finally he was able to validate the rare absence of Jr a, present in most blood-groups but missing in some Japanese-Hawaiians and Samoans. The little girl's name was Sherry Tualaulelei. When the homicide investigators learned that the pastry chef, his wife, and their three children had gone to New York City on vacation four days before the hit-and-run, and were able to produce ticket stubs that placed them seventh row center of the Martin Beck Theater, enjoying the revival of *Guys and Dolls,* at the precise moment the Mercedes struck the children, the Organized Crime Unit was called in, and the scope of the investigation was broadened. Sherry Tualaulelei was instrumental in the conviction and thirty-three-year imprisonment of the pastry chef's boss, Sinio "Sally Comfort" Conforte, who had "borrowed" a car to sneak out for a visit to his mistress.

LEVENDIS: On Wednesday the 9th of October, he sent a fruit basket to Patricia and Faustino Evangelista, a middle-aged couple in Norwalk, Connecticut, who had given to the surviving son, the gun his beloved older brother had used to kill himself. The accompanying note read: *Way to go, sensitive Mom and Dad!*

LEVENDIS: On Thursday the 10th of October, he created a cure for bone-marrow cancer. Anyone could make it: the juice of fresh lemons, spiderwebs, the scrapings of raw carrots, the opaque and whitish portion of the toenail called the *lunula,* and carbonated water. The pharmaceutical cartel quickly hired a prestigious Philadelphia PR firm to throw its efficacy into question, but the AMA and FDA ran accelerated tests, found it to be potent, with no deleterious effects, and recommended its immediate use. It had no effect on AIDS, however. Nor did it work on the common cold. Remarkably, physicians praised the easing of their workload.

LEVENDIS: On Friday the 11th of October, he lay in his own filth on the sidewalk outside the British Embassy in Rangoon, holding a begging bowl. He was just to the left of the gate, half-hidden by the angle of the high wall from sight of the military guards on post. A woman in her fifties, who had been let out of a jitney just up the street, having paid her fare and having tipped as few rupees as necessary to escape a strident rebuke by the driver, smoothed the peplum of her shantung jacket over her hips, and marched imperially toward the Embassy gates. As she came abaft the derelict, he rose on one elbow and shouted at her ankles, "Hey, lady! I write these pomes, and I sell 'em for a buck inna street, an' it keeps juvenile delinquents offa the streets so's they don't spit on ya! So whaddaya think, y'wanna buy one?" The matron did not pause, striding toward the gates, but she said snappishly, "You're a businessman. Don't talk art."

This is a story titled

The Route of Odysseus

"You will find the scene of Odysseus's wanderings when you find the cobbler who sewed up the bag of the winds."
Eratosthenes, late 3rd century, B.C.

LEVENDIS: On Saturday the 12th of October, having taken the sidestep, he came to a place near Weimar in southwest Germany. He did not see the photographer snapping pictures of the scene. He stood among the cordwood bodies. It was cold for the spring; and even though he was heavily clothed, he shivered. He walked down the rows of bony corpses, looking into the black holes that had been eye sockets, seeing an endless chicken dinner, the bones gnawed clean, tossed like jackstraws in heaps. The stretched-taut groins of men and women, flesh tarpaulins where passion had once smoothed the transport from sleep to wakefulness. Entwined so cavalierly that here a woman with three arms, and there a child with the legs of a sprinter three times his age. A woman's face, looking up at him with soot for sight, remarkable cheekbones, high and lovely, she might have been an actress. Xylophones for chests and torsos, violin bows that had waved goodbye and hugged grandchildren and lifted in toasts to the passing of traditions, gourd whistles between eyes and mouths. He stood among the cordwood bodies and could not remain merely an instrument himself. He sank to his haunches, crouched and wept, burying his head in his hands, as the photographer took shot after shot, an opportunity like a gift from the editor. Then he tried to stop crying, and stood, and the cold cut him, and he removed his heavy topcoat and placed it gently over the bodies of two women and a man lying so close and intermixed that it easily served as coverlet for them. He stood among the cordwood bodies, 24 April 1945, Buchenwald, and the photograph would appear in a book published forty-six years later, on Saturday the 12th of October. The photographer's roll ran out just an instant before the slim young man without a topcoat took the sidestep. Nor did he hear the tearful young man say, "Sertsa." In Russian, *sertsa* means soul.

LEVENDIS: On Sunday the 13th of October, he did nothing. He rested. When he thought about it, he grew annoyed. "Time does not become sacred until we have lived it," he said. But he thought: *to hell with it; even God knocked off for a day.*

LEVENDIS: On Monday the 14th of October, he climbed up through the stinking stairwell shaft of a Baltimore tenement, clutching his notebook, breathing through his mouth to block the smell of mildew, garbage, and urine, focusing his mind on the apartment number he was seeking, straining through the evening dimness in the wan light of one bulb hanging high above, barely illuminating the vertical tunnel, as he climbed and climbed, straining to see the numbers on the doors, going up, realizing the tenants had pulled the numbers *off* the doors to foil him and welfare investigators like him, stumbling over something oily and sobbing jammed into a corner of the last step, losing his grip on the rotting bannister and finding it just in time, trapped for a moment in the hopeless beam of washed-out light falling from above, poised in mid-tumble and then regaining his grip, hoping the welfare recipient under scrutiny would not be home, so he could knock off for the day, hurry back downtown and crosstown and take a shower, going up till he had reached the topmost landing, and finding the number scratched on the doorframe, and knocking, getting no answer, knocking again, hearing first the scream, then the sound of someone beating against a wall, or the floor, with a heavy stick, and then the scream again, and then another scream so closely following the first that it might have been one scream only, and he threw himself against the door, and it was old but never had been well-built, and it came away, off its hinges, in one rotten crack, and he was inside, and the most beautiful young black woman he had ever seen was tearing the rats off her baby. He left the check on the kitchen table, he did not have an affair with her, he did not see her fall from the apartment window, six storeys into a courtyard, and never knew if she came back from the grave to escape the rats that gnawed at her cheap wooden casket. He never loved her, and so was not there when what she became flowed back up through the walls of the tenement to absorb him and meld with him and become one with him as he lay sleeping penitently on the filthy floor of the topmost apartment. He left the check, and none of that happened.

LEVENDIS: On Tuesday the 15th of October, he stood in the Greek theatre at Aspendos, Turkey, a structure built two thousand years earlier, so acoustically perfect that every word spoken on its stage could be heard with clarity in any of its thirteen thousand seats, and he spoke to a little boy sitting high above him. He uttered Count Von Manfred's dying words, Schumann's overture, Byron's poem: "Old man, 'tis not so difficult to die." The child smiled and waved. He waved back, then shrugged. They became friends at a distance. It was the first time someone other than his mother, who was dead, had been kind to the boy. In years to come it would be a reminder that there was a smile out there on the wind. The little boy looked down the rows and concentric rows of seats: the man 'way down there was motioning for him to come to him. The child, whose name was Orhon, hopped and hopped, descending to the center of the ring as quickly as he could. As he came to the core, and walked out across the orchestra ring, he studied the man. This person was very tall, and he needed a shave, and his hat had an extremely wide brim, like the hat of Kül, the man who made weekly trips to Ankara, and he wore a long overcoat far too hot for this day. Orhon could not see the man's eyes because he wore dark glasses that reflected the sky. Orhon thought this man looked like a mountain bandit, only dressed more impressively. Not wisely for a day as torpid as this, but more impressively than Bilge and his men, who raided the farming villages. When he reached the tall man, and they smiled at each other, this person said to Orhon, "I am an unlimited person living in a limited world." The child did not know what to say to that. But he liked the man. "Why do you wear such heavy wool today? I am barefoot." He raised his dusty foot to show the man, and was embarrassed at the dirty cloth tied around his big toe. And the man said, "Because I need a safe place to keep the limited world." And he unbuttoned his overcoat, and held open one side, and showed Orhon what he would inherit one day, if he tried very hard not to be a despot. Pinned to the fabric, each with the face of the planet, were a million and more timepieces, each one the Earth at a different moment, and all of them purring erratically like dozing sphinxes. And Orhon stood there, in the heat, for quite a long while, and listened to the ticking of the limited world.

LEVENDIS: On Wednesday the 16th of October, he chanced upon three skinheads in Doc Martens and cheap black leatherette, beating the crap out of an interracial couple who had emerged from the late show at the La Salle Theater in Chicago. He stood quietly and watched. For a long while.

LEVENDIS: On Thursday the 17th of October he chanced upon three skinheads in Doc Martens and cheap black leatherette, beating the crap out of an interracial couple who had stopped for a bite to eat at a Howard Johnson's near King of Prussia on the Pennsylvania Turnpike. He removed the inch-and-a-half-thick ironwood dowel he always carried beside his driver's seat and, holding the 2½′ long rod at its centerpoint, laid alongside his pants leg so it could not be seen in the semi-darkness of the parking lot, he came up behind the three as they kicked the black woman and the white man lying between parked cars. He tapped the tallest of the trio on his shoulder, and when the boy turned around — he couldn't have been more than seventeen — he dropped back a step, slid the dowel up with his right hand, gripped it tightly with his left, and drove the end of the rod into the eye of the skinhead, punching through behind the socket and pulping the brain. The boy flailed backward, already dead, and struck his partners. As they turned, he was spinning the dowel like a baton, faster and faster, and as the stouter of the two attackers charged him, he whipped it around his head and slashed straight across the boy's throat. The snapping sound ricocheted off the dark hillside beyond the restaurant. He kicked the third boy in the groin, and when he dropped, and fell on his back, he kicked him under the chin, opening the skinhead's mouth; and then he stood over him, and with both hands locked around the pole, as hard as he could, he piledrove the wooden rod into the kid's mouth, shattering his teeth, and turning the back of his skull to flinders. The dowel scraped concrete through the ruined face. Then he helped the man and his wife to their feet, and bullied the manager of the Howard Johnson's into actually letting them lie down in his office till the State Police arrived. He ordered a plate of fried clams and sat there eating pleasurably until the cops had taken his statement.

LEVENDIS: On Friday the 18th of October, he took a busload of Mormon schoolchildren to the shallow waters of the Great Salt Lake in Utah, to pay homage to the great sculptor Smithson by introducing the art-ignorant children to the *Spiral Jetty,* an incongruously gorgeous line of earth and stone that curves out and away like a thought lost in the tide. "The man who made this, who dreamed it up and then *made* it, you know what he once said?" And they ventured that no, they didn't know what this Smithson sculptor had said, and the man who had driven the bus paused for a dramatic moment, and he repeated Smithson's words: "Establish enigmas, not explanations." They stared at him. "Perhaps you had to be there," he said, shrugging. "Who's for ice cream?" And they went to a Baskin-Robbins.

LEVENDIS: On Saturday the 19th of October, he filed a thirty-million-dollar lawsuit against the major leagues in the name of Alberda Jeanette Chambers, a 19-year-old lefthander with a fadeaway fast ball clocked at better than 96 mph; a dipsy-doodle slider that could do a barrel-roll and clean up after itself; an ERA of 2.10; who could hit from either side of the plate with a batting average of .360; who doubled as a peppery little shortstop working with a trapper's mitt of her own design; who had been refused tryouts with virtually every professional team in the United States (also Japan) from the bigs all the way down to the Pony League. He filed in Federal District Court for the Southern Division of New York State, and told Ted Koppel that Allie Chambers would be the first female player, mulatto or otherwise, in the Baseball Hall of Fame.

LEVENDIS: On Sunday the 20th of October, he drove out and around through the streets of Raleigh and Durham, North Carolina, in a rented van equipped with a public address system, and he endlessly reminded somnambulistic pedestrians and families entering eggs 'n' grits restaurants (many of these adults had actually voted for Jesse Helms and thus were in danger of losing their *sertsa*) that perhaps they should ignore their bibles today, and go back and reread Shirley Jackson's short story, "One Ordinary Day, with Peanuts."

This is a story titled

The Daffodils that Entertain

LEVENDIS: On Monday the 21st of October, having taken the sidestep, he wandered through that section of New York City known as the Tenderloin. It was 1892. Crosstown on 24th Street from Fifth Avenue to Seventh, then he turned uptown and walked slowly on Seventh to 40th. Midtown was rife with brothels, their red lights shining through the shadows, challenging the wan gaslit streetlamps. The Edison and Swan United Electric Light Co., Ltd., had improved business tremendously through the wise solicitations of a salesman with a Greek-sounding name who had canvassed the prostitution district west of Broadway only five years earlier, urging the installation of Mr. Joseph Wilson Swan and Mr. Thomas Alva Edison's filament lamps: painted crimson, fixed above the ominously yawning doorways of the area's many houses of easy virtue. He passed an alley on 36th Street, and heard a woman's voice in the darkness complaining, "You said you'd give me two dollars. You have to give it to me first! Stop! No, *first* you gotta give me the two dollars!" He stepped into the alley, let his eyes acclimate to the darkness so total, trying to hold his breath against the stench; and then he saw them. The man was in his late forties, wearing a bowler and a shin-length topcoat with an astrakhan collar. The sound of horse-drawn carriages clopped loudly on the bricks beyond the alley, and the man in the astrakhan looked up, toward the alley mouth. His face was strained, as if he expected an accomplice of the girl, a footpad or shoulder-hitter or bully-boy pimp to charge to her defense. He had his fly unbuttoned and his thin, pale penis extended; the girl was backed against the alley wall, the man's left hand at her throat; and he had hiked up her apron and skirt and petticoats, and was trying to get his right hand into her drawers. She pushed against him, but to no avail. He was large and strong. But when he saw the other man standing down there, near the mouth of the alley, he let her garments drop, and fished his organ back into his pants, but didn't waste time buttoning-up. "You there! Like to watch your betters at work, do you?" The man who had done the sidestep spoke softly: "Let the girl go. Give her the two dollars, and let her go." The man in the bowler took a step toward the mouth of the alley, his hands coming up in a standard pugilist's extension. He gave a tiny laugh that was a snort that was rude and derisive: "Oh so, fancy yourself something of the John L. Sullivan, do you, captain? Well, let's see how you and I and the Marquis Q get along . . ." and he danced forward, hindered considerably by the bulky overcoat. As he drew within double arm's-length of his opponent the younger man drew the taser from his coat pocket, fired at point-blank range, the barbs striking the pugilist in the cheek and neck, the charge lifting him off his feet and driving him back into the brick wall so hard that the filaments were wrenched loose, and the potential fornicator fell forward, his eyes rolled up in his head. Fell forward so hard he smashed three of his front teeth, broken at the gum-line. The girl tried to run, but the alley was a dead end. She watched as the man with the strange weapon came to her. She could barely see his face, and there had been all those killings with that Jack the Ripper in London a few years back, and there was talk this Jack had been a Yankee and had come back to New York. She was terrified. Her name was Poppy Skurnik, she was an orphan, and she worked way downtown as a pieceworker in a shirtwaist factory. She made one dollar and sixty-five cents a week, for six days of labor, from seven in the morning until seven at night, and it was barely enough to pay for her lodgings at Baer's Rents. So she "supplemented" her income with a stroll in the Tenderloin, twice a week, never more, and prayed that she could continue to avoid the murderous attentions of gentlemen who liked to cripple girls after they'd topped them, continue to avoid the pressures of pimps and boy friends who wanted her to work for them, continue to avoid the knowledge that she was no longer "decent" but was also a long way from winding up in one of these red-light whorehouses. He took her gently by the hand, and started to lead her out of the alley, carefully stepping over the unconscious molester. When they reached the street, and she saw how handsome he was, and how young he was, and how premierely he was dressed, she also smiled. She was extraordinarily attractive, and the young man tipped his hat and spoke to her kindly, inquiring as to her name, and where she lived, and if she would like to accompany him for some dinner. And she accepted, and he hailed a carriage, and took her to Delmonico's for the finest meal she had ever had. And later, much later, when he brought her to his townhouse on upper Fifth Avenue, in the posh section, she was ready to do anything he required of her. But instead, all he asked was that she allow him to give her a hundred dollars in exchange for one second of small pain. And she felt fear, because she knew what these nabobs were like, *but a hundred dollars*! So she said yes, and he asked her to bare her left buttock, and she did it with embarrassment, and there was exactly one second of mosquito bite pain, and then he was wiping the spot where he had injected her with penicillin, with a cool and fragrant wad of cotton batting. "Would you like to sleep the night here, Poppy?" the young man asked. "My room is down the hall, but I think you'll be very comfortable in this one." And she was worried that he had done something awful to her, like inject her with a bad poison, but she didn't *feel* any different, and he seemed so nice, so she said yes, that would be a dear way to spend the evening, and he gave her ten ten-dollar bills, and wished her a pleasant sleep, and left the room, having saved her life, for she had contracted syphilis the week before, though she didn't know it; and within a year she would have been unable, by her appearance alone, to get men in the streets; and would have been let go at the shirtwaist factory; and would have been seduced and sold into one of the worst of the brothels; and would have been dead within another two years. But this night she slept well, between cool sheets with hand-embroidered lace edging, and when she rose the next day he was gone, and no one told her to leave the townhouse, and so she stayed on from day to day, for years, and eventually married and gave birth to three children, one of whom grew to maturity, married, had a child who became an adult and saved the lives of millions of innocent men, women, and children. But that night in 1892 she slept a deep, sweet, recuperative and dreamless sleep.

LEVENDIS: On Tuesday the 22nd of October, he visited a plague of asthmatic toads on Iisalmi, a small town in Finland; a rain of handbills left over from World War II urging the SS troops to surrender on Chejudo, an island off the southern coast of Korea; a shock wave of forsythia on Linares in Spain; and a fully-restored 1926 Ahrens-Fox model RK fire engine on a mini-mall in Clarksville, Arkansas.

LEVENDIS: On Wednesday the 23rd of October, he corrected every history book in America so that they no longer called it The Battle of Bunker Hill, but rather Breeds Hill where, in fact, the engagement of 17 June 1775 had taken place. He also invested every radio and television commentator with the ability to differentiate between "in a moment" and "momentarily," which were not at all the same thing, and the misuse of which annoyed him greatly. The former was in his job description; the latter was a matter of personal pique.

LEVENDIS: On Thursday the 24th of October, he revealed to the London *Times* and *Paris-Match* the name of the woman who had stood on the grassy knoll, behind the fence, in Dallas that day, and fired the rifle shots that killed John F. Kennedy. But no one believed Marilyn Monroe could have done the deed and gotten away unnoticed. Not even when he provided her suicide note that confessed the entire matter and tragically told in her own words how jealousy and having been jilted had driven her to hire that weasel Lee Harvey Oswald, and that pig Jack Ruby, and how she could no longer live with the guilt, goodbye. No one would run the story, not even the *Star,* not even *The Enquirer,* not even *TV Guide.* But he tried.

LEVENDIS: On Friday the 25th of October, he upped the intelligence of every human being on the planet by forty points.

LEVENDIS: On Saturday the 26th of October, he lowered the intelligence of every human being on the planet by forty-two points.

This is a story titled

At Least One Good Deed a Day, Every Single Day

LEVENDIS: On Sunday the 27th of October, he returned to a family in Kalgoorlie, SW Australia, a five-year-old child who had been kidnapped from their home in Bayonne, New Jersey, fifteen years earlier. The child was no older than before the family had immigrated, but he now spoke only in a dialect of Etruscan, a language that had not been heard on the planet for thousands of years. Having most of the day free, however, he then made it his business to kill the remaining seventeen American GIs being held MIA in an encampment in the heart of Laos. Waste not, want not.

LEVENDIS: On Monday the 28th of October, still exhilarated from the work and labors of the preceding day, he brought out of the highlands of North Viet Nam Capt. Eugene Y. Grasso, USAF, who had gone down under fire twenty-eight years earlier. He returned him to his family in Anchorage, Alaska, where his wife, remarried, refused to see him but his daughter whom he had never seen, would. They fell in love, and lived together in Anchorage, where their story provided endless confusion to the ministers of several faiths.

LEVENDIS: On Tuesday the 29th of October, he destroyed the last bits of evidence that would have led to answers to the mysteries of the disappearances of Amelia Earhart, Ambrose Bierce, Benjamin Bathurst and Jimmy Hoffa. He washed the bones and placed them in a display of early American artifacts.

LEVENDIS: On Wednesday the 30th of October, he traveled to New Orleans, Louisiana, where he waited at a restaurant in Metairie for the former head of the Ku Klux Klan, now running for state office, to show up to meet friends. As the man stepped out of his limousine, wary guards on both sides of him, the traveler fired a Laws rocket from the roof of the eatery. It blew up the former KKK prexy, his guards, and a perfectly good Cadillac Eldorado. Leaving the electoral field open, for the enlightened voters of Louisiana, to a man who, as a child, had assisted Mengele's medical experiments, a second contender who had changed his name to avoid being arrested for child mutilation, and an illiterate swamp cabbage farmer from Baton Rouge whose political philosophy involved cutting the throats of peccary pigs, and thrusting one's face into the boiling blood of the corpse. Waste not, want not.

LEVENDIS: On Thursday the 31st of October, he restored to his throne the Dalai Lama, and closed off the mountain passes that provided land access to Tibet, and caused to blow constantly a cataclysmic snowstorm that did not affect the land below, but made any accessibility by air impossible. The Dalai Lama offered a referendum to the people: should we rename our land Shangri-La?

LEVENDIS: On Friday the 32nd of October, he addressed a convention of readers of cheap fantasy novels, saying, "We invent our lives (and other people's) as we live them; what we call 'life' is itself a fiction. Therefore, we must constantly strive to produce only good art, absolutely entertaining fiction." (He did *not* say to them: "I am an unlimited person, sadly living in a limited world.") They smiled politely, but since he spoke only in Etruscan, they did not understand a word he said.

LEVENDIS: On Saturday the 33rd of October, he did the sidestep and worked the oars of the longboat that brought Christopher

Columbus to the shores of the New World, where he was approached by a representative of the native peoples, who laughed at the silly clothing the great navigator wore. They all ordered pizza and the man who had done the rowing made sure that venereal disease was quickly spread so that centuries later he could give a beautiful young woman an inoculation in her left buttock.

LEVENDIS: On Piltic the 34th of October, he gave all dogs the ability to speak in English, French, Mandarin, Urdu, and Esperanto; but all they could say was rhyming poetry of the worst sort, and he called it *doggerel.*

LEVENDIS: On Sqwaybe the 35th of October, he was advised by the Front Office that he had been having too rich a time at the expense of the Master Parameter, and he was removed from his position, and the unit was closed down, and darkness was penciled in as a mid-season replacement. He was reprimanded for having called himself Levendis, which is a Greek word for someone who is full of the pleasure of living. He was reassigned, with censure, but no one higher up noticed that on his new assignment he had taken the name Sertsa.

This has been a story titled

Shagging Fungoes

JANE SHAPIRO

Poltergeists

FROM THE NEW YORKER

THE OTHER EVENING, after talking on the phone with my daughter, Nora, who lives in Rome, I walked over to the Mexican place, the nearest restaurant to my apartment, where I had a narrow escape — I almost stepped into a deeply strange, forgotten, familiar world. I stopped on the threshold, looking in at the stucco room hung with striped rugs and dusty sequin-trimmed sombreros; it was early, but the place was packed, unnaturally so, and the mood was wrong — not loud but still too keyed up. Then I saw why the restaurant seemed to have shrunk: all the patrons were high school kids. They looked gigantic; even the girls appeared to need a place with higher ceilings and more commodious chairs. They weren't braying or throwing food or dropping their pants or anything; in the intense attitudes that were normal for them, they were eating burritos. I backed out. Moments later, when I came to, I was strolling toward the Thai place, remembering a lost time, my children's high school days.

In 1985, I was still living in New Jersey in the house Willie and I had bought when the kids were small, and when Zack and Nora got into their senior and junior years the three of us were suddenly agitated and constantly struggling to appear serene. I was alone. That's what it felt like: I'm living alone, with only my adolescent children and our hair-trigger adrenal glands. The epinephrine was cycling through our nervous systems with no outlet. Since Nora and Zack had started high school, there had been a few occasions when I went over the top and screamed. It came on only once or twice a year, and afterward I was ground down by ordinary guilt. Still, I understood perfectly the state of mind of the parents who shrieked and frothed daily, tried to rip the earrings out of their children's ears, and rolled around with the kids in mortal combat on the rug. With even the most hysterical of the parents of teenagers I knew, I felt a sort of tender affiliation: they had been blindfolded and poked until maddened; they were flying, on an adrenaline high that couldn't be contained.

Mornings were O.K. In the mornings, things were normal, with the indefinable heightened quality we were getting used to: supranormal, metanormal. Zack and Nora were glossily beautiful, standing in the kitchen in pure ringing silence, conserving their deep reserves of energy. Zack's breakfast was four pieces of toast and a quart of milk; Nora's was a Diet Coke. Every few days I squeezed oranges and carried the glasses of juice to their bedrooms, where they were blow-drying their marvelous hair. *Oh, thanks,* they'd call patiently, through the dryers' roar. While I watched, they'd take a sip.

That year, I was really busy. I spent a fair number of evenings going out with my women friends, all of us wearing our earrings, and suits with big shoulders, and being glamorous, irrepressible modern American divorcées together, then straggling home. And I was still working full-time at a training school for bad boys (breaking and entering, assault with intent, car thefts), a place where I had a role to play that was simple and made sense: I was trying to teach kids to read. On my way to work I'd drop my own kids at the high school and I'd watch as they crossed the lawn; they looked dynamic but pacific — they were washed to a shine, arrayed in calculated, shabby, sexy black. I had a persistent, weird feeling: I couldn't prove it, but I thought that those were not my children. The crossing guard looked like the same guy he had always been. But the kids had been replaced by Martians.

Daytime was the Martian time, when all the normal stuff happened. Graciously, they did the usual things: Nora did gymnastics, and Zack played his guitar; they were both lacrosse players, student council representatives, actors, and members of the Black Literature Club. After school, Zack worked at a health food restaurant, making sandwiches invented during the sixties; Nora helped run a theater program for tiny children, walking the kids to the bathroom, tying their masks onto their little faces, restraining the biter. If I got home late from work, the house would already be thumping, a giant heartbeat in the walls — Nora's Jane Fonda video. This was still daytime. Nora and Zack were doing the well-known, complicated adolescent impersonation of people fully engaged with the daytime things. In fact, everything happened at night.

They were going to concerts. Some Saturdays, they set out in the morning and rode long distances, to faraway venues. Hours before the show, there'd be a city of cars in the parking lot, and packs of young people in the late sun and then in the gathering darkness, lurching around and handling each other, and buying and selling and consuming loose joints, pills, the standard seductive killer drugs, and a fluid called Liquid Lady. Nora and Zack told me about these events. Of course I asked, Did their friends drink and take drugs? Zack had long been a master of the noncommittal amiable remark. He said, "The bottles to beware of are the ones that look like cologne."

Other Saturdays, they stayed home. After dinner they walked around their rooms for three hours, dressing and phoning. At ten, scrubbed as if for surgery and artfully got up, they rushed out. At two, hoarse and depleted, they staggered home.

At parties, muscular, stoic boys would kneel and take a piece of tubing deep into their mouths and tip their heads back like sword swallowers, and their friends would pour whole beers through a motor-oil funnel, straight down their throats. Girls did it, too — Nora reported that when this happened she sometimes left the room. This was dangerous, I said; drinking like that, those boys could get very sick. "Get sick?" Zack said. "Actually, Mom, that's pretty euphemistic. They could die." I planned to call the parents of the beer swallowers, to inform them. Which parents would you single out, the kids said. It happens all the time. Please, Mom. It's the least of it.

"Mom," Zack said. "Here's a typical incident, but you can't do any phoning."

"What is it?" I said.

"We can't tell you these things if you start talking about calling people."

"What is it?"

"Is it about Benjy?" Nora asked, starting to laugh. "Oh, it's ridiculous! It's nothing, Mom."

"*What?*"

They were laughing so happily, so healthily. They pounded each other, stamped their feet, wiped their eyes. They both cried, "*Benjy drank three beers through his nose!*"

Zack's girlfriend, Bibi, looked as much like Nora as somebody else could — a sexier, ruder Nora, in muddy cowboy boots. In the daytime, Bibi smelled like a puppy — she was working after school for a veterinarian, planning to become one. She liked to tell long, bloody, oddly arousing stories about veterinarian life. Bibi was very beautiful and sloppy. I was jealous of her. The first time she came to our house, she immediately picked up our cat, pressed him to her, and licked his fur; Zack sat down suddenly, as if to avoid swooning. Now, whenever she had a chance, Bibi would come over and stay for many hours, with her jeans straining to cover her strong, elegant legs. She would slip off the boots and lie down with her feet in Zack's lap. Then she would fondle the cat in several remarkably inventive ways, and Zack would watch her. She drove me nuts.

Nora suddenly got a boyfriend — a deep-voiced guy named Mark. He was less annoying than Bibi — shallower, less clever, and not around much. I kind of liked him, and he may have kind of liked me. A sophomore, he was already planning to be a surgeon. On our first meeting, I asked how he knew that for sure, and he said sonorously, "I have a special aptitude," and wiggled his fingers. He grinned. Nora blushed horribly. We all stared at Mark's jiggling, dexterous hands.

I had a boyfriend myself; that is to say, there was someone I'd been seeing since a few months after Willie and I divorced. Steven and I weren't by any means in love, but we were certainly old enough to be placid together, reasonably happy in the way recommended by best-selling books: we didn't expect too much. The only thing I had ever tried to change about him was early on, when I made him cut back on the after-shave.

Steven stayed over on the Saturdays he didn't have his son with him. Every other Sunday morning he drove out and bought eight bagels, and he and I ate two of them in the wonderful silence, and by the time the kids stumbled from their beds he had usually gone home. "Where's Dome?" they said. (His only unusual physical characteristic was a slightly over-rounded forehead, and you really had to be paying attention to notice it.) Once a month or so, he'd still be there when they woke, and they'd say things like "Hi, Steve. Thanks for the bagels — these six bagels as well as the last nine hundred bagels."

On a back road late on Halloween night, driving home from a party at about ninety miles an hour, two kids rolled a car. They climbed out, stood up, vomited on their ghost costumes, and walked away in the moonlight. After that, some parents of party-givers started making all the guests sleep at their houses so they wouldn't drive home drunk; when you arrived at the party you had to surrender your car keys before you could repair to the keg or upend the bottle through your nose. Zack didn't have his driver's license yet; Bibi did. Zack and Bibi and Nora got in the habit of pretending that they'd been driven by someone else, and in the middle of the night, after everybody had fallen down on the mattresses, they'd slip out and meet on the lawn and run for Bibi's car and make their getaway. The three of them would drive out to the diner, comb their smoky hair, eat platters of scrambled eggs, and, when they felt coherent enough, drive on home.

"Do any of these parents happen to refuse to serve alcohol?" I asked once, kind of wearily.

Zack said that the parents didn't serve marijuana and cocaine, but that inhospitality had virtually no impact on events.

"*Cocaine?* Is that a *common* thing?"

He looked at me absently. He said it was a pain, because cocaine traditionally happens in the bathroom, so anytime you wanted to go to the bathroom you had to go out in the yard.

Nora laughed. "It's really true!" she said. "Julie comes to be lookout."

"So what would happen if no alcohol was served? Would anybody go to the party?"

"Sure," they said. "It happens. Everybody goes."

"And then nobody drinks?"

Zack said, "People bring vodka and drink it in cups of tea."

"I don't want you to drink and drive!"
"We never do," they said. "Are you crazy?"
"Do you smoke joints?"
"Mom," they said kindly, holding my gaze.
"I don't want you to drink or smoke at all."
"We know that, Mom. We know you don't."

My pal Annie came over to have tea and talk about our lives — what we used to do, what we would do later, when all this was over. Annie's daughter was a Saturday gymnast, like Nora; her son worked alongside Zack at Tempting Treats, squeezing the carrots, massing the sprouts in the pitas, melting the Monterey Jack — killing a little of their enormous surplus of time. Annie and I had been banking on these pursuits to keep the kids safe. In fact, Annie had gone further — had got her former husband to ante up a lot of support money to keep their kids in the private day school instead of the public school. So we considered her children marginally safer than mine: they were receiving *individual attention.* Now Annie and I sat in the dining room with the teapot in its ineffectual little cozy, giving each other keen looks. Zack was in his room. His door was closed, and through the door came, instead of sound, the usual waves of sexual energy pouring into the house and agitating the air. I imagined him in there finishing his college essays, desperately pulling on his hair. "Probably not his hair," Annie said glumly. She said she used to worry that when they reached high school they'd start having lots of sex — dangerous, fifties sex — and that would be traumatic, and now there was AIDS, which was unimaginably worse. Still, if they wore their condoms and chose their partners carefully, she had decided, the safest illicit activity currently available to the kids was making love. "At least while they're having sex they can't be driving the car a hundred miles an hour," she said.

Passing the dining room, Nora called pleasantly, "Why can't they?"

After an eventful New Year's Eve, when Zack got his butt squeezed by a mystery girl, and also underwent a conversion and rededication to academic excellence, he devoted eighteen consecutive nights to studying for his third round of S.A.T.s, like somebody possessed. Then he and Nora stayed over with friends and came home on Saturday morning gray and staring. Here's what they said:

We watched "Love Connection." Then "The People's Court" — a case about a beagle and some rat poison. Then the five-o'clock news — Lou Gossett was on. Then "World News Tonight" — we love it. Reagan was real happy down in Mexico, shaking hands with the Mexican president. Then we got souvlaki and took it to the party. We left early and went back to Holly's mom's and watched "The Shining." Then "Repo Man" came on. Then Robbie said "I'm Robertson Parson Shattuck III" about forty times and tiptoed out and tried to walk on the edge of the upper terrace with his eyes closed and fell onto the bluestone lower terrace and broke his arm. Then we took him to the emergency room and waited for his dad, and his dad rode over in his Jaguar with his Haitian driver. Then two guys from the high school came in; they had been beaten up and their faces were meat. Then "Tom and Jerry." Then morning came.

"Then what happened?" I asked.

Zack: "Sun came up."

As the year progressed, the parties seemed to grow more drastic, more extreme. Shooting the Boot was introduced — each guest gulped a sneakerful, out of the host's high-top. Vomiting, of course, was perennially big: the Technicolor yawn, riding the porcelain bus, talking to Ralph on the big white phone. Urination was big: a kid named Soup liked to go into the bathroom immediately and piss into the shampoo. One couple or another always had to have a fight, and one or both of the lovers had to run out of the house, and maybe the girl would key-scratch the guy's car. There was always the abused guy. There was always the depressed girl who pulled guys seriatim into a bedroom or closet. Something valuable always had to get broken. If, as could happen, the parents were fools enough to leave town, everybody showed up, and then there'd be the trashed house and weird things going around in the dryer, and maybe the whole population of the high school outside on the deck, some of them in mid-urination when the deck fell down.

Nora didn't drink. She reported that a boy had asked, When did you stop? I never drank, she said. Never? Unsteadily, he held out his big strong feverish hand for a crunching handshake. He nodded sagely. He said, *I'm very impressed.*

Some narcs came to school. Nora said that the narcs — a man and a woman — were wearing amazing disguises: bell-bottoms, fringed vests, *hair.* They looked about thirty-five. Nora claimed the narcs had sidled up and asked where to buy "stuff," and she'd said, "Officers, I have no idea."

In fact, you could buy your drugs in the auditorium. Or outside the gym, against the wall, where the regular daytime dope-smokers stood dreaming. Every Friday, a blue van pulled up behind the gym, and the dealers, three seniors — Jason, George, and Robbie — ran out, got in, and in two turns around the block bought the school's supplies for the week. From Nora, their pal, I got a clear impression of the dealers: Robbie was a neglected, handsome, depressed rich boy; George was a gentle, skinny, cocaine-dependent poor boy; and Jason was a hardened criminal.

I made an appointment with the principal. He was a tall fellow, always as precisely turned out as one of his students, as clean-shaven as a person can be. The skin of his cheeks shone like a baby's, and he had a baby's clear, guiltless eyes. When I arrived, he turned this face toward me and looked pleasant. "What are you doing about the drug problem?" I said, and he held his pleasing expression. "Please sit down," he said. As for the narcotics, the administration was aware, they were paying steadily close attention, there'd been marked improvement, hopes were high. "A van comes every week to sell dope," I said. He said he wasn't at liberty to say publicly what was being done about that possibility. "Have you considered stopping it?" I said. "That seems pretty straightforward."

It wasn't that simple, he said amicably.

"It *is* that simple. You pick up the phone, you dial, you tell the cops. They drive out and they arrest the drug dealers."

This was a community of very concerned parents, he said. It was a community full of resources.

"I don't get it."

We gazed at each other with hatred.

He said that no parent in this community — perhaps, and he certainly thought so, myself included — would want to see the future of any local student jeopardized by what many might argue could be a very unnecessary police presence.

I said, "You mean Robbie Shattuck is too rich to bust."

He told me that the concern of parents like me was a source of support and nourishment for the high school administration, and he could only impress upon me that they were continuously at work on addressing the pressing problems facing us, not just narcotics-related, not just alcohol-related, not just violence-related, not just prejudice-related, but across the board. While saying this, he stood, and all the wrinkles fell out of his suit. He said some more. Meanwhile, I imagined him studious in cruel bathroom light, scraping the razor time and again over his cowardly face. I lunged across the desk and we shook hands — our hands were wet. He promised to keep me and people like me apprised. At last we gave up and said a brief, loud, disgusted goodbye, like lovers who were sickened to recall they had ever shared a moment.

Steven turned forty-five and started bringing in a lot more money. He began to mutter about changing his already extremely rewarding life. His son was ten, so he had energy for this remaking — I was bitter about that and laughed a lot. The result of his deliberations was, for somebody in his situation, an ordinary one: he upgraded from a Honda to a metallic Porsche. Whenever he came over, the kids looked for new ways to compliment him on the phallic nature of his choice: "*Commanding,*" they'd say. "*Potent. Really smooth and rounded.*" Steven and I shared friendly sex, a desire to be with another person, and a talent for not causing trouble — was there more? This year I had been surprised to develop, by imperceptible increments, an awareness that Steven and I might actually part; I couldn't face it. Meanwhile, every other Saturday night the new Porsche stood all night in the driveway, gleaming, solid, dependable, a still point in a shifting universe.

Zack, to Nora, when he thought I was out: "It's stifling. It's stifling here. It's so *stifling* living in this house! There's not enough air in this house to support life!"

Nora wanted to go to Florida with her boyfriend. "You've got to be kidding," I said. She said, "That is *not* a nice tone." I was drawing some flash cards for school, using basketball terms and the names of Knicks. I printed "HOOK SHOT."

Her boyfriend had two plane tickets to Fort Myers and an uncle's empty condo on Captiva Island. I said that was economical but cut no ice with me.

She said, "Well, I want to go."

"Ask your father," I said. Saying this gave me a tiny, standard sort of thrill: let *him* deal with it. Wreck *his* week. Nora snorted — she and Willie were getting along badly. She was secretly not talking to him; that is, technically she spoke with him, but meanwhile she knew she was only pretending to speak.

While I printed "FOUL LINE," "FAST BREAK," "TOUCH PASS," and "RORY SPARROW," Nora explained my philosophy to me: that I took the position that they had to make their own decisions, always balancing their decisions against my concerns and feelings, that that's how we'd arrived at their curfews, that's how we'd arranged things for years — I trusted them. This was no different. I said, "Well, my feelings are very strong. I don't want you to go."

"Excuse me, Mom, but I think that's kind of hypocritical."

"And why is that?"

"Because Mark is already my boyfriend, and we're not going to do" — ominously — "anything in Florida that we *can't do here*."

That didn't matter, I said, even if true, which I doubted: what mattered was the intensity of the honeymoon-like situation, the five days alone, my sense that although I didn't need to intervene in their inevitable sexual life, I did need to make my own statement about precisely what my hopes and, yes, I said bravely, my expectations were for her, and what my own values continued to be, and so on. I warmed to my topic and, hoping to gain the advantage, lavishly gesturing with my Magic Marker, jawed on.

"Well, I'm sorry, Mommy!" she said finally, and she began to cry.

"Why are you crying?"

"You're a wonderful mother," Nora squeaked. "And I really feel bad about this."

"There's no harm done," I said.

"I can see that you and me are going to have to have different views."

"We certainly do."

"I feel so bad. I hate to not do what you want!"

"I'm sure you'll do the right thing," I said.

"That's why I'm upset!"

"Why?"

She said miserably, "Because I'm going!" Then she dried her face and went to phone her friends to borrow their many infinitesimal iridescent G-string-based bathing suits.

I yelled after her, into the next room, "Don't you kids ever have any *real* problems?"

Nora, a week later, at dinner, apropos nothing: "Mom, I hate to say it. But I don't know what's wrong with you. It's like you're turning into a different person."

I now had, of course, a psychiatrist. My psychiatrist was cautious, stubborn, wily, deft, like somebody whose survival in a hostile world depended on extreme cunning and vigilance. It made sense: he was a Freudian — his type was supposed to have already vanished, like the theater and Yiddish. His office contained a prominent couch, which I wouldn't consider lying on; a couple of kilims, like Freud's; a small card thanking the patients for not smoking; a tissue box decorated with kitty cats entangled in their yarn balls. Early on, he had accidentally revealed that he loved Cheech and Chong, and then nothing for months. I had been talking to him all year: he appeared sometimes drowsy or faintly addled, sometimes alert; behind him the light falling through the window brightened, dimmed, brightened; the newest rug seemed to fade slightly; a humidifier joined us and the air grew moist. The most comforting thing my psychiatrist ever said to me, and it was extremely comforting, wasn't even a full sentence. He murmured, "The inevitable disquietude of spirit in a house where adolescents live."

Zack was in "Three Sisters": a shortened version, cut by the drama teacher — three acts, fewer military men, and only half the pronouncements about life. The kids called it "Two and a Half Sisters." After the play's run, eight of the cast members came for dinner and sat at our round dining table wearing idiosyncratic and sexy clothes, flushed and attentive like a ring of children at a birthday party. I served a turkey, although it was February, and one bottle of California champagne for all of them — for a toast to Chekhov and themselves. When I brought in the platter, their dilated pupils shone and they all cried, "Turkey! My favorite food!" They pantomimed abject disbelief — all their lives, they'd had turkey only once a year. Vivaciously, they toasted the turkey, as if he were a pal. They all had to go to the bathroom constantly; each time, whoever left said goodbye to the turkey carcass. After dinner they drank many cups of tea. Then everybody strolled to the front door, and they all stood there and looked at Zack overintently while he said to me, "Oh, where is it, where has it all gone, my past, when I was young, gay, clever, when I dreamed and thought with grace, when my present and my future were lighted up with hope?" Then the others took turns thanking me with lines from "Two and a Half Sisters," tossed their hairdos, and rushed into the night. Zack went with them. This was a good moment. I stood on the step a long time, staring out into total darkness.

Steven was away for the weekend — no Porsche, no bagels. At midnight, after a video outing, Nora got home, looking sensible. Her planned mock honeymoon was still three weeks away; we weren't talking about it. She had been lying low, leading a remarkably staid life. She seemed to be playing a character in an imaginary young person's novel: "Nora Green, Good High School Girl." Now she pulled on her boxers, yanked back her hair, washed her face for half an hour, kissed me twice, and went to bed.

At two, Zack's expected arrival time, he wasn't home. I decided to read. At two-thirty, he wasn't home. At three, he wasn't home. At three-fifteen, the phone rang once, then stopped. At three-thirty, I heard Bibi's car slowly approaching, coasting in — she was driving with admirable care, and they were almost home. But they weren't. The car paused, then moved on. When I went to look out, it was gone. Empty street, in quiet darkness.

I thought I could call Willie and wake him, to say — what? I could call the parents of Zack's fellow actors. Half an hour more, and I'd be willing to go that far.

I waited. I could wake Nora and ask her where Zack had planned to go. Of all the alternatives, that seemed preferable —

waking a young person instead of some parents who, troubled, compromised, were still somehow managing in the middle of a Saturday night to catch a few pathetic winks. At four, I tapped at Nora's door, then tiptoed in. Her lamp was on, casting soft light on her tangled bed. Nora was gone.

I dialed Willie, let it ring. He was out. I enjoyed one moment of resentment, very brief and rich.

I phoned the parents.

Three of the actors were in their beds. Nora's boyfriend, Mark, wasn't in his bed. Bibi wasn't. Tim, the senior class president, wasn't; Katya, the eager environmentalist, wasn't; Jessica, the mathematician, wasn't. Beebop, the boy with four earrings, wasn't. Holly, the girl with the shredded jeans and visible underpants, wasn't. Alan, the tall weight-lifting boy with the velvet hat, who was going into the army, wasn't. It was four in the morning. Almost all the parents answered on the first ring; struggling to awaken, they were remarkably gracious, as if genuinely welcoming my call. None of them were curt with me, and none sounded at all resentful. They didn't sound as though they bore any resemblance to the parents I'd imagined encouraging crowds of future Ivy Leaguers to ingest beer through gas station funnels and vomit onto their shoes. One couple, whom I'd never met, and whose son was home and sleeping, offered to come over and sit with me because I was a single parent. Two of the fathers offered to drive out and look, but we couldn't think where they should go. One of the fathers offered to go out, find them, and run them over with the car, and his wife and I laughed hysterically for a long time. Bibi's mother called the police, who had no information. Let's get off the phones, we said. Maybe they'll call.

At six, in birdsong and rising light, they arrived. Nora slipped her key in the lock like a safecracker, slid the door open, and stepped in. Her lips were rosy and puffy, prominent in her ravaged face. "Oh Mom!" she said groggily. "Oh no! You're up!"

And I was also *really disappointed* and I was also *really mad,* I cried. How could they do this? Hadn't it occurred to them I'd be worried? What was in their minds? Half the parents in this town had been awake half the night! *"And I cannot believe not one of you had the consideration to call! It's absolutely incredible that —"*

"One of who?" she said.

"*All of you!*" I cried, and I stamped my foot in its fuzzy slipper. *"I have had it! I can't believe you guys would betray my trust like this! You go out there right now and tell Zack to send Bibi home and get in here!"*

She looked horribly confused. "What do you mean?" she said.

"What do *you* mean?"

"Isn't Zack here?" she said.

"Zack wasn't with you?" I said.

Pause. Tiny voice. "I was with Mark."

"What a surprise," I said. "But where is Zack?"

"Well, Mom, I'm sorry," she said. Then she added mildly, the way she had said the same thing to the hippie narcs, "I have no idea."

I recalled something funny the psychiatrist had said. The Kleenex box was over near the couch. Occasionally, sitting across the room, I threatened to sniffle, and then we both half rose and he shoved the box toward me through the empty air. Once, he murmured in consolation, while shoving the box, that a poltergeist was like a sort of ectoplasmic manifestation of adolescent libido.

"What?" I said.

"Poltergeist," he said.

I snuffled.

"The ghost that makes noises and throws plates off the shelves," he said.

I said damply, "Please. It's really not helping. I could use some *advice*."

He said, "Fine. Here it is: Put the babies up for adoption."

I was standing on the driveway in my bathrobe and coat, looking at the frosted lawn and the ascending sun, when Bibi's car, one fender crumpled, pulled in. Zack and Bibi got out and walked toward me slowly. They'd both been crying. One of Zack's shirtsleeves was torn off and wrapped around his arm as a bandage. He dropped Bibi's hand and put his arms around me, and for a moment I laid my head on his shoulder and hugged him back. "Oh, I hope you weren't worrying," he said softly. And he said that the line had been busy when they'd called last night — four tries and then they had thought it was too late.

I said that was ridiculous, I was furious at all of them, and where the hell had they been?

"Oh no. I hope you weren't up worrying," he said again.

Of course I had been, I said, and so had Bibi's mother. What had happened?

"Gee, I'm sorry." He looked exhausted, and so disheartened that it made me feel quiet. "Your sister has just taken all the flak for you," I said, but my heart wasn't in it. "What *happened*?"

He said to Bibi, "Will you come in with me?" When he reached to take her hand, she pulled it away — her palms were covered with little cuts. Inside, the cat threw himself against her legs, and she looked at him absently but didn't pick him up. We sat down, and they started telling their story moment by moment.

A long tangled night. Implausible, undoubtedly real events. It had taken on a life of its own — it *unfolded.* First they'd started to drive to Washington to see the Vietnam Memorial — to show it to Alan, who'd been threatening for months to join the army. They were going to call me from the road. Holly's father, a doctor, lived in Philadelphia, and she wanted to stop at his apartment to show Alan a photograph of him, taken twenty-five years earlier: her handsome young dad in green beret and full regalia, in Panama, in front of a grocery store, giving the camera his typical look of confidence. In two cars they drove down to Philadelphia. On South Street, Bibi's car got a flat. It seemed a little menacing — many guys in shadowy doorways. Bibi drove Holly's car to a phone and called me, but my line was busy.

Still in my coat, sitting at the kitchen table, I was listening hard. They were across from me, leaning slightly against each other. Zack's good hand was in Bibi's jacket pocket. Their story was oddly persuasive, told in those intense soft voices.

Zack and Tim and Alan changed the flat; they all drove to the divorced father's apartment, he was gone for the week, they couldn't find the photograph, they ate some English muffins out of his freezer, thought of calling me but got distracted, then it was too late to call, they got exhausted, lay down.

"Eight of you lay down?"

Well, yes, they said.

They slept awhile. Some people were smoking recreational amounts of dope in quiet darkness on the living room rug; the others were in the father's room, on the bed and in the chair, under their jackets, sleeping. Later, the living room people slept, and the bedroom people woke up. The apartment smelled like dusty smoke. Holly was gone. There was confusion. Much later it turned out she'd been outside, wearing her father's navy blue overcoat, walking around the block — Spruce, Fifth, Pine, Fourth, over and over again. It was cold out, with a high, white moon. When Bibi and Zack got organized and went out to look for Holly, they stepped out into the dark street and there she was!

They reorganized themselves as a group, turned on some lamps, brushed their teeth with the absent father's toothbrush, opened, then closed, the windows, patted at the cushions. Alan was upset — maybe he was planning to make the wrong move. Holly was upset — this short night in her father's apartment, surrounded by his furniture, was in some strange, powerful way the most intimate time she'd ever had there. Some of the group wanted to debate with Alan; others talked quietly with Holly. After a long time standing in the foyer, they went out.

They found their cars. ("Why did you have to *find* your cars?" For a moment his wry self, Zack said, "Suffice it to say, we had to.") As usual, they drove to a diner. Holly was agitated and trembly and afraid people were looking at her; Alan was crying. Alan had been drinking a lot of tequila. While he cried, he held his velvet hat on his head.

Some were starving for pancakes. Others couldn't eat. It was late — they gave up the Washington trip and decided to turn back. When they came out of the diner and into the huge parking lot, Alan suddenly wanted to drive — he grabbed Bibi's keys and jumped behind the wheel of her car. They yelled, "Alan! You can't drive!" But he started off, slowly.

To stop him, Zack stepped in front of the car. Tim and Bibi stood to the rear, so he couldn't back up.

But Alan locked the doors and started calling increasingly loud warnings out the almost shut window into the freezing night. They were all jumping around when he finally eased into second and started toward Zack. Before Zack could jump away, Alan speeded up. When the car touched him, Zack did a strange thing: he put his hands against the hood and tried to push it back.

Alan had the windows up now; he was calling something, his

friends were running alongside yelling, he accelerated; Zack was backing up fast, pushing at the car, and through the windshield he could see the tears on Alan's face. Zack jumped on the bumper and flung himself forward onto the hood. ("Like Harrison Ford," Bibi said fondly, and I blinked at her. I thought she was talking about an American president whose face I had temporarily forgotten.)

Zack was face down across the car, and he grabbed the wipers and the edge of the hood right under the windshield and held on with his fingertips. Two of the guys were reaching for him to help him off, but the car was going too fast and Zack was going to lose his grip and fall under the wheels. Alan speeded up. Zack laid his face on the metal — it reminded him of lying with your face against sand and hearing footsteps. He thought, This is ridiculous. I'm gonna get killed. He would be this year's high school death — age seventeen, in front of a gleaming diner. He closed his eyes. The parking lot spun around him. He could hear Bibi's voice, feel the cold metal under his weirdly hot face. When, instead of turning out onto the highway, Alan rammed a wall sideways and the car stopped, Zack flew off almost slowly, he thought, and he could see behind his eyes the arc being described in the black air by his body — arms, legs, gelled hair — before, at last, he landed.

He passed out. Under his forearm was half a wine bottle. There was glass all around on the ground, like confetti, and Bibi knelt and brushed it away from him, making many little cuts in her hands, which showed up only later, after the others had pulled Alan out of the car and embraced him, and Zack had opened his eyes, and they were seated inside the diner again, ordering huge doughnuts and lots of cups of coffee, like long-distance truckers. They were all squeezed into one big booth, pressed against each other. They punched the buttons on the jukebox. They felt light and almost cheerful now. Zack laid his head back on the vinyl and tried to take Bibi's hand, and all the little cuts started to bleed. Then, Zack said, he and Bibi both began to cry.

It was morning. Outside, it was cold and sunny and still. I thought about their friend Alan, about his habit of holding the velvet hat on his head, as if against a stiff wind. We were still sitting at the table in our coats. "Look, I know this sounds crazy," Zack said. I was about to say it certainly does, how dangerous, how unwise, and also you passed out, you should be looked at by a doctor. Instead I said, "You seem so sad."

Zack said, "Well, we are sad. That's just it. We really are."

After that, things changed. Nora didn't go to Florida; five days before, she broke up with Mark and unpacked. Zack got into college in Vermont; we drove to the mall and bought long underwear and Arctic boots. Then something seemed to drift out of the house, like fog breaking up, almost as if the kids were already gone.

Spring came. I took to spying on them. On Saturdays I'd walk past Tempting Treats and try to catch a glimpse of Zack in his green apron behind the counter. Or a couple of times on the way home from work I drove to the grade school where Nora ran the theater program; I stood in the bushes outside the window and watched her apply makeup to the exalted faces of five first graders. She'd live at home one more year, a placid, celibate girl. In three months Zack would leave for college, never to return.

And then for the rest of the year nothing much happened — I expected it to, but it didn't — and we started living in a sort of timeless present. Things were as calm as they had been obscurely turbulent. At first this was unnerving, and we waited for more volatility. Finally, we settled down, but by then June had come and it all was essentially over. Zack graduated. The entire graduating class wore sunglasses with their caps and gowns; they threw their caps and bellowed; they patiently stood on the lawn for a long time being grinned at by their triumphant, exhausted, over-experienced families, then went out to get shitfaced.

I remember standing there on the grass watching Zack and Nora and their friends strolling away. At that moment, as I might have expected but hadn't, a wave of feeling broke over me; it was an unfamiliar combination — real, deep sadness and heart-stopping relief. I would miss them so much I'd never get over it — I couldn't live without them! At the same time, for my purposes they weren't leaving fast enough. I couldn't wait another minute to start not caring so much.

I looked around. Willie was standing with some other people, laughing like a maniac. Steven, with whom I would amicably part, had gone to get the still unblemished Porsche. For the moment, I was alone. I remember I was wearing a lot of jewelry and a beige silk dress. It was hot. But I shivered. I think I started thinking about a circus, imagining a life on the high wire — I shuddered, the way I bet you would if you had just crossed the wire for the first time, and now you were safe on the platform, folding your parasol, looking back, suddenly recognizing that you had recently been walking in air.

SUSAN POWER

Red Moccasins

FROM STORY

MY NIECE BERNARDINE BLUE KETTLE, the one I called Dina, was thirteen — too old to be sitting on my lap. But there she was, her long legs draped over mine and her feet scraping the ground. Our fingers were laced together, both sets of arms wrapped around her pole waist. My four-year-old son, Chaske, was sitting on the floor, drumming a pillow with my long wooden cooking spoon. He covered one ear with his hand and twisted his face to imitate the Sioux singers he worshipped, old men who singed their vocal cords on high notes. He pounded his song into the pillow, making the Sioux lullaby sound energetic as a powwow song.

"Dance for me," I told Dina. I wanted her to play along with Chaske. Dina left my lap and danced around her cousin as if he were a drummer at the powwow grounds. She was serious, aware of her posture, light on her feet, tucking sharp elbows into her sides. Max, my son's pet owlet, watched Dina circle the room. He bobbed forward on the offbeat from his perch atop the mantel clock. My husband had discovered him wandering through a prairie dog town.

"Look at Max," I told the children. "You've got him dancing, too." But Max quickly tired of the game and used his long legs to turn himself around, so all we could see were his feathered back and hunched shoulders.

I clapped and clapped when the song ended, and Chaske gave up the spoon so I could stir his supper, another batch of the watery potato soup we'd been eating for weeks.

It was 1935 and a good portion of North Dakota had dried up and blown away. Grit peppered our food, coated our teeth, and silted our water. We heard that cities as distant as Chicago and New York were sprinkled with Plains topsoil. I thought it was fitting, somehow. I imagined angry ancestors fed up with Removal grabbing fistfuls of parched earth to fling toward Washington, making the president choke on dust and ashes. We prayed for rain, and when it did not come, when instead we were strangled by consumption, many people said the end of the world had come to the Standing Rock Sioux Reservation. I was not a doomsday disciple. I wouldn't let the world end while my son, Chaske, still had so much living to do.

"Bet you can't guess what's for supper," I teased Chaske, who was perched on Dina's shoulders.

"Potato soup!" he shouted, delighted to be suddenly taller than me. Dina rolled her eyes but didn't say anything. She bounced Chaske up and down, stooped over and then lifted on her toes like a horse rearing on its hind legs.

They looked like two opposites, like people with blood running from separate rivers. Chaske, whose baptism name was Emery Bauer, Jr., after his German father, was sturdy and tall for his age, his powerful calf muscles bulging like little crab apples under the skin. His hair was creamy yellow, the color of beeswax, and his eyes were a silvery gray, so pale they were almost white.

I couldn't trace Chaske's Sioux blood or find evidence of his father in his features and coloring. It was as if he came from his own place, having sidestepped all the family tracks laid out before him. Dina, on the other hand, was a blueprint of the women in our family, long-legged and graceful, thick braids grazing her narrow hips. Her little heart-shaped face was dark brown, the color of a full-blood, and her eyes black as onyx studs. Dina had been with me when I delivered Chaske, holding my hand while old women assisted me. Dina was the one who placed him in my arms, and I remember thinking, as she held him, that he looked like a bundle of sunflowers, yellow against her dusky skin. I placed the children together in my mind, couldn't imagine one without the other.

After supper Dina washed the dishes. It was so easy it was like a game to her because in my modern house, fit for a white woman, she could pump water directly into my kitchen sink and watch it drain away. She didn't have to go outside and haul buckets. I pulled out my sewing basket and let Chaske play with a jar full of buttons.

"Have you finished my costume?" Dina called over her shoulder.

"You'll be the first to know," I said. I laughed because she was so impatient, more impatient every day. I was sewing Dina her first complete Sioux costume. Ordinarily a mother would do this, but Dina's was the next thing to useless. Joyce Blue Kettle had never gotten close enough to a needle to stick herself, let alone sew a costume. As a child she'd been restless and boy-crazy, so she never learned to tan hides or do beadwork. If her mother scolded her, saying, "Look at your little cousin. Look at her fine beadwork," Joyce would puff out her bottom lip and squeeze round tears onto her flat cheeks. She would say, "You know I can't see right," pointing to her left eye, which was crossed, permanently focused on her nose. Of course, she managed to see well enough to paint her face and read movie magazines she swiped from the Lugers' store. Joyce and I were first cousins, which in our tribe made us sisters, despite our differences.

When Dina finished stacking the clean plates, I called her into the sitting room. "I'm almost ready to start your moccasins," I said. I traced the outline of her foot onto a scrap of cardboard so that the soles would match perfectly her fine narrow feet.

"Will you make me rattlesnake hair ties?" Dina asked. I dropped the paring knife I was using to cut the pattern from cardboard.

"Where did you see hair ties like that?" I was careful to leave the blade in my lap because my hands were shaking.

"I've dreamt about the Red Dress woman," she whispered. "And she had rattlesnake rattles tied in her hair. She shook them at me. She told me I could wear my hair like that."

"You can't," I said. I knew I sounded too angry. "When she comes after you, you should turn the other way."

"Have you seen her?" asked Dina, staring at me.

"Yes. But I discouraged her from coming." I didn't tell my niece that at her age I had dreamt about Čuwígnaka Ša, Red

Dress, my dead grandmother. I had heard her insistent voice, crackling with energy, whispering promises of a deadly power passed on through the bloodlines from one woman to the next. I had seen her kneeling beside a fire, feeding it with objects stolen from her victims: buttons, letters, twists of hair. She sang her spells, replacing the words of an ancient honor song with those of her own choosing. She doused the flames.

"Could she really control people?" Dina asked.

"That's what they say. But it didn't do her any good. She spelled one too many and he killed her."

My niece held her unfinished costume in her hands. She stroked the blue trade cloth material and pinched the cowrie shells sprinkled across the dress and leggings. I'd hidden the beaded belt and the flour-sack cape covered with inch-long bugle beads to surprise her with later.

There was a knock at the kitchen door. Dina's father, Clifford Blue Kettle, poked his head into the kitchen and waved at me.

"Come on in," I said. He shook his head and twisted the doorknob like he was trying to wring it loose. Black bangs hid his eyes.

"Dina here?" he asked me, so whispery he had to clear his throat and ask me again. Dina stepped into the doorway between the sitting room and kitchen. "Your ma says to get home now," he told her.

"He's so shy around you," Dina said, laughing softly.

I waved off her comment as if I disagreed, but she was right; my cousin's husband had feelings for me. When we were children, he had followed me everywhere, helping me with my chores and bringing me little treasures he'd discovered: seashells, fool's gold, ripe chokecherries. One time he brought me a round glass eye he'd poked from the socket of his sister's doll. It was too much for Joyce. She intercepted the gift, snatched it from the palm of my hand as I studied the green iris. She took Clifford over the same way, ordering him around, demanding his attention, and because I didn't love Clifford, I let her keep him. It never seemed to occur to him that he could protest. He was amiable and slow-minded. He longed to please. Even now he brought me little gifts or fashioned toys for Chaske, like my son's first baby rattle, and I could see he had something for me. One hand was hidden behind his back.

"What have you got there?" I asked. I walked to the door and tried to peek over his shoulder, which made him grin.

"Got these in a giveaway. Know Joyce can't use them." He handed me a mason jar full of red beads tiny as poppy seeds. I poured a few of them into my hand and admired their rich color, scarlet as a fresh wound sliced into my palm. I spilled them back into the jar.

"Thank you. I can put these to good use."

Having given me the gift, Clifford relaxed. He kicked the back steps with the toe of his boot. "Come on now," he called to his daughter.

Dina kissed Chaske's plump cheek before she left, and he smiled at her, kissing his fist and popping it against her arm.

I meant to stay up late to finish sewing Dina's leggings, but Chaske started coughing. He clenched his hands over his chest as if he had captured something between them, a sawing cricket or fluttering moth. I knew the odd gesture was a way he dealt with pain, trying to hammer it down. I carried Chaske to my lumpy brass bed and curled beside him. His coughing finally tapered off and he murmured, "Max."

"Max is fine," I said. "Go to sleep." I rubbed Chaske's back, my hand moving in circles, unable to relax while I listened to his breathing. His hair smelled like sweet grass, and his little body, changing too quickly from plump to wiry, warmed the bed. I guarded his sleep, forcing my breath into a perfect rhythm as if I could breathe for him, and in the morning I was weary but triumphant, having kept the world in orbit.

I had been a widow for two months, since the end of November. Dr. Kessler, a notorious alcoholic but the only doctor on the reservation, had diagnosed Emery as consumptive and told him he should go to the white sanatorium in Rapid City, South Dakota.

"I better not," my husband said, terse as always. But after seven years of marriage, I could practically read Emery's mind. He didn't want to split up our family. If I became ill, I would never be admitted to the hospital Dr. Kessler had suggested; I would be sent to the inferior Sioux sanatorium where few patients recovered. And our son Chaske wasn't really an appropriate candidate for either place. Who knew where he would end up?

"We'll take our chances," Emery said, and so we did. Emery remained at home where I was to keep him well fed and well rested. Consumption was rampant by this time, hitting nearly every family on our reservation, and no attempts were made to quarantine the sick from the healthy. My husband was a successful rancher, in partnership with his two brothers, and I couldn't keep him from work for very long. In the end it wasn't consumption that killed him but a wild horse he called Lutheran. Emery's two brothers brought my husband's body to me, stumbling beneath his bear weight. They were crying, promising me they would shoot that devil horse who had thrown Emery and broken his neck.

"No!" I said, and they looked suddenly wary. They grabbed my arms as if they expected me to pitch forward. "That horse did him a kindness." I wanted them to leave so I could comb Emery's hair and wash his face. "He didn't waste away from the consumption. He went quickly."

Later that night I sat on the edge of Chaske's cot. I told him that his sleeping father, laid out in the next room on our brass bed, was having such good dreams he didn't want to wake up.

"Is he dreaming about Max?" Chaske asked me.

"Yes," I said. "He's dreaming about all of us."

I panicked that night when I realized I didn't own a single photograph of my husband. It wasn't my memory I worried about, but Chaske's. He was so young I couldn't trust that he would remember Emery, the shape of his black beard, his tremendous wingspan and silent laugh. As Chaske slept I told him about his father, chanting our history until it became a songstory I hoped he would follow in his dreams.

I told him about the day I met Emery Bauer. It was the winter of 1928, and I was eighteen years old. I had been snowbound for several days in my family's cabin and was desperate to be outdoors where I could work the cramps out of my legs and fill my lungs with fresh air. I went for a long walk, fighting through high drifts, pausing only to search for landmarks.

I wandered onto the leased land of the Bauer ranch, thinking I was heading toward town. I came to a shallow frozen pond.

The ice was uneven, marred by tangled clumps of weeds, but I noticed a man skimming across it as if on a smooth pane of glass. He balanced on silver blades slim as butter knives, propelling his barrel body forward and then magically backward, skirting the weeds and chiseling the ice with his skates. I had heard about ice-skating, but I'd never seen it done. I'd never seen a man spin like a top. I hunched beside a frozen bush, hoping he wouldn't notice me. But I was framed in white and difficult to miss. The graceful man suddenly skated toward me, stopping so quickly his blades spit a spray of ice. He towered over me, smiling, alternately fingering his black beard and tapping the heavy workboots slung around his neck.

"You like to dance on water?" he asked me. I shook my head. I didn't know what else to do. "I'm Emery," he said. He waited, staring directly into my eyes, which made me uncomfortable.

"I'm Anna Thunder," I finally answered.

"Now *that's* a name to live up to." He clapped his large hands together. "Come here, this will be fun." Emery removed his skates, which I saw were metal blades screwed onto a pair of workboots. He donned the shoes he'd been carrying and knelt in the snow. Even down on one knee he was tall.

"Give me your foot," he said. He was the only white man other than the doctor and reservation priest I had ever spoken to, but I trusted him completely. Ironically, I think it was his size that calmed me. He was such a giant he seemed uncomfortable in his body; his posture, an accommodating stoop, and his gestures, apologetic. Off the ice he shambled awkwardly. So I did as he requested. I watched him stuff one of his mittens in the toe of each boot and then fit the skates on my feet. He held my hands and pulled me across the ice. At first I was rigid and tottered on the slippery surface, but eventually I relaxed and pushed off the blades, cutting the ice with confident strokes.

"God made you to skate," Emery breathed in my ear.

Our courtship was an ice dance, and Emery's wedding present to me was my own set of silver blades he'd ordered from the Sears catalogue. He attached them to a new pair of ankle-high laced boots cut out of fancy thin leather.

Emery and I married despite disapproval from both sides. Joyce Blue Kettle protested the loudest, flapping her tongue so much I thought she might wear it thin as a hair ribbon. Joyce had been married for several years by that time and was already a mother, but she was jealous.

"People will say you're greedy," Joyce confided to me the night before my wedding.

"What do you mean?" I only half listened, distracted as I was by the last minute details of polishing my shoes and combing my damp hair with a clump of sage to scent it.

"They say you're marrying him to get things. What about the seven new dresses, one for each day of the week, he bought you? What about the horsehair sofa and the brass bed? Didn't he even build you a house?"

Earlier that day I had taken Joyce on a tour of the new house, a neat clapboard structure made of planed lumber. I felt guilty as we moved through the rooms, the number of my possessions suddenly overwhelming me. All my life I had been taught that material goods were dispensable, things to be shared with friends and family. We were not supposed to have more than we needed, so there were endless rounds of giveaways at our dances, where people unburdened themselves of accumulated objects. But Emery was not Sioux, and his affection for me resulted in lavish offerings.

Let them say what they want, I decided. I repeated this aloud to my cousin Joyce, who was pinching the ivory-colored velvet fabric of my wedding cap.

"They know Emery has different ways," I said.

"Whatever you say." Joyce shrugged her shoulders, and the next day when I pinned the elegant cap to my newly bobbed black hair, I noticed sharp creases in the pile that no amount of smoothing could repair.

On our first wedding anniversary, Emery and I gave a feast for my Sioux relatives. I'd thought time would set things right for Joyce, but she remained bitter about the match. She trailed after me at the feast, pretending to help me in the kitchen where she sat idle, letting her mouth do all the work.

"Čuwígnaka Ša was really looking out for you," she said, fighting a sly smile. She was referring to our grandmother, Red Dress. Joyce liked to tell people that Emery hadn't fallen for me, but for the old magic I had used to spell him. I ignored her, knowing that I'd never tested these powers. If they really existed, I figured they must have atrophied like an unused muscle. Besides, I'd heard people say the same thing about Joyce and her conquest of Clifford. I struggled for something pleasant to say.

"That Bernardine's getting smarter every day, and Clifford looks like he's doing real good."

"That's because I keep him happy." Joyce smoothed a narrow hand across her wiry hair.

"You know, it works differently in my house," I said. "Emery comes up with so many ways to please me." I ran my own narrow hand from my waist to the round edge of my hip.

Later, I forgave Joyce because when she heard about my husband's sudden death she sent Bernardine to the house to watch over Chaske. Clifford accompanied his daughter, offering to take Emery's personal stock of two horses and one cow to his own place where he could tend them. I was grateful to my cousin for letting her family assist me.

Before his brothers buried him, I bathed Emery's face and trimmed his beard. I filled his pockets with the lemon drop candies he favored and the deck of cards we used to play gin rummy. Then I packed both pairs of ice skates in the coffin so that he would be waiting for me by a shallow frozen pond, ready to strap skates on my feet and take me ice-dancing.

The first day of February was mild, so I opened the windows to air out the house. I'd traded two of my dresses for a scrawny chicken, and I was relieved to be cooking something other than potato soup. Max pecked at the chicken's liver, winking at me from his perch beside the stove.

I overheard Chaske talking to Max. "Atéwaye," my father, he called the young owl. I understood then that this was Chaske's way of keeping his father alive. "Atéwaye, look at this," he said, holding up a blue-and-white-swirled marble. He chattered for a long time, disturbing Max's sleep, until he started coughing. I moved to hold him, murmuring, "You aren't sick," because his eyes looked afraid, round as the owlet's.

He was racked by coughing fits most of the day, and his cheeks were flushed. By the time we finished supper, I considered bundling him up and trying to get him to Dr. Kessler's place, three miles away. But the wind changed. The sky was suddenly a heavy gray, and it seemed to be lowering itself, ready to flatten our reservation. Without the horses, I was afraid to set out on foot.

"Close the windows!" I shouted and felt foolish. I was the only one who could heed the command. So I sealed our house against a kicking wind and a crushing mantle of snow. Chaske and I went to bed early. I slept through the night for the first time in many weeks.

Chaske was worse the next day. The pain in his chest made him cry. I gave him castor oil, which Dr. Kessler had recommended for my husband, but it didn't seem to help. No one I knew had a phone, so I put on several layers of clothes and started to walk the half mile to Dina's place, thinking someone there could contact the doctor. But I realized it would take a long time to make it through such deep snow. I couldn't leave Chaske alone for very long.

I told him stories to take his mind off the pain. I even unpacked the baby rattle he'd given up years before, the rattlesnake rattle Clifford had made for him. I shook it beside his ear, punctuating my singing with its sliding rasp. I sang him funny songs, even dirty songs, and when the pain had exhausted him, I sang the Sioux lullaby he had so recently performed. He was too weak to raise his own voice, but he wielded the wooden cooking spoon in his hand and banged it against the wall. The brass bed rocked with our desperate rhythm, we churned the air with our noise. For a moment, I wondered if I could save Chaske myself, summon a healing magic. But I remembered Joyce's futile attempts to cure her crossed eye, the hours she spent as a child pointing her finger at the offending organ while staring at her reflection in a cracked mirror. I knew we did not have the healing touch.

The house was dark and my voice was almost gone when I heard a knock at the front door.

"Coming!" I croaked.

It was my cousin Joyce, standing on my porch. I could see Emery's sorrel mare at the gate and Dina seated on my slender palomino. I waved to her.

"I come about the costume," Joyce said. At first I didn't know what she was talking about. "There's that powwow tonight," she continued, "up at the hall. Dina was hoping her costume was ready so she could wear it."

"Chaske is real sick. He needs the doctor. Could you stop at Kessler's place and tell him to come?"

Joyce promised to fetch him. She patted my arm.

I returned to Chaske warm with confidence. "Everything will be okay," I crooned, my voice clear and strong again. I rocked Chaske in the brass bed, held his body against mine as if I could absorb the tearing coughs. At least an hour passed. I was sinking into the dark and feeling hope drain away. I could actually *feel* it, a trickle of heat on my hands.

All this time I had pictured Joyce driving the horse through wet snow as high as its chest. I could see the horse swimming across snowfields to reach Dr. Kessler. But the picture changed. I saw my cousin and her daughter break through snow walls, pound the flakes to slush beneath the horses' hooves, but only as far as the community hall. They were inside the flat building, their cheeks pink and fingers warming in their jacket pockets. They were dancing together around the drum, their feet moving in a perfect mother-daughter symmetry. Then it was Dina, dancing alone as her mother watched from the sidelines, tracking the girl with the eye she could control. Her lips were pinched with satisfaction, she held herself stiff and straight in the wooden folding chair, proud. The picture dazzled my eyes as I sat in the dark room, burned itself against the backs of my eyelids. I imagined I could even hear the song that moved Bernardine's feet. It swept across the snow and spilled its notes against the bedroom window. The glass shrieked.

Finally I lit the lamp. I saw my reflection in the windowpane and noticed new lines etched in my face, drawn from nose to chin. I lifted the lamp high to regard the rest of the room. I nearly dropped it. Patches of brilliant red speckled the walls beside my bed and the faded quilts. My own hands were covered with blood from Chaske's lungs. His eyes were truly white now, as if his spirit were the only thing that had given them pigmentation. I knew I had lost him. But before I moved to wash his body, I poked my finger in his mouth, deep in a pool of black blood. I swallowed the fluid because wherever he had gone I wanted to follow close behind.

My son's coffin was carried to town and stored in an icehouse. The ground was frozen, so we couldn't bury him just yet. Joyce

Blue Kettle showed up at my door with small pails of food and wet eyes. She said Dina was so upset she couldn't get out of bed. I didn't let her inside the house.

"Get away," I said. I refused to open the door wider than an inch.

"I'm just sick about it. I didn't know how bad he was."

"You were dancing, weren't you? You were dancing."

Her eyes sparked and lit like a flash fire. "Who do you think you are? If Dina was sick you know that doctor wouldn't lift a finger to make it over here. He'd tell me to bring her in. What makes you think he'd come for yours? Is yours better than mine?"

I left the door cracked open and went to my room. I removed every dress from the wardrobe, even stepped out of the blue calico I was wearing. I rushed down the stairs in my cotton slip.

"Here!" I said, throwing the dresses at my cousin who waited, curious, on my front porch. "You always wanted them. Take them! Take them!"

Joyce backed down the steps and hurried away. She nearly tripped over the skirt of one dress, the one I wore at my wedding. I watched her run across the frozen yard, my five remaining dresses clutched to her chest.

I was as frozen as the ground, frost on my upper lip, my tongue a chunk of ice. My mind was numb, but my fingers still worked. I dug out the red beads Clifford had given me. Originally I'd planned to find dark blue beads as well, intending to decorate Dina's moccasins with the two contrasting colors. But now I just wanted to finish the slippers.

It took me three full days to bead the moccasins. I beaded the upper half, the sides, the leather tongue, even the soles, using all but a handful of beads. The moccasins were pure red. In those three days, I didn't eat a single morsel of food. I kept my stomach filled with water. The pump had frozen so I had to drink gritty, melted snow. I let Max pick at the meals the community had cooked for me.

I remember the night I finished beading Dina's moccasins the way I remember stories I have read in books — from a distance, from behind a barrier, perhaps a sheet of ice. I folded Dina's costume and placed the moccasins on top. Then I wrapped the bundle in a pillowcase. I dressed to go outdoors, wearing Emery's workboots, and I fastened Chaske's baby rattle to my braid with a leather thong. I tossed the braid over my shoulder and heard its warning rasp. It was after midnight, but I didn't take a lantern; the moon was a chilly night-light. I picked up the package and was about to set off when something stopped me, a sudden prick of heat deep inside my body. The snow attracted my gaze as I paused in the doorway. It looked clean, as though it could deaden the spark. So I covered my head and arms with snow, molding it to my thighs. I didn't feel the chill or the moisture. I moved on like a snow queen.

I can still hear my footsteps crackling through the drifts. I stopped several feet from the door of the Blue Kettle place.

"Cŭwígnaka Ša, you help me now," I implored. I hunched in the snow.

Bernardine, I called with my mind. *Bernardine.* I didn't speak aloud, but my head buzzed with her name, the syllables filled my throat. My teeth clicked her name. *Bernardine.*

She was wearing the flannel nightdress I'd given her for Christmas, and she was barefoot. She came right up to me. *We must dress you,* I said, still silent. She was obedient, her eyes glazed and swollen from crying. She lifted her arms so I could remove the nightdress. Her skin shriveled in the cold, but she didn't shiver. I dressed her then, in the trade cloth dress and leggings. I tied the belt around her waist and slipped the cape over her head. I smoothed her thick braids. Finally I knelt before her and fit the beaded moccasins on her feet. I tied the laces.

"You dance," I hissed. The words were white smoke in the air.

No one will ever know how many hours Bernardine danced in the snow. She danced herself into another world. Clifford found her the next day about a mile from their house, at the edge of a circular track she'd worn through high snowdrifts. People said she was frozen to a young hackberry tree, embracing it as if she had given up on her powwow steps and commenced waltzing.

I heard Joyce wanted someone to remove the shreds of leather and beads, all that remained of Dina's red moccasins. But the pieces were fused to her daughter's skin. One old woman started to cut them off, slicing into flesh, which was the moment Joyce stumbled out of her mind. So they left them on Dina's feet.

For two months she and my son, Chaske, rested side by side in the icehouse. People avoided me and my cousin after an initial round of visits. But everyone turned out for the joint burial.

Joyce and Clifford and I stood near the open graves. I noticed everyone else had pulled back. I don't remember a single word uttered by the Catholic priest. I don't even remember walking to the tiny cemetery behind the church. But I can hear the sound of Joyce's laughter. She giggled into a white handkerchief, tears rolling down her flat cheeks. Her short hair was patchy, singed in several places, and I guessed that Clifford had tried to set her hair with a curling iron. She looked years younger, her face smooth and empty, so different from my own face, which I hardly recognized anymore. My skin was parched and lined as the bottom of a dry creek bed.

That spring, after the children were buried, I discovered that magic let loose can take on a life of its own. I had made my niece dance, and there was no one to tell her to stop. Bernardine Blue Kettle was still dancing, this time around my pretty clapboard house. I didn't actually see her; I was too afraid to look, afraid I would see Chaske riding on her shoulders. But I heard the stamp and shuffle of her steps. She never visited at the same time, teasing me with her unpredictability, and there were no footprints in the dirt. But each time the noise ended and I found the courage to step onto my porch, I saw the flash of red beads that had fallen on the ground. I didn't touch them. I kicked the dirt to hide their gleam.

I noticed that even the magpies, always greedy for shimmering objects, scavenged in some other yard. They did not covet the sparkling red beads scattered outside my house.

THOM JONES

I Want to Live!

FROM HARPER'S MAGAZINE

SHE WONDERED how many times a week he had to do this. Plenty, no doubt. At least every day. Maybe twice . . . three times. Maybe, on a big day, five times. It was the ultimate bad news, and he delivered it dryly, like Sergeant Joe Friday. He was a young man, but his was a tough business and he had gone freeze-dried already. Hey, the bad news wasn't really a surprise! She . . . *knew*. Of course, you always hope for the best. She heard but she didn't hear.

"What?" she offered timidly. She had hoped . . . for better. Geez! Give me a break! What was he saying? Breast and uterus? Double trouble! She *knew* it would be the uterus. There had been the discharge. The bloating, the cramps. The fatigue. But it was common and easily curable provided you got it at stage one. Eighty percent cure. But the breast — that one came out of the blue and that could be really tricky — that was fifty-fifty. Strip out the lymph nodes down your arm and guaranteed chemo. God! Chemo. The worst thing in the world. Good-bye hair — there'd be scarves, wigs, a prosthetic breast, crying your heart out in "support" groups. Et cetera.

"Mrs. Wilson?" The voice seemed to come out of a can. Now the truth was revealed and all was out in the open. Yet how — tell me this — how would it ever be possible to have a life again? The voice from the can had chilled her. To the core.

"Mrs. Wilson, your last CA 125 hit the ceiling," he said. "I suspect that this could be an irregular kind of can . . . cer."

Some off-the-wall kind of can . . . cer? A kind of wildfire cancer! Not the easygoing, 80 percent cure, tortoise, as-slow-as-molasses-in-January cancer!

January. She looked past the thin oncologist, wire-rimmed glasses, white coat, inscrutable. Outside, snowflakes tumbled from the sky, kissing the pavement — each unique, wonderful, worth an hour of study, a microcosm of the Whole: awe-inspiring, absolutely fascinating, a gift of divinity gratis. Yet how abhorrent they seemed. They were white, but the whole world had lost its color for her now that she'd heard those words. The shine was gone from the world. Had she been Queen of the Universe for a million years and witnessed glory after glory, what would it have mattered now that she had come to this?

She . . . came to . . . went out, came back again . . . went out. There was this . . . wonderful show. Cartoons. It was the best show. This wasn't so bad. True, she had cancer but . . . these wonderful cartoons. Dilaudid. On Dilaudid, well, you live, you die — that's how it is . . . life in the Big City. It happens to everyone. It's part of the plan. Who was she to question the plan?

The only bad part was her throat. Her throat was on fire. "Intubation." The nurse said she'd phone the doctor and maybe he'd authorize more dope.

"Oh, God, please. Anything."

"Okay, let's just fudge a little bit, no one needs to know," the nurse said, twisting a knob on Tube Control Central. Dilaudid. Cartoons. Oh, God, thank God, Dilaudid! Who invented that drug? Write him a letter. Knight him. Award the Nobel Prize to Dilaudid Man. Where was that knob? A handy thing to know. Whew! Whammo! Swirling, throbbing ecstasy! And who was that nurse? Florence Nightingale, Mother Teresa would be proud . . . oh, boy! It wasn't just relief from the surgery; she suddenly realized how much psychic pain she had been carrying and now it was gone with one swoop of a magic wand. The cartoons. Bliss . . .

His voice wasn't in a can, never had been. It was a normal voice, maybe a little high for a man. Not that he was effeminate. The whole problem with him was that he didn't seem real. He wasn't a flesh-and-blood kinda guy. Where was the *empathy?* Why did he get into this field if he couldn't empathize? In this field, empathy should be your stock-in-trade.

"The breast is fine, just a benign lump. We brought a specialist in to get it, and I just reviewed the pathology report. It's nothing to worry about. The other part is not . . . so good. I'm afraid your abdomen . . . it's spread throughout your abdomen . . . it looks like little Grape-Nuts, actually. It's exceedingly rare and it's . . . it's a rapid form of . . . can . . . cer. We couldn't really take any of it out. I spent most of my time in there untangling adhesions. We're going to have to give you cisplatin . . . if it weren't for the adhesions, we could pump it into your abdomen directly — you wouldn't get so sick that way — but those adhesions are a problem and may cause problems further along." Her room was freezing, but the thin oncologist was beginning to perspire. "It's a shame," he said, looking down at her chart. "You're in such perfect health . . . otherwise."

She knew this was going to happen yet she heard herself say, "Doctor, do you mean . . . I've got to take —"

"Chemo? Yeah. But don't worry about that yet. Let's just let you heal up for a while." He slammed her chart shut and . . . whiz, bang, he was outta there.

Good-bye, see ya.

The guessing game was over and now it was time for the ordeal. She didn't want to hear any more details — he'd said something about a 20 percent five-year survival rate. Might as well bag it. She wasn't a fighter, and she'd seen what chemo had done to her husband, John. This was it. Finis!

She had to laugh. Got giddy. It was like in that song — *Freedom's just another word for nothing left to lose* . . . When you're totally screwed, nothing can get worse, so what's to worry? Of course she could get lucky . . . it would be a thousand-to-one, but maybe . . .

The ovaries and uterus were gone. The root of it all was out. Thank God for that. Those befouled organs were gone. Where? Disposed of. Burned. In a dumpster? Who cares? The source was destroyed. Maybe it wouldn't be so bad. How could it be that bad? After all, the talk about pain from major abdominal surgery was overdone. She was walking with her little cart and tubes by the third day — a daily constitutional through the ward.

Okay, the Dilaudid was permanently off the menu, but morphine sulfate wasn't half bad. No more cartoons but rather a mellow glow. Left, right, left, right. Hup, two, three, four! Even a journey of a thousand miles begins with the first step. On the morphine she was walking a quarter of an inch off the ground and everything was . . . softer, mercifully so. Maybe she could hack it for a thousand miles.

But those people in the hospital rooms, gray and dying, that was her. Could such a thing be possible? To die? Really? Yes, at some point she guessed you did die. But her? Now? So soon? With so little time to get used to the idea?

No, this was all a bad dream! She'd wake up. She'd wake up back in her little girl room on the farm near Battle Lake, Minnesota. There was a Depression, things were a little rough, but big deal. What could beat a sun-kissed morning on Battle Lake and a robin's song? There was an abundance of jays, larks, bluebirds, cardinals, hummingbirds, red-winged blackbirds in those days before acid rain and heavy-metal poisoning, and they came to her yard to eat from the cherry, apple, plum, and pear trees. What they really went for were the mulberries.

Ah, youth! Good looks, a clean complexion, muscle tone, a full head of lustrous hair — her best feature, although her legs were pretty good, too. Strength. Vitality. A happy kid with a bright future. Cheerleader her senior year. Pharmacy scholarship at the college in Fergus Falls. Geez, if her dad hadn't died, she could have been a pharmacist. Her grades were good, but hard-luck stories were the order of the day. It was a Great Depression. She would have to take her chances. Gosh! It had been a great, wide, wonderful world in those days, and no matter what, an adventure lay ahead, something marvelous — a handsome prince and a life happily ever after. Luck was with her. Where had all the time gone? How had all the dreams . . . fallen away? Now she was in the Valley of the Shadow. The morphine sulfate was like a warm and friendly hearth in Gloom City, her one and only consolation.

He was supposed to be a good doctor, one of the best in the field, but he had absolutely no bedside manner. She really began to hate him when he took away the morphine and put her on Tylenol 3. Then it began to sink in that things might presently go downhill in a hurry.

They worked out a routine. If her brother was busy, her daughter drove her up to the clinic and then back down to the office, and the thin oncologist is . . . called away, or he's . . . running behind, or he's . . . *something.* Couldn't they run a business, get their shit together? Why couldn't they anticipate? It was one thing to wait in line at a bank when you're well, but when you've got cancer and you're this cancer patient and you wait an hour, two hours, or they tell you to come back next week . . . come back for something that's worse than anything, the very worst thing in the world! Hard to get up for that. You really had to brace yourself. Cisplatin, God! Metal mouth, restlessness, pacing. Flop on the couch, but that's no good; get up and pace, but you can't handle that, so you flop on the couch again. Get up and pace. Is this really happening to me? *I can't believe this is really happening to me!* How can such a thing be possible?

Then there were the episodes of simultaneous diarrhea and vomiting that sprayed the bathroom from floor to ceiling! Dry heaves and then dry heaves with bile and then dry heaves with blood. You could drink a quart of tequila and then a quart of rum and have some sloe gin too and eat pink birthday cakes and five pounds of licorice, Epsom salts, a pint of kerosene, some Southern Comfort — and you're on a Sunday picnic compared to cisplatin. Only an archfiend could devise a dilemma where to maybe *get well* you first had to poison yourself within a whisker of death, and in fact if you didn't die, you wished that you had.

There were visitors in droves. Flowers. Various intrusions at all hours. Go away. Leave me alone . . . please, God, leave me . . . alone.

Oh, hi, thanks for coming. Oh, what a lovely — such beautiful flowers . . .

There were moments when she felt that if she had one more episode of diarrhea, she'd jump out of the window. Five stories. Would that be high enough? Or would you lie there for a time and die slowly? Maybe if you took a header right onto the concrete. Maybe then you wouldn't feel a thing. Cisplatin: she had to pace. But she had to lie down, but she was squirrelly as hell and she couldn't lie down. TV was no good — she had double vision, and it was all just a bunch of stupid shit, anyhow. Soap operas — good grief! What absolute crap. Even her old favorites. You only live once, and to think of all the time she pissed away watching soap operas.

If only she could sleep. God, couldn't they give her Dilaudid?

No! Wait! Hold that! Somehow Dilaudid would make it even worse. Ether then. Put her out. Wake me up in five days. Just let me sleep. She *had* to get up to pace. She *had* to lie down. She *had* to vomit. *Oh, hi, thanks for coming. Oh, what a lovely — such beautiful flowers.*

The second treatment made the first treatment seem like a month in the country. The third treatment — oh, damn! The whole scenario had been underplayed. Those movie stars who got it and wrote books about it were stoics, valiant warriors compared to her. She had no idea anything could be so horrible. Starving in Bangladesh? No problem, I'll trade. Here's my MasterCard and the keys to the Buick — I'll pull a rickshaw, anything! Anything but this. HIV-positive? Why just sign right here on the dotted line and you've got a deal! I'll trade with anybody! Anybody.

The thin oncologist with the Bugs Bunny voice said the CA 125 number was still up in the stratosphere. He said it was up to her if she wanted to go on with this. What was holding her up? She didn't know, and her own voice came from a can now. She heard herself say, "Doctor, what would you do . . . if you were me?"

He thought it over for a long time. He pulled off his wire rims and pinched his nose, world-weary. "I'd take the next treatment."

It was the worst by far — square root to infinity. Five days: no sleep, pacing, lying down, pacing. Puke and diarrhea. The phone. She wanted to tear it off the wall. After all these years, couldn't they make a quiet bell? — did they have shit for brains or what? *Oh, hi, well . . . just fine. Just dandy. Coming by on Sunday? With the kids? Well . . . no, I feel great. No. No. No. I'd love to see you . . .*

And then one day the thin-timbre voice delivered good news. "Your CA 125 is almost within normal limits. It's working!"

Hallelujah! Oh my God, let it be so! A miracle. Hurrah!

"It is a miracle," he said. He was almost human, Dr. Kildare, Dr. Ben Casey, Marcus Welby, M.D. — take your pick. "Your CA is down to rock bottom. I think we should do one, possibly two more treatments and then go back inside for a look. If we do too few, we may not kill it all but if we do too much — you see, it's toxic to your healthy cells as well. You can get cardiomyopathy in one session of cisplatin and you can die."

"One more is all I can handle."

"Gotcha, Mrs. Wilson. One more and in for a look."

"I hate to tell you this," he said. Was he making the cartoons go away? "I'll be up front about it, Mrs. Wilson, we've still got a problem. The little Grape-Nuts — fewer than in the beginning, but the remaining cells will be resistant to cisplatin, so our options are running thin. We could try a month of an experimental form of hard chemotherapy right here in the hospital — very, very risky stuff. Or we could resume the cisplatin, not so much aiming for a cure but rather as a holding action. Or we could not do anything at all . . ."

Her voice was flat. She said, "What if I don't do anything?"

"Dead in three months, maybe six."

She said, "Dead how?"

"Lungs, liver, or bowel. Don't worry, Mrs. Wilson, there won't be a lot of pain. I'll see to that." Bingo! He flipped the chart shut and . . . whiz, bang, he was outta there!

She realized that when she got right down to it, she wanted to live, more than anything, on almost any terms, so she took more cisplatin. But the oncologist was right, it couldn't touch those resistant rogue cells; they were like roaches that could live through atomic warfare, grow and thrive. Well then, screw it! At least there wouldn't be pain. What more can you do? She shouldn't have let him open her up again. That had been the worst sort of folly. She'd let him steamroll her with Doctor Knows Best. Air had hit it. No wonder it was a wildfire. A conflagration.

Her friends came by. It was an effort to make small talk. How could they know? How could they *know* what it was like? They loved her, they said, with liquor on their breath. They had to get juiced before they could stand to come by! They came with casseroles and cleaned for her, but she had to sweat out her nights alone. Dark nights of the soul on Tylenol 3 and Xanax. A lot of good that was. But then when she was in her loose, giddy *freedom's just another word for nothing left to lose* mood, about ten days after a treatment, she realized her friends weren't so dumb.

They knew that they couldn't really *know*. Bugs Bunny told her there was no point in going on with the cisplatin. He told her she was a very brave lady. He said he was sorry.

A month after she was off that poison, cisplatin, there was a little side benefit. She could see the colors of the earth again and taste food and smell flowers — it was a bittersweet pleasure, to be sure. But her friends took her to Hawaii, where they had this great friend ("You gotta meet him!") and he . . . he made a play for her and brought her flowers every day, expensive roses, et cetera. She had never considered another man since John had died from can . . . cer ten years before. How wonderful to forget it all for a moment here and there. A moment? Qualify that — make that ten, fifteen seconds. How can you forget it? Ever since she got the news she could . . . not . . . forget . . . it.

Now there were stabbing pains, twinges, flutterings — maybe it was normal everyday stuff amplified by the imagination or maybe it was real. How fast would it move, this wildfire brand? Better not to ask.

Suddenly she was horrible again. Those nights alone — killers. Finally one night she broke down and called her daughter. Hated to do it, throw in the towel, but this was the fifteenth round and she didn't have a prayer.

"Oh, hi. I'm just fine" — *blah blah blah* — "but I was thinking maybe I could come down and stay, just a while. I'd like to see Janey and —"

"We'll drive up in the morning."

At least she was with blood. And her darling granddaughter. What a delight. Playing with the little girl, she could forget. It was even better than Hawaii. After a year of sheer hell, in which all of the good stuff added up to less than an hour and four minutes total, there was a way to forget. She helped with the dishes. A little light cleaning. Watched the game shows, worked the *Times* crossword, but the pains grew worse. Goddamn it, it felt like nasty little yellow-tooth rodents or a horde of translucent termites — thousands of them, chewing her guts out! Tylenol 3 couldn't touch it. The new doctor she had been passed to gave her Dilaudid. She was enormously relieved. But what she got was a vial of little pink tablets and after the first dose she realized it wasn't much good in the pill form; you could squeeze by on it but they'd *promised* — no pain! She was losing steam. Grinding down.

They spent a couple of days on the Oregon coast. The son-in-law — somehow it was easy to be with him. He didn't pretend that things were other than they were. He could be a pain in the bun, like everyone, bitching over trivialities, smoking Kool cigarettes, strong ones — jolters! A pack a day easy, although he was considerate enough to go outside and do it. She wanted to tell him, "Fool! Your health is your greatest fortune!" But she was the one who'd let six months pass after that first discharge.

The Oregon coast was lovely, although the surf was too cold for actual swimming. She sat in the hotel whirlpool and watched her granddaughter swim a whole length of the pool all on her own, a kind of dog-paddle thing but not bad for a kid going on seven. They saw a show of shooting stars one night but it was exhausting to keep up a good front and not to be morbid, losing weight big time. After a shower, standing at the mirror, scars zigzagging all over the joint like the Bride of Frankenstein, it was just awful. She was bald, scrawny, ashen, yet with a bloated belly. She couldn't look. Sometimes she would sink to the floor and just lie there, too sick to even cry, too weak to even get dressed, yet somehow she did get dressed, slapped on that hot, goddamn wig, and showed up for dinner. It was easier to do that if you pretended that it wasn't real, if you pretended it was all on TV.

She felt like a naughty little girl sitting before the table looking at meals her daughter was killing herself to make — old favorites that now tasted like a combination of forty-weight Texaco oil and sawdust. It was a relief to get back to the couch and work crossword puzzles. It was hell imposing on her daughter but she was frightened. Terrified! They were her blood. They *had* to take her. Oh, to come to this!

The son-in-law worked swing shift and he cheered her in the morning when he got up and made coffee. He was full of life. He was real. He was authentic. He even interjected little pockets of hope. Not that he pushed macrobiotics or any of that foolishness, but it was a fact — if you were happy, if you had something to live for, if you loved life, you lived it. It had been a mistake for her to hole up there in the mountains after John died. The Will to Live was more important than doctors and medicines. You had to reinvigorate the Will to Live. The granddaughter was good for that. She just couldn't go the meditation-tape route, imagining microscopic, ravenous, good-guy little sharks eating the bad cancer cells, et cetera. At least the son-in-law didn't suggest that or come on strong with a theology trip. She noticed he read the King James Bible, though.

She couldn't eat. There was a milk-shake diet she choked down. Vanilla, chocolate fudge, strawberry — your choice. Would Madame like a bottle of wine with dinner? Ha, ha, ha.

Dilaudid. It wasn't working, there was serious pain, especially in her chest, dagger thrusts — *Et tu, Brute?* She watched the clock like a hawk and had her pills out and ready every four hours — and that last hour was getting to be murder, a morbid sweat began popping out of her in the last fifteen minutes. One morning she caved in and timidly asked the son-in-law, "Can I take three?"

He said, "Hell, take four. It's a safe drug. If you have bad pain, take four." Her eyes were popping out of her head. "Here, drink it with coffee and it will kick in faster."

He was right. He knew more than the doctor. You just can't do everything by the book. Maybe that had been her trouble all along — she was too compliant, one of those "cancer" personalities. She believed in the rules. She was one of those kind who wanted to leave the world a better place than she found it. She had been a good person, had always done the right thing — this just wasn't right. It wasn't fair. She was so . . . angry!

The next day, over the phone, her son-in-law bullied a prescription of methadone from the cancer doctor. She heard one side of a lengthy heated exchange while the son-in-law made a persuasive case for methadone. He came on like Clarence Darrow or F. Lee Bailey. It was a commanding performance. She'd never heard of anyone giving a doctor hell before. God bless him for not backing down! On methadone tablets a warm orange glow sprung forth and bloomed like a glorious, time-lapse rose in her abdomen and then rolled through her body in orgasmic waves. The sense of relief shattered all fear and doubt though the pain was still there to some extent. It was still there but — so what? And the methadone tablets lasted a very long time — no more of that *every four hours* bullshit.

*

Purple blotches all over her skin, swollen ankles. Pain in her hips and joints. An ambulance trip to the emergency room. "Oh," they said, "it's nothing . . . vascular purpura. Take aspirin. Who's next?"

Who's next? Why hadn't she taken John's old .38 revolver the very day she heard that voice in the can? Stuck it in the back of her mouth and pulled the trigger? She had no fear of hellfire. She was a decent, moral person but she did not believe. Neither was she the Hamlet type — what lies on the other side? It was probably the same thing that occurred before you were born — zilch. And zilch wasn't that bad. What was wrong with zilch?

One morning she waited overlong for the son-in-law to get up, almost smashed a candy dish to get him out of bed. Was he going to sleep forever? Actually, he got up at his usual time.

"I can't. Get. My breath," she told him.

"You probably have water in your lungs," the son-in-law said. He knew she didn't want to go to the clinic. "We've got some diuretic. They were Boxer's when she had congestive heart failure — dog medicine, but it's the same thing they give humans. Boxer weighed fifty-five pounds. Let me see . . . take four, no, take three. To be cautious. Do you feel like you have to cough?"

"Yes." Kaff, kaff, kaff.

"This might draw the water out of your lungs. It's pretty safe. Try to eat a banana or a potato skin to keep your potassium up. If it doesn't work, we can go over to the clinic."

How would he know something like that? But he was right. It worked like magic. She had to pee like crazy but she could breathe. The panic to end all panics was over. If she could only go . . . number two. Well, the methadone slows you down. "Try some Metamucil," the son-in-law said.

It worked. Kind of, but it sure wasn't anything to write home about.

"I can't breathe. The diuretics aren't working."

The son-in-law said they could tap her lung. It would mean another drive to the clinic, but the procedure was almost painless and provided instantaneous relief. It worked but it was three days of exhaustion after that one.

The waiting room. Why so long? Why couldn't they anticipate? You didn't have to be a genius to know which way the wildfire was spreading. Would the methadone keep that internal orange glow going or would they run out of ammo? Was methadone the ultimate or were there bigger guns? Street heroin? She'd have to put on her wig and go out and score China White.

The little girl began to tune out. Gramma wasn't so much fun anymore; she just lay there and she gave off this smell. There was no more dressing up; it was just the bathrobe. In fact, she felt the best in her old red-and-black tartan pattern, flannel, ratty-ass bathrobe, not the good one. The crosswords — forget it, too depressing. You could live the life of Cleopatra but if it came down to this, what was the point?

The son-in-law understood. Of all the people to come through. It's bad and it gets worse and so on until the worst of all. "I don't know how you can handle this," he'd say. "What does it feel like? Does it feel like a hangover? Worse than a hangover? Not like a hangover. Then what? Like drinking ten pots of boiled coffee? Like that? Really? Jittery! Oh, God, that must be awful. How can you stand it? Is it just like drinking too much coffee or is there some other aspect? Your fingers are numb? Blurred vision? It takes eight years to watch the second hand sweep from twelve to one? Well, if it's like that, how did you handle *five days?* I couldn't — I'd take a bottle of pills, shoot myself. Something. What about the second week? Drained? Washed out? Oh, brother! I had a three-day hangover once — I'd rather die than do that again. I couldn't ride out that hangover again for money. I know I couldn't handle chemo . . ."

One afternoon after he left for work, she found a passage circled in his well-worn copy of Schopenhauer: "In early youth, as we contemplate our coming life, we are like children in a theater before the curtain is raised, sitting there in high spirits and eagerly waiting for the play to begin. It is a blessing that we do not know what is really going to happen." Yeah! She gave up the crosswords and delved into *The World As Will and Idea.* This Schopenhauer was a genius! Why hadn't anyone told her? She was a reader, she had waded through some philosophy in her time — you just couldn't make any sense out of it. The problem was the terminology! She was a crossword ace, but words like *eschatology* — hey! Yet Schopenhauer got right into the heart of all the important things. The things that really mattered. With Schopenhauer she could take long excursions from the grim specter of impending death. In Schopenhauer, particularly in his aphorisms and reflections, she found an absolute satisfaction, for Schopenhauer spoke the truth and the rest of the world was disseminating lies!

Her son-in-law helped her with unfinished business: will, mortgage, insurance, how shall we do this, that, and the other? Cremation, burial plot, et cetera. He told her the stuff that her daughter couldn't tell her. He waited for the right moment and then got it all in — for instance, he told her that her daughter loved her very much but that it was hard for her to say so. She knew she cringed at this revelation, for it was ditto with her, and she knew that he could see it. Why couldn't she say to her own daughter three simple words, "I love you"? She just couldn't. Somehow it wasn't possible. The son-in-law didn't judge her. He had to be under pressure, too. Was she bringing everyone in the house down? Is that why he was reading Schopenhauer? No, Schopenhauer was his favorite. "Someone had to come out and tell it like it is," he would say of the dour old man with muttonchops whose picture he had pasted on the refrigerator. From what she picked up from the son-in-law, Schopenhauer wrote his major work by his twenty-sixth birthday — a philosophy that was ignored almost entirely in his lifetime and even now, in this day and age, it was thought to be more of a work of art than philosophy in the truest sense. A work of art? Why, it seemed irrefutable! According to the son-in-law, Schopenhauer spent the majority of his life in shabby rooms in the old genteel section of Frankfurt, Germany, that he shared with successions of poodles to keep him company while he read, reflected, and wrote about life at his leisure. He had some kind of small inheritance, just enough to get by, take in the concerts, do a little traveling now and then. He was well versed in several languages. He read virtually everything written from the Greeks on upward, including the Eastern writers, a classical scholar, and had the mind to chew things over and make something of the puzzle of life. The son-in-law, eager to discourse, said Freud called Schopenhauer one of the six greatest men who ever lived. Nietzsche, Thomas Mann, and Richard Wagner all paid tribute to this genius who had been written off with one word — pessimist. The son-in-law lamented that his works were going out of print, becoming increasingly harder to find. He was planning a trip to Frankfurt, where he hoped to find a little bust of his hero. He had written to officials in Germany making inquiries. They had given him the brush-off. He'd have to fly over himself. And she, too, began to worry that the works of this writer would no longer be available . . . she, who would be worms' meat any day.

Why? Because the *truth* was worthwhile. It was more important than anything, really. She'd had ten years of peaceful retirement, time to think, wonder, contemplate, and had come up with nothing. But new vistas of thought had been opened by the curiously ignored genius with the white muttonchops, whose books were harder and harder to get and whom the world would consider a mere footnote from the nineteenth century — a crank, a guy with an ax to grind, a hypochondriac, a misogynist, an alarmist who slept with pistols under his pillow, a man with many faults. Well, check anyone out and what do you find?

For God's sake, how were you supposed to make any sense out of this crazy-ass shit called life? If only she could simply push a button and never have been born.

The son-in-law took antidepressants and claimed to be a melancholiac, yet he always seemed upbeat, comical, ready with a laugh. He had a sense of the absurd that she had found annoying back in the old days when she liked to pretend that life was a stroll down Primrose Lane. If she wasn't walking down the "sunny side of the street" at least she was "singin' in the rain." Those were the days.

What a fool!

She encouraged the son-in-law to clown and philosophize, and he flourished when she voiced a small dose of appreciation or barked out a laugh. There was more and more pain and discomfort, but she was laughing more too. Schopenhauer: "No rose without a thorn. But many a thorn without a rose." The son-in-law finessed all of the ugly details that were impossible for her. Of all the people to come through!

With her lungs temporarily clear and mineral oil enemas to regulate her, she asked her daughter one last favor. Could they take her home just once more?

They made an occasion of it and drove her up into the mountains for her granddaughter's seventh birthday party. Almost everyone in the picturesque resort town was there, and if they were appalled by her deterioration they did not show it. She couldn't go out on the sun porch, had to semi-recline on the couch, but everyone came in to say hello and all of the bad stuff fell away for . . . an entire afternoon! She was deeply touched by the warm affection of her friends. There were . . . so many of them. My God! They loved her, truly they did. She could see it. You couldn't bullshit her anymore; she could see deep into the human heart; she knew what people were. What wonderful friends. What a perfect afternoon. It was the last . . . good thing.

When she got back to her daughter's she began to die in earnest. It was in the lungs and the bowel, much as the doctor said it would be. Hell, it was probably in the liver even. She was getting yellow, not just the skin but even the whites of her eyes. There was a week in the hospital, where they tormented her with tests. That wiped out the last of her physical and emotional stamina.

She fouled her bed after a barium lower G.I. practically turned to cement and they had to give her a powerful enema. Diarrhea in the bed. The worst humiliation. "Happens all the time, don't worry," the orderly said.

She was suffocating. She couldn't get the least bit of air. All the main players were in the room. She knew this was it! Just like that. Bingo! There were whispered conferences outside her room. Suddenly the nurses, those heretofore angels of mercy, began acting mechanically. They could look you over and peg you, down to the last five minutes. She could see them give her that *anytime now* look. A minister dropped in. There! That was the tip-off — the fat lady was singing.

When the son-in-law showed up instead of going to work she looked to him with panic. She'd been fighting it back but now . . . he was there, he would know what to do without being asked, and in a moment he was back with a nurse. They cranked up the morphine sulfate, flipped it on full-bore. Still her back hurt like hell. All that morphine and a backache . . . just give it a minute . . . ahhh! Cartoons.

Someone went out to get hamburgers at McDonald's. Her daughter sat next to her holding her hand. She felt sorry for them. They were the ones who were going to have to stay behind and play out their appointed roles. Like Schopenhauer said, the best they would be able to do for themselves was to secure a little room as far away from the fire as possible, for Hell was surely in the here and now, not in the hereafter. Or was it?

She began to nod. She was holding onto a carton of milk. It would spill. Like diarrhea-in-the-bed all over again. Another mess. The daughter tried to take the carton of milk away. She . . . held on defiantly. Forget the Schopenhauer — what a lot of crap that was! She did not want to cross over. She wanted to live! She wanted to live!

The daughter wrenched the milk away. The nurse came back and cranked up the morphine again. They were going for "comfort." Finally the backache . . . the cartoons . . . all of that was gone.

(She was back on the farm in Battle Lake, Minnesota. She was nine years old and she could hear her little red rooster, Mr. Barnes, crowing at first light. Then came her brother's heavy work boots clomping downstairs and the vacuum swoosh as he opened up the storm door, and then his boots crunch-crunching through the frozen snow. Yes, she was back on the farm all right. Her brother was making for the outhouse and presently Barnes would go after him, make a dive-bomb attack. You couldn't discourage Mr. Barnes. She heard her brother curse him and the thwap of the tin feed pan hitting the bird. Mr. Barnes's frontal assaults were predictable. From the sound of it, Fred walloped him good. As far as Mr. Barnes was concerned, it was his barnyard. In a moment she heard the outhouse door slam shut and another tin thwap. That Barnes — he was something. She should have taken a lesson. Puffed out her chest and walked through life — "I want the biggest and the best and the most of whatever you've got!" There were people who pulled it off. You really could do it if you had the attitude.

Her little red rooster was a mean little scoundrel, but he had a soft spot for her in his heart of steel and he looked out for her, cooed for her and her alone. Later, when young men came to see her, they soon arranged to meet her thereafter at the drugstore soda fountain uptown. One confrontation with Barnes, even for experienced farm boys, was one too many. He was some kind of rooster all right, an eccentric. Yeah, she was back on the farm. She . . . could feel her sister shifting awake in the lower bunk. It was time to get up and milk the cows. Her sister always awoke in good humor. Not her. She was cozy under a feather comforter and milking the cows was the last thing she wanted to do. Downstairs she could hear her mother speaking cheerfully to her brother as he came back inside, cursing the damn rooster, threatening to kill it. Her mother laughed it off; she didn't have a mean bone in her body.

She . . . could smell bacon in the pan, the coffee pot was percolating, and her grandmother was up heating milk for her Ovaltine. She hated Ovaltine, particularly when her grandmother overheated the milk — burned it — but she pretended to like it, insisted that she needed it for her bones, and forced it down so she could save up enough labels to get a free decoder ring to get special messages from Captain Cody, that intrepid hero of the airwaves. She really wanted to have that ring, but there was a Great Depression and money was very dear, so she never got the decoder or the secret messages or the degree in pharmacology. Had she been more like that little banty rooster, had she been a real go-getter . . . Well — it was all but over now.)

The main players were assembled in the room. She . . . was nodding in and out but she could hear. There she was, in this apparent stupor, but she was more aware than anyone could know. She heard someone say somebody at McDonald's put "everything" on her hamburger instead of "cheese and ketchup only." They were making an issue out of it. One day, when they were in her shoes, they would learn to ignore this kind of petty stuff, but you couldn't blame them. That was how things were, that's all. Life. That was it. That was what it was. And here she lay . . . dying.

Suddenly she realized that the hard part was all over now. All she had to do was . . . let go. It really wasn't so bad. It wasn't . . . anything special. It just was. She was trying to bring back Barnes one last time — that little memory of him had been fun, why not go out with a little fun? She tried to remember his coloring — orange would be too bright, rust too drab, scarlet too vivid. His head was a combination of green, yellow, and gold, all blended, and his breast and wings a kind of carmine red? No, not carmine.

He was just a little red rooster, overly pugnacious, an ingrate. He could have been a beautiful bird if he hadn't gotten into so many fights. He got his comb ripped off by a raccoon he'd caught stealing eggs in the henhouse, a big bull raccoon that Barnes had fought tooth and nail until Fred ran into the henhouse with his .410 and killed the thieving intruder. Those eggs were precious. They were income. Mr. Barnes was a hero that day. She remembered how he used to strut around the barnyard. He always had his eye on all of the hens; they were his main priority, some thirty to forty of them, depending. They were his harem and he was the sheik. Boy, was he ever. She remembered jotting down marks on a pad of paper one day when she was home sick with chicken pox. Each mark represented an act of rooster fornication. In less than a day, Mr. Barnes had committed the sexual act forty-seven times that she could see — and she didn't have the whole lay of the land from her window by any means. Why, he often went out roving and carousing with hens on other farms. There were bitter complaints from the neighbors. Barnes really could stir things up. She had to go out on her bicycle and round him up. Mr. Barnes was a legend in the county. Mr. Barnes thought the whole world belonged to him and beyond that — the suns, the stars, and the Milky Way — all of it! Did it feel good or was it torment? It must have been a glorious feeling, she decided. Maybe that was what Arthur Schopenhauer was driving at in his theory about the Will to Live. Mr. Barnes was the very personification of it.

Of course it was hard work being a rooster, but Barnes seemed the happiest creature she had ever known. Probably because when you're doing what you really want to do, it isn't work. No matter how dull things got on the farm, she could watch Barnes by the hour. Barnes could even redeem a hot, dog-day afternoon in August. He wasn't afraid of anything or anybody. Did he ever entertain a doubt? Some kind of rooster worry? Never! She tried to conjure up one last picture of him. He was just a little banty, couldn't have weighed three pounds. Maybe Mr. Barnes would be waiting for her on the other side and would greet her there and be her friend again.

She nodded in and out. In and out. The morphine was getting to be too much. Oh, please God. She hoped she wouldn't puke

. . . So much left unsaid, undone. Well, that was all part of it. If only she could see Barnes strut his stuff one last time. "Come on, Barnes. Strut your stuff for me." Her brother, Fred, sitting there so sad with his hamburger. After a couple of beers, he could do a pretty good imitation of Mr. Barnes. Could he . . . would he . . . for old time's sake? Her voice was too weak, she couldn't speak. Nowhere near. Not even close. Was she dead already? Fading to black? It was hard to tell. "Don't feel bad, my darling brother. Don't mourn for me. I'm okay" . . . and . . . one last thing — "Sarah, I do love you, darling! Love you! Didn't you know that? Didn't it show? If not, I'm so, so very sorry . . ." But the words wouldn't come — couldn't come. She . . . was so sick. You can get only so sick and then there was all that dope. Love! She should have shown it to her daughter instead of . . . assuming. She should have been more demonstrative, more forthcoming. . . . That's what it was all about. *Love your brother as yourself and love the Lord God almighty with all your heart and mind and soul.* You were sent here to love your brother. Do your best. Be kind to animals, obey the Ten Commandments, stuff like that. Was that it? Huh? Or was that all a lot of horseshit?

She . . . nodded in and out. Back and forth. In and out. She went back and forth. In and out. Back and forth . . . in and out. There wasn't any tunnel or white light or any of that. She just . . . died.

TONY EARLEY

Charlotte

FROM HARPER'S MAGAZINE

THE PROFESSIONAL WRESTLERS are gone. The professional wrestlers do not live here anymore. Frannie Belk sold the Southeastern Wrestling Alliance to Ted Turner for more money than you would think, and the professional wrestlers sold their big houses on Lake Norman and drove in their BMWs down I-85 to bigger houses in Atlanta.

Gone are the Thundercats, Bill and Steve, and the Hidden Pagans with their shiny red masks and secret signs; gone is Paolo the Peruvian who didn't speak English very well but could momentarily hold off as many as five angry men with his flying bare feet; gone are Comrade Yerkov the Russian Assassin and his bald nephew Boris, and the Sheik of the East and his Harem of Three, and Hank Wilson Senior the Country Star with his beloved guitar Leigh Ann; gone is Naoki Fujita who spit the mysterious Green Fire of the Orient into the eyes of his opponents whenever the referee turned his back; gone are the Superstud, the MegaDestroyer, the Revenger, the Preacher, Ron Rowdy, Tom Tequila, the Gentle Giant, the Littlest Cowboy, Genghis Gandhi, and Bob the Sailor. Gone is Big Bill Boscoe, the ringside announcer, whose question "Tell me, Paolo, what happened in there?" brought forth the answer that all Charlotteans still know by heart — "Well, Beel, Hidden Pagan step on toe and hit head with chair and I no can fight no more"; gone are Rockin' Robbie Frazier, the Dreamer, the Viking, Captain Boogie Woogie, Harry the Hairdresser, and Yee-Hah O'Reilly the Cherokee Indian Chief. And gone is Lord Poetry and all that he stood for, his archrival Bob Noxious, and Darling Donnis — the Sweetheart of the SWA, the Prize Greater Than Any Belt — the girl who had to choose between the two of them, once and for all, during THE FINAL BATTLE FOR LOVE.

Gone. Now Charlotte has the NBA, and we tell ourselves we are a big deal. We dress in teal and purple and sit in traffic jams on the Billy Graham Parkway so that we can yell in the new coliseum for the Hornets, who are bad, bad, bad. They are hard to watch, and my seats are good. Whenever any of the Hornets come into the bar, and they do not come often, we stare up at them like they were exotic animals come to drink at our watering hole. They are too tall to talk to for very long, not enough like us, and they make me miss the old days. In the old days in Charlotte we did not take ourselves so seriously. Our heroes had platinum blond hair and twenty-seven-inch biceps, but you knew who was good and who was evil, who was changing over to the other side, and who was changing back. You knew that sooner or later the referee would look away just long enough for Bob Noxious to hit Lord Poetry with a folding chair. You knew that Lord Poetry would stare up from the canvas in stricken wonder, as if he had never once in his life seen a folding chair. (In the bar we screamed at the television, Turn around, ref, turn around! Look out, Lord Poetry, look out!) In the old days in Charlotte we did not have to decide if the Hornets should trade Rex Chapman (they should not) or if J. R. Reid was big enough to play center in the NBA (he is, but only sometimes). In the old days our heroes were as superficial as we were — but we knew that — and their struggles were exaggerated versions of our own. Now we have the Hornets. They wear uniforms designed by Alexander Julian, and play hard and lose, and make us look into our souls. Now when we march disappointed out of the new coliseum to sit unmoving on the parkway, in the cars we can't afford, we have to think about the things that are true: Everyone in Charlotte is from somewhere else. Everyone in Charlotte tries to be something they are not. We spend more money than we make, but it doesn't help. We know that the Hornets will never make the playoffs, and that somehow it is our fault. Our lives are small and empty, and we thought they wouldn't be, once we moved to the city.

*

My girlfriend's name is Starla. She is beautiful, and we wrestle about love. She does not like to say she loves me, even though we have been together four and a half years. She will not look at me when I say I love her, and if I wanted to, I could ball up those three words and use them like a fist. Starla says she has strong lust for me, which should be enough; she says we have good chemistry, which is all anyone can hope for. Late in the night, after we have grappled until the last drop of love is gone from our bodies, I say, "Starla, I can tell that you love me. You wouldn't be able to do it like that if you didn't love me." She sits up in bed, her head tilted forward so that her red hair almost covers her face, and picks the black hair that came from my chest off of her breasts and stomach. The skin across her chest is flushed red, patterned like a satellite photograph; it looks like a place I should know. She says, "I'm a grown woman and my body works. It has nothing to do with love." Like a lot of people in Charlotte, Starla has given up on love. In the old days Lord Poetry said to never give up, to always fight for love, but now he is gone to Atlanta with a big contract and a broken heart, and I have to do the best that I can. I hold on, even though Starla says she will not marry me. I have heard that Darling Donnis lives with Bob Noxious in a big condo in Buckhead. Starla wants to know why I can't be happy with what we have. We have good chemistry and apartments in Fourth Ward and German cars. She says it is enough to live with and more than anyone had where we came from. We can eat out whenever we want.

Yet Starla breaks my heart. She will say that she loves me only at the end of a great struggle, after she is too tired to fight anymore, and then she spits out the words, like vomit, and calls me bastard or fucker or worse, and asks if the thing I have just done has made me happy. It does not make me happy, but it is what we do. It is the fight we fight. The next day we have dark circles under our eyes like the makeup truly evil wrestlers wear, and we circle each other like animals in a cage that is too small, and what we feel then is nothing at all like love.

I manage a fern bar on Independence Boulevard near downtown called P. J. O'Mulligan's Goodtimes Emporium. The regulars call the place PJ's. When you have just moved to Charlotte from McAdenville or Cherryville or Lawndale, it makes you feel good to call somebody up and say, Hey, let's meet after work at PJ's. It sounds like real life when you say it, and that is a sad thing. PJ's has fake Tiffany lampshades above the tables, with purple and teal hornets belligerent in the glass. It has fake antique Coca-Cola and Miller High Life and Pierce-Arrow Automobile and Winchester Repeating Rifle signs screwed on the walls, and imitation brass tiles glued to the ceiling. (The glue occasionally lets go and the tiles swoop down toward the tables, like bats.) The ferns are plastic because smoke and people dumping their drinks into the planters kill the real ones. The beer and mixed drinks are expensive, but the chairs and stools are cloth-upholstered and plush, and the ceiling lights in their smooth, round globes are low and pleasant enough, and the television set is huge and close to the bar and perpetually tuned to ESPN. Except when the Hornets are on Channel 18 or wrestling is on TBS.

In the old days in Charlotte a lot of the professional wrestlers hung out at PJ's. Sometimes Lord Poetry stopped by early in the afternoon, after he was through working out, and tried out a new poem he had found in one of his thick books. The last time he came in, days before THE FINAL BATTLE, I asked him to tell me a poem I could say to Starla. In the old days in Charlotte you would not think twice about hearing a giant man with long red hair recite a poem in a bar, even in the middle of the afternoon. I turned the TV down, and the two waitresses and the handful of hard cores who had sneaked away from their offices for a drink saw what was happening and eased up close enough to hear. Lord Poetry crossed his arms and stared straight up, as if the poem he was searching for was written on the ceiling or somewhere on the other side, in a place we couldn't see. His voice was higher and softer than you would expect the voice of a man that size to be, and when he nodded and finally began to speak, it was almost in a whisper, and we all leaned in even closer. He said,

We sat grown quiet at the name of love;
We saw the last embers of daylight die,
And in the trembling blue-green of the sky
A moon, worn as if it had been a shell
Washed by time's waters as they rose and fell
About the stars and broke in days and years.

I had a thought for no one's but your ears:
That you were beautiful, and that I strove
To love you in the old high way of love;
That it had all seemed happy, and yet we'd grown
As weary-hearted as that hollow moon.

P. J. O'Mulligan's was as quiet then as you will ever hear it. All of Charlotte seemed suddenly still and listening around us. Nobody moved until Lord Poetry finally looked down and reached again for his beer and said, "That's Yeats." Then we all moved back, suddenly conscious of his great size and our closeness to it, and nodded and agreed that it was a real good poem, one of the best we had ever heard him say. Later, I had him repeat it for me, line for line, and I wrote it down on a cocktail napkin. Sometimes, late at night, after Starla and I have fought, and I have made her say I love you like uncle, even as I can see in her eyes how much she hates me for it, I think about reading the poem to her, but some things are just too true to ever say out loud.

In PJ's we watch wrestling still, even though we can no longer claim it as our own. We sit around the big screen without cheering and stare at the wrestlers like favorite relatives we haven't seen in years. We say things like, Boy, the Viking has really put on weight since he moved down there, or When did Rockin' Robbie Frazier cut his hair like that? We put on brave faces when we talk about Rockin' Robbie, who was probably Charlotte's most popular wrestler, and try not to dwell on the fact that he has gone away from us for good. In the old days he dragged his stunned and half-senseless opponents to the center of the ring and climbed onto the top rope, and after the crowd counted down from five (Four! Three! Two! One!) he would launch himself into the air, his arms and legs spread like wings, his blond hair streaming out behind him like a banner, and fly ten, fifteen feet, easy, and from an unimaginable height drop with a crash like an explosion directly onto his opponent's head. He called it the Rockin' Robbie B-52. ("I'll tell you one thing, Big Bill. Come next Saturday night in the Charlotte Coliseum I'm gonna B-52 the Sheik of the East like he ain't never been B-52ed before.") And after Rockin' Robbie's B-52 had landed, while his opponent flopped around on the canvas like a big fish, waiting only to be mounted and pinned, Rockin' Robbie leaped up and stood over him, his body slick with righteous sweat, his face a picture of joy. He held his hands high in the air, his fingers spread wide, his pelvis thrusting uncontrollably back and forth in the electric joy of the moment. Then he tossed his head back and howled like a dog, his lips a gleeful red O turned toward the sky. Those were glorious days. Whenever Rockin' Robbie walked into PJ's, everybody in the place raised their glasses and pointed their noses at the fake bronze of the ceiling and bayed at the stars we knew spun, only for us, in the high, moony night above Charlotte. Nothing like that happens here anymore. Frannie Belk gathered up all the good and evil in our city and sold it four hours south. These days the illusions we have left are the small ones of our own making, and in the vacuum the wrestlers left behind, those illusions have become too easy to see through; we now have to live with ourselves.

About once a week some guy who's just moved to Charlotte from Kings Mountain or Chester or Gaffney comes up to me where I sit at the bar, on my stool by the waitress station, and says, Hey man, are you P. J. O'Mulligan? They are never kidding, and whenever it happens I don't know what to say. I wish I could tell them whatever it is they need in their hearts to hear, but P. J. O'Mulligan is fourteen lawyers from Richmond with investment capital. What do you say? New people come to Charlotte from the small towns every day, searching for lives that are bigger than the ones they have known, but what they must settle for, once they get here, are much smaller hopes: that maybe this year the Hornets might really have a shot at the Celtics, if Rex Chapman has a good game; that maybe there really is somebody named P. J. O'Mulligan, and that maybe that guy at the bar is him. Now that the wrestlers are gone, I wonder about these things. How do you tell somebody how to find what they're looking for when ten years ago you came from the same place and have yet to find it yourself? How do you tell somebody from Polkville or Aliceville or Cliffside, who just saw downtown after sunset for the first time, not to let the beauty of the skyline fool them? Charlotte is a place where a crooked TV preacher can steal money and grow like a sore until he collapses from the weight of his own evil by simply promising hope. So don't stare at the NCNB Tower against the dark blue of the sky; keep your eyes on the road. Don't think that Independence Boulevard is anything more than a street. Most of my waitresses are college girls from UNCC and CPCC, and I can see the hope shining in their faces even as they fill out applications. They look good in their official P. J. O'Mulligan's khaki shorts and white sneakers and green aprons and starched, preppy blouses, but they are still mill-town girls through and through, come to the city to find the answers to their prayers. How do you tell them Charlotte isn't a good place to look? It is a place where a crooked TV preacher can pray that his flock will send him money so that he can build a giant water slide — and they will.

But PJ's still draws a wrestling crowd. They are mostly good-looking and wear lots of jewelry. The girls do aerobics like religion and have big, curly hair, stiff with mousse. They wear short, tight dresses — usually black — and dangling earrings and spiked heels and lipstick with little sparkles in it, like stars, that you're not even sure you can see. (You catch yourself staring at their mouths when they talk, waiting for their lips to catch the light.) The guys dye their hair blond and wear it spiked on top, long and permed in back, and shaved over the ears. They lift weights and take steroids. When they have enough money they get coked up. They wear stonewashed jeans and open shirts and gold chains thick as ropes and cowboy boots made from python skin, which is how professional wrestlers dress when they relax. Sometimes you will see a group of guys in a circle, with their jeans pulled up over their calves, arguing about whose boots were made from the biggest snake. The girls have long, red fingernails and work mostly in the tall offices downtown. Most of the guys work outdoors — construction usually; there still is a lot of that, even now — or in the bodybuilding gyms, or the industrial parks along I-85. Both sexes are darkly and artificially tanned, even in the winter, and get drunk on shooters and look vainly in PJ's for love.

Around midnight on Friday and Saturday, before everyone clears out to go dancing at The Connection or Plum Crazy's, where the night's hopes become final choices, PJ's gets packed. The waitresses have to move sideways through the crowd with their trays held over their heads. Everybody shouts to be heard over one another and over the music — P. J. O'Mulligan's official contemporary jazz, piped in from Richmond — and if you close your eyes and listen carefully you can hear in the voices the one story they are trying not to tell: how everyone in Charlotte grew up in a white house in a row of white houses on the side of a hill in Lowell or Kannapolis or Spindale, and how they had to be quiet at home because their daddies worked third shift, how a black oil heater squatted like a gargoyle in the middle of their living room floor, and how the whole time they were growing up the one thing they always wanted to do was leave. I get lonesome sometimes, in the buzzing middle of the weekend, when I listen to the voices and think about the shortness of the distance all of us managed to travel as we tried to get away, and how when we got to Charlotte the only people we found waiting for us were the ones we had left. Our parents go to tractor pulls and watch *Hee Haw.* My father eats squirrel brains. We tell ourselves that we are different now, because we live in Charlotte, but know that we are only making do.

The last great professional wrestling card Frannie Belk put together — before she signed Ted Turner's big check and with a diamond-studded wave of her hand sent the wrestlers away from Charlotte for good — was ARMAGEDDON V — THE LAST EXPLOSION, which took place in the new coliseum three nights after the Hornets played and lost their first NBA game. ("Ohhhhhh," Big Bill Boscoe said in the promotional TV ad, his big voice quavering with emotion, "Ladies and Gentlemen and Wrestling Fans of All Ages: See an unprecedented galaxy of SWA wrestling stars collide and explode in the Charlotte Coliseum . . .") And for a while that night — even though we knew the wrestlers were moving to Atlanta — the world still seemed young and full of hope, and we were young in it, and life in Charlotte seemed close to the way we had always imagined it should be: Paolo the Peruvian jerked his bare foot out from under the big, black boot of Comrade Yerkov and then kicked the shit out of him in a flying frenzy of South American feet; Rockin' Robbie Frazier squirted a water pistol into Naoki Fujita's mouth before Fujita could ignite the mysterious Green Fire of the Orient, and then launched a B-52 from such a great height that even the most jaded wrestling fans gasped with wonder (and if that wasn't enough, he later ran from the locker room in his street clothes, his hair still wet from his shower, his shirttail out and flapping, and in a blond fury B-52ed not one but *both* of the Hidden Pagans, who had used a folding chair to gain an unfair advantage over the Thundercats, Bill and Steve). And we saw the Littlest Cowboy and Chief Yee-Hah O'Reilly, their wrists bound together with an eight-foot leather thong, battle nobly in an Apache Death Match, until neither man was able to stand and the referee called it a draw and cut them loose with a long and crooked dagger belonging to the Sheik of the East; Hank Wilson Senior the Country Star whacked Captain Boogie Woogie over the head with his beloved guitar Leigh Ann, and earned a thoroughly satisfying disqualification and a long and heartfelt standing O; one of the Harem of Three slipped the Sheik of the East a handful of Arabian sand, which he threw into the eyes of Bob the Sailor to save himself from the Sailor's Killer Clam Hold — from which no bad guy ever escaped, once it was locked — but the referee saw the Sheik do it (the rarest of wrestling miracles) and awarded the match to the Sailor; and in the prelude to the main event, like the thunder before a storm, the Brothers Clean — the Superstud, the Viking, and the Gentle Giant — outlasted the Three Evils — Genghis Gandhi, Ron Rowdy, and Tom Tequila — in a six-man Texas Chain-Link Massacre Match in which a ten-foot wire fence was lowered around the ring, and bald Boris Yerkov and Harry the Hairdresser patrolled outside, eyeing each other suspiciously, armed with bullwhips and folding chairs, to make sure that no one climbed out and no one climbed in.

Now, looking back, it seems prophetic somehow that Starla and I lined up on opposite sides during THE FINAL BATTLE FOR LOVE. ("Sex is the biggest deal people have," Starla says. "You think about what you really want from me, what really matters, the next time you ask for a piece.") In THE FINAL BATTLE, Starla wanted Bob Noxious, with his dark chemistry, to win Darling Donnis away from Lord Poetry once and for all. He had twice come close. I wanted Lord Poetry to strike a lasting blow for love. Starla said it would never happen, and she was right. Late in the night, after it is over, after Starla has pinned my shoulders flat against the bed and held them there, after we are able to talk, I say, "Starla, you have to admit that you were making love to me. I could tell." She runs to the bathroom, her legs stiff and close together, to get rid of part of me. "Cave men made up love," she calls out from behind the door. "After they invented laws they had to stop killing each other, so they told their women they loved them to keep them from screwing other men. That's what love is."

Bob Noxious was Charlotte's most feared and evil wrestler, and on the night of THE FINAL BATTLE, we knew that he did not want Darling Donnis because he loved her. Bob Noxious was scary: He had a cobalt blue, spiked mohawk, and if on his way to the ring a fan spat on him, he always spat back. He had a neck like a bull, and a fifty-six-inch chest, and he could twitch his pectoral muscles so fast that his nipples jerked up and down like pistons. Lord Poetry was almost as big as Bob Noxious, and scary in different ways. His curly red hair was longer than Starla's, and he wrestled in paisley tights — pink and magenta and lavender — specially made in England. He read a poem to Darling Donnis before and after every match while the crowd yelled for him to stop. (Charlotte did not know which it hated more: Bob Noxious with his huge and savage evil or the prancing Lord Poetry with his paisley tights and fat book of poems.) Darling Donnis was the picture of innocence (and danger, if you are a man) and hung on every word Lord Poetry said. She was blonde, and wore a low-cut, lacy white dress (but never a slip), and covered her mouth with her hands whenever Lord Poetry was in trouble, her moist green eyes wide with concern.

Darling Donnis's dilemma was this: She was in love with Lord Poetry, but she was mesmerized by Bob Noxious's animal power. The last two times Bob Noxious and Lord Poetry fought, before THE FINAL BATTLE, Bob Noxious had beaten Lord Poetry with a folding chair until Lord Poetry couldn't stand, and then he turned to Darling Donnis and put his hands on his hips and threw his shoulders back, revealing enough muscles to make several lesser men. Darling Donnis's legs visibly wobbled, and she steadied herself against the ring apron, but she did not look away. While the crowd screamed for Bob Noxious to Shake 'em! Shake 'em! Let 'em go! he began to twitch his pectorals up and down, first just one at a time, just once or twice — teasing Darling Donnis — then the other, then in rhythm, faster and faster. It was something you had to look at, even if you didn't want to, a force of nature, and at both matches Darling Donnis was transfixed. She couldn't look away from Bob Noxious's chest and would have gone to him (even though she held her hands over her mouth and shook her head no, the pull was too strong) had it not been for Rockin' Robbie Frazier. At both matches before THE FINAL BATTLE, Rockin' Robbie ran out of the locker room in his street clothes and tossed the prostrate Lord Poetry the book of poetry that Darling Donnis had carelessly dropped on the apron of the ring. Then he climbed through the ropes and held off the enraged and bellowing Bob Noxious long enough for Lord Poetry to crawl out of danger and read Darling Donnis one of her favorite sonnets, which calmed her. But the night of THE FINAL BATTLE, all of Charlotte knew that something had to give. We did not think that even Rockin' Robbie could save Darling Donnis from Bob Noxious three times. Bob's pull was too strong. This time Lord Poetry had to do it himself.

They cleared away the cage from the Texas Chain-Link Massacre, and the houselights went down slowly until only the ring was lit. The white canvas was so bright that it hurt your eyes to look at it. Blue spotlights blinked open in the high darkness beneath the roof of the coliseum, and quick circles of light skimmed across the surface of the crowd, showing in an instant a hundred, two hundred, expectant faces. The crowd could feel the big thing coming up on them, like animals before an earthquake. Rednecks in the high, cheap seats stomped their feet and hooted like owls. Starla twisted in her seat and stuck two fingers into her mouth and cut loose with a shrill whistle. "Ohhhhh, Ladies and Gentlemen and Wrestling Fans," Big Bill Boscoe said from everywhere in the darkness, like the very voice of God, "I hope you are ready to hold on to your seats" — and in their excitement 23,000 people screamed *Yeah!* — "Because the earth is going to shake and the ground is going to split open" — *YEAH!*, louder now — "and hellfire will shoot out of the primordial darkness in a holocaust of pure wrestling fury" — they punched at the air with their fists and roared, like beasts, the blackness they hid in their hearts, *YEAHHHHHH!* "Ohhhhhh," Big Bill

Boscoe said when they quieted down, his voice trailing off into a whisper filled with fear (he was afraid to unleash the thing that waited in the dark for the sound of his words, and they screamed in rage at his weakness, *YEAHHHHHHHH!*). "Ohhhhhh, Charlotte, ohhhhhhh, Wrestling Fans and Ladies and Gentlemen, I hope, I pray, that you have made ready" — *YEAHHHHHHH!* — "for . . . the FINAL . . . BATTLE . . . FOR . . . LOOOOOOOOOVE!"

At the end of regulation time (nothing really important ever happens in professional wrestling until the borrowed time after the final bell has rung) Bob Noxious and Lord Poetry stood in the center of the ring, their hands locked around each other's thick throat. Because chokeholds are illegal in SWA professional wrestling, the referee had ordered them to let go and, when they refused, began to count them out for a double disqualification. Bob Noxious and Lord Poetry let go only long enough to grab the referee, each by an arm, and throw him out of the ring, where he lay prostrate on the floor. Lord Poetry and Bob Noxious again locked on to each other's throat. There was no one there to stop them, and we felt our stomachs falling away into darkness, into the chaos. Veins bulged like ropes beneath the skin of their arms. Their faces were contorted with hatred, and turned from pink to red to scarlet. Starla jumped up and down beside me and shouted, "*KILL* Lord Poetry! *KILL* Lord Poetry!"

Darling Donnis ran around and around the ring, begging for someone, anyone, to make them stop. At the announcer's table, Big Bill Boscoe raised his hands in helplessness. Sure he wanted to help, but he was only Big Bill Boscoe, a voice. What could he do? Darling Donnis rushed away. She circled the ring twice more until she found Rockin' Robbie Frazier keeping his vigil in the shadows near the entrance to the locker room. She dragged him into the light near the ring. She pointed wildly at Lord Poetry and Bob Noxious. Both men had started to shake, as if cold. Bob Noxious's eyes rolled back in his head, but he didn't let go. Lord Poetry stumbled, but reached back with a leg and regained his balance. Darling Donnis shouted at Rockin' Robbie. She pointed again. She pulled her hair. She doubled her hands under her chin, pleading. "*CHOKE* him!" Starla screamed. "*CHOKE* him!" She looked sideways at me. "HURRY!" Darling Donnis got down on her knees in front of Rockin' Robbie and wrapped her arms around his waist. Rockin' Robbie stroked her hair but stared into the distance and shook his head no. Not this time. This was what it had come to. This was a fair fight between men and none of his business. He walked back into the darkness.

Darling Donnis was on her own now. She ran to the ring and stood at the apron and screamed for Bob Noxious and Lord Poetry to stop it. The sound of her words was lost in the roar that came from up out of our hearts, but we could feel them. She pounded on the canvas, but they didn't listen. They kept choking each other, their fingers a deathly white. Darling Donnis crawled beneath the bottom rope and into the ring. "NO!" Starla yelled, striking the air with her fists. "Let him DIE! Let him DIE!" Darling Donnis took a step toward the two men and reached out with her hands, but stopped, unsure of what to do. She wrapped her arms around herself and rocked back and forth. She grabbed her hair and started to scream. She screamed as if the earth really had opened up and hellfire had shot up all around her — and that it had been her fault. She screamed until her eyelids fluttered closed, and she dropped into a blonde and white heap on the mat, and lay there without moving.

When Darling Donnis stopped screaming, it was as if the spell that had held Bob Noxious and Lord Poetry at each other's throat was suddenly broken. They let go at the same time. Lord Poetry dropped heavily to his elbows and knees, facing away from Darling Donnis. Bob Noxious staggered backward into the corner, where he leaned against the turnbuckles. He held on to the top rope with one hand and with the other rubbed his throat. "Go GET her!" Starla screamed at Bob Noxious. "Go GET her!" For a long time nobody in the ring moved, and in the vast, enclosed darkness surrounding the ring, starting up high and then spreading throughout the building, 23,000 people began to stomp their feet. Tiny points of fire, hundreds of them, sparked in the darkness. But still Bob Noxious and Lord Poetry and Darling Donnis did not move. The crowd stomped louder and louder (BOOM! BOOM! BOOM! BOOM!) until finally Darling Donnis weakly raised her head and pushed her hair back from her eyes. We caught our breath and looked to see where she looked. It was at Bob Noxious. Bob Noxious glanced up, his dark power returning. He took his hand off of his throat and put it on the top rope and pushed himself up higher. Darling Donnis raised herself onto her hands and knees and peeked quickly at Lord Poetry, who still hadn't moved, and then looked back to Bob Noxious. "DO it, Darling Donnis!" Starla screamed. "Just DO it!" Bob Noxious pushed off against the ropes and took an unsteady step forward. He inhaled deeply and stood up straight. Darling Donnis's eyes never left him. Bob Noxious put his hands on his hips and with a monumental effort threw his great shoulders all the way back. *No,* we saw Darling Donnis whisper. *No.* High up in the seats beside me, Starla screamed, "*YES!*"

Bob Noxious's left nipple twitched once. Twitch. Then again. Then the right. The beginning of the end. Darling Donnis slid a hand almost imperceptibly toward him across the canvas. But then, just when it all seemed lost, Rockin' Robbie Frazier ran from out of the shadows to the edge of the ring. He carried a thick book in one hand and a cordless microphone in the other. He leaned under the bottom rope and began to shout at Lord Poetry, their faces almost touching. (*Lord Poetry! Lord Poetry!*) Lord Poetry finally looked up at Rockin' Robbie and then slowly turned to look at Bob Noxious, whose pectoral muscles had begun to twitch regularly, left-right, faster and faster, like heartbeats. Darling Donnis raised a knee from the canvas and began to crawl toward Bob Noxious. Rockin' Robbie reached in through the ropes and helped Lord Poetry to his knees. He gave the book and the microphone to Lord Poetry. Lord Poetry turned around, still kneeling, until he faced Darling Donnis. She didn't even look at him. Five feet to Lord Poetry's right, Bob Noxious's huge chest was alive, pumping, a train picking up speed. Lord Poetry opened the book and turned to a page and shook his head. No, that one's not right. He turned farther back into the book and shook his head again. What is the one thing you can say to save the world you live in? How do you find the words? Darling Donnis licked her red lips. Rockin' Robbie began flashing his fingers in numbers at Lord Poetry. Ten-eight. Ten-eight. Lord Poetry looked over his shoulder at Rockin' Robbie, and his eyebrows moved up in a question: Eighteen? "Yes," screamed Rockin' Robbie. "Eighteen." "Ladies and Gentlemen," Big Bill Boscoe's huge voice suddenly said, filled now with hope,

"I think it's going to be Shakespeare's Sonnet Number Eighteen!" and a great shout of *NOOOOO!* rose up in the darkness like a wind.

Lord Poetry flipped through the book, and studied a page, and reached out and touched it, as if it were in Braille. He looked quickly at Darling Donnis, flat on her belly now, slithering toward Bob Noxious. Lord Poetry said into the microphone, "Shall I compare thee to a summer's day?" Starla kicked the seat in front of her and screamed, "NO! Don't do it! Don't do it! He's after your soul! He's after your soul!" Lord Poetry glanced up again and said, "Thou art more lovely and more temperate," and then faster, more urgently, "Rough winds do shake the darling buds of May," but Darling Donnis crawled on, underneath the force of his words, to within a foot of Bob Noxious. Bob Noxious's eyes were closed in concentration and pain, but still his pectorals pumped faster. Lord Poetry opened his mouth to speak again, but then buried his face in the book and slumped to the mat. Rockin' Robbie pulled on the ropes like the bars of a cage and yelled in rage, his face pointed upward, but he did not climb into the ring. He could not stop what was happening. *Please,* we saw Darling Donnis say to Bob Noxious. *Please.* The panicked voice of Big Bill Boscoe boomed out like a thunder: "Darling Donnis! Darling Donnis! And summer's lease hath all too short a date: sometime too hot the eye of heaven shines, and often is his gold complexion dimm'd!" But it was too late: Bob Noxious reached down and lifted Darling Donnis up by the shoulders. She looked him straight in the eye and reached out with both hands and touched his broad, electric chest. Her eyes rolled back in her head. Starla dropped heavily down into her seat and breathed deeply, twice. She looked up at me and smiled. "There," she said, as if it was late in the night, as if it was over. "There."

JANET PEERY

What the Thunder Said

FROM BLACK WARRIOR REVIEW

IT WAS WINTER when I first saw Call Lucas, though I'd seen him, sure, before. Ours was more a sudden notice, like a secret thought grown big, then bigger, till you blurt it out and nearly jump inside your skin to hear it said. He was milking Boss, his flat man-rump on a T-bar stool, knees higher, spraddle-legged, shouldered into Boss's flank, arm hoist round her leg to hobble her, neck craned sideways, looking up at nothing, at the pigeons in the rafters, then at me; at me, at Mackie Spoon, eighteen, come in to gather eggs. His wife had a hen that roosted in the barn, and I'd gone out to find the nest.

What we did was wrong, though there can be a way of turning something, seeing how what happens after can add up to make it right. It was milking time, five-thirty, warm inside from cattle, from the little things that live in hay to make it give its own green breathing heat. The sun was tabby-orange through the slats, dust and motes around me like I'd walked into a spangled halo, bars of orange slid across me smooth and light as water. I smelled the warm grass smell of hay not cured and dust and cattle, linseed oil and harness leather, swallows' nests of mud and straw and feathers, mice, the foam of milk from Call's pail when he set it down and milk lapped into the dirt as he came toward me, unwashed work when he got closer, myself in my wool coat with wet snow melting on the shoulders where it fell upon me from the eaves, myself under my dress; and we lay down in all of it, in a way that felt like all the world was gathered into one sweet skin, and though you know it's wrong, down deep, in bone and blood and muscle, you want the one thing your head tells you you're not supposed to want, and in that wanting, in that knowing it's wrong, there is a stillness at the center, calm and full and sly, that comes from knowing you will do it anyway, and you tell your head to cease its thinking, to let the bone and blood and muscle have their way, glad, for in that time when everything's afight within you, you are whole as you will ever be, and how I knew the first went gladly out of Eden.

Call was quiet after, gave out one shiver, gathered up his pail and eased back through the stanchion bars to turn Boss out, looked back at me as though he knew me to the center yet had never seen me in his life before, and in his eyes there was a blue-eyed look of staring too long toward the sun, as though they hurt him.

I lived on the place in a little side house. I'd come up in answer to an ad to help Missus in the house. My people lived across the Oklahoma line, but I had had enough of home and of the church I had grown up in. I knew there could be something more. I knew a man could love a woman better than he loved his belt, his Bible, and the way his mouth fit round the word *abomination.* I knew that copperheads and bullsnakes were a proof of nothing, that tongues of flame would not consume me if I kissed a boy whose mouth had tasted sweet and clean as broom straw. I had my own idea of things, and so I left.

Call's was not a rich farm, mostly wheat, alfalfa, flax. He'd been hurt by the dust storms, but not as much as some. The farm was bottomland, sandy loam along the Ninnescah, and willow brakes and cottonwoods and sandplum trees had kept the damage down. Still, you could see it in the scoured look of things.

Missus was a tiny woman, bones frail as a squab's, her hair fine blond, like chick fluff, and she wore dresses in a baby shade of blue. She was sickly, and the Hannah Circle doted on her, bringing covered dishes, cakes and pies to tempt her. They were in the kitchen with her when I got back with the eggs, twelve whites, six brown, two banty.

"Put them on the drainboard, Mackie," Missus told me. "You can wash them later."

"Try some of this peach pie, Lila," one of the ladies offered her.

"Oh, thank you, no," she said. "Maybe after a while." I heard her sigh. "Right now I'm not too pert."

The Hannahs clucked around her while I stood at the sink and scalded dishes I'd let sit after supper. I felt my neck go as pink as the spots of rouge on Missus's cheeks. I'd been there four weeks then.

One of the ladies asked after her health. "Poorly," Missus said, "and tired. But I'll bear up."

"Call's so good to hire you help," another said.

"Yes," said Missus. "There's so much work, and we weren't blessed with children."

They started in on female trouble, and I tried to close my ears. I dried the dishes in a hurry, wanting to get out because I knew Call would be bringing in the house milk and I didn't want the warm new smell of it to rise into that kitchen where I stood, my head gone giddy as it ever went at any spirit hoodoo, everybody watching.

Things just went along. I worked in the house and around the yard and with the chickens. I took portions of what I cooked, and ate alone at my own place, so the three of us sitting together at the table didn't happen. It was all the bumping into each other. I'd be at the sink and he'd bring in the milk to skim and there we'd be, working, breathing, so close we could smell the things we both remembered, but neither of us would speak. Neither of us acted like the other was alive, but in that ignoring there was more than if we'd tried to talk.

I made up my own world, the one I knew could be, pretending we were married, that I was the wife and he the husband, that I ran the house and saw to things in such a way that didn't need reminding. When we met each other in the barn, I stopped all my pretending and just let be, then afterward went back to the silent way it was. I came to feel a power over Missus, that I was strong and she was weak and this was only right. I took to slamming things — her teacup at her place, a pair of scissors she had asked for — pretending accident, my slamming, and she would take it with a narrowing of eyes, but say just, "Lightly, Mackie, lightly."

This went on about a year, the three of us moving around, bumping into each other, not talking much, but busy and working, like a boxhive full of bees, until the idea of what was going on became an almost buzzing in my ears.

Then two things happened. Call took Missus to the doctor in Belle Plaine and when they came back she went to bed and didn't get up anymore. To care for her, I moved into the spare room. We put a bell beside her bed so she could call for me. She took this fine, but with her small mouth tightened, and it seemed her belly swelled as though her tumor fed itself on what it knew of me. But until the night in March when Boss had trouble calving and Call yelled out for me to come, I think she just suspected.

Boss bawled and bellowed like the earth was heaving, and we worked by lantern light to turn her calf, me kneading at her hardened belly, Call naked to the waist, his arm full up inside her, wrenching till I felt a give and shifting, slid his arm out red and warm and steaming, and we saw the baby crown. Then, above our breathing, we heard another sound, Missus's bell, but close outside, and when we looked around we saw her in her pale blue nightgown, coming through the doorway toward us in the cold, ringing, calling in a whisper. She cried that she'd forgotten something, cried because she couldn't think of what it was, and then we all three knew she knew, but none of us would say it, and so things went along with Call and me inside the house like man and wife, with Missus as our child.

"I got some broth down her," I'd tell him. "She fussed, but took it."

"She never did eat much," he'd say, and this was how we talked about her, nothing deeper, and we never talked about ourselves and what we were doing or the names we'd have to bear, but my heart sang at the way things worked out, because the second thing that happened was that I was pregnant.

It had happened one winter night the second year when I'd gone to bathe. I'd heated water at the house and carried a ewer out to my place. I lit the lamp and stood at the table washing. I heard him outside, and in my young pride and what I'd learned about desire, I knew the sight of me could stir him, so I didn't move to cover myself, only turned a bit because we still had never seen each other without clothes. When he came in, I helped him take off his things and washed him until the water went cool.

At first I just ignored the signs that even as Missus lay there I was incubating something of my own. My feet grew sore and swollen waiting on her, and I lost my breakfast soon as I could get it down, but I tried to be kind, and stopped the slamming ways. I didn't tell Call about what I was carrying, but planned to wait for it to grow big enough for him to notice and when she died do the right thing and marry me and just go on. For in that quiet grief-struck house I was happy, and the days could not be long enough. I saw the rightness of the world in everything. When the brood sow farrowed twenty piglets, I knew that number meant my age. If I gathered thirty-seven eggs, it stood for Call's. In April, lightning hit the walnut tree and forked it to the roots, and I knew this meant she would go within a month.

The Hannahs were all over us then, bringing things. More than one looked askance at me, but I kept my eyes down so they couldn't say a word against me for want of charity. "That Mackie Spoon's not missing any meals," one said, but they didn't say more because Call was known to be an upright man.

One asked me, "Where will you go when Lila passes?"

"Don't know," I said. But I knew.

"You might find a place over at the Costin farm," another said. "Bitty Costin's half worn out with all those children."

Another suggested the cafe out on the highway.

"I'll worry about it when the time comes," I said.

"Call looks bad," one said, but I said nothing.

"Feed him, Mackie," they told me. "That's all you can do."

One night in early May I sat beside her bed, sponging her with lemon water. She was wracked, her body meager as an empty grain sack, her skin the color of wet ash, gray-blue and drowned. She asked if I would put the pillow on her face, her nose and mouth, if I would hold it there. "Please, Mackie."

It was the only thing she wanted, the last thing left in her to want. For her, I wanted to, but for everything I'd wanted that I'd taken from her, I couldn't. "I can't," I said.

"A kindness. Please."

I cried into my hands, "I can't," and she cried with me, petting me and saying, "Child, I know."

Call went on about his work all through this time, but I could hear him pounding on the anvil in the toolshed late at night, I saw the blisters on his palms, the axe marks gouged like splintered wounds out on the granary floor. He stayed out of her room all that month, and though I understood it, though I didn't love him any less, I hated him a little.

I was in the kitchen after the service, after all the mourners had gone, wrapping food in dishtowels and covering bowls with dinner plates when I heard a sound coming through the open windows from the barn, like the wind used to sound before the dust began to blow. I ran outside with my apron still around my middle, across the yard and toward the sound. I looked inside the barn. He was on his knees beside the hay, and I knew he'd maybe started out to pray but ended up just howling. I saw her pale blue nightgown and I saw that he was stuffing it with hay then tearing at it, stuffing it again and moaning and I watched and listened till I couldn't stand it any longer and I turned and ran with my hands over my ears and the hard weight of the baby like a stone inside me. I ran inside the house and slammed the door and cried, for me, for her, for him, for anyone who ever wanted something that was gone.

In the morning when I got up he was asleep on the floor beside her bed. I went around the kitchen quiet, fixing his breakfast. I went outside. The day was fine and beautiful. Swallows flew in and out of the barn with wisps of straw to build new nests. Off in the timber I heard the bawling of a calf. Cottonwoods were sending off their seedling puffs to gather on the clothesline wires like batting. I went to turn the chickens out, feeling wifely and washed clean as the bedding I had hung upon the line. In the air I felt a message for me that Lila was happier, and I began to feel happy for myself. I knew I could make Call happy, too, and I began to sing the Do Lord song — *oh, do remember me* — and I began to feel remembered in all the turning world, and when I came to the part about the home in gloryland which outshines the sun, the sun itself rose over the barn and glinted off the roof until it looked as red as flame. I took this as a sign that the world had turned itself to right again, all wrongs forgiven, and when the rooster crowed it was the trumpet blowing in the Year of Jubilee.

When I went back to the house, the door was locked. I knew better than to try the front because it was sealed shut always, since the dust storms. My suitcase was on the step. On top of it was a square white envelope, no writing on it or inside it, not my name, just five smooth twenty-dollar bills.

I've worked at every cafe from Blackwell to the Waco Wego at least once, some more. I didn't marry. I didn't tell a soul what really happened. I told my son his father was a boy I'd loved who'd moved away before he knew, and only I see Call's straight chin in my son's son. I waited thirty years for Call to speak to me, to say he knew me. I stopped the world with waiting, not to start again until he walked through the door of whatever place I worked and told me, "Mackie Spoon, I'm sorry," for I believed that day would come.

I waited for it, and in the turning of a hundred seasons I saw only Call come begging. Winters moved through springs and summers, and I waited. Sandplums fell, their ripeness gone to bruise, so he could see the shame in waste. Leaves blew from their bare and reaching branches just to show him that the wrong he'd done me was a grievous one. Frost was to remind him of a harsher cold; ice, the sharp, cracked color of his heart. But I, I would forgive him. All he had to do was ask. This moment I could see in rain, and we would then be whole again and new, and he would melt with gladness at the way I had forgiven him.

I saw him many times, caught glimpses of his truck, of him, but only once in thirty years did he look back at me, last summer when Costin's old place caught heat and burned and everybody gathered there. The barn was still burning, but the house had gone. People shone flashlights over the ash pile, but there was nothing left to see but charred wood and one lone teapot on a blackened stove. Across the ashes that had been the house, against the blaze that was the barn, stood Call. I thought I'd gone past fleshly things, but deep inside me something moved at seeing his remembered mouth. He looked at me across the burned-out house, full face, the fire behind him hot and whipping in the wind, the flames so bright they made his eyes a shadow I could not see into, and I knew the day had come.

There is a way a summer storm will come up from the west, from mountains I have never seen but know are there, a sudden way that, seeing the dark cloud tower, you can almost think the walls of dust have come again until you feel the wind is sharp and clean and you catch the smell of coming-closer rain.

In the storm head rolling high and heavy over us, rising like a warning, there was something of a waiting, of a watching of the goings-on on earth, something in the clouds of wrong that will not be forgotten, and I waited for the lightning to appear, for the flash of reckoning that would scorch Call for what he'd done.

But on the last night I was to see him, I saw instead the message of the fool I was on earth to try to fit the signs of heaven toward the purpose of my will, and when the lightning flashed upon his eyes I saw, instead, my own, by awful trick of light, the hard and high and mighty vision of my own.

I felt my bones grow laden at the sight, with years, and with the sudden want of mercy and the very ground to hold me so I wouldn't fall, and I called out to him, "I'm sorry."

What was in him I can never know, but what was in him made him turn away.

I didn't think. I ran into the rubble and the ashes and I grabbed the teapot. The handle seared my skin but I held on and ran toward him as he walked away. The sound my throat made was a noise like none I'd ever heard — a terrible dark language or another tongue — that wouldn't cease until I threw the teapot at him, hard. It struck him in the back, a clank, a rattle hollow as a far-off clap of thunder. He stopped, stood still, began to turn, then caught himself and kept on walking into rain that came in short, quick gusts and then began to fall like rain, like only rain.

ANTONYA NELSON

Naked Ladies

FROM THE NEW YORKER

LAURA'S FAMILY was going to Easter brunch at the Houses'. They were invited every year by Mr. House, but this was the first time Laura's mother could accept. Mr. House called the party his Easter Frolic, and Laura's father never wanted to go. "Frolic at the House house?" he always said. "We'll pass." The family was going this year because he was away showing his paintings at spring arts fairs. He had got lucky, securing more booth spaces than ever before. Already he'd been gone for a month, traveling in his old Land Cruiser, among his canvases, phoning home every few nights to report on his sales. Of the eight checks he'd sent to them, only one had proved rubber. Laura's mother mailed a letter to the woman who'd written it, chastising her for behaving badly. The letter came back from Las Vegas marked "NO LONGER AT THIS ADDRESS," and Laura intercepted it and burned it in the back yard before her mother got home.

Laura's mother raised other people's children — that was her job. She departed each weekday morning in order to arrive at the Houses' before the three school-age children left, which meant that her own family had to fend for itself. The youngest House child, four-year-old Mikey, had Down's syndrome and was her main responsibility. Mrs. House, who blamed herself for his condition, could not be counted upon; she sometimes spent the whole day lying in bed circling catalogue merchandise and punching 800 numbers.

There were four House children, two boys and two girls, just like Laura's family. Except not like them at all. The House children were neatly spaced, like elections, every two years — ten, eight, six, four — while Laura's family was helter-skelter, seventeen, thirteen, eight, and seven, testimony to their parents' ambivalent feelings about kids. In fact, the two youngest — her brothers — were the same age from October until December, which made Laura acutely embarrassed about the obvious recklessness of her parents' lovemaking. When she was younger, when her mother first began working for the Houses, Laura longed for the same tidy procession of children, longed to recite the healthy even numbers of their ages. If she could have, she would have arranged for a new sibling to arrive every two years, until there were eight or ten of them, because she loved quantity as well as orderliness. It proved stability, something aggressively substantial.

The Houses did not call Laura's mother Mrs. Laughlin but Nana, a name Laura found irritatingly intimate. Laura's father said that it made her sound like the family sheepdog. More than he hated the name, he hated the almost-uniform she wore, a large green smock with four square pockets. "Cover those breasts, Broom Hilda," he would say when she brought it home to launder. "Hide that butt."

"This gruesome thing pays the rent," she would say to him, wadding it into a ball and throwing it among the dirty clothes. Her husband would turn out his lower lip like a child. Though his paintings sold only sporadically, when they did sell the family was rich for a week or two. This seemed, to him, to make up for the other, anxious times.

Always as part of Laura's consciousness was the worry that her parents would divorce. They weren't volatile and didn't fight — not the way married people fought in books or movies — but instead picked at one another in a sly, monkeylike manner, each baiting the other until one of them might be forced to slam a door or yell at the dog. Laura both looked forward to and dreaded what her parents called *scenes*. They didn't like to make them, but after one had played itself out Laura felt a kind of humming glee, as if she had seen a vision of the future, a moment of her womanly life briefly revealed to her. From her parents Laura had learned to attach weight to the most subtle vocal inflection, the most fleeting glance. She often lay awake at night replaying the day, hearing again and again words that might have been meant, or taken, unkindly, biting her nails until she could go no farther down.

To the Easter Frolic the five Laughlins wore their good clothes. Their mother debated about a hat — hats, at Easter, seemed necessary to her — and decided upon a turquoise beret, which sat tilted like a dinner plate on her head. She wore a simple silk dress, a lighter shade of turquoise, belted at her hips with a Guatemalan scarf that Mrs. House had given her after their trip over Christmas.

"You look pretty," said Laura's younger sister, Pammy, who was thirteen. "The Houses probably never saw you in anything but your ugly green shirt. Won't they be surprised?"

"Won't they?" Laura agreed, proud that her forty-year-old mother still had a figure to show off.

Admiring herself in the mirror, lifting her chin to draw her throat taut, their mother said, "And at the front door, no less."

They were the first to arrive. The day was a perfect midwestern spring day, sunny and still. The Houses' neighborhood was incorporated, a city unto itself in the middle of Wichita. Traffic had to slow to parade speed in order to pass through; Eastborough had its own police department, whose officers drove understated, cream-colored sedans instead of the typical black-and-white ones, and whose only responsibility was to issue speeding tickets. Laura's father complained because residents here did not have to pay Wichita city taxes; Laura's friends, crawling through at twenty miles per hour, bemoaned the fact that of course the best mall would be built on the other side of Eastborough. Laura tried to pinpoint what, exactly, distinguished it from her neighborhood, Riverside, because the houses there were older and more stately. The difference seemed to have to do with the small details — the clusters of pansies and antique park benches along the street, the absence of loud city buses and delivery trucks, the long path of black mushroom lights that led to the House door. Nothing stirred this Sunday morning but the songbirds.

The Laughlins stood on the flagstone front porch while Laura's mother rang the bell. Inside the House home a long, elegant bonging sounded — the Big Ben tune, their mother told them — and then Mr. House opened the door wearing a tuxedo jacket over a sweatsuit. Laura understood that this was his outfit.

His running shoes were brand-new, the kind you could pump air into.

"Nana!" he exclaimed. "Well, well, Nana, aren't you a piece of work!" He was a large-featured, sinister-looking man. His nose was long and wide, his dark hair oiled back from a vampirish widow's peak. His face had the sleek eagerness of a wet dog's. "For Godsakes, come in!" he roared.

Their mother had big breasts, which neither Laura nor her sister had inherited. Mr. House stared at them now, revealed as they were beneath the thin silk. Under his gaze, she lifted her hand to her throat, covering her chest with her forearm. Her face was flushed, and her silver-blond hair shone underneath her rakish hat. She led her children through the foyer of her employer's house.

Mr. House offered them drinks. Laura's mother allowed the three youngest children Cokes and accepted a cocktail of champagne and orange juice for herself, turning her wrist to check her delicate dress watch for the time. "So early," she laughed. When Mr. House tried to give Laura the same kind of drink, her mother shook her head, so that Laura was left with nothing, because she was too embarrassed to take a Coke in consolation.

They were gathered awkwardly in what appeared to be a modern ballroom, done in uncompromising black and white and red. An ebony grand piano gleamed in the corner like an advertisement for furniture polish. Beside it stood a brilliant white statue, a life-size naked woman whose head was coyly ducked. A marble drape fell lazily from her fingertips to pool at her ankles. The expanse of bright red tiled floor was broken only by white fur throw rugs, which floated on it like clouds. Mr. House seemed to recall that he, too, had a family, and turned his head to shout out their names.

Pammy nudged Laura, pointing above their heads to the walls. They were lined with ink drawings, also of naked women, but for one astonishing exception: a painting of their father's, a piece from his "Over the Shoulder" series. Though there could be no mistake, Laura looked for his signature in the corner just to be sure. There it was, "Luke Laughlin," in his typically impatient penmanship. The painting stood out among the women like a beggar. She wondered how it had got here. It was of a winter field, silos and shredded haystacks, wind through bare trees, all of it seen over the large foreground shoulder of a scruffy jacket. For this series her father had been using dental tools to scrape paint onto the canvas. He'd come up with a polished-steel tone by mixing molten aluminum foil with his oils. It gave the effect of frozen metal, a surface your warm finger might stick to. Laura's arms broke out in goose bumps. Around her father's painting and its sober subject, the naked women seemed to preen, silly and moneyed. To them, his painting took itself too seriously, like a street character preaching doom on a sunny day. Loosen up, the naked figures implored, their curves and arches like a languorous cat in the sun. Laura's stomach turned with tension, and she began marking time until it would be permissible for her to suggest they go home.

The House children trooped in wearing jeans and T-shirts, high-tops and spandex. Mrs. House wore peacock colors — a fashion trick Laura recognized from the discarded French magazines her mother brought home from here. The plumage was supposed to distract from her bulk, but still she looked as if she were filled with sand. Like Mr. House, she entered in high spirits, grinning in surprise at Mrs. Laughlin, eyeing the four children in such a way that the two boys stepped behind their older sisters. Laura felt ridiculous in her dress and hose. Her brothers wore neckties and dark suits from a grandfather's funeral last fall; of course their wrists stuck out, their pants were too short, their shoes were unbearably squeaky. Only Mikey House, unkempt as the retarded often seem, kept Laura from burning up in shame. He had loped over to her mother and thrown his arms around her knees. Mrs. Laughlin ran her fingers through his stiff hair and Laura saw she loved him at least as much as she did her own children. In what was obviously a ritual, he reached for her wedding band, wrestled it from her finger and slid it on his own thumb.

"He misses his Nana — don't you, Mikey?" said Mrs. House, unjealous. "And here she is, come to see you on a Sunday. What do you think?"

Mikey snuggled into Mrs. Laughlin's dress once more, this time leaving a large wet spot at her crotch. No one else seemed to notice, though Laura saw her mother's lips crimp as she brushed her palm over her lap. This, Laura realized, was the reason for the smock. Gently, Mrs. Laughlin directed Mikey's mouth away from her. Now that he had attached himself to her, she seemed more at home, and she asked the other House boy, Frank, Jr., to show her family around.

"Kitchen," he said as he led Laura and the others rapidly through the house. "Dining room." "Pantry." The doorbell began bonging again, and shrill greetings could be heard, women's voices rising in exclamation, then falling into confidences, Mr. House booming out, "Well, come on in, you old son of a such-and-such!" The tour terminated at the back of the house, in a plushly carpeted bedroom that had no windows. They had gone too quickly for Laura's taste, ten-year-old Frank gliding through each room in a bored, mature manner, reciting square footage, flipping on lights for a moment, then extinguishing them. He'd gestured toward paintings and statues, mentioning the names of artists, until he realized his guests had never heard of them and were not impressed. This bedroom with no natural light was his, and it was with true enthusiasm that he now showed Laura's brothers his *Playboys,* stacked beside his small television.

"I have my own subscription," he said, pointing out his name on the mailing label. "Dad got it for me."

"He did?" the boys asked in unison.

Frank nodded. "He was tired of me stealing his."

Laura's brothers settled happily on the rug, each with a magazine. Pammy, who often didn't know if she ought to stay with her brothers or go with her sister, finally gave in to curiosity and shyly hefted December's issue, folding herself into a cross-legged position on the floor.

Left alone, Laura returned by the route Frank had just taken, moving slowly this time through the rooms. The house was full of things, each wall hidden by furniture or art and by beautiful and unbeautiful clutter like department-store displays, pillows and decorative knickknacks, large vases sporting wheat stalks, needlepoint footrests, porcelain dolls, exotic foreign masks and figurines. Laura wondered if her mother was tempted, as she was, to pretend she lived in this modern palace. It was cavelike, and there were many rooms that seemed without function, merely pretty; rooms one retreated to for contemplation. They appealed to Laura for that reason — that, and their cleanliness. Each had a peaceful view of the vast lawn — "the grounds," she imagined it was called — where guests now clustered like floral arrangements.

In one of the rooms rested an immaculate easel, and Laura pictured Mrs. House sitting here, looking out over her estate, using a pristine set of watercolors to render a sunset. The stool before the easel was padded and spun smoothly around; in the corner stretched an old-fashioned chaise longue, rosewood and velvet. Laura could not help comparing this to her father's studio, which was the back porch, and which stank of mineral spirits, oil paints, and cat litter. His easels, all of them, were chaotic with splattered color and were mended with duct tape. Plastic weatherproofing covered the windows, obscuring the outdoors. From the ceiling hung bare two-hundred-watt bulbs; beside his feet he kept an electric space heater turned on — a fire hazard, her mother always claimed. When her father was home, Laura often sat in his studio with him, listening to him talk about his unsavory and impoverished Oklahoman family, his dismal yet serendipitous life's journey. She was the only one of his children he allowed to stay while he painted; the others always wanted him to paint a particular thing, or, if not that, then to explain what he *was* painting, and then felt free to criticize. But Laura was too nervous to do anything more than simply watch him. She brought him his Earl Grey tea with a squirt of honey in it, and sat on a small metal stepladder until her back ached. With the heater on, the porch provided a cozy and heady atmosphere. She'd cried when the gallery in Chicago that showed him had gone under, leaving him and his work to the mercy of arts-and-crafts fairs.

Out of Mrs. House's painting room led two closed doors. The first Laura tried opened into a bathroom.

"Hey!" shouted Mrs. House, who sat inside with her jumpsuit around her knees. Laura slammed the door and stood squinting, willing the thing to unhappen. From the lawn she heard a group of men laugh together, as if at a punch line. A beach ball thwapped the window, then rolled away. Mrs. House's bare flesh, in the glimpse Laura had, was astonishing, plentiful, melting over her like vanilla ice cream. The second door — she opened it tentatively — revealed the kitchen, where the caterers were heating food. They looked at Laura with disdain, as if she must live in this house or one like it.

Laura moved briskly through the ballroom, through vaporous clouds of different strong perfumes. A glass fell from a woman's slim fingers and popped neatly into shards. "My word," the woman said to Laura, and then walked off, leaving the sparkling mess. Laura found her mother outside, away from the party, and stood in her shadow, safe haven. She and Mr. House were beneath a pink magnolia tree, peering up. Laura had the strange impression that they had been touching, though at the moment they weren't. Little Mikey sat on the ground at Mrs. Laughlin's feet, playing with a basket of toys. He had tiny Guatemalan "trouble dolls" — the Houses had brought back sets for Laura and Pammy, too — a Lego doorway, a small plastic reindeer whose legs had been gnawed off, the connector from a Hot Wheels track, a white barrette, and two metal keys, along with Mrs. Laughlin's wedding ring. He had created a game for himself, walking the keys through the doorway, slipping the connector into his mouth to make a tongue, babbling around it to the trouble dolls.

"See him?" Mr. House was saying as he pointed to the tree's branches. "Get out of there, you sneaky shit!" Laura looked up. A squirrel stared placidly down at the humans below, his head protruding from a small wooden house. The fur at his neck ruffled like a mane; the hole was not large enough to accommodate him, and Laura wondered aloud if he was stuck. "He chewed his way in," Mr. House said, swinging his arm as if opening a door. "Right into a wren house. Impertinent little shit." He went on smiling.

To Laura, Mrs. Laughlin said, "Mr. House loves birds. He builds them houses in his spare time." To him, she said, "You'll have to cultivate a taste for squirrels." She took a last sip from her glass, spinning the ice as she finished off the drink.

Mr. House went, "Ah ha ha ha," his face distorted with cracks and crevices. He seemed to laugh frequently, whether a thing was funny or not. Laura did not like him, but for some reason her mother did. At home she poked fun at him, imitating his monstrous guffaw, his incessant cursing. But here she smiled serenely at him as he sighted along his pointed finger, which he aimed at the squirrel like a gun. Mikey looked up when he heard his father laugh and now followed the motion attentively, as if real bullets might emerge from the big hand.

Mr. House said, "This the one who wants to be a model?"

"That's Pammy," her mother told him. "Pammy's been prancing around in her underwear since she was two or three. No," she said. She paused, and rolled her hip toward Laura, then recited the familiar line, "This one is the thinker."

Mr. House instantly fell into a pose, bent at the waist, resting his elbow on his raised knee, fist under his chin. He grimaced as if in pain. His tux tail touched the pale spring grass. "Get it?" he asked. "Row Dan? 'The Thinker'?"

Her mother laughed again. Laura couldn't tell if it was with him or at him. Mrs. Laughlin was sly, in her own way — unpredictable and sometimes unkind. At home she had said, "He's no Einstein but at least he's jolly. At least he knows how to have fun."

" 'Jolly,' " Laura's father had repeated, tasting the word.

"Of course you two know Rodin," Mr. House said, rising and unself-consciously reaching inside his sweatpants to make an adjustment. "What with an artist in the house." This time it was *his* tone she couldn't read. "Maybe Laura will be an artist herself. You paint, Laura?"

She shook her head.

"Draw?" he persisted. "Play an instrument? Compose song lyrics?"

"She debates," Mrs. Laughlin told him. "She has trophies — don't you, sweetheart?"

He made a sour face. "Careful, you might end up a lawyer, like yours truly." He emptied his glass of ice by throwing it out over the lawn. "But probably in public defense, am I right?"

Laura shrugged. Mrs. Laughlin squatted to put Mikey's toys back in their basket, her thighs pressed together in the tight silk dress, the fabric between them tense. Mikey snuffled disconsolately until Mrs. Laughlin gave him a kiss on the nose. Mr. House turned his fat, gleaming face to Laura again and winked. "Quit this debating baloney," he advised as they approached the house and the other guests. "You're pretty — nothing wrong with that — so be pretty! Wear nice clothes, be a model. You could make a wonderful model — you just have to smile."

It was a tradition of the Easter Frolic to have an egg hunt, Mr. House told them in the ballroom. He had been playing requests at the piano, his long, wide fingers gliding over the keys while people hummed along. The sun shone without remorse through large, clean windows, reflecting blindingly off the red floor, off the crystal glasses and ice cubes. Every song had an identical choppy rhythm meant to sound jazzy and light, like one-liners. Beside Laura a woman snapped her fingers a little too slowly. A small man with a strange lump on his forehead danced with whoever would consent. He liked to spin his partners with his fingertips so their dresses flared. Mr. House tinkled a few high keys — like a bird trill — and then abruptly stopped playing.

"The hunt!" he announced. Weakly, the woman next to Laura snapped once more. Mr. House patted her rump when he stood up, as if in consolation.

"He's crude," Laura told her sister as they wandered around the swimming pool, looking halfheartedly for eggs. The first they'd found was plastic and contained a cheap necklace and pendant: turned one way, Betty Boop smiled under her long lashes; turned the other way, her mouth became an "O" and her dotted dress disappeared. Pammy put the necklace on. They found hard-boiled eggs with the beginnings of riddles on them ("How many Catholics does it take to change a light bulb?") or with the answers ("Because it was a *hung jury*"), and they found chocolates in the shape of naked women — buxom, foil-wrapped little candies nestled in the tender crocuses.

"He sure likes naked ladies," Pammy observed. She, like Laura's brothers, was enjoying the morning. To them it did not spell disaster but adventure — something they would tell all their friends about.

"I think he's having an affair with Mom," Laura told Pammy by the pool. She said it in order to feel her heart race, not entirely concerned with whether she believed it.

"Bullshit," Pammy said. After she'd thought for a moment, she added, "Dad is a lot better-looking, and younger and skinnier and everything. Mr. House is kind of" — she searched for the right word — "gross."

"Like that matters," Laura told her. The prospect of her mother's affair would give Laura a headache — it was her nature to keep peace — but a small, evolving, renegade emotion made her want something extraordinary to happen. She and Pammy sat by the pool and took their shoes and stockings off, dangling their feet in the icy water. On the other side of the lawn, guests crawled along the shrubbery, still seeking eggs, absurd in their good clothes. Laura's brothers and Frank held grocery sacks for easy collection. Her mother helped Mikey while Mr. House stood on the porch yelling, "You're getting hot, very hot, even hotter!" and laughing loudly.

"I bet anything she tells us not to tell Dad we were here," Pammy said suddenly, as if the whole party had come clear to her.

"No," Laura said, "she'll let us tell him. This is her way of getting back at him for being gone so much. While he's away we're all out here with Mr. House, like he's our other dad, the pervert one." But his compliment — telling her she could be a model — kept lightening Laura's opinion of him. Unlike most people, he seemed to have faith in something besides her intelligence, and she was not above feeling flattered.

"Isn't this place funny?" Pammy said. "So funny and weird. I never thought there could be a place like this. And Mom comes here every day — that's the weirdest part of all." She pulled her pale legs from the water and brushed off the drops that clung to them. "Do you think Dad knows one of his paintings is here?"

"No. If he knew, he'd come steal it off the wall." Laura was positive he had not given it to the Houses. Perhaps her mother had made a gift of it, but that was unlikely. For all their curious bickering, she would not have betrayed him this way, through his work. So Laura deduced that Mr. House had bought the painting, without her father knowing, possibly as a way of pleasing her mother, though Laura understood that it would not please her, and she understood that Mr. House knew it, too.

"It looks so funny with those other pictures," Pammy went on. "So depressing and . . . brown."

"It's not depressing," Laura said. "It's just more realistic."

"Naked ladies are real," Pammy said. "They're just as real as a blizzard on a farm, only prettier."

Laura didn't want to argue with Pammy, so she repeated what they agreed upon: "His painting is all wrong here."

Pammy lifted her plastic pendant from between her new, small breasts and fingered it in the sunlight. "If I was Mom," she said, "I think I'd like to work here. It's cool."

"Girls!" Mr. House shouted out at them, waving his arms toward himself like a coach. The lawn was so wide that his voice seemed out of synch. "Come on, you bathing beauties! Come eat, drink, be merry, and limbo!"

They joined the party on the deck, passing through a croquet game. The people playing made the game seem glamorous, the disproportion of their size to their mallets not at all silly. Bright wooden balls rolled quietly through the grass and went *clok* against one another. Mrs. House sat watching the game, feeding a fat black dog on her lap. Laura averted her eyes, hoping that Mrs. House had been too stunned to recognize her when she opened the bathroom door. "Here you go," Mrs. House told the dog, handing him a Jordan almond.

Everyone was eating. Plates decorated every surface; a melting ice swan swam in a sea of ripe fruit. In a budding tree whose two largest branches reached like arms toward the sky, a young man sat with his shirt off, feet above his head, popping stuffed mushrooms into his mouth. Mr. House stood below him, tossing up more. "Handle a beer?" he asked the boy, who nodded agreeably in answer. At one barbecue a side of beef spun while at another a whole pig revolved, big and pink as a fat child. The caterers circulated with champagne and miniature quiches, studiously ignoring the goings-on.

Laura found her mother again. She had grown dreamy with drink and lay on a padded lounge chair at the far end of the deck, her beret tilted over her eyes to block the sun. Her bare legs were white as eggshell, pale blue veins beneath the mildly translucent skin like splintering cracks. Mikey lay asleep beside her, his feet tucked beneath her knees for warmth. His ordinarily strange features appeared normal in sleep — freckled and pug — and this made Laura briefly sad.

From inside, Laura heard the doorbell ring. Until it sounded, she had thought she might want something to happen; now she knew otherwise. No one else seemed to have heard the long chime, and she waited for it to begin again before she went to answer it herself.

Her father stood on the flagstone porch, investigating the House mailbox, to which an enormous, black, screaming eagle was attached at the claws.

"Dad."

"Hi, honey. How's the Frolic?"

"Awful, really."

"Got you answering the door?" He stepped gently past her, moving quietly, as he always did, as if someone might jump out and surprise him.

"I was the only one who heard the bell," she told him. "We didn't think you'd be home until tonight," she added.

"You don't say?" he said.

"How was Oregon?"

"Wet," he said. "Earthy and impoverished, though happy. They have happy industries out there — Christmas trees and vineyards, happy, happy. I preferred Nevada — you ought to see the neon."

"That's too bad," Laura said, just to say something.

He gave his shoulders and head a slight shake, as if to wake up. "I've been driving since yesterday afternoon." He looked at his paint-dirtied plastic watch. "Twenty-four hours. I was ready to be home." He ran a thumbnail behind his earlobe. "And then nobody was there."

"Want to wait here while I get Mom and everybody?"

"No." He looked around the dark foyer for the first time. He was unshaven and smelled of his vehicle and the road. "No, I certainly don't want to wait here."

Laura took his hand, which was callused and warm, like a work glove, and led him along the circuitous route she'd discovered earlier instead of through the ballroom where his painting hung. He followed, grunting in amusement every now and then, dropping her hand to study an abstract painting in one room.

"Some of it's nice," Laura said, about the clutter, "but most of it's junk." She waited for him to agree.

"That's your opinion?" He spoke without looking at her, tipping his face so close to the painting that he seemed to be smelling it. "This is a marvelous piece," he said, sighing. "Absolutely marvelous." Art he admired made him melancholy, Laura had noticed. Her father had once spent nine thousand dollars on a painting. That was before the children were born. It now hung in his and Mrs. Laughlin's bedroom at home where no one but the family ever saw it.

"I interrupted Mrs. House on the toilet," Laura told him as they left the room, trying to cheer him up.

He smiled distractedly.

"Have you been here before?" she asked when they came to a patio door.

"Never," he said, stepping onto the deck.

"But not," Mr. House boomed beside them, "for lack of an invitation."

Her mother was where Laura had last seen her, asleep on the lounge chair next to Mikey. Her turquoise dress was hiked halfway up her bare thighs and her arms were crossed — as if she were carrying on an angry conversation in her dream. She was deeply asleep and looked cold, with Mikey curled against her so trustingly that Laura forgave her — whatever the infraction, whether it was preferring this child and home to her own or loving peculiar Mr. House or something else, something private between her parents which Laura might and might not wish to understand.

"You must be the mister," Mr. House had gone on when he had so suddenly materialized beside her and her father.

Mr. Laughlin showed his teeth like a hyena, the expression he reserved for people to whom he felt superior.

"Lemme buy you a drink," Mr. House said, waving in the direction of a passing caterer.

"O.K.," Mr. Laughlin agreed. "Get your brothers and sister," he said to Laura, nodding toward the pool, where all the party's children sat eating chocolate and comparing parents.

As she hurried, fearing a fight, she felt the headache she had expected descend like a hat over her skull. "Dad's here," she hissed to Pammy.

Pammy's eyebrows jumped. "Oh, man."

They each grabbed a brother and headed back. Mr. House and their father were standing over their mother's chair looking at her as she slept.

"Hey, Dad!" the youngest Laughlin greeted his father.

"Son."

"Guess what? I won third prize in the — what's his name?"

"Bacchus," Mr. House supplied.

"Bacchus Look-Alike Contest." He held up a Polaroid photo of himself wearing a crown of rubber purple grapes and holding a plastic set of pipes. "I got a prize," he added, pulling a fluorescent-orange feather boa from his suit-jacket pocket.

Mr. Laughlin accepted the boa, studying it as it slid like water through his fingers and onto the ground.

"First prize was Royals tickets," Laura's brother went on, bending to retrieve the wrap. "But we couldn't go all the way to Kansas City, anyway. Could we?" He looked up at his father, who shook his head.

On the chair Mikey jolted awake, his face becoming the familiar flattened, pink-eyed one of Down's syndrome once more.

"Nana," he snuffled, to warn her, and Mrs. Laughlin turned toward him without opening her eyes, nuzzling, attempting to close him in her arms. When he would not comply, she pushed aside her beret and squinted up.

Her husband waved his fingers down at her.

"Surprise, surprise!" said Mr. House.

When Mr. and Mrs. Laughlin agreed the family had to be going ("Oh, it's a school day tomorrow, and he's been driving all night." "I've been driving all night." "All night, honey, really?" "Really, all night."), Mr. House said he would walk them to the door. He led them toward the ballroom, and Pammy and Laura gave each other agonized looks. Now the crisis would come, the painting would be discovered.

Curiously, Laura's mother seemed unfazed by what was happening. She yawned and then shivered, crossing her arms and allowing Mr. House to put his tuxedo jacket around her shoulders as they moved toward the house, Mr. Laughlin in front walking with his nose tilted toward the ground, a pained grin lifting the left side of his mouth.

"Goodbye, goodbye!" the boys shouted to Frank, Jr., who stood with his legs spread on the other side of the lawn, waving and laughing — a perfect, reduced replica of his father.

"Thank you, Mrs. House," Pammy told the hostess, whom they met at the ballroom door. The group stopped to give her space to pass.

"You're surely welcome, baby," Mrs. House said to Pammy. "See you Monday," she said over her shoulder to Laura's mother as she joined her other guests outside.

They could have moved quickly through the room; Mr. Laughlin could have kept staring at the floor, walking on the lipstick red tile, thinking, smirking. But from the yard came a terrible wail; Mikey House had discovered that his Nana had left, and as he barreled at her, running lopsidedly, Mr. Laughlin raised his eyes to take in the pictures on the walls.

Without breathing, Laura watched him see them, the naked women, one drawing after another, their rolling, seductive ease, and then his own painting among them like a slammed door. What surprised her was that his eyes jumped over his painting — no alarm, no anger, not even, it seemed, recognition — and concentrated on the nudes. She looked up again. They were not very well rendered, obviously done by a hobbyist — or, as her father would say, "a draw-er, as in chest of." Laura tried to see what he saw — the round bottoms, the heavy breasts, the faces half hidden in ink smudge. Then her father turned to his wife, who had bent over Mikey once more, calming him. Her hat fell to the floor and her pale hair covered her eyes.

Laura blinked. It could be her, she thought. The woman in the pictures could be her mother — which would make Mr. House the artist. She saw them in a flash, together in the House studio, her mother on the chaise, Mr. House staring at her ardently, scratching away with his pens. She wanted to meet her father's eyes for confirmation, but he would not look at Laura. He waited for his wife, patiently.

In the foyer, Mr. Laughlin removed Mr. House's enormous tuxedo jacket from Mrs. Laughlin's shoulders.

"She can wear it home," Mr. House said magnanimously.

"She *can,*" Mr. Laughlin agreed, handing over the dark garment. "But she won't."

Mrs. Laughlin never went back. She began working for the phone company a few days later. They didn't divorce, and, after Laura left home — when she was in college and then law school — she found herself alternately proud of and annoyed by her parents' enduring marriage. As to the significance of what had happened at the Houses', Laura could only look to the fact that soon her father acquired a partner to share booth space with and represent him — a single man, a photographer who lived on the road anyway and didn't mind the traveling — and to her mother's fierce tears one dinnertime when Laura's youngest brother carelessly asked what in the world would happen to Mikey House.

On the drive across town that Easter, Mr. Laughlin told them the story of his trip west, of how he'd had to spend the nights in his Land Cruiser — he illustrated by curling himself spasmodically as he steered — because he'd run out of hotel money, of his stiff back and stinky clothes, the way he'd eaten at restaurants that offered two-for-one meals. He kept turning to check Mrs. Laughlin's expression, but she was still sleepy, sluggish, looking blankly out the window, shivering. Even without Mr. House's jacket, every now and then Laura caught a whiff of his cologne — so powerful it was as if he were among them for a moment. Mr. Laughlin's stories weren't pathetic tales; he managed to have Laura and Pammy and their brothers laughing at his bad luck by the time they reached their driveway on the other side of the city.

Later, he and Laura drove back to the Houses' to pick up Mrs. Laughlin's car; her old Maverick had been hopelessly trapped in the overcrowded driveway, Mercedeses and Cadillacs and BMWs packed four-deep behind and beside it. "We'll get it tonight," Laura's father had said, guiding Mrs. Laughlin to his boxy vehicle parked across the street. When he and Laura returned for the car, they didn't speak, as if they were in agreement — as if he, too, she thought, had recognized his pretty wife in the mediocre art. It would be easy to say something, and Laura nearly did: a little evidence would go a long way, would twist tight whatever was already tense.

Her father pulled up in front of the Houses' once more. The driveway was empty except for Mrs. Laughlin's car. The windows of the house were dark, as if the family had all gone to bed early. Or as if they didn't want to be seen.

"Your mother's left headlight is out," Mr. Laughlin said to Laura.

It was the first thing he'd said in thirty minutes, and Laura tried to make some symbolic sense of his words but couldn't. "What do you mean?" she asked tentatively.

"Her Mav, the left headlight. You ought to just follow me home." He stretched his arms and tapped the ceiling of the Land Cruiser with his fingers. The smell of his sweat filled the front seat. Then he laughed. "Man, have I driven enough today or what?" And Laura saw that nothing was going to happen. They were going to go home and watch television with the rest of the family. The Easter Frolic was over. "Hoppity hop," her father said, which was his way of prodding her into action.

Laura continued to intercept the mail, which one day led her to think about the woman who'd taken her mother's place at the Houses'. Because the envelope with the Eastborough return address was so light, Laura had thought it might be empty; instead, a slim gold ring slid out. Nothing more. Had her father even noticed its absence, Laura wondered. She slipped the ring on her pinkie and imagined another woman, interviewing for the position of Nana, marveling at her odd employer, and, after taking the job, playing with Mikey, loving him, wondering at his eclectic basket of toys — at the barrette and the black tongue, the swinging red door and the legless reindeer, the two keys and trouble dolls, someone's mysterious, modest wedding band.

STEPHEN DIXON

Man, Woman and Boy

FROM WESTERN HUMANITIES REVIEW

THEY'RE SITTING. "It's wrong," she says. He says, "I know." She stands, he does right after her. "It's all wrong," she says. "I know," he says, "but what are we going to do about it?" She goes into the kitchen, he follows her. "It almost couldn't be worse," she says. "Between us — how could it be? I don't see how." "I agree," he says, "and I'd like to change it from bad to better but I don't know what to do." She pours them coffee. She puts on water for coffee. She fills the kettle with water. She gets the kettle off the stove, shakes it, looks inside and sees there's only a little water in it, turns on the faucet and fills the kettle halfway and then. And then? "Do you want milk, sugar?" she says. This after the water's dripped through the grounds in the coffeemaker, long after she said "I'm making myself coffee, you want some too?" He nodded. Now he says, "You don't know how I like it by now?" "Black," she says. "Black as soot, black as ice. Black as the ace of spades, as the sky, a pearl, black as diamonds." "Whatever," he says, "whatever are you talking about?" "Just repeating something you once said. How you like your coffee." "I said that? Those, I mean — I said any of them? Never. You know me. I don't say stupid or foolish things, I try not to talk in clichés, I particularly dislike similes in my speech, and if I'm going to make a joke, I know beforehand it's going to get a laugh. But to get back to the problem." "The problem is this," she says. "We're two people, in one house, with only one child, and I'm not pregnant with a second. We have a master bedroom and one other bedroom, so one for us and one for the child. We have no room for guests. We have no guestroom. The sofa's not comfortable enough to sleep on and doesn't pull out into a bed. We have no sleeping bag for one of us to sleep on the floor. I don't want our boy to sleep in the master bed with one of us while the other sleeps in his bed. One of us has to go, is what I'm saying." "I understand you," he says. "The problem's probably what you said. It is, let's face it. One of us has to go because both of us can't stay and traditionally it's been the man. But I don't want to go, I'd hate it. Not so much to leave you but him. Not at all to leave you. I'm being honest. Don't strike out against me for it, since it's not something I'm saying just to hurt you." "I wouldn't," she says. "I like honesty. And the feeling's mutual, which I'm also not saying just to get back at you for what you said. But I'm not leaving the boy and traditionally the man is, in situations like this, supposed to, or simply has. We've seen it. Our friends and friends of friends we've heard of who have split up. The child traditionally stays with the woman. And it's easier, isn't it, for the one without the child to leave than the one who stays with it, and also ends up being a lot easier on the child. So I hope that's the way it'll turn out. I think we both agree on that or have at least agreed on it in our conversation just now." "Our conversation which is continuing," he says. "Our conversation which should conclude. It wouldn't take you too long to pack, would it?" "You know me," he says, "I never acquired much. Couple of dress shirts, two T-shirts, three pairs of socks, not counting the pair I'm wearing, three or four handkerchiefs, a tie. Two undershorts, including the one on me, pair of work pants in addition to the good pants I've on. Sports jacket to match the good pants, work jacket and coat, hat, muffler, boots, sneakers and the shoes I'm wearing and that should be it. Belt, of course. Bathing suit and running shorts. Anything I leave behind — some books but the one I'm reading and will take — I can pick up some other time. The tie, in fact, I can probably leave here; I never use it." "You might," she says. "Anyway, it's small enough to take and not use. Take everything so you'll be done with it. So you're off then? Need any help packing?" "For that amount of stuff? — nah. But one last time?" "What, one last time?" she says. "A kiss, a smooch, a feel, a hug, a little bit of pressing the old family flesh together, okay?" "You want to make me laugh? I'll laugh. Cry? — I'll do that too.

Which do you want me to do?" "Okeydoke, I got the message and was only kidding." "Oh yes, for sure, only kidding, you." "What's that supposed to mean?" he says. "Oh you don't know, for sure, oh yes, you bet." "If you're referring to that smooch-talk, what I meant was I'd like to be with my child for a few minutes before I go. To hug, squeeze, kiss and explain that I'm not leaving him but you. That I'll see him periodically, or really as much as I can — every other day if you'll let me. You will let me, right?" "For the sake of him, of course, periodically. More coffee?" "No thanks," he says. "Then may I go to my room while you have this final get-together with him? Not final; while you say good-bye for now?" "Go on. I won't steal him."

They move backward, she to the couch, he to the chair. They never drank coffee, never made it; never had that conversation. They're both reading, or she is and he has the book on his lap. Their son's on the floor putting a picture puzzle together. It's a nice domestic scene, he thinks, quiet, the kind he likes best of all. Fire going in the fireplace — he made it. A good one too, though fires she makes are just as good. It doesn't give off much heat, fault of the fireplace's construction, but looks as if it does and is beautiful. Thermostat up to sixty-eight, so with the fire, high enough to keep the house warm, cosy. He has a tea beside him on the side table. On the side table beside him. Beside his chair. A Japanese green tea, and he's shaved fresh ginger into it. Tea's now lukewarm. Tastes it; it is. He's been thinking these past few minutes and forgot about the tea. She has a cup of hot water with lemon in it. Not hot now — she might even have finished it — but was when he gave it to her. About ten minutes ago she said, "Strange as this must sound" — he'd said he was making himself tea, would she like some or anything with boiling water? — "it's all I want. I wonder if it means I'm coming down with something." He said, "You feel warm?" "No." "Anything ache — limbs, throat, extremities?" "Nope, I guess I'm not," and resumed reading. "What could you be coming down with, Mommy?" the boy said. "Your mommy means with a cold," he said. "Oh," the boy said and went back to his puzzle. I wonder, the man thinks, what that long parting scene I imagined means. It's not like that with us at all. We're a happy couple, a relatively happy one. Hell, happier than most it seems, more compatible and content and untroubled than most too. I still love her. Do I? Be honest. I still do. Very much so. Very much? Oh, well, not as passionately or crazily most days as I loved her when I first met her or the first six months or so of our being together before we got married or even the first six months or so of our marriage, but close enough to that. She still excites me. Very much so. Physically, intellectually. We make love a lot. About as much as when we first met, or after the first month we met. She often initiates it. Not because I don't. Lots of times she does when I'm thinking of initiating it but she starts it first. She doesn't seem dissatisfied. I'm not too. What's there to be dissatisfied about? A dozen or so years since we met and we still go at it like kids, or almost like kids — like adults, anyone — what I'm saying is almost as if sometimes it's the first. I have fantasies about other women but what do they mean? Meaning, they don't mean much: I had them a week after I met her, they're fleeting and they probably exist just to make it even better with her, but probably not. They exist. That's the way I am. So long as I don't act on them, which I'd never do, for why would I? which is what I'm saying. And she tells me she loves me almost every day. Tells me almost every day. And almost every night one of the last things she says to me, in the dark or just before or after she turns off the light, is "I love you, dearest." And I usually say, "I love you too," which is true; very much so: I do, and then we'd briefly kiss and maybe later, maybe not, after I put down my reading, make love. So why'd I think that scene? Just trying it out? Wondering how I'd feel? How would I? Awful, obviously. I couldn't live without her. Or I could but it'd be difficult, very extremely trying, probably impossible, or close. And without the boy? Never. As I said in the scene, I want to see him every day. He's such a good kid. I want to make him breakfast every morning till he's old enough to make his own, help him with his homework when he wants me to and go places with him — museums, the park, play ball with him, take walks with him — with him and her: summer vacations, two to three weeks here or there, diving off rafts, long swims with him alongside me. Things like that. Libraries. He loves libraries and children's bookstores. Really odd I thought that scene then. Just trying it out as I said, that's all, or I suppose.

He gets up and gets on the floor and says, "Need any help?"

"No, Dad, thanks. If I do I'll tell you." "Sure now?" "Positive. I like to figure things out myself. That's the object of the puzzle, isn't it?" "Well, sometimes it's nice to do it with other people — it can be fun. But do what you want. And you're pretty good at this." "So far I am. I want to get up to one with a thousand pieces. This is only five hundred. But that's still two hundred more than the last one I did, which was two hundred fifty." "Two hundred fifty more than the last one," he says. "Two hundred fifty times two hundred fifty — no, I mean times two; or two hundred fifty plus another two hundred fifty equals —" "Five hundred." "I know. Two hundred fifty times two hundred fifty is probably fifty thousand, or a hundred." "That's good. You're so smart." He touches the boy's cheek. "Okay, but if you need any help, whistle." "What for?" "I mean — it's just an expression like what you said before: if you want me to help you'll tell me."

He goes over to his wife. She's reading and correcting manuscripts from her class. He puts his hand on top of her head. First he stood there thinking, "Should I stay here till she notices me and looks up or should I put my hand on her head? On her head. Just standing here might seem peculiar to her. I'm sure if I was able to stand back and see myself standing here like this, it would seem peculiar." Now with his hand on her head he thinks, "Actually, standing here with my hand on top of her head must also seem peculiar to her." Just as he's about to take his hand off, she looks up and grabs his hand with the one holding the pen. "Hello," she says. "Hello." "What's up?" she says. "Just admiring you." "You're a dear," she says. "You're the dear, a big one. I love you." "And I love you, my dearest." "And I love you very much," he says. "Very very." "Same with me, my dearest," she says. "Is that all? I mean, it's a lot and I like your hand here and holding it," and she squeezes it, "but may I return to my schoolwork unless you have anything further to say?" "Return, return," he says and she pulls her hand away and holds the other side of the manuscripts with it. "Oh, Daddy and Mommy said they love each other," the boy says. "That's right, we did," he says. "We said it and we do." "Are you just saying that to me?" the boy says. "Ask your mother." "Well, Mom?" "Well, what?" she says, looking up from her manuscripts. "Do you really love Daddy or are you —" "Yes, of course, such a question, what do you think? Now may I return to my work? Eight more essays to grade in a little bit under an hour. That's when I think I'll be too sleepy for anything but sleep." "Oh yes?" he says. "Leave your mother then to her reading." "Not before you both kiss on the lips." "You ask for so much," he says. "All right with you, ma'am?" he says to her. "Come ahither and adither," she says and moves her head up, he bends over and puts his lips on hers. He sticks the tip of his tongue in in a way where he's sure the boy won't be able to see it. Their tongues touch, eyes close. His do he knows — the eyes. He opens his and sees hers are closed. Closes his and opens them quickly: still closed. "Okay, you proved it," the boy says. "You can stop now."

They move into the dining room. About an hour earlier, two. The three of them. They're seated, eating. He avoids looking at her, she him. He doesn't want to talk. When he wants something near her he nudges his son and points to it and his son gives it to him or he just reaches over, sometimes even has to stand up, and get it himself. When she wants something near him she asks their son, though he always puts the thing he took back in the spot it was on. He's angry at her and doesn't want to just talk to his son and ignore her. Something she said. That he doesn't do enough of the housework. "Hell I don't," he said. "I do at least half or most of the work most of the time." That wasn't it. He and she didn't say that. What then? Said to her, "You know, I hate saying this, but the house could be neater. You going to take umbrage, take." Said this to her about an hour before dinner. Soon after he came home from work. She'd got home from work a couple of hours earlier. The boy was in his room doing homework. Or that's what she said he was supposed to be there for. "You know I like order. That the chaos you prefer, or simply don't mind living with, gets to me viscerally sometimes. Forget the 'viscerally.' I can't stand chaos, it makes me nervous, temperamental, like cigarette smoke does. Forget the cigarette smoke. I just can't stand it." "Then tidy up the place," she said. "It's not just tidying up that's needed; it's also the dirt and dust." "Then clean up the place too." "I don't clean up enough? I do most of the cleaning, it seems, plus most of the clothes washing and shopping and making the beds and fixing up the boy's room and cleaning the bird's cage and feeding it every night and our food cooking and dish washing and all that crap and I just think it's your turn. The food I see you've done, though I made the salad before I left. But the rest." "Okay, I'll clean up," she said. "I've been busy, I am busy, I did the dinner except the salad, set the table, it's been a rough day at school, I've helped our son with his long division for an hour and still have a mess of essays to grade, but if you think the distribution of housework's been unequal, I'll do what you say. I wanted to say 'what the boss said,' but you might take umbrage. Umbrage; what a word." She cleaned up the living room and dining room. When she started to, he said, "I don't mean now." Tidied up, swept the floors and rugs, dusted and polished the furniture, straightened the many books on the shelves, rubbed some stains on the wooden floor with a solution till she got them out. It looks and smells a lot better, he thought, place isn't a complete jumble, but she's making me feel guilty and she knows it. Why doesn't she do it periodically, as I do, and then it wouldn't come to this. "Do," meaning the cleaning; "this," being the disorder, dirty house, argument. The food was cooking, dinner was. He didn't want to eat with the two of them feeling about each other like this, but what could he say: "I don't want to eat right now, you go ahead without me," after she'd cooked it and just cleaned part of the house and he'd, so to speak, started the argument? He'd come home mad because of something that happened at the office — more pettiness there, nothing that should have upset him. He took it out on her — might have taken it out on the boy if he'd been around — which isn't to say the place wasn't a visual assault when he got there, but it certainly wasn't enough of one to start an argument over, especially when he knew she'd taught most of the day and he could see she'd done some work at home: dinner, scrap paper scattered about showing she'd helped the boy with his long division. Besides, it just wasn't something that warranted arguing over any time. He'd gone to work mad because this morning in bed — it all could have stemmed from this — he'd wanted to make love. One of those mornings: dreamt of lovemaking, woke up thinking of lovemaking, wanted very much to do it. She mumbled, "Too tired, sweetie," and moved her neck away from his lips. He persisted. "I said I'm tired, too much so, don't want to, please let me sleep, I need it." Usually she gave in, even when she didn't feel like it. She knew it'd only take him a few minutes when he was like this and she could take the easiest and least involved position and wouldn't even have to move to it since she was in it now: on her side with her back to him, and that he'd want to get out of bed right after to wash up, exercise, have coffee and read the paper, and prepare the breakfast table for their son and her. He pressed into her, put a hand on her breast through the nightgown, other hand between her legs. She had panties on. He hadn't known. He started to pull them down. "What, huh?" she said, as if startled awake. "Don't, damnit. I said I didn't want to and I certainly feel less like it now. Do it to yourself if you're so horny, but with me it'd be like with a corpse." "A corpse isn't warm." "Please?" "And I'm not horny; I just want you." "Sure," she said. "Oh yeah, you bet, oh boy," and moved a few inches away from him. "Bloody Christ," he said and got out of bed. "Bitch," he said softly but he thought loud enough for her to hear. She didn't respond, eyes were closed, she looked asleep. Faking it maybe, but who cares? They didn't talk at breakfast, which he ate standing up at the stove, she at the table he'd set. And he didn't look at her when he left for work. Put on his coat, got his briefcase, kissed his son, left. The previous day during dinner they'd had an argument. Her mother had said to him on the phone, "Are you treating my daughter nicely? Remember, she's our only child, one in a zillion, and I always want her treated well because nobody in the world deserves it better." "Have you asked either of us if she's been treating me nicely?" he said. "What a question," she said, and then, "Let me talk to her if she's there — it's why I called." His wife later asked him what he'd said that made her mother so mad, and it started. "She's too nosy sometimes and she expects sensible gentle answers to these impossible often hostile questions, and then she dismisses me as if I'm her houseboy-idiot." "You don't know how to talk to her and you never liked her and you don't know how to act civilly to anyone you don't like." "Is that right?" he said, and so on. That morning he'd wanted to make love and they did. After, she said, "Nothing really gets started with me when we make it lately and I end up so frustrated. Do you mind my saying this? — for the most part you do it too quickly. You have to warm me up more and concentrate on the right spots, especially if you suddenly come on me unprepared, like when I'm asleep." "Listen, we're all responsible for our own orgasms," he said. "The hell we are." "I didn't mean it the way it might have come out, but we are to a certain degree, don't you think?" "You meant it and you show it," she said. "Just get yours, buster, and let whoever it is burn." "What whoever-it-is?" he said. "It's only you." "Don't bullshit you don't know what I mean," she said, and so on. The previous day they fought about something, he forgets what: that she's been letting the gas gauge go almost to empty, that she took his stapler the other day and now he can't find it, that her personal trash in the bathroom wastebasket is starting to stink and it's her responsibility to dump it in the can outside or at least tie it up and stick it in the kitchen garbage bag. "So I forgot." "So from now on remember." "Don't fight," their son said. "Please don't shout, please don't yell." They stopped but didn't talk to each other for a few hours. The previous night, when he was reading and at the same time falling asleep, she got into bed naked and said, "You don't have to if you don't want to — no obligation," and he said, "No no, I can probably do it," and they made love and went to sleep holding each other, she kissing his hand, he the back of her head. Further back. The boy's born and he drops to his knees in the birthing room he's so excited. Further. They're getting married and they both break down during the ceremony and cry. Further. They meet. Sees her at a cocktail party, introduces himself: "You probably have better things to do than talk to me," and she says, "What a line — no, why?" His first wife, girlfriends, first he was smitten with in grade school. He's a boy and his parents are arguing bitterly at the dinner table. He puts his hands over his ears and yells, "Stop, can't you ever stop screaming at yourselves?" "Don't do that," his father says, pulling his hands off his ears. "What are you, crazy?" and he says, "Yes," or "You made me," or "Why shouldn't I be?" and runs out of the room. "Go after the maniac," and his brother goes after him and says, "It's not good for me either when they're like that, so come on back." Hears further back. From his mother's stomach. "Filthy rotten bitch." "And you. Stupid, cheap, pigheaded, a pill. Get lost. I hate your guts." "Not as much as I hate yours. Here." "And what's that?" "What you wanted so much. Your allowance. Take it and stick it up your ass," and so on. "Why'd I marry you?" and so on. "You don't think I ask that question too? With all I had and never any lip from anyone, what'd I need it for?" and so on.

He's in his chair, the man, wishing he'd made himself coffee or tea. Something hot to drink. He can think better with it. Son plays, wife reads. They'll probably make love tonight, he thinks. He's been nice all day, no arguments, she's smiled lovingly at him several times the last few hours. Kissed her when he got home and she said, "Ooh, that's some kiss; I love it." He can't wait. He's sure she'll come to bed ready. If she doesn't — well, how will he know? He can go to the bathroom and shake the case. Sometimes he can smell it on her too. The cream. Anyway, he can say — he's usually first in bed, usually reading — "I hope you're ready, I know I am." "Sure," she'll say if she isn't ready and go back to the bathroom. He loves her. They have their fights and disputes and sometimes he tells himself he hates her and doesn't want to live another second with her, but he really loves her. He should remember that. So beautiful. Still a very beautiful face. Her body still excites him. She's so smart, so good. He's lucky, particularly when he's so often a sonofabitch and fool. He should remember all that. He should call his mother now. Doesn't want to budge. Just wants to sit here remembering, digesting — something — the thoughts he just had about her. That he loves her. That no matter what, he loves her. "Time for bed," she says to their son. "Oh, I don't want to go yet," the boy says. "Do what your mother tells you," he says. "Okay," the boy says, "okay, but you don't have to talk rough." "I wasn't. And please clean up your puzzle. — Nah, just forget it, it's late and you're going to bed; I'll do it." He looks at her. She's standing, her manuscripts are on the couch. Smiles at her. She smiles at him, he smiles back. The boy gets up and heads for the stairs. "Look," he says to her, "he's really going to bed without a fuss. What a kid." "I'll run his bath, you'll tell him a story after?" "I don't need anyone for that," the boy says. "I can fill my own tub — I know how much to — and I want to read by myself before I go to sleep." "You read?" the man says. "He reads?" to her. "Since when? I don't want him to. Soon I won't be able to do anything for him. He'll be brushing his own hair, combing his own teeth." "Daddy, you got those wrong. And I've been doing them a long time." "That's what I'm saying," he says. "Next you'll be cooking your own shoelaces, tying your own food. Go, go, don't let me stop you, big man," and blows a kiss at him. He didn't mean those first two to be switched around, but turned out to be a good joke.

The boy runs upstairs. He gets on the floor, puts the what-do-you-call-them? — isolated, or incomplete, or unassembled or just-not-put-in-the-puzzle-yet pieces in their box, doesn't know what to do with the partly completed puzzle, carefully slides it against the wall. Hears water running in the tub, lots of padding back and forth on the ceiling. "He's growing up so much," he says. "You haven't noticed before?" she says. "Of course, but the way he phrases things, and just now — no remonstrating." He sits beside her. "Mind?" "Go on." Puts his arm around her shoulder, pulls her to him. She looks at him. "Yes?" "This is the life," he says, "everything but the kid asleep." "Yes, it's very nice," and kisses his lips and goes back to reading. He continues looking at her. Wants to say, "You're beautiful, you know; beautiful." Takes his arm away for he feels it might be bothering her. She wants to concentrate. Good, she should. He leans his head back on the couch, looks at the ceiling. I go upstairs, he thinks. My son's in bed reading. He smells washed, his room's neat, he tidied it up without anyone asking. "All done for now?" I say. He puts the book on the floor and says, "Forty-six; please remember the page for me?" "Will do. Good night, my sweet wonderful child," I say and kiss his lips, make sure the covers are over his shoulders. "Pillows all comfortable?" and he says, "You could get them right, I don't mind." I fix the pillows, rest his head on them, turn the light off and go downstairs. "Like a beer or glass of wine?" I say. "If you'll share a bottle of beer with me," she says. We do. "I'm tired," I say. "Let's go to bed then," she says. We do. I'm in bed, naked, clothes piled beside me on the floor, glasses and book on my night table. She's still in — She's sitting on the other side of the bed, taking her clothes off. She was just in the bathroom a few minutes. "Dear," I say. "Not to worry," she says, "it's all taken care of. What's on your mind's on mine." All her clothes are off. I breathe deeply to see if I can smell her. I can: a little fresh cologne, cream she put on, something from her underarms. Or mine. I smell one when she's looking away. Nothing. Can I shut off the light?" I say. "Please, I'm finished." I shut it off. She gets under the covers with me. We hug, kiss, rub each other very hard. She grabs me and I grab her. Something tells me it's going to be one of the best for me.

"Like a glass of wine, some beer?" he asks. "I don't want to get too sleepy," she says. "Maybe I can read a couple of more papers than I thought I could, so I won't have to do too many tomorrow." "Dad?" his son shouts from upstairs. "We're all out of toilet paper up here." "You checked the bathroom closet, the cabinet under the sink?" "Everyplace." "To the rescue," and he gets a roll out of the downstairs bathroom, runs upstairs, puts the roll in. He goes into his son's room. The boy's drawing at his desk and he says, "Don't you have to use the toilet?" "I did, but I was thinking of you and Mom." "That's very thoughtful, very. Come on now, though, you have to go to bed." The boy gets into bed. "Teeth all combed?" "Everything," the boy says. "You don't want the night light on?" "I don't need it anymore." "Good, that's fine, but if you change your mind, okay too. Good night, my sweet wonderful kid," and he bends down and kisses him on the lips, turns the light off.

He undresses, brushes his teeth, flosses, washes his face, washes his penis and behind with a washrag, washes the washrag with soap and hangs it on the shower rod, walks a few steps downstairs and says softly, "Sweetheart, I'm going to bed now, to read — you coming up soon?" "No. And don't wait up for me. I'm thinking now I'll just do the whole bunch of them, no matter how long it takes. Good night." "Good night." He gets into bed, opens a book, reads, feels sleepy, puts the book down, looks at her side of the bed and thinks, "Remember what you promised to think about before? What was it? Bet you forgot." Thinks. "Ah," he says when he remembers what it was. "It's true," he thinks, "I really love her." "You hear that, dear," he says low, "do you hear that? I can't wait till you get into bed so I can hold ya." He puts the book and glasses on the night table, shuts off the light, lies on his back to see if anything else comes into his head, shuts his eyes, turns over on his side, falls asleep.

ANDREA LEE

Winter Barley

FROM THE NEW YORKER

1. The Storm

NIGHT; a house in northern Scotland. When October gales blow in off the Atlantic, one thinks of sodden sheep huddled downwind and of oil cowboys on bucking North Sea rigs. Even a large, solid house like this one feels temporary tonight, like a hand cupped around a match. Flourishes of hail, like bird shot against the windows; a wuthering in the chimneys, the sound of an army of giants charging over the hilltops in the dark.

In the kitchen a man and a woman sit eating a pig's foot. Edo and Elizabeth. Together their years add up to ninety, of which his make up two-thirds. Edo slightly astonished Elizabeth by working out this schoolboy arithmetic when they first met, six months ago. He loves acrostics and brain teasers, which he solves with the fanatical absorption common to sportsmen and soldiers — men used to long, mute waits between bursts of violence. Edo has been both mercenary and white hunter in the course of an unquiet life passed mainly between Italy and Africa, between privilege and catastrophe. He is a prince, one of a swarm exiled from an Eastern European kingdom now extinct, and this house, his last, is a repository of fragments from ceremonial lives and the web of cousinships that link him to most of the history of Europe.

The house is full of things that seem to need as much care as children: pieces of Boulle and Caffiéri scattered among the Scottish furniture bought at auction, a big I.B.M. computer programmed to trace wildfowl migrations worldwide, gold flatware knobby with crests, an array of retrievers with pernickety stomachs in the dog run outside, red Venetian goblets that for washing require the same intense concentration one might use in restoring a Caravaggio. In the afternoons Edo likes to sit down with a glass — a supermarket glass — of vermouth and watch reruns of "Fame" magically sucked from the wild Scottish air by the satellite dish down the hill. With typical thoroughness he has memorized the names and dispositions of the characters from Manhattan's High School of Performing Arts and has his favorites: the curly-haired musical genius, the beautiful dance instructor he calls "la mulâtresse." The television stands in a thicket of silver frames that hold photographs of men who all resemble Edward VII, and women with the oddly anonymous look of royalty. Often they pose with guns and bearers on swards blanketed with dead animals, and their expressions, like Edo's, are invariably mild.

To Elizabeth, Edo's kitchen looks unfairly like a men's club: brown, cavernous, furnished with tattered armchairs, steel restaurant appliances, charts of herbs, dogs in corners, Brobdingnagian pots for feeding hungry grouse shooters, and green baize curtains, which, as they eat tonight, swell and collapse slowly with the breath of the storm. The pig's foot is glutinous and spicy, cooked with lentils, the way Romans do it at Christmastime. Edo cooked it, as he cooks everything. When Elizabeth visits, he doesn't let her touch things in the kitchen — even the washing up is done in a ritual fashion by the housekeeper, a thin Scottish vestal.

"These lentils are seven years old," he announces, taking another helping.

"Aren't you embarrassed to be so stingy?"

Dried legumes never go bad, he tells her, and it's a vulgar trait to disdain stinginess. His mother fed her children on rice and coffee during the war, even though they crossed some borders wearing vests so weighted with hidden gold pieces that he and his sisters walked with bent knees. Edo grew up with bad teeth and an incurable hunger, like the man in the fairy tale who could eat a mountain of bread. He has a weakness for trimmings and innards, the food of the poor.

Elizabeth knows she adopts an expression of intense comprehension whenever Edo reminisces; it pinches her features, as if they were strung on tightening wires. Still, she doesn't want to be one of those young women befuddled by lives lived before their own. She grew up in Dover, Massachusetts, went to Yale, and hopes that one day she'll believe in more than she does now. At the same time she has a curiously Latin temperament — not the tempestuous but the fatalistic kind — for someone with solid layers of Dana and Hallowell ancestors behind her. This trait helps her at work; she is a vice president at an American bank in Rome. Tonight under a long pleated skirt she is wearing, instead of the racy Italian underwear she puts on at home, a pair of conventual white underpants and white cotton stockings held up with the kind of elastic garters her grandmother's Irish housemaid might have worn. Edo has been direct, and as impersonal as someone ticking off a laundry list, about what excites him. She is excited by the attitude in itself: an austere erotic vocabulary far removed from the reckless sentiment splashed around by the men she knows in Rome, Boston, and Manhattan.

Elizabeth discovered early on that the world of finance, far from moving like clockwork, is full of impulse and self-indulgence, which extend into private life. When she met Edo she had just come out of a bad two years with a married former client from Milan, full of scenes and abrupt cascades of roses, and a cellular phone trilling at all hours. In contrast, this romance is orderly. She supposes it is an idyll when she thinks about it, which, strangely, is almost never; it flourishes within precise limits of ambition, like a minor work of art. The past he sets before her in anecdotes — for he is a habitual raconteur, though rarely a tedious one — keeps the boundaries clear.

Africa; dust-colored Tanzania. Edo is telling her how his mother once got angry on safari, blasted a rifle at one of the bearers, missed, and hit a small rhinoceros. Under a thatch of eyebrows Edo's hooded blue eyes glow with a gentle indifference, as if to him the story means nothing; the fact is that he couldn't live without invoking these memories, which instead of fading or requiring interpretation have grown more vivid and have come to provide a kind of textual commentary on the present. His hair is white, and he has a totemic Edwardian mustache. His cheeks are eroded from years of shooting in all weathers on all continents. It's the face of a crusty old earl in a children's book, of Lear, and he is appropriately autocratic, crafty, capricious, sentimental.

He watches Elizabeth and thinks that her enthusiasm for the gluey pig's foot and the rhino story both grow out of a snobbish American need to scrabble about for tradition. Americans are romantics, he thinks — "romantic" for him is the equivalent of "middle-class" — and she is no exception, even if she does come from a good family. Accustomed to judging livestock and listening to harebrained genetic theories at gatherings of his relatives, he looks at her bone structure with the eye of an expert. She is beautiful. Her posture has the uncomplicated air of repose which in Europe indicates a well-born young girl. But there is an unexpected quality in her — something active, resentful, uncertain, desirous. He likes that. He likes her in white stockings.

She says something in a low voice. "Speak up!" he says, cupping his ear like a deaf old man. He is in fact a bit deaf, from years of gunpowder exploding beside his ear. He often claims it turned his hair prematurely white and permanently wilted his penis, but only the first is true. "You're a gerontophile," he tells her.

She'd said something about storms on Penobscot Bay. The rattling windows here remind her of the late August gales that passed over Vinalhaven, making her grandmother's summer house as isolated from the world outside as a package wrapped in gray fabric. She recalls the crystalline days that came after a storm, when from the end of the dock she and her cousins, tanned Berber color and feverish with crushes, did therapeutic cannonballs into the frigid water. She sees her grandmother in long sleeves and straw hat, for her lupus, dashing down a green path to the boathouse with a hammer in her hand: storm damage. In the island house, as in Edo's, is a tall clock whose authoritative tick seems to suspend time.

Elizabeth and Edo finish the pig's foot and stack the dishes in the sink. Then they go upstairs and on his anchorite's bed make love with a mutual rapacity that surprises both of them, as it always does. Each one has the feeling that he is stealing something from the other, snatching pleasure with the innocent sense of triumph a child has in grabbing a plaything. Each feels that this is a secret which must be kept from the other, and this double reserve gives them a rare harmony.

Later Edo lies alone, under the heavy linen sheets, his lean body bent in a frugal half crouch evolved from years of sleeping on cots and on bare, cold ground. He sent out the dogs for a last pee beside the kitchen door, and now they sleep, twitching, in front of the embers in his fireplace. He has washed down the sleeping pill with a glass of Calvados that Elizabeth left for him and lies listening to a pop station from Aberdeen and feeling the storm shuddering through the house, through his bones. He imagines Elizabeth already asleep in the bedroom with the Russian engravings, or — hideous American custom — having a bedtime shower. He has never been able to share a bed with a woman, not during his brief marriage, not during love affairs with important and exigent beauties. It gives him a peculiar sense of squalor to think of all the women who protested or grew silent when he asked them to leave or got up and left them. Alone among them, Elizabeth seems to break away with genuine pleasure; her going is a blur of white legs flashing under his dressing gown. Attractive.

After immersion in that smooth body, he feels not tired but oddly tough, preserved. An old salt cod, he says to himself, but for some reason what he envisions instead is a burl on a tree. At Santa Radegonda, a vast country house in Gorizia that nowadays exists only in the heads of a few old people, there was in the children's garden an arbor composed of burled nut trees trained together for centuries. The grotesque, knobby wood, garish with green leaves, inspired hundreds of nursemaids' tales of hobgoblins. Inside were a rustic table and chairs made of the same arthritic wood. The quick and the dead. A miracle of craft in the garden of a house where such miracles were common — and all of them grist for Allied and German bombs. He seems to see that arbor with something inside flashing white, like Elizabeth's legs, but then the Tavor takes hold and he sleeps.

2. *Remembering Easter*

The storm has blown itself out into a brilliant blue morning, and Elizabeth lies in bed below an engraving of a cow-eyed Circassian bride and reads the diary of Virginia Woolf. Volume II, 1920–1924. She imagines Bloomsbury denizens with long faces and droopy, artistic clothes making love with the lighthearted anarchy of Trobriand islanders. Through the window she can hear Edo talking in his surprisingly awful English to the gardener about damage to *Cruciferae* in the kitchen plot. Rows of broccoli, brussels sprouts, and a rare black Tuscan cabbage have been flattened. The gardener replies in unintelligible Scots, and Elizabeth laughs aloud. She finds it shocking that she can feel so happy when she is not in love.

They met when she was depressed over the terrible, commonplace way things had ended with her married lover from Milan, with all her friends' warnings coming true one by one like points lighting up on a pinball machine. She had sworn off men — Italians in particular — when a gay friend of hers, Nestor, who spoke Roman dialect but was really some kind of aristocratic mongrel, invited her to Scotland to spend Easter with him and some other friends at the house of a mad old uncle of his. Nestor and the others didn't show up for their meeting at Gatwick, so Elizabeth bought a pair of Argyle socks at the airport shop and took the flight up to Aberdeen on her own. It didn't feel like an adventure, more like stepping into a void. After the tawny opulence of Rome, the obstinate cloud cover through which she caught glimpses of tweed-colored parcels of land far below suggested a mournful Protestant thrift even in scenery. She listened to the Northern British accents around her and recalled her mother's tales of a legendary sadistic Nanny MacKenzie. In her head ran a rhyme from childhood:

> There was a naughty boy,
> And a naughty boy was he
> He ran away to Scotland,
> Scotland for to see.

Nestor was not in Aberdeen, had left no word, and the mad uncle was disconcerting: white-haired, thin-legged, with the pitiless eyes of an old falcon. He was exquisitely unsurprised about her coming alone, as if it were entirely usual for him to have unknown young women appear for Easter weekend. Jouncing along with her in a green Land Rover, he smoked one violent, unfiltered cigarette after another as she talked to him about Rome, trying to conceal her embarrassment and her anger at Nestor. Air of a near polar purity and chilliness blew in through the window and calmed her, and she saw in the dusk that the landscape wasn't bundles of tweed but long, rolling waves of woodland, field, and pasture under a sky bigger than a Colorado sky, a glassy star-pricked dome that didn't dwarf the two of them but rather conferred on them an almost ceremonial sense of isolation. No other cars appeared on the road. They passed small granite villages and plowed fields full of clods the size of a child's head, and Elizabeth felt the man beside her studying her without haste, without real curiosity, his cold gaze occasionally leaving the road and passing over her like a beam from a lighthouse.

Edo was wondering whether his young jackass of a nephew had for once done him a favor. But he himself had offered no kindness that merited return, and Nestor was ungenerous, like the rest of Edo's mother's family. Perhaps the girl's arriving like this was a practical joke: he remembered the time in Rome when a half-clothed Cinecittà starlet had appeared on his terrace at dawn, sent by his friends but claiming to have been transported there by group telekinesis during a séance. But Elizabeth's irritation, barely lacquered with politeness, was genuine, and lent a most profound resonance to her odd entrance. In the half light he admired the gallant disposition of her features below her short, fair hair, the way she talked in very good Italian, looking severely out of the window, from time to time throwing her neck to one side in her camel hair collar, like a young officer impatient with uniforms.

"We're on my land now," he said after forty minutes, and she observed ridges of pleated dark forest and a jumble of blond hills. Down a slope behind a wall of elms was the house — a former grange, two hundred years old, long and low, with wings built on around a courtyard. With windows set deeply below an overhanging slate roof, it looked defensive and determined to endure; on each wing, black support beams of crudely lapped pine gave it the air of an archaic fortification. When Edo opened the Land Rover's door for her and she stepped out onto the gravel, the air struck her lungs with a raw freshness that was almost painful.

"Why do you live here?" Elizabeth had changed from jeans into a soft, rust-colored wool dress that she wore to the bank on days when she felt accommodating and merciful. She stood in front of the fire with one of the red Venetian goblets in her hand, feeling the airiness of the crystal, balancing it like a dandelion globe she was about to blow, watching the firelight reflecting on all the small polished objects in the long, low-ceilinged room so that they sparkled like the lights of a distant city. She knew the answer: gossipy Nestor had gone on at length about Byzantine inheritance disputes, vengeful ex-wives, and drawn-out tantrums in climacteric princes. However, with Edo standing before her so literally small and slight but at the same time vibrant with authority, so that one noticed his slightness almost apologetically — with him playing host with immaculate discretion, yet offering, subtly, an insistent homage — she felt strangely defenseless. She felt, in fact, that she had to buy time. Already she was deliberately displaying herself, as the fire heated the backs of her legs. Before she let everything go she wanted to understand why suddenly she felt so excited and so lost and so unconcerned about both.

"Why do I live here? To get clear of petty thieves," he said with a smile. "The daily sort, the most sordid kind — family and lovers. When I got fed up with all of them a few years ago, it occurred to me that I didn't have to go off to live in Geneva like some dismal old fool of an exile. Africa was out, because after a certain age one ends up strapped to a gin bottle there. So I came up here among the fog and the gorse. I like the birds in Scotland, and the people are tightfisted and have healthy bowels, like me." He paused, regarding her with the truculent air of a man accustomed to being indulged as an eccentric, and Elizabeth looked back at him calmly. "Are you hungry?" he asked suddenly.

"I'm very hungry. Since breakfast I've only had a horrible scone."

"Horrible scones are only served in this house for tea. I have something ready which I'll heat up for you. No, I don't want any help; I'll bring it to you as you sit here. It will be the most exquisite pleasure for me to wait on you. There is some snipe that a nephew of mine, not Nestor, shot in Sicily last fall."

"What do you think happened to Nestor?" asked Elizabeth. "Could you call him?"

"I'd never call that bad-mannered young pederast. He was offensive enough as an adolescent flirting with soldiers. Now he's turned whimsical."

When Edo went off to the kitchen Elizabeth walked back and forth, glancing at photographs and bonbonnières, touching a key on the computer, looking over the books on cookery and game birds, the racecar magazines, the worn, pinkish volumes of the *Almanach de Gotha;* and she smiled wryly at how her heart was beating. In the kitchen Edo coated the small bodies of the snipe in a syrupy, dark sauce while from her corner the Labrador bitch looked at him beseechingly. His thought was: How sudden desire makes solitude — not oppressive but unwieldy, and slightly ludicrous. It was a thought that had not come to him in the last few years — not since his last mistress had begun the inevitable transformation into a sardonic and too knowledgeable friend. Randy old billy goat, he said genially to himself, employing the words of that outspoken lady; and with the alertness he used to follow trails or sense changes in weather he noted that his hand was unsteady as he spooned the sauce.

The next day, Good Friday, they drove a hundred miles to Loch Ness and stood in the rain on a scallop of rocky shore. Edo broke off a rain-battered narcissus and handed it to Elizabeth in silence. He was wearing a khaki jacket with the collar turned up, and suddenly she saw him as he must have been forty years earlier: a thin, big-nosed young man with a grandee's posture — an image now closed within the man in front of her, like something in a reliquary.

On the drive back, he asked her abruptly whether she knew who he was, told her that his curious first name (Edo was the third in a procession) had set a prewar fashion for hundreds of babies whose mothers wanted to copy the choice of a princess. It was a rather pathetic thing to say, thought Elizabeth, who from

Nestor knew all about him and the family, even down to alliances with various unsavory political regimes. Long beams of sunlight broke through over pastures where lambs jumped and ewes showed patches of red or blue dye on their backs, depending on which ram had covered them; shadows of clouds slid over the highlands in the distance. Edo drove her across a grouse moor and talked about drainage and pesticides and burning off old growth, about geese and partridge and snipe.

Then he said: "I want the two of us to have some kind of love story. Am I too old and deaf?"

"I don't know," said Elizabeth.

"I've quarreled with nearly everyone, I'm solitary and selfish, and I understand dogs better than women. I have been extremely promiscuous, but I have no known disease. That's just to prevent any misunderstanding."

"It doesn't sound very appealing."

"No, but I have a foolish, optimistic feeling that it might appeal to you. The thing I like most is a girl from a good family who dresses vulgarly once in a while. Nothing flashy — just the cook's night out. And schoolgirl underclothes, the kind the nuns made my sisters wear. Do you think you'd be willing to do that for me?"

"I might." Elizabeth felt as if she were about to burst with laughter. Everything seemed overly simple — as it did, she knew, at the beginning of the most harrowing romances. Yet, laughing inside, she felt curiously tender and indulgent toward him and toward herself. Why not? she thought. During the rest of the trip home they traded stories about former lovers with a bumptious ease startling under the circumstances, as if they were already old friends who themselves had gotten over the stage of going to bed. His were all bawdy and funny: making love to a fat Egyptian princess on a bathroom sink, which broke; an actress who cultivated three long, golden hairs on a mole in an intimate place.

The telephone rang before dinner that night, and it was Nestor. He was in France, in some place where there were a lot of people and the line kept dropping; he wanted to know whether Elizabeth had arrived. His uncle swore at him and said that no one — male, female, fish, or fowl — had arrived and that he was spending Easter alone. Then Edo slammed the phone down and looked at Elizabeth. "Now you're out of the world," he told her. "You're invisible and free."

They stood looking out of the sitting room windows toward the northwest, where a veil of daylight still hung over the Atlantic, and he told her that when seals came ashore on the town beaches people went after them with rifles. He came closer to her, felt desire strike his body like a blow, called himself an old fool, and began to kiss her face. Her hair had a bland fragrance like grain, which called up a buried recollection of a story told him by his first, adored nurse (a Croat with a cast in one eye), about a magic sheaf of wheat that used to turn into a girl, he couldn't remember why or how. Elizabeth remained motionless and experienced for the first time the extraordinary sensation she was to have ever after with Edo: of snatching pleasure and concealing it. "We won't make love tonight," he said to her. "I've already had you in a hundred ways in my mind; I want to know if I can desire you even more. Prolonging anticipation — it's a very selfish taste I have. But without these little devices, I'll be honest with you, things get monotonous too quickly."

Later he told her not to worry, and she said happily, "But I'm not at all worried. In a few months we'll be sick to death of each other."

This arrival at Easter has become currency in Elizabeth's sentimental imagination, but unlike other episodes with other men it doesn't pop up to distract her during work or even very often when she's not working. She has never been anxious about Edo, but she wants to see him often. Though he is never calm, he calms her. When he sends for her and she takes the now familiar flight up to Aberdeen, she feels her life simplified with every moment in the air. It's a feeling like clothes slipping off her body.

She thinks of it this morning as she sits in the sunlight with her knees up under the covers, and she takes possession, a habit of hers, of a phrase from the book she is reading. "So the days pass," she reads, half aloud, "and I ask myself whether one is not hypnotized, as a child by a silver globe, by life, and whether this is living."

3. Sportsmen

For the last ten minutes Elizabeth, the old prince, and three young men have been sitting around the table talking about farts. The young men are Nestor and two cousins of his, whom Elizabeth knows slightly from parties in Rome. All three are tall and thin, with German faces and resonant Italian double last names; they wear threadbare American jeans and faded long-sleeved knit shirts. They are here for a few days' shooting, and in the front hall stand their boots — magnificent boots the color of chestnuts, handmade, lace-up, polished and repolished into the wavering luster of old furniture. The front hall itself is worth a description: wide, bare, pine boards, a worn, brocade armchair, antique decoys, a pair of antlers twenty thousand years old dug from a Hungarian bog, ten green jackets on wall pegs, exhaling scents of rubberized canvas and dog.

The three young men worship Edo — since their nursery days he has been a storybook rakehell uncle, wreathed in a cloud of anecdote unusually thick even for their family. They are also very interested in Elizabeth — two of them because she's so good-looking, and Nestor from a piqued curiosity mixed with sincere affection. She has stopped confiding in him since he mischievously threw her together with his uncle at Easter. He owns the condominium next to the one she rents in Via dei Coronari and knows that she has been using a lot of vacation time going up to Scotland; he assumes that the old skinflint is laying out money for the tickets and that they're sleeping together, but he can't understand what they do for each other, what they do with each other. She is not an adventuress (in his world they still talk about adventuresses), and she is clearly not even infatuated. Elizabeth's non-whim, as he is starting to call it, serves only to confirm in Nestor's frivolous mind the impenetrable mystery that is America.

Elizabeth sits among them like a sphinx — something she learned from watching fashionable Italian women. But she feels conflicted, torn between generations. Edo feels a growing annoyance at seeing how her fresh face fits in among the fresh faces of the young men. Her presence makes the gathering effervescent and unstable, and all the men have perversely formed an alliance and are trying with almost touching transparency to shock her.

"It's a sixteenth-century gadget in copper called *'la péteuse,'* " continues Edo in a gleeful, didactic tone. "It consists of a long, flexible metal tube that was used to convey nocturnal flatus out from between the buttocks, under the covers of the seigneurial bed, into a pot of perfumed water where rose petals floated. I own three of them — one in Paris and the other two in Turin. I keep them with the chastity belts."

Everyone is crunching and sucking the tiny bones of larks grilled on skewers, larks that the guests brought in a neat, foil-wrapped parcel straight from Italy, it being illegal to shoot song-birds in Great Britain. They eat them with toasted strips of polenta, also imported. Elizabeth hates small birds but is determined this evening to hold up the female side; she draws the line at the tiny, contorted heads, which make her think of holocausts and Dantean hells. Game, she thinks, is high in the kind of amino acids that foster gout and aggressive behavior.

"The worst case of flatulence I know of," Edo says, "was the Countess Pentz, a lady-in-waiting to my mother. She was a charming woman with nice big breasts, but she was short and ugly, and farted continuously. It was funny at receptions to see everyone pretending not to notice. I believe she used to wear a huge pair of padded bloomers that muffled the noise to a rumble like distant thunder."

They go on to discuss Hitler and meteorism. One of Nestor's cousins, Giangaleazzo, sends Elizabeth a swift glance of inquiry, perhaps of apology. There is something sweet about that look. Edo sees it and glowers. Elizabeth seizes the opportunity to contribute, mentioning — she realizes it's a mistake the minute she does — Chaucer. Blank looks from the men, although only Edo is truly uneducated. Edo says: "The middle classes always quote literature. It makes them feel secure."

Elizabeth has lived in Rome long enough to be able to throw back a cold-blooded barb of a retort, the kind they don't expect from an American woman. She knows that the young men aren't even surprised by Edo's remark, since it seems to be a family tradition to savage one another like a pack of wolf cubs. But she is looking at the row of restaurant knives and cleavers stuck in back of the long, oiled kitchen counter, and she is imagining the birds heaped in the freezer — small, gnarled bodies the color of cypress bark. She decides that she would like not simply to kill Edo but to gut him swiftly and surgically, the way she has watched him so many times draw a grouse.

When they have finished the larks and the young men are eating Kit Kat bars and drinking whiskey, they complete the fraternal atmosphere by launching into a *canzone goliarda,* a bawdy student song. This one has nearly twenty verses and is about a monk who confesses women on a stormy night and the various obscene penances he has them perform:

Con questa pioggia, questo vento,
Chi è chi bussa a mio convento?

Between verses Edo looks at her without remorse. He's thinking, She's tough, she holds up — which is one of his highest compliments. "You look like a wild animal when you get angry," he tells her, and she hates herself for the way her heart leaps. Just before midnight she lies in bed wondering whether he will come down to her. She will not go to him; she wants him to come to her room so she can treat him badly. She lies there feeling vengeful and willfully passive, imagining herself a Victorian servant girl waiting for the master to descend like Jove; at any minute she expects the doorknob to turn. But he doesn't come, and she falls asleep with the light on. At breakfast the next morning he greets her with great tenderness and tells her that he sat up till dawn with Nestor, discussing fishing rights on a family property in Spain.

4. *Halloween*

Bent double, Edo and Elizabeth creep through a stand of spindly larch and bilberry toward the pond where the wild geese are settling for the night. It is after four on a cold, clear afternoon, with the sun already behind the hills and a concentrated essence of leaf meal and wet earth rising headily at their footsteps — an elixir of autumn. Edo moves silently ahead of Elizabeth, never breaking a twig. His white head is drawn down into the collar of his green jacket, and his body is relaxed and intent, the way he has held it stalking game over the last fifty years in Yugoslavia, Tanzania, Persia.

Even before they could see the pond, when they were still in the Land Rover, chivying stolid Hertfordshire cows, and then on foot working open a gate that the tenant farmer had secured sloppily with a clothesline and a piece of iron bedstead — even then the air reverberated with the voices and wingbeats of the geese. The sound created a live force around the two of them, as if invisible spirits were bustling by in the wind. Now, from the corner of the grove, Edo and Elizabeth spy on two or three hundred geese in a crowd as thick and raucous as bathers on a city beach: preening, socializing, some pulling at sedges in the water of the murky little pond, others arriving from the sky in unraveling skeins, calling, wheeling, landing. Sometimes during the great fall and spring migrations, over two thousand at a time stop at Edo's pond.

He brought them here himself, using his encyclopedic knowledge of waterfowl to create a landscape he knew would attract them. He selected the unprepossessing, scrubby countryside after observation of topography and migratory patterns, and enlarged the weedy pond to fit an exact mental image of the shape and disposition needed to work together in a kind of sorcery to pull the lovely winged transients, pair by pair, out of the sky. After three years, the visiting geese have become a county curiosity. Local crofters have lodged repeated complaints. Edo doesn't shoot the geese; he watches them. This passion for the nobler game birds is the purest, most durable emotion he has known in his life; it was the same when he used to lie in wait for hours in order to kill them. Now he's had enough shooting, but the passion remains.

He grips Elizabeth's arm as he points out a pair of greylags in the garrulous crowd on the water. His hand on her arm is like stone, and Elizabeth, who loves going to watch the geese, nevertheless finds something brittle and old-maidish in the fixity of his interest. Crouching beside him, she experiences an arid sense of hopelessness, of jealousy — she isn't sure of what. Casting about, she thinks of his ex-lovers who sometimes call or visit — European women near his own age who seem to have absorbed some terrible erotic truth that they express in throaty laughter and an inhuman poise in the smoking of cigarettes and in the crossing of their still beautiful legs. They are possessive of Edo, and they make her feel raw as a nursery child brought out on display. But she knows they aren't the real reason that she feels cold around the heart.

"You're not interested in getting married, are you?" He says it abruptly, once they have returned to the Land Rover. He says it in French, his language for problems, reasoning, and resolution. He hears his own terror and looks irritably away from her. It is six months since they met.

"No, I'm not," replies Elizabeth. She is embarrassed by the fatuous promptness with which the words bound out, like a grade-school recitation. Yet she hadn't prepared them. She hadn't prepared anything. They are bouncing across stubble, and to the west, where the evening light is stronger, a few green patches shine with weird intensity among the autumn browns: barley fields planted this month to be harvested in January or February. On the horizon, below a small, spiky gray cloud, a bright planet regards them equably. Without another word, Edo stops the motor and reaches over to unzip her jacket and unbutton her shirt. With the same rapt, careful movements he used in approaching the geese, he bends his head and kisses her breasts. Then he straightens up and looks at her and a strange thing happens: each understands that they've both been stealing pleasure. For a second they are standing face-to-face in a glass corridor; they see everything. It's a minor miracle that is over before they can realize that it is the most they will have together. Instantly afterward, there is only the sense of a bright presence already departed, and the two of them faltering near the edge of an indefinable danger. As Elizabeth buttons her shirt and Edo turns the ignition key, they are already engaged in small, expert movements of denial and retreat. The jeep pulls out onto the darkening road, and neither finds a further word to say.

A tumult of wind and dogs greets them as they pull up ten minutes later to the house. Dervishes of leaves spin on the gravel beside the rented Suzuki that Nestor and his cousins used to get to that day's shoot, near Guthrie. Both Elizabeth and Edo stare in surprise at the kitchen windows, where there is an unusual glow. It looks like something on fire, and for an instant Edo has the sensation of disaster — a conflagration not of his house, nothing so real, but a mirage of a burning city, a sign transplanted from a dream.

"What have they gotten up to, the young jackasses?" he says, climbing hurriedly out of the jeep. But Elizabeth sees quite clearly what Nestor and his cousins have done and, with an odd sense of relief, starts to giggle. They've carved four pumpkins with horrible faces, put candles inside, and lined them up on the windowsills. She interprets it as a message to her, since yesterday she and Giangaleazzo, who went to Brown, had been talking about Halloween in New England. "It's Halloween," she says, in a voice pitched a shade too high. She feels a sudden defensive solidarity with the jumble of young men in the kitchen, who are drinking Guinness and snuffing like hungry retrievers under the lids of the saucepans.

"Jackasses," repeats Edo, who at the best of times defines as gross presumption any practical joke he hasn't thought up himself. In this mood, his superstitious mind is shaken, and he can't cast off that disastrous first vision. He hurries inside, telling her to follow him.

Instead, Elizabeth lets the door close and lingers outside, looking at the glowing vegetable faces and feeling the cold wind shove her hair back from her forehead. She wills herself not to think of Edo. Instead she thinks of a Halloween in Dover when she was eight or nine and stood for a long time on the doorstep of her own house after her brothers and everyone else had gone inside. The two big elms leaned over the moon, and the jack-o'-lantern in the front window had a thick dribble of wax depending from its grin, and she had had to pee badly, but she had kept standing there, feeling the urine pressing down in her bladder, clutching a cold hand between her legs where the black cheesecloth of her witch costume bunched together. She'd stood there feeling excitement and terror at the small, dark world she had created around herself simply by holding back. It's an erotic memory that she has always felt vaguely ashamed of, but at the moment it seems curiously appropriate, a pleasure she'd enjoyed without guessing its nature.

Edo opens the kitchen door and calls her, and she comes toward him across the gravel. For a moment before he can see her clearly, he has the idea that there is a difference in the way she is moving, that her face may hold an expression that will change everything. Once, thirty years ago, in Persia, he and his brother Prospero saw a ball of dust coming toward them over the desert, a ball of dust that pulled up in front of them and turned into a Rolls-Royce, with a body made, impossibly, of wicker, and, inside, two young Persian noblemen, their friends, laughing, with falcons on their wrists. He and his brother and the gunbearers had stood there as if in front of something conjured up by djinns. He watches Elizabeth come with the same stilling of the senses as he had that afternoon in the desert. When she gets closer, though, the dust, as it were, settles, and his wavering perspective returns to normal, there on the doorstep of his last, his favorite house, in the cold October night. He thinks of the unspoken bargain she has kept so magnificently for a woman of her age, for any woman, and he says to himself, Very well. He has studied nature too long to denigrate necessity. Then why the word thudding inside him, first like an appeal, then a pronouncement: "Never, never, never"? Never, then.

Laughter comes from behind him. His nephews to summon him have launched into the ribald student song from the other night. When Elizabeth reaches him he doesn't look anymore but takes her arm firmly, draws her inside, and shuts the door.

JOANNA SCOTT

Concerning Mold upon the Skin, Etc.

FROM ANTAEUS

HE WAS A MAN distracted by his ignorance, acutely aware of the limits of his knowledge and therefore superior, in his own opinion, to his ignorant and complacent neighbors. He wanted to know what he didn't know and since his youth had devoted himself to the effort of knowing more. Not Faustian ambition but fresh wonder kept him awake at night, caused him to break out in a cold sweat when he held up a finished lens to a candle flame, displaced all other appetites. And even though his neglected wife took to entertaining suitors in her own bedroom and his horns were visible to everyone, he didn't care. He cared only about what was invisible, knew that what the human eye could see or the ideas that the mind could conceive constituted a mere fraction of the world. Most of his contemporaries were satisfied with the dual concepts of substance and spirit. But even as a child he had sensed that the world of substances did not end with man's perception of it. Just as the sky disappeared into the invisible heavens, the material world disappeared into its invisible parts and so could never be examined in its entirety.

The obscurity of minutiae thrilled and maddened him — literally drove him mad. When he was a young man of twenty-six he built a laboratory in the back of his dry goods shop, at first simply a room where he could be alone with his experiments but eventually the room in which he ate, drank, and slept. And on the day he dragged his bedding into the laboratory, his wife stopped pleading with him and offered herself to an eager gallant. Too distracted by love and lust ever to give her husband a second thought again, she left it to her eldest daughter, Marie, to carry in her father's meals, which he hardly touched, and, later in his life, to bring him his mail, which he devoured with insane, carnivorous impatience.

Born in 1632, he was a citizen of Delft, a linen-draper by profession as well as an official of the Delft City Council. And it must be said on his behalf that for many years he continued dutifully to measure and cut and sell his bolts of cloth, despite his consuming passion. Every day but Sunday he worked in the shop, and he spent three evenings out of the week examining the newest weights and measures in the City Hall. He worked at these jobs that he detested with stoical persistence in order to support his family so that they would leave him alone.

Alone. How he loved the solitude of winter nights, his laboratory lined with candelabra, concave lenses trapping the reflections so the flames seemed buried inside the thin glass disks like fish in ice. He loved the silence, the cold, even the stiffness of his fingers because the discomfort reminded him that he was alive, and as long as he remained alive he could extend the perimeter of his knowledge a little further, could know just a little more, could see what he could see, each night something new and, in its newness, astonishing.

He had learned the rudiments of grinding lenses from a spectacle-maker in Amsterdam. He bought his glass from alchemists and apothecaries. He made his oblong mounts of copper and gold himself. While the people of Delft sniggered at him behind his back, he perfected his craft and after years of painstaking experiment found a method for making a magnifying lens less than an eighth of an inch across. It took him three months to grind and polish fine a single tiny lens, and when he had two such lenses he mounted one above the other between adjustable metal plates. He was twenty-seven when he finished assembling the world's first microscope, yet his hands shook like an old man's. Even as he bent to look through the lenses he had a suspicion that nothing he'd seen before had prepared him for this.

"So symmetrical, so perfect, that it shows little things to me with a fantastic clear enormousness," he wrote in his diary, in

Dutch. Dutch. The language of fishermen, of ditchdiggers, of shopkeepers. He couldn't speak Latin, so he could not — *would not* — tell anyone about how he had invented an instrument far more powerful than Hook's microscope, an instrument that made the invisible world visible. His account would have seemed not only unbelievable, but vulgar, too. Better to keep his discoveries to himself, to hoard them with a miser's glee. He had contrived the microscope for his own use — he would relish his discoveries with a pleasure that was all the more intoxicating because it was secret.

Entirely on his own, for his own benefit, deriving his own conclusions, he examined shreds of cabbage, ox eyes, chicken livers, beaver hides, fingernail clippings, mustache whiskers, the sting of a flea, the legs of a louse, dry skin scraped from his arm. He took to stalking flies during the day in his dry goods shop, climbing over counters and up shelves, trapping the insects between cupped hands and closing them in glass jars so that they died — intact — from suffocation. At first his customers stared with the scornful delight of a fool's audience, then with increasing impatience, and soon they stopped watching him at all. They left the shop without waiting for their fabric and would never have come back again if it hadn't been for Marie.

Lovely Marie, with ruddy cheeks always aglow, like her father's fine lenses. Marie coaxed the women of Delft to return to the shop, and she gave up her study of French so she could wait on the customers herself. She rescued her father's business, but not because she loved him. More than she loved her father she resented him, along with the rest of Delft believed him to be insane. But she had a strong, seventeenth-century sense of obligation. She was a daughter. Unlike her mother, who had stopped being a proper wife when her husband stopped being a husband, Marie would always be the eldest daughter of the mad lensgrinder of Delft, would cling to the identity through her father's long (sometimes she feared it would be endless) life, until he died at the ripe old age of eighty-one and she, herself an old woman of sixty by then, could close up the shop and with her small inheritance live quietly, reclusively, depended upon by no one.

"Steady elfkin, Papa's dearest." He'd say this not to her nor to her brothers and sisters, but to a dead fly as he carefully dissected its head and stuck its brain on the tip of a needle. *Papa's dearest.* What a mockery of paternal solicitude. Marie would set down his tray with his dinner and turn away in disgust, leaving her crazed father alone with his purposeless instruments.

Deliciously alone in his invisible world.

There is nothing more aesthetically satisfying than form that convinces us of its perfection, Marie's father believed, nothing more incredible than perfection in miniature. So even if he had wanted to tell someone — and gradually, over the years, the urge to tell began to displace the urge to protect his secret — who would believe him? He would have to tell it in Dutch. An incredible story in Dutch! They would laugh at him, and their laughter would seduce him like the Sirens' song until he started laughing, too, laughing along with them, laughing at himself.

But if he couldn't tell them, he could show them. He had to show them before he died. Or show one of them, one man, someone he could trust, a scientist, yes, he knew a worthy man: Regnier de Graaf, the only man in Delft who was a corresponding member of the Royal Society. He was forty-one years old when he invited de Graaf into his laboratory; he felt like a four-year-old child, though, as de Graaf bent down to look through his microscope at the strand of hair — Marie's hair, which she had generously plucked for them. She watched too, not with her father's anxious anticipation but with an air of disapproval, as though she were the mother of the four-year-old boy, tapping her foot as steadily as a clock's pendulum, waiting for de Graaf to get on with it.

He was slow. Annoyingly slow, in Marie's opinion. Terrifyingly slow to her father. But when de Graaf finally straightened his stooped back, took off his spectacles, wiped his rheumy eyes, he said, shaking his head, exactly what Marie's father had hoped to hear.

"Good God."

Yes, God was good. So good that after Marie's father, with de Graaf's recommendation, wrote a rambling eight-page letter to the Royal Society of London, they wrote back. The Royal Society. They had proven false many superstitions of the day, including, most famously, this: that a spider in a circle made of the powder of a unicorn's horn cannot crawl out. Indeed, it can and will crawl out, and very quickly! The Royal Society had performed the experiment themselves in London. Marvelous men. And these same scientists were not only interested in the lens-grinder of Delft but wanted to know more.

So he told them what he'd seen, told them almost everything. In Dutch, no less! Now when he wasn't looking through his microscope he was answering their questions, describing the "little things" in careful detail. Yet he still refused, despite the repeated requests of the Royal Society, to explain how to assemble his powerful microscope. This could wait. The eminent gentlemen far away in London hadn't earned his trust yet. He didn't trust anything or anyone he hadn't seen.

And then one night a year later, after fourteen days of constant rain, the dampness inside the house so dense that bedclothes were soaked by morning, he turned his instrument upon a drop of water from a cistern. Why he hadn't done this before he couldn't say — later in his life he would regret nothing as much as the fact that he'd wasted so many years examining dead and inanimate things. Because what he saw that night was more wonderful than anything else — yes, it was the nourishment that wonder seeks: life.

He tried to restrain his passion as he wrote to the Royal Society:

> I saw, with great amazement, that this material contained many tiny animals which moved about in a most amusing fashion, some spinning around like tops; others, exceedingly tiny, moved so rapidly helter-skelter that they looked like a confused swarm of dancing gnats or flies.

He showed no such restraint, however, when his daughter, Marie, entered the laboratory. He stood up from his desk with such haste that he knocked over his inkwell, and the dark liquid spread over his unfinished letter until it assumed the shape of a man's boot. Beautiful black liquid. Life in liquid. With his microscope he would examine all kinds of watery substances — well water, canal water, sugar water, saliva, perspiration, semen, blood! He would investigate every form of liquid in the world.

He rushed at his daughter, and she managed to set down the tray with the flask of wine before he grabbed her. "Marie!" he sobbed, burying his face in her neck.

Was he weeping? Marie wondered. Had he, at long last, come

to his senses and recognized that he'd been neglecting his family? Was this the anguish of remorse? No, he'd lost what little sense he had left, Marie realized when he lifted up his face. He was a small man and she a tall woman, so in her adult years she towered above him. She looked down on him then. He was laughing, his lips peeled back as though drawn by thread. A puppet's face made of wood and velvet, that's what she was reminded of right then, and the laughter seemed to come from a separate source across the room — from another man, a stranger, the devil hiding in the shadows, laughing for her father, through her father. And if she still fought to recognize her father in that grotesque face, she knew he was lost to her forever as soon as he spoke.

"Marie, dearest Marie. Give me a tear."

Ah, what a plaintive voice, what a pathetic man. He would always be mad — there was no chance of recovery and therefore he would never feel remorse. She despised him right then. He would never feel remorse for what he'd done to her and would never feel gratitude for all that she'd done for him. Yet she was obligated to her father, or to the demon who had taken possession of him. Without her obligation she would have been nothing — this was the fault of the century, not her own fault, not even her father's. She didn't blame him for the obligation, only for his selfishness. His selfishness. Yes, for this she despised him, this mad, cloying, wooden toy of a man. She tried to push him away.

"Marie!" He held her face, brought his lips to hers, kissed her not like a father should kiss a daughter, but like the devil kisses. Marie struggled to free herself. He tasted her with his thin, warm tongue and for a few horrible seconds she couldn't stop him. And then they separated with a gasp and stared at each other in amazement and mutual confusion, mirror images, father and daughter.

What just happened?

It was Marie who understood first. She did not move, only closed her eyes so she would not have to see him. And for a moment her father understood, too. Looking at Marie he couldn't help but understand and was ashamed. But his shame flickered and went out when he saw — *oh, gracious Marie!* — the thing he most desired: a large, milky tear that seeped from between her eyelids and slid down her cheek.

He caught the tear on the knuckle of his thumb and transferred it to a specimen slide. He set the slide on the table. While he was adjusting the glass Marie slipped from the laboratory. He didn't try to stop her, although if he were her, he would have wanted nothing more than to look at this aspect of himself, this expression of modesty, magnified a hundredfold. Filled with generosity, he decided that if she came back he would let her have a peek at this extraordinary image. He reached for the slide again, noticing that in the candlelight the opaque tear was the inimitable color of fire. He admired it for a moment, then positioned the slide below the metal plates, hardly able to manage even this since his hands were trembling so. Even before he had examined the tear he started to compose in his head the letter he would write to the Royal Academy: "an incredible number of little animals of various sorts, which move very prettily, which tumble about and sidewise, this way and that" — words of a man who had neither wealth nor fame but a success far more extraordinary, the freedom to tell the most amazing stories and to be believed. This was the lasting consequence of his invention: He had forever changed the nature of belief. Nothing visible to the naked eye could be trusted anymore, for everything had a secret microscopic life. He, the master of magnification, had made visible the unimaginable.

An incredible number of little animals of various sorts, which move very prettily. Ghosts and demons were pale fantasies compared to these thousands of tiny worms alive in a droplet of water. Among all the minute marvels that he had discovered, this universe inside a tear would be the most marvelous of all — no more astonishing sight had ever come into focus beneath the glass. To the lens-grinder of Delft, there was hardly a difference between discovering life and creating it.

WENDELL BERRY

Pray Without Ceasing

FROM THE SOUTHERN REVIEW

MAT FELTNER WAS MY GRANDFATHER on my mother's side. Saying it thus, I force myself to reckon again with the strangeness of that verb *was*. The man of whom I once was pleased to say, "He is my grandfather," has become the dead man who was my grandfather. He was, and is no more. And this is a part of the great mystery that we call time.

But the past is present also. And this, I think, is a part of the greater mystery we call eternity. Though Mat Feltner has been dead for twenty-five years and I am now older than he was when I was born and have grandchildren of my own, I know his hands, their way of holding a hammer or a hoe or a set of checklines, as well as I know my own. I know his way of talking, his way of cocking his head when he began a story, the smoking pipe stem held an inch from his lips. I have in my mind, not just as a memory but as a consolation, his welcome to me when I returned home from the university and, later, from jobs in distant cities. When I sat down beside him, his hand would clap lightly onto my leg above the knee; my absence might have lasted many months, but he would say as though we had been together the day before, "Hello, Andy." The shape of his hand is printed on the flesh of my thigh as vividly as a birthmark. This man who was my grandfather is present in me, as I felt always his father to be present in him. His father was Ben. The known history of the Feltners in Port William begins with Ben.

But even the unknown past is present in us, its silence as persistent as a ringing in the ears. When I stand in the road that passes through Port William, I am standing on the strata of my history which go down through the known past into the unknown: the blacktop rests on state gravel, which rests on county gravel, which rests on the creek rock and cinders laid down by the town when it was still mostly beyond the reach of the county; and under the creek rock and cinders is the dirt track of the town's beginning, the buffalo trace that was the way we came. You work your way down, or not so much down as within, into the interior of the present, until finally you come to that beginning in which all things, the world and the light itself, at a word welled up into being out of their absence. And nothing is here that we are beyond the reach of merely because we do not know about it. It is always the first morning of Creation and always the last day, always the now that is in time and the now that is not, that has filled time with reminders of itself.

When my grandfather was dying, I was not thinking about the past. My grandfather was still a man I knew, but as he subsided day by day he was ceasing to be the man I had known. I was experiencing consciously for the first time that transformation in which the living, by dying, pass into the living, and I was full of grief and love and wonder.

And so when I came out of the house one morning after breakfast and found Braymer Hardy sitting in his pickup truck in front of my barn, I wasn't expecting any news. Braymer was an old friend of my father's; he was curious to see what Flora and I would do with the long-abandoned Harford Place that we had bought and were fixing up, and sometimes he visited. His way was not to go to the door and knock. He just drove in and stopped his old truck at the barn and sat looking around until somebody showed up.

"Well, you ain't much of a Catlett," he said, in perfect good humor. "Marce Catlett would have been out and gone two hours ago."

"I do my chores *before* breakfast," I said, embarrassed by the lack of evidence. My grandfather Catlett would, in fact, have been out and gone two hours ago.

"But," Braymer said in an explanatory tone, as if talking to himself, "I reckon your daddy is a late sleeper, being as he's an office man. But that Wheeler was always a shotgun once he *got* out," he went on, clearly implying, and still in excellent humor, that the family line had reached its nadir in me. "But maybe you're a right smart occupied of a night, I don't know." He raked a large cud of tobacco out of his cheek with his forefinger and spat.

He looked around with the air of a man completing an inspection, which is exactly what he was doing. "Well, it looks like you're making a little headway. You got it looking some better. Here," he said, pawing among a litter of paper, tools, and other odds and ends on top of the dashboard and then on the seat beside him, "I brought you something." He eventually forcepped forth an old newspaper page folded into a tight rectangle the size of a wallet and handed it through the truck window. "You ought to have it. It ain't no good to me. The madam, you know, is hell for an antique. She bought an old desk at a sale, and that was in one of the drawers."

I unfolded the paper and read the headline: BEN FELTNER, FRIEND TO ALL, SHOT DEAD IN PORT WILLIAM. "Ben Feltner was your great-granddaddy."

"Yes. I know."

"I remember him. He was fine as they come. They never made 'em no finer. The last man on earth you'd a thought would get shot."

"So I've heard."

"Thad Coulter was a good kind of feller, too, far as that goes. I don't reckon he was the kind you'd a thought would shoot somebody, either."

He pushed his hat back and scratched his forehead. "One of them things," he said. "They happen."

He scratched his head some more and propped his wrist on top of the steering wheel, letting the hand dangle. "Tell you," he said, "there ain't a way in this world to know what a human creature is going to do next. I loaned a feller five hundred dollars once. He was a good feller, too, wasn't a thing wrong with him far as I knew, I liked him. And dogged if he didn't kill himself 'fore it was a week."

"Killed himself," I said.

"*Killed* himself," Braymer said. He meditated a moment, looking off at his memory of the fellow and wiggling two of the fingers that hung over the steering wheel. "Don't you know," he said, "not wishing him no bad luck, but I wished he'd a done it a week or two sooner."

I laughed.

"Well," he said, "I know you want to be at work. I'll get out of your way."

I said, "Don't be in a hurry," but he was starting the truck and didn't hear me. I called, "Thanks!" as he backed around. He raised his hand, not looking at me, and drove away, steering with both hands, with large deliberate motions, as if the truck were the size of a towboat.

There was an upturned feed bucket just inside the barn door. I sat down on it and unfolded the paper again. It was the front page of the Hargrave *Weekly Express*, flimsy and yellow, nearly illegible in some of the creases. It told how, on a Saturday morning in July of 1912, Ben Feltner, who so far as was known had had no enemies, had been killed by a single shot to the head from a .22 caliber revolver. His assailant, Thad Coulter, had said, upon turning himself in to the sheriff at Hargrave soon after the incident, "I've killed the best friend I ever had." It was not a long article. It told about the interment of Ben Feltner and named his survivors. It told nothing that I did not know, and I knew little more than it told. I knew that Thad Coulter had killed himself in jail, shortly after the murder. And I knew that he was my grandfather Catlett's first cousin.

I had learned that much not from anyone's attempt, ever, to tell me the story, but from bits and pieces dropped out of conversations among my elders, in and out of the family. Once, for instance, I heard my mother say to my father that she had always been troubled by the thought of Thad Coulter's lonely anguish as he prepared to kill himself in the Hargrave jail. I had learned what I knew, the bare outline of the event, without asking questions, both fearing the pain that I knew surrounded the story and honoring the silence that surrounded the pain.

But sitting in the barn that morning, looking at the old page opened on my knees, I saw how incomplete the story was as the article told it, and as I knew it. And seeing it so, I felt incomplete myself. I suddenly wanted to go and see my grandfather. I did not intend to question him. I had never heard him speak so much as a word about his father's death, and I could not have imagined breaking his silence. I wanted only to be in his presence, as if in his presence I could somehow enter into the presence of an agony that I knew had shaped us all.

With the paper folded again in my shirt pocket, I drove the two miles to Port William and turned in under the old maples beside the house. When I let myself in, the house was quiet, and I went as quietly as I could to my grandfather's room, thinking he might be asleep. But he was awake, his fingers laced together on top of the bedclothes. He had seen me drive in, and was watching the door when I entered the room.

"Morning," I said.

He said, "Morning, son," and lifted one of his hands.

"How're you feeling?"

"Still feeling."

I sat down in the rocker by the bed and told him, in Braymer's words, the story of the too-late suicide.

My grandfather laughed. "I expect that grieved Braymer."

"Is Braymer pretty tight?" I asked, knowing he was.

"I wouldn't say 'tight,' but he'd know the history of every dollar he ever made. Braymer's done a lot of hard work."

My grandmother had heard us talking, and now she called me. "Oh, Andy!"

"I'll be back," I said, and went to see what she wanted.

She was sitting in the small bedroom by the kitchen where she had always done her sewing, and where she slept now that my grandfather was ill. She was sitting by the window in the small cane-bottomed rocking chair that was her favorite. Her hands were lying on her lap and she was not rocking. I knew that her arthritis was hurting her; otherwise, at that time of day, she would have been busy at something. She had medicine for the arthritis, but it made her feel unlike herself; up to a certain point of endurability, she preferred the pain. She sat still and let the pain go its way and occupied her mind with thoughts. Or that is what she said she did. I believed, and I was as sure as if she had told me, that when she sat alone that way, hurting or not, she was praying. Though I never heard her pray aloud in my life, it seems to me now that I can reproduce in my mind the very voice of her prayers.

She had called me in to find out things, which was her way. I sat down on the stool in front of her and submitted to examination. She wanted to know what Flora was doing, and what the children were doing, and when I had seen my mother, and what she had been doing. She asked exacting questions that called for much detail in the answers, watching me intently to see that I withheld nothing. She did not tolerate secrets, even the most considerate ones. She had learned that we sometimes omitted or rearranged facts to keep her from worrying, but her objection to that was both principled and passionate. If we were worried, she wanted to worry with us; it was her place, she said.

After a while, she quit asking questions, but continued to look at me. And then she said, "You're thinking about something you're not saying. What is it? Tell Granny."

She had said that to me many times in the thirty years I had known her. By then, I thought it was funny. But if I was no longer intimidated, I was still compelled. In thirty years I had never been able to deceive her when she was looking straight at me. I could have lied, but she would have known it, and then would have supposed that somebody was sick. I laughed and handed her the paper out of my pocket.

"Braymer Hardy brought that to me this morning."

She unfolded it, read a little of the article, but not all, and folded it back up. Her hands lay quiet in her lap again, and she looked out the window, though obviously not seeing what was out there that morning. Another morning had come to her, and she was seeing it again through the interval of fifty-three years.

"It's a wonder," she said, "that Mat didn't kill Thad Coulter that morning."

I said, "Granddad?"

And then she told me the story. She told it quietly, looking through the window into that July morning in 1912. Her hands lay in her lap and never moved. The only effect her telling had on her was a glistening that appeared from time to time in her eyes. She told the story well, giving many details. She had a good memory, and she had lived many years with her mother-in-law, who also had a good one. I have the impression that they, but not my grandfather, had pondered together over the event many times. She spoke as if she were seeing it all happen, even the parts of it that she had not in fact seen.

"If it hadn't been for Jack Beechum, Mat *would* have killed him," my grandmother said.

That was the point. Or it was one of the points — the one, perhaps, that she most wanted me to see. But it was not the beginning of the story. Adam and Eve and then Cain and Abel began it, as my grandmother depended on me to know. Even in Thad Coulter's part of the story, the beginning was some years earlier than July of 1912.

Abner Coulter, Thad's only son, had hired himself out to a grocer in Hargrave. After a few years, when he had (in his own estimation) learned the trade, he undertook to go into business for himself in competition with his former employer. He rented a building right on the courthouse square. He was enabled to do this by a sizable sum of money borrowed from the Hargrave bank on a note secured by a mortgage on his father's farm.

And here Thad's character enters into the story. For Thad not only secured his son's note with the farm that was all he had in the world, and that he had only recently finished paying for, but he further committed himself by bragging in Port William of his son's new status as a merchant in the county seat.

"Thad Coulter was not a bad man," my grandmother said. "I believed then, and I believe now, that he was not a bad man. But we are all as little children. Some know it and some don't."

She looked at me to see if I was one who knew it, and I nodded, but I was thirty then and did not know it yet.

"He was as a little child," she said, "and he was in serious trouble."

He had in effect given his life and its entire effort as hostage to the possibility that Abner, his only son, could be made a merchant in a better place than Port William.

Before two years were out, Abner repaid his father's confidence by converting many small private fritterings and derelictions into an undisguisable public failure, and thereupon by riding off to somewhere unknown on the back of a bay gelding borrowed ostensibly for an overnight trip to Port William. And so Thad's fate was passed from the reckless care of his son to the small mercy of the law. Without more help than he could confidently expect, he was going to lose his farm. Even with help, he was going to have to pay for it again, and he was close to sixty years old.

As he rode home from his interview with the Hargrave banker, in which the writing on the wall had been made plain to him, he was gouging his heel urgently into the mule's flank. Since he had got up out of the chair in the banker's office, he had been full of a desire as compelling as thirst to get home, to get stopped, to get low to the ground, as if to prevent himself from falling off the world. For the country that he had known all his life and had depended on, at least in dry weather, to be solid and steady underfoot, had suddenly risen under him like a wave.

Needing help as he did, he could not at first bring himself to ask for it. Instead, he spent most of two days propped against a post in his barn, drinking heavily and talking to himself about betrayal, ruin, the coldheartedness of the Hargrave bankers, and the poor doings of damned fools, meaning both Abner and himself. And he recalled, with shocks of bitterness that only the whiskey could assuage, his confident words in Port William about Abner and his prospects.

"I worked for it, and I come to own it," he said over and over again. "Now them will own it that never worked for it. And him that stood on it to mount up into the world done run to perdition without a patch, damn him, to cover his ass or a rag to hide his face."

When his wife and daughter begged him to come into the house, he said that a man without the sense to keep a house did not deserve to be in one. He said he would shelter with the dogs and hogs, where he belonged.

The logical source of help was Ben Feltner. Ben had helped Thad to buy his farm — had signed his note and stood behind him. Ben was his friend, and friendship mattered to Ben; it may have mattered to him above all. But Thad did not go to Ben until after his second night in the barn. He walked to Ben's house in Port William early in the morning, drunk and unsteady, his mind tattered and raw from repeated plunges through the thorns and briars of his ruin.

Ben was astonished by the look of him. Thad had always been a man who used himself hard, and he had grown gaunt and stooped, his mouth slowly caving in as he lost his teeth. But that morning he was also soiled, sagging, unshaved and uncombed, his eyes bloodshot and glary. Ben said, "Come in, Thad. Come in and sit down." And he took him by the arm, led him in to a chair, and sat down facing him.

"They got me, Ben," Thad said, the flesh twitching around his eyes. "They done got me to where I can't get loose." His eyes glazed by tears that never fell, he made as much sense of his calamity as he was able to make: "A poor man don't stand no show." And then, his mind lurching on, unable to stop, he fell to cursing, first Abner, and then the Hargrave bank, and then the ways of the world that afforded no show to a poor man.

Ben listened to it all, sitting with his elbow on the chair arm and his forefinger pointed against his cheek. Thad's language and his ranting in that place would not have been excusable had he been sober. But insofar as Thad was drunk, Ben was patient. He listened attentively, his eyes on Thad's face, except that from time to time he looked down at his beard as if to give Thad an opportunity to see that he should stop.

Finally Ben stopped him. "Thad, I'll tell you what. I don't believe I can talk with you anymore this morning. Go home, now, and get sober and come back. And then we'll see."

Thad did not have to take Ben's words as an insult. But in his circumstances and condition, it was perhaps inevitable that he would. That Ben was his friend made the offense worse — far worse. In refusing to talk to him as he was, Ben, it seemed to Thad, had exiled him from the society of human beings, had withdrawn the last vestige of a possibility that he might find anywhere a redemption for himself, much less for his forfeited land. For Thad was not able then to distinguish between himself as he was and himself as he might be sober. He saw himself already as a proven fool, fit only for the company of dogs and hogs. If he could have accepted this judgment of himself, then his story would at least have been different, and would perhaps have been better. But while he felt the force and truth of his own judgment, he raged against it. He had fled to Ben, hoping that somehow, by some means that he could not imagine, Ben could release him from the solitary cage of his self-condemnation. And now Ben had shut the door.

Thad's whole face began to twitch and his hands to move aimlessly, as if his body were being manipulated from the inside by some intention that he could not control. Patches of white appeared under his whiskers. He said, "I cuss you to your damned face, Ben Feltner, for I have come to you with my hat in my hand and you have spit in it. You have throwed in your lot with them sons of bitches against me."

At that Ben reached his limit. Yet even then he did not become angry. He was a large, unfearful man, and his self-defense had something of merriment in it. He stood up. "Now, Thad, my friend," he said, "you must go." And he helped him to the door. He did not do so violently or with excessive force. But though he was seventy-two years old, Ben was still in hearty strength, and he helped Thad to the door in such a way that Thad had no choice but to go.

But Thad did not go home. He stayed, hovering about the front of the house, for an hour or more.

"It seemed like hours and hours that he stayed out there," my grandmother said. She and my great-grandmother, Nancy, and old Aunt Cass, the cook, had overheard the conversation between Ben and Thad, or had overheard at least Thad's part of it, and afterward they watched him from the windows, for his fury had left an influence. The house was filled with a quiet that seemed to remember with sorrow the quiet that had been in it before Thad had come.

The morning was bright and still, and it was getting hot, but Thad seemed unable to distinguish between sun and shade. There had got to be something fluttery or mothlike about him now, so erratic and unsteady and unceasing were his movements. He was talking to himself, nodding or shaking his head, his hands making sudden strange motions without apparent reference to whatever he might have been saying. Now and again he started resolutely toward the house and then swerved away.

All the while the women watched. To my grandmother, remembering, it seemed that they were surrounded by signs that had not yet revealed their significance. Aunt Cass told her afterward, "I dreamed of the dark, Miss Margaret, all full of the sound of crying, and I knowed it was something bad." And it seemed to my grandmother, as she remembered, that she too had felt the house and town and the bright day itself all enclosed in that dreamed darkness full of the sounds of crying.

Finally, looking out to where the road from upriver came over the rise into town, they saw a team and wagon coming. Presently they recognized Thad Coulter's team, a pair of mare mules, one black and the other once gray but now faded to white. They were driven by Thad's daughter, wearing a sunbonnet, a sun-bleached blue cotton dress, and an apron.

"It's Martha Elizabeth," Nancy said.

And Aunt Cass said, "Poor child."

"Well," Nancy said, relieved, "she'll take him home."

When Martha Elizabeth came to where Thad was she stopped the mules and got down. So far as they could see from the house, she did not plead with him; she did not say anything at all. She took hold of him, turned him toward the wagon, and led him to it. She held onto him as he climbed unsteadily up into the wagon and sat down on the spring seat, and then, gathering her skirts in one hand, she climbed up and sat beside him. And all the while she was gentle with him. Afterward, and always, my grandmother remembered how gentle Martha Elizabeth had been with him.

Martha Elizabeth turned the team around, and the Feltner women watched the wagon with its troubled burden go slowly back along the ridgeline. When it had disappeared, they went back to their housework.

Ben, who had meant to go to the field where his hands were at work, did not leave the house as long as Thad was waiting about outside. He saw no point in antagonizing Thad when he did not have to, and so he sat down with a newspaper.

When he knew that Thad was gone and out of sight, Ben got up and put on his hat and went out. He was worried about the state both of Thad's economy and of his mind. He thought he might find some of the other Coulters in town. He didn't know that he would, but it was Saturday, and he probably would.

The Feltner house stood, as it still does, in the overlap of the northeast corner of the town and the southwest corner of Ben's farm. There was a farmstead at each of the town's four corners. There was, as there still is, only the one road, which climbed out of the river valley, crossed a mile of ridge, passed through the town, and, after staying on the ridge another half mile or so, went back down into the valley again. For most of its extent, at that time, it was little more than a wagon track. Most of the goods that reached the Port William merchants still came to the town landing by steamboat and then up the hill by team and wagon. The town itself consisted of perhaps two dozen houses, a church, a blacksmith shop, a bank, a barber shop, a doctor's office, a hotel, two saloons, and four stores that sold a variety of merchandise from groceries to dry goods to hardware to harness. The road that passed through town was there only as a casual and hardly foreseen result of the comings and goings of the inhabitants. An extemporaneous town government had from time to time caused a few loads of creek rock to be hauled and knapped and spread over it, and the townspeople had flung their ashes into it, but that was all. It had never thought of calling itself a street.

Though the houses and shops had been connected for some time by telephone lines carried overhead on peeled and whitewashed locust poles, there was as yet not an automobile in the town. There were times in any year still when Port William could not have been reached by an automobile unless that was accompanied by a team of mules to pull it across the creeks and out of the mud holes.

Except for the telephone lines, the town, as it looked to Ben Feltner on that July morning seventy-eight years ago, might have been unchanged for many more years than it had existed. It looked older than its history. And yet in Port William, as everywhere else, it was already the second decade of the twentieth century. And in some of the people of the town and the community surrounding it, one of the characteristic diseases of the twentieth century was making its way: the suspicion that they would be greatly improved if they were someplace else. This disease had entered into Thad Coulter and into Abner. In Thad it was fast coming to crisis. If Port William could not save him, then surely there was another place that could. But Thad could not just leave, as Abner had; Port William had been too much his life for that. And he was held also by friendship — by his friendship for Ben Feltner, and for himself as a man whom Ben Feltner had befriended — a friendship that Ben Feltner seemed now to have repudiated and made hateful. Port William was a stumbling block to Thad, and he felt he must rid himself of it somehow.

Ben, innocent of the disease that afflicted his friend yet mortally implicated in it and not knowing it, made his way down into the town, looking about in order to gauge its mood — for Port William had its moods, and they needed watching. More energy was generated in the community than the work of the community could consume, and the surplus energy often went into fighting. There had been cuttings and shootings enough. But usually the fighting was more primitive, and the combatants simply threw whatever projectiles came to hand: corncobs, snowballs, green walnuts, or rocks. In the previous winter, a young Coulter by the name of Burley had claimed that he had had an eye blackened by a frozen horse-turd thrown, so far as he could determine, by a Power of the Air. But the place that morning was quiet. Most of the crops had been laid by and many of the farmers were already in town, feeling at ease and inclined to rest now that their annual battle with the weeds had ended. They were sitting on benches and kegs or squatting on their heels under the shade trees in front of the stores, or standing in pairs or small groups among the hitched horses along the sides of the road. Ben passed among them, greeting them and pausing to talk, enjoying himself, and all the while on the lookout for one or another of the Coulters.

Martha Elizabeth was Thad's youngest, the last at home. She had, he thought, the levelest head of any of his children, and was the best. Assuming the authority that his partiality granted her, she had at fifteen taken charge of the household, supplanting her mother, who was sickly, and her three older sisters, who had married and gone. At seventeen, she was responsible beyond her years. She was a tall, rawboned girl, with large hands and feet, a red complexion, and hair so red that, in the sun, it appeared to be on fire.

"Everybody loved Martha Elizabeth," my grandmother said. "She was as good as ever was."

To Thad it was a relief to obey her, to climb into the wagon under the pressure of her hand on his arm and to sit beside her as she drove the team homeward through the rising heat of the morning. Her concern for him gave him shelter. Holding to the back of the seat, he kept himself upright and, for the moment, rested in being with her.

But when they turned off the ridge onto the yet narrower road that led down into the valley called Cattle Pen and came into sight of their place, she could no longer shelter him. It had long been, to Thad's eye, a pretty farm — a hundred or so acres of slope and ridge on the west side of the little valley, the lower, gentler slopes divided from the ridge land by a ledgy bluff that was wooded, the log house and other buildings occupying a shelf above the creek bottom. Through all his years of paying for it, he had aspired toward it as toward a Promised Land. To have it, he had worked hard and long and deprived himself, and Rachel, his wife, had deprived herself. He had worked alone more often than not. Abner, as he grew able, had helped, as the girls had, also. But Abner had been reserved for something better. Abner was smart — too smart, as Thad and Rachel agreed without ever much talking about it, to spend his life farming a hillside. Something would have to be done to start him on his way to something better, a Promised Land yet more distant.

Although he had thought the farm not good enough for Abner, Thad was divided in his mind; and for himself he loved it. It was what he had transformed his life into. And now, even in the morning light, it lay under the shadow of his failure, and he could not bear to look at it. It was his life, and he was no longer in it. Somebody else, some other thing that did not even know it, stood ready to take possession of it. He was ashamed in its presence. To look directly at it would be like looking Martha Elizabeth full in the eyes, which he could not do either. And his shame raged in him.

When she stopped in the lot in front of the barn and helped him down, he started unhitching the team. But she took hold of his arm and drew him away gently toward the house.

"Come on, now," she said. "You've got to have you something to eat and some rest."

But he jerked away from her. "Go see to your mammy!"

"No," she said. "Come on." And she attempted again to move him toward the house.

He pushed her away, and she fell. He could have cut off his hand for so misusing her, and yet his rage at himself included her. He reached into the wagon box and took out a short hickory stock with a braid of rawhide knotted to it. He shook it at her.

"Get up," he said. "Get yonder to that house 'fore I wear you out."

He had never spoken to her in such a way, had never imagined himself doing so. He hated what he had done, and he could not undo it.

The heat of the day had established itself now. There was not a breeze anywhere, not a breath. A still haze filled the valley and redoubled the light. Within that blinding glare he occupied a darkness that was loud with accusing cries.

Martha Elizabeth stood at the kitchen door a moment, looking back at him, and then she went inside. Thad turned back to the team then, unhitched them, did up the lines, and led the mules to their stalls in the barn. He moved as if dreaming through these familiar motions that had now estranged themselves from him. The closer he had come to home, the more the force of his failure had gathered there to exclude him.

And it was Ben Feltner who had barred the door and left him without a friend. Ben Feltner, who owed nothing, had turned his back on his friend, who now owed everything.

He said aloud, "Yes, I'll come back sober, God damn you to hell!"

He lifted the jug out of the white mule's manger, pulled the cob from its mouth, and drank. When he lowered it, it was empty. It had lasted him three days, and now it was empty. He cocked his wrist and broke the jug against an upright.

"Well, that does for you, old holler-head."

He stood, letting the whiskey seek its level in him, and felt himself slowly come into purpose; for now he had his anger full and clear. Now he was summoned by an almost visible joy.

He went to the house, drank from the water bucket on the

back porch, and stepped through the kitchen door. Rachel and Martha Elizabeth were standing together by the cookstove, facing him.

"Thad, honey, I done fixed dinner," Rachel said. "Set down and eat."

He opened the stairway door, stepped up and took down his pistol from the little shelf over the door frame.

"No, now," Martha Elizabeth said. "Put that away. You ain't got a use in this world for that."

"Don't contrary me," Thad said. "Don't you say another damned word."

He put the pistol in his hip pocket with the barrel sticking up and turned to the door.

"Wait, Thad," Rachel said. "Eat a little before you go." But she was already so far behind him that he hardly heard her.

He walked to the barn, steadying himself by every upright thing he came to, so that he proceeded by a series of handholds on doorjamb and porch post and gatepost and tree. He could no longer see the place, but walked in a shifting aisle of blinding light through a cloud of darkness. Behind him now was almost nothing. And ahead of him was the singular joy to which his heart now beat in answer.

He went into the white mule's stall, unbuckled hamestrap and bellyband, and shoved the harness off her back, letting it fall. He unbuckled the collar and let it fall. Again his rage swelled within him until it seemed to tighten the skin of his throat, as though his body might fail to contain it, for he had never before in his life allowed a mule's harness to touch the ground if he could help it. But he was not in his life now, and his rage pleased him.

He hooked his finger in the bit ring and led the mule to the drinking trough by the well in front of the barn. The trough was half an oak barrel, nearly full of water. The mule wanted to drink, but he jerked her head up and drew her forward until she stood beside the trough. The shorn stubble of her mane under his hand, he stepped up onto the rim. Springing, he cast himself across the mule's back, straddled her, and sat upright as darkness swung around him. He jerked hard at the left rein.

"Get up, Beck," he said.

The mule was as principled as a martyr. She would have died

before she would have trotted a step, and yet he urged her forward with his heel. Even as the hind feet of the mule lifted from their tracks, the thought of Martha Elizabeth formed itself within the world's ruin. She seemed to rise up out of its shambles, like a ghost or an influence. She would follow him. He needed to hurry.

On the fringe of the Saturday bustle in front of the business houses, Ben met Early Rowanberry and his little boy, Arthur. Early was carrying a big sack, and Art a small one. They had started out not long after breakfast; from the log house on the ridgetop where the Rowanberrys had settled before Kentucky was a state, they had gone down the hill, forded the creek known as Sand Ripple, and then walked up the Shade Branch hollow through the Feltner place and on to town. Early had done his buying and a little talking, had bought a penny's worth of candy for Art, and now they were starting the long walk back. Ben knew that they had made the trip on foot to spare their mules, though the sacks would weigh sorely on their shoulders before they made it home.

"Well, Early," Ben said, "you've got a good hand with you today, I see."

"He's tol'ble good company, Ben, and he packs a little load," Early said.

Ben liked all the Rowanberrys, who had been good neighbors to him all his life, and Early was a better-than-average Rowanberry — a quiet man with a steady gaze and a sort of local fame for his endurance at hard work.

Ben then offered his hand to Art, who shyly held out his own. But then Ben said, "My boy, are you going to grow up to be a wheelhorse like your pap?" and Art answered without hesitation, "Yes, sir."

"Ah, that's right," Ben said. And he placed his hand on the boy's unladen shoulder.

The two Rowanberrys then resumed their homeward journey, and Ben walked on down the edge of the dusty road into town.

Ben was in no hurry. He had his mission in mind and was somewhat anxious about it, but he gave it its due place in the order of things. Thad's difficulty was not simple; whatever it was possible to do for him could not be done in a hurry. Ben passed slowly through the talk of the place and time, partaking of it. He liked the way the neighborhood gathered into itself on such days. Now and then, in the midst of the more casual conversations, a little trade talk would rouse up over a milk cow or a pocketknife or a saddle or a horse or mule. Or there would be a joke or a story or a bit of news, uprisings of the town's interest in itself that would pass through it and die away like scurries of wind. It was close to noon. It was hot even in the shade now, and the smells of horse sweat and horse manure had grown strong. On the benches and kegs along the storefronts, pocketknives were busy. Profound meditations were coming to bear upon long scrolls of cedar or poplar curling backward over thumbs and wrists and piling over shoetops.

Somebody said, "Well, I can see the heat waves a-rising."

Somebody else said, "Ain't nobody but a lazy man can see them heat waves."

And then Ben saw Thad's cousin, Dave Coulter, and Dave's son, Burley, coming out of one of the stores, Dave with a sack of flour on his shoulder and Burley with a sack of meal on his. Except for his boy's face and grin, Burley was a grown man. He was seventeen, a square-handed, muscular fellow already known for the funny things he said, though his elders knew of them only by hearsay. He and his father turned down the street toward their wagon, and Ben followed them.

When they had hunched the sacks off their shoulders into the wagon, Ben said, "Dave?"

Dave turned to him and stuck out his hand. "Why, howdy, Ben."

"How are you, Dave?"

" 'Bout all right, I reckon."

"And how are you, Burley?"

Dave turned to his boy to see that he would answer properly, and Burley, grinning, said, "Doing about all right, thank you, sir," and Dave turned back to Ben.

"Had to lay in a little belly timber," he said, " 'gainst we run plumb out. And the boy here, he wanted to come see the sights."

"Well, my boy," Ben said, "have you learned anything worthwhile?"

Burley grinned again, gave a quick nod, and said, "Yessir."

"Oh, hit's an educational place," Dave said. "We hung into one of them educational conversations yonder in the store. That's why we ain't hardly going to make it back home by dinnertime."

"Well, I won't hold you up for long," Ben said. And he told Dave as much as he had understood of Thad's trouble. They were leaning against the wagon box, facing away from the road. Burley, who had gone to untie the mules, was still standing at their heads.

"Well," Dave said, "hit's been norated around that Abner weren't doing just the way he ought to. Tell you the truth, I been juberous about that loan proposition ever since Thad put his name to it. Put his whole damned foothold in that damned boy's pocket is what he done. And now you say it's all gone up the spout."

"He's in a serious fix, no question about it."

"Well, is there anything a feller can do for him?"

"Well, there's one thing for certain. He was drunk when he came to see me. He was cussing and raring. If you, or some of you, could get him sober, it would help. And then we could see if we can help him out of his scrape."

"Talking rough, was he?"

"Rough enough."

"I'm sorry, Ben. Thad don't often drink, but when he does he drinks like the Lord appointed him to get rid of all of it."

Somebody said, "Look out!"

They turned to see Thad and the white mule almost abreast of them. Thad was holding the pistol.

"They said he just looked awful," my grandmother said. "He looked like death warmed over."

Ben said, without raising his voice, in the same reasonable tone in which he had been speaking to Dave, "Hold on, Thad."

And Thad fired.

Dave saw a small round red spot appear in the center of Ben's forehead. A perplexed look came to his face, as if he had been intending to say something more and had forgotten what it was. For a moment, he remained standing just as he had been, one hand on the rim of the wagon box. And then he fell. As he went down, his shoulder struck the hub of the wagon wheel so that he fell onto his side, his hat rolling underneath the wagon.

Thad put the pistol back into his hip pocket. The mule had stood as still after he had halted her as if she were not there at all, but at home under a tree in the pasture. When Thad kicked her, she went on again.

Ben Feltner never had believed in working on Sunday, and he did not believe in not working on workdays. Those two principles had shaped all his weeks. He liked to make his hay cuttings and begin other large, urgent jobs as early in the week as possible in order to have them finished before Sunday. On Saturdays, he and Mat and the hands worked in the crops if necessary; otherwise, that day was given to the small jobs of maintenance that the farm constantly required, and to preparations for Sunday, when they would do nothing except milk and feed. When the work was caught up and the farm in order, Ben liked to have everybody quit early on Saturday afternoon. He liked the quiet that descended over the place then, with the day of rest ahead.

On that Saturday morning he had sent Old Smoke, Aunt Cass's husband, and their son, Samp, and Samp's boy, Joe, to mend a fence back on the river bluff. Mat he sent to the blacksmith shop to have the shoes reset on Governor, his buggy horse. They would not need Governor to go to church; they walked to church. But when they had no company on Sunday afternoon, and the day was fair, Ben and Nancy liked to drive around the neighborhood, looking at the crops and stopping at various households to visit. They liked especially to visit Nancy's brother, Jack Beechum, and his wife, Ruth, who lived on the Beechum home place, the place that Nancy would always refer to as "out home."

And so Mat, that morning, after his chores were done, had slipped a halter on Governor and led him down through town to the blacksmith's. He had to wait — there were several horses and mules already in line — and so he tied Governor to the hitch rail in front of the shop and went in among the others who were waiting and talking, figuring that he would be late for dinner.

It was a good place. The shop stood well back from the street, leaving in front of it a tree-shaded, cinder-covered yard, which made room for the hitch rail and for the wagons, sleds, and other implements waiting to be repaired. The shop itself was a single large, dirt-floored room, meticulously clean — every surface swept and every tool in place. Workbenches went around three walls. Near the large open doorway were the forge and anvil.

The blacksmith — a low, broad, grizzled man by the name of Elder Johnson — was the best within many miles, a fact well known to himself, which sometimes made him difficult. He also remembered precisely every horse or mule he had ever nailed a shoe on, and so he was one of the keepers of the town's memory.

Elder was shoeing a colt that was nervous and was giving him trouble. He was working fast so as to cause the colt as little discomfort as he could. He picked up the left hind hoof, caught it between his aproned knees, and laid the shoe on it. The shoe was too wide at the heel, and he let the colt's foot go back to the floor. A small sharp-faced man smoking a cob pipe was waiting, holding out a broken singletree for Elder's inspection as he passed on his way back to the forge.

Elder looked as if the broken tree were not the sort of thing that could concern him.

"Could I get this done by this evening?" the man asked. His name was Skeets Willard, and his work was always in some state of emergency. "I can't turn a wheel," he said, "till I get that fixed."

Elder let fall the merest glance at the two pieces of the singletree, and then looked point-blank at the man himself as if surprised not only by his presence but by his existence. "What the hell do you think I am? A hammer with a brain? Do you see all them horses and mules tied up out there? If you want that fixed, I'll fix it when I can. If you don't, take it home."

Skeets Willard elected to lay the pieces down in a conspicuous place by the forge. And Elder, whose outburst had not interrupted the flow of talk among the bystanders, caught the shoe in his tongs and shoved it in among the coals of the forge. He cranked the bellows and made small white flames spike up out of the coals. As he turned the handle, he stared in a kind of trance at the light of the open doorway, and the light shone in his eyes, and his face and his arms were shining with sweat. Presently he drew the shoe, glowing, out of the coals and, laying it on the horn of the anvil, narrowed the heel. He then plunged it into the slack tub from which it raised a brief shriek of steam.

Somebody turned out of the conversation and said, "Say, Elder, do you remember that little red mule come in here with a bunch of yearlings Marce Catlett bought up around Lexington? Ned, I think they called him."

"Newt," Elder said in so even a voice that Skeets Willard might never have been there. "You bet I remember him."

He took the cooled shoe from the slack tub and, picking up the colt's foot and straddling it again, quickly nailed one nail in each side, raking the points over with the claws of his hammer. He let the colt stand on his foot again to see how the shoe set. "You bet I remember him," he said. "That mule could kick the lard out of a biscuit."

And then they heard the single voice raised in warning out in the road, followed immediately by the shot and by a rising murmur of excited, indistinguishable voices as the whole Saturday crowd turned its attention to the one thing.

Mat hurried out with the others and saw the crowd wedged in between the storefronts and Dave Coulter's wagon. He began to realize that the occasion concerned him only when the crowd began to make way for him as he approached.

"Let him through! Let him through!" the crowd said.

The crowd opened to let him through, turning its faces to him, falling silent as it saw who he was. And then he saw what was left of the man who had been his father lying against the wagon wheel. Those nearest him heard him say, "Oh!" and it did not sound like him at all. He stepped forward and knelt and took his father's wrist in his hand to feel for the pulse that he did not expect, having seen the wound and the fixed unsighted eyes. The crowd now was as quiet around him as the still treetops along the road. For what seemed a long time Mat knelt there with his father's dead wrist in his hand, while his mind arrived and arrived and yet arrived at that place and time and that body lying still on the bloodied stones. When he looked up again he did not look like the man they had known at all.

"Who did this?" he said.

And the crowd answered, "Thad Coulter, he done it."

"Where'd he go?"

"He taken down the road yonder towards Hargrave. He was on that old white mule, old May."

When Mat stood up again from his father's side, he was a man new-created by rage. All that he had been and thought and done gave way to his one desire to kill the man who had killed his father. He ached, mind and body, with the elation of that one thought. He was not armed, but he never thought of that. He would go for the horse he had left tied at the blacksmith's. He would ride Thad Coulter down. He would come up beside him and club him off the mule. He would beat him down out of the air. And in that thought which lived more in his right arm than in his head, both he and his enemy were as clear of history as if newborn.

By the time Mat was free of the crowd, he was running.

Jack Beechum had sold a team of mules the day before, and so he had a check to carry to the bank. He also had a list of things that Ruth wanted from town, and now that he had money ahead he wanted to settle his account at Chatham's store. His plan was to do his errands in town and get back home by dinner; that afternoon he wanted to mow a field of hay, hoping it would cure by Monday. He rode to town on a good black gelding called Socks for his four white pasterns.

He tied the horse some distance from the center of town in a place of better shade and fewer flies. He went to the bank first, and then went about gathering the things that Ruth needed, ending up at Chatham's. He was sitting by Beater Chatham's desk in the back, watching Beater total up his account, when they heard the shot out in the street.

"Sounds like they're getting Saturday started out there," Jack said.

"I reckon," Beater said, checking his figures.

"They're going to keep on until they shoot somebody who don't deserve it."

Beater looked at him then over the tops of his glasses. "Well, they'll have to look around outside town to find somebody, won't they?" He filled out a check for the amount of the bill and handed the check to Jack for him to sign.

And then someone who had just stepped out of the store stepped back in again and said, "Jack, you'd better come. They've shot Ben Feltner."

Jack never signed the check that day or for several days. He ran to the door. When he was outside, he saw first the crowd and then Mat running toward him out of it. Without breaking his own stride, he caught Mat and held him.

They were both moving at some speed, and the crowd heard the shock of the impact as the two men came together. Jack could hardly have known what he was doing. He had no time to think. He may have been moved by an impulse simply to stop things until he *could* think. Or perhaps he knew by the look on Mat's face that he had to be obstructed. At any rate, as soon as Jack had taken hold of Mat, he understood that he *had* to hold him. And he knew that he had never taken hold of any such thing before. He had caught Mat in a sideways hug that clamped his arms to his sides. Jack's sole task was to keep Mat from freeing his arms. But Mat was little more than half Jack's age; he was in the prime of his strength. And now he twisted and strained with the concentration of fury, uttering cries that could have been either grunts or sobs, forcing Jack both to hold him and to hold him up. They strove there a long time, heaving and staggering, hardly moving from the tracks they had stood in when they came together, and the dust rose up around them. Jack felt that his arms would pull apart at the joints. He ached afterward. Something went out of him that day, and he was not the same again.

And what went out of Jack came into Mat. Or so it seemed, for in that desperate embrace he became a stronger man than he had been. A strength came into him that held his grief and his anger as Jack had held him. And Jack knew of the coming of this strength, not because it enabled Mat to break free but because it enabled Jack to turn him loose. Mat ceased to strive, and Jack let go his hold. He stepped away, allowing himself to be recognized, and Mat stood. To Jack, it was as though he had caught one man and let another go.

But he put his eye on Mat, not willing yet to trust him entirely to himself, and waited.

They both were winded, wet with sweat, and for a moment they only breathed, watched by the crowd, Jack watching Mat, Mat looking at nothing.

As they stood so, the girl, Martha Elizabeth, walked by in the road. She did not look at them or at the wagon or at the body crumpled on the ground. She walked past it all, looking ahead, as if she already saw what she was walking toward.

Coming aware that Jack was waiting on him, Mat looked up;

he met Jack's gaze. He said, "Pa's dead. Thad Coulter has shot him."

They waited, looking at each other still, while the earth shook under them.

Mat said, "I'll go tell Ma. You bring Pa, but give me a little time."

Dinner was ready, and the men were late.

"It wasn't usual for them to be late," my grandmother said, "but we didn't think yet that anything was wrong. Your mother was just a little girl then, and she was telling us a story about a doll and a dog and a horse."

Aunt Cass stood by the stove, keeping an eye on the griddle. Nancy was sweeping the floor under the firebox of the stove; she was a woman who was always doing. Margaret, having set the table, had turned one of the chairs out into the floor and sat down. All three were listening to Bess, who presently stopped her story, rolled her eyes, and said, "I hear my innards a-growling. I reckon I must be hungry."

They laughed.

"I 'spect so, I 'spect so," Aunt Cass said. "Well, you'll get something to eat 'fore long."

When she heard Mat at the kitchen door, Aunt Cass said, "Miss Nancy, you want to take the hoecake up?" And then seeing the change in Mat's face, which was new to it but old to the world, she hushed and stood still. Nancy, seeing the expression on Cass's face, turned to look at Mat.

Bess said, "Goody! Now we can eat!"

Mat looked at his mother, and then down at Bess and smiled. "You can eat directly," he said.

And then he said, "Margaret, take Bess and go upstairs. I think she's got a book up there she wants you to read to her."

"I knew what it was then," my grandmother said. "Oh, I felt it go all over me before I knew it in my mind. I just wanted to crawl away. But I had your mother to think about. You always have somebody to think about, and it's a blessing."

She said, "Come on, Bess, let's go read a story. We'll eat in a little bit."

As soon as he heard their footsteps going up the stairs, Mat looked at his mother again. As the silence gathered against him, he said, "Ma, I'm sorry, Pa's dead. Thad Coulter has shot him."

She was already wearing black. She had borne four children and raised one. Two of her children she had buried in the same week of a diphtheria epidemic, of which she had nearly died herself. After the third child had died, she never wore colors again. It was not that she chose to be ostentatiously bereaved. She could not have chosen to be ostentatious about anything. She was, in fact, a woman possessed of a strong native cheerfulness. And yet she had accepted a certain darkness that she had lived in too intimately to deny.

She stood, looking at Mat, while she steadied herself, and steadied the room around her, in the quiet that, having suddenly begun there, would not end for a long time. And then she said to Mat, "Sit down."

She said, "Cass, sit down."

They turned chairs away from the table and sat down, and then he did.

"Now," she said, "I want to know what happened."

In the quiet Mat told as much, as little, as he knew.

As if to exert herself against the silence that too quickly filled the room, Nancy stood again. She laid her hand on the shoulder of Mat's wet shirt and patted it once.

"Cass," she said, "we mustn't cry," though there were tears on her own face.

"Mat," she said, "go get Smoke and Samp and Joe. Tell them, and tell them to come here."

To Aunt Cass again, she said, "We must fix the bed. They'll need a place to lay him."

And then they heard the burdened footsteps at the door.

In his cresting anger in the minutes before he stopped the mule in the road in Port William and fired the one shot that he ever fired in anger in his life, Thad Coulter knew a fierce, fulfilling joy. He saw the shot home to the mark, saw Ben Feltner stand a moment and go down, and then he heeled the mule hard in the side and rode on. He went on because all behind him that he might once have turned back to was gone from his mind, and perhaps even in his joy he knew that from that time there was to be no going back.

Even before the town was out of sight behind him, his anger and his joy began to leave him. It was as if his life's blood were running out of him, and he tried to stanch the flow by muttering aloud the curses of his rage. But they had no force, and his depletion continued.

His first thought beyond his anger was of the mule. She was thirsty, he knew, and he had denied her a drink.

"When we get to the creek," he said.

The mule followed the windings of the road down off the upland. Below the cleared ridges, they passed through woods. On the gentler open slopes below, they came into the blank sunlight again, and he could see the river winding between its wooded banks toward its meeting with the Ohio at Hargrave.

At the foot of the hill, the road dipped under trees again and forded a creek. Thad rode the mule into the pool above the ford, loosened the rein, and let her drink. It was a quiet, deeply shaded place, the water unrippled until the mule stepped into it. For the first time in three days Thad could hear the quiet, and a bottomless sorrow opened in him, causing him suddenly to clutch his belly and groan aloud.

When the mule had finished drinking, he rode her out of the pool, dismounted, and, unbuckling one end of the rein from the bit, led her into a clump of bushes and tall weeds and tied her there. For now the thought of pursuit had come to him, and he knew he would have to go the rest of the way on foot. The mule could not be hurried, and she would be difficult to hide.

He went back to the pool and knelt at the edge of it and drank, and then he washed his hands and in his cupped hands lifted the clear water time and again to his face.

Presently, he became still, listening. He could hear nothing but the cicadas in the surrounding trees. And then he heard, coming fast, the sound of loud talking and the rapid hooftread of horses. He stepped into a patch of weeds and watched several riders go by on the road. They were boys and young men from the town who, having waited through the aftermath of the shooting, had now been carried by their excitement into pursuit of him. Boys, he thought. He felt in no danger from them — he did not think of the pistol — and yet he feared them. He now imagined himself hurrying on foot along the road, while the young riders picked and pecked at him.

The quiet returned, and he could feel, as if in the hair roots and pores of his skin, that Martha Elizabeth was coming near. He went back to the road again.

The walking and the water drying on his face cleared his mind, and now he knew himself as he had been and as he was, and knew that he was changed beyond unchanging into something he did not love. Now that his anger had drained away, his body seemed to him not only to be a burden almost too heavy to carry, but to be on the verge of caving in. He walked with one hand pressed to his belly, where the collapse seemed already to have begun.

The best route between Port William and Hargrave was still the river. The road found its way as if by guess, bent this way and that by the whims of topography and the convenience of landowners. At intervals, it was interrupted by farm gates.

After a while, hearing several more horses coming behind him, he stepped out of the road and lay down in a small canebrake. When they had passed, he returned to the road and went on. Always he was watchful of the houses he passed, but he stayed in the road. If he was to protect the one choice of which he was still master, he had to hurry.

And now, as he had not been able to do when he left it, he could see his farm. It shone in his mind as if inwardly lighted in the darkness that now surrounded both him and it. He could see it with the morning sun dew-bright on the woods and the sloping pastures, on the little croplands on the ridge and in the bottoms along the creek. He could see its cool shadows stretching out in the evening and the milk cows coming down the path to the barn. It was irrevocably behind him now, as if a great sword had fallen between him and it.

He was slow and small on the long road. The sun was slow overhead. The air was heavy and unmoving. He watched the steady stepping of his feet, the road going backward beneath them. He had to get out of the road only twice again: once for a family in a spring wagon coming up from Hargrave and once for another horse and rider coming down from Port William. Except for those, nothing moved in the still heat but himself. Except for the cicadas, the only sounds he heard were his own steady footfalls on the dry dust.

He seemed to see always not only the changing road beneath his feet but also that other world in which he had lived, now lighted in the dark behind him, and it came to him that on that day two lives had ended for a possibility that never had existed: for Abner Coulter's mounting up to a better place. And he felt the emptiness open wider in him and again heard himself groan. He wondered, so great was the pain of that emptiness, that he did not weep, but it exceeded weeping as it exceeded words. Beyond the scope of one man's grief, it cried out in the air around him, as if in that day's hot light, the trees and the fields and the dust of the road all grieved. An inward pressure that had given his body its shape seemed to have been withdrawn, and he walked, holding himself, resisting step by step the urge to bend around the emptiness opening in his middle and let himself fall.

Where the valley began to widen toward the river's mouth, the road passed a large bottom planted in corn. Thad looked back, expecting that he would see Martha Elizabeth, and he did see her. She was maybe three-quarters of a mile behind him, small in the distance, and the heat rising off the field shimmered and shook between them, but he knew her. He walked faster, and he did not look back again. It seemed to him that she knew everything he knew, and loved him anyhow. She loved him, minute by minute, not only as he had been, but as he had become. It was a wonderful and a fearful thing to him that he had caused such a love for himself to come into the world, and then had failed it. He could not have bowed low enough before it and remained above ground. He could not bear to think of it. But he knew that she walked behind him — balanced across the distance, in the same hot light, the same darkness, the same crying air — ever at the same speed that he walked.

Finally he came to the cluster of houses at Ellville, at the end of the bridge, and went across into Hargrave. From the bridge to the courthouse, he went ever deeper into the Saturday crowd, but he did not alter his gait or look at anybody. If anybody looked at him, he did not know it. At the cross streets, he could see on the river a towboat pushing a line of barges slowly upstream, black smoke gushing from its stacks. The walks were full of people, and the streets were full of buggies and wagons. He crossed the courthouse yard where people sat on benches or stood talking in little groups under the shade trees. It seemed to him that he walked in a world from which he had departed.

When he went through the front door of the courthouse into the sudden cool darkness of the hallway, he could not see. Lights swam in his eyes in the dark, and he had to prop himself against the wall. The place smelled of old paper and tobacco and of human beings, washed and unwashed. When he could see again, he walked to a door under a sign that said "Sheriff" and went in. It was a tall room lighted by two tall windows. There was a row of chairs for people to wait in, and several spittoons, placed for the presumed convenience of spitters, had been as much missed as hit. No one was there but a large man in a broad-brimmed straw hat and a suit somewhat too small, who was standing behind a high desk, writing something. At first he did not look up. When he finally did look up, he stared at Thad for some time as if not sufficiently convinced of what he saw.

"In a minute," he said, and looked down again and finished what he was writing. There was a badge pinned lopsidedly to the pocket of his shirt, and he held an unlit cigar like another pen in his left hand. He said as he wrote, "You been drove hard and put up wet, I reckon."

"Yes," Thad said. "I have killed a man."

The sheriff laid the pen on the blotter and looked up. "Who?"

Thad said, "Ben Feltner, the best friend ever I had." His eyes suddenly brimmed with tears, but they did not fall. He made no sound and he did not move.

"You're a Coulter, ain't you? From up about Port William?"

"Thad," Thad said.

The sheriff would have preferred that Thad had remained a fugitive. He did not want a self-confessed murderer on his hands — especially not one fresh from a Saturday killing in Port William. He knew Ben Feltner, knew he was liked, and feared there would be a commotion. Port William, as far as he was concerned, was nothing but trouble, almost beyond the law's reach and certainly beyond its convenience — a source, as far as he was concerned, of never-foreseeable bad news. He did not know what would come next, but he thought that something would, and he did not approve of it.

"I wish to hell," he said, "that everybody up there who is going to kill each other would just, by God, go ahead and do it." He looked at Thad for some time in silence, as if giving him an opportunity to disappear.

"Well," he said, finally, "I reckon you just as well give me the pistol."

He gestured toward Thad's sagging hip pocket, and Thad took out the pistol and gave it to him.

"Come on," the sheriff said.

Thad followed him out a rear door into the small paved yard of the jail, where the sheriff rang for the jailer.

The sheriff had hardly got back into the office and taken up his work again when a motion in the doorway alerted him. He looked and saw a big red-faced girl standing just outside the door as if uncertain whether or not it was lawful to enter. She wore a sunbonnet, a faded blue dress that reached to her ankles, and an apron. Though she was obviously timid and unused to public places, she returned his look with perfect candor.

"Come in," he said.

She crossed the threshold and again stopped.

"What can I do for you, miss?"

"I'm a-looking for Mr. Thad Coulter from up to Port William, please, sir."

"You his daughter?"

"Yes, sir."

"Well, he's here. I got him locked up. He claims he killed a fellow."

"He did," the girl said. "Is it allowed to see him?"

"Not now," the sheriff said. "You come back in the morning, miss. You can see him then."

She stood looking at him another moment, as if to make sure that he had said what he meant, and then she said, "Well, I thank you," and went out.

An hour or so later, when he shut the office and started home to supper, she was sitting on the end of one of the benches under the shade trees, looking down at her hands in her lap.

"You see," my grandmother said, "there are two deaths in this — Mr. Feltner's and Thad Coulter's. We know Mr. Feltner's because we had to know it. It was ours. That we know Thad's is because of Martha Elizabeth. The Martha Elizabeth you know."

I knew her, but it came strange to me now to think of her — to be asked to see her — as a girl. She was what I considered an old woman when I first remember her; she was perhaps eight or ten years younger than my grandmother, the fire-red long gone from her hair. She was a woman always near to smiling, sometimes to laughter. Her face, it seemed, had been made to smile. It was a face that assented wholly to the being of whatever and whomever she looked at. She had gone with her father to the world's edge and had come back with this smile on her face. Miss Martha Elizabeth, we younger ones called her. Everybody loved her.

When the sheriff came back from supper, she was still there on the bench, the Saturday night shoppers and talkers, standers and passers leaving a kind of island around her, as if unwilling to acknowledge the absolute submission they sensed in her. The sheriff knew as soon as he laid eyes on her this time that she was not going to go away. Perhaps he understood that she had no place to go that she could get to before it would be time to come back.

"Come on with me," he said, and he did not sound like a sheriff now but only a man.

She got up and followed him through the hallway of the courthouse, past the locked doors of the offices, out again, and across the little iron-fenced courtyard in front of the jail. The sheriff unlocked a heavy sheet-iron door, opened it, and closed it behind them, and they were in a large room of stone, steel, and concrete, containing several cages, barred from floor to ceiling, the whole interior lighted by one kerosene lamp hanging in the corridor.

Among the bars gleaming dimly and the shadows of bars thrown back against concrete and stone, she saw her father sitting on the edge of a bunk that was only an iron shelf let down on chains from the wall, with a thin mattress laid on it. He had paid no attention when they entered. He sat still, staring at the wall, one hand pressed against his belly, the other holding to one of the chains that supported the bunk.

The sheriff opened the cell door and stood aside to let her in. "I'll come back after while," he said.

The door closed and was locked behind her, and she stood still until Thad felt her presence and looked up. When he recognized her, he covered his face with both hands.

"He put his hands over his face like a man ashamed," my grandmother said. "But he was like a man, too, who had seen what he couldn't bear." She sat without speaking a moment, looking at me, for she had much to ask of me. "Maybe Thad saw his guilt full and clear then. But what he saw that he couldn't bear was something else."

And again she paused, looking at me. We sat facing each other on either side of the window; my grandfather lay in one of his lengthening sleeps nearby. The old house in that moment seemed filled with a quiet that extended not only out into the whole broad morning but endlessly both ways in time.

"People sometimes talk of God's love as if it's a pleasant thing. But it is terrible, in a way. Think of all it includes. It included Thad Coulter, drunk and mean and foolish, before he killed Mr. Feltner, and it included him afterwards."

She reached out then and touched the back of my right hand with her fingers; my hand still bears that touch, invisible and yet indelible as a tattoo.

"That's what Thad saw. He saw his guilt. He had killed his friend. He had done what he couldn't undo; he had destroyed what he couldn't make. But in the same moment he saw his guilt included in love that stood as near him as Martha Elizabeth and at that moment wore her flesh. It was surely weak and wrong of him to kill himself — to sit in judgment that way over himself. But surely God's love includes people who can't bear it."

The sheriff took Martha Elizabeth home with him that night; his wife fed her and turned back the bed for her in the spare room. The next day she sat with her father in his cell.

"All that day," my grandmother said, "he would hardly take his hands from his face. Martha Elizabeth fed him what little he would eat and raised the cup to his lips for what little he would drink. And he ate and drank only because she asked him to, almost not at all. I don't know what they said. Maybe nothing."

At bedtime again that night Martha Elizabeth went home with

the sheriff. When they returned to the courthouse on Monday morning, Thad Coulter was dead by his own hand.

"It's a hard story to have to know," my grandmother said. "The mercy of it was Martha Elizabeth."

She still had more to tell, but she paused again, and again she looked at me and touched my hand.

"If God loves the ones we can't," she said, "then finally maybe we can. All these years I've thought of him sitting in those shadows, with Martha Elizabeth standing there, and his work-sore old hands over his face."

Once the body of Ben Feltner was laid on his bed, the men who had helped Jack to carry him home went quietly out through the kitchen and the back door, as they had come in, muttering or nodding their commiseration in response to Nancy's "Thank you." And Jack stayed. He stayed to be within sight or call of his sister when she needed him, and he stayed to keep his eye on Mat. Their striving with each other in front of Chatham's store, Jack knew, had changed them both. Because he did not yet know how or how much or if it was complete, it was not yet a change that he was willing, or that he dared, to turn his back on.

Someone was sent to take the word to Rebecca Finley, Margaret's mother, and to ask her to come for Bess.

When Rebecca came, Margaret brought Bess down the stairs into the quiet that the women now did their best to disguise. But Bess, who did not know what was wrong and who tactfully allowed the pretense that nothing was, knew nevertheless that the habits of the house were now broken, and she had heard that quiet that she would never forget.

"Grandma Finley is here to take you home with her," Margaret said, giving her voice the lilt of cheerfulness. "You've been talking about going to stay with her, haven't you?"

And Bess said, dutifully supplying the smile she felt her mother wanted, "Yes."

"We're going to bake some cookies just as soon as we get home," Rebecca said. "Do you want to bake a gingerbread boy?"

"Yes," Bess said.

She removed her hand from her mother's hand and placed it in her grandmother's. They went out the door.

The quiet returned. From then on, though there was much that had to be done and the house stayed full of kin and neighbors coming and going or staying to help, and though by midafternoon women were already bringing food, the house preserved a quiet against all sound. No voice was raised. No door was slammed. Everybody moved as if in consideration not of each other, but of the quiet itself — as if the quiet denoted some fragile peacefulness in Ben's new sleep that should not be intruded upon.

Jack Beechum was party to that quiet. He made no sound. He said nothing, for his own silence had become wonderful to him and he could not bear to break it. Though Nancy, after the death of their mother, had given Jack much of his upbringing and had been perhaps more his mother than his sister, Ben had never presumed to be a father to him. From the time Jack was eight years old, Ben had been simply his friend — had encouraged, instructed, corrected, helped, and stood by him; had placed a kindly, humorous, forbearing expectation upon him that he could not shed or shirk and had at last lived up to. They had been companions. And yet, through the rest of that day, Jack had his mind more on Mat than on Ben.

Jack watched Mat as he would have watched a newborn colt weak on its legs that he had helped to stand, that might continue to stand or might not. All afternoon Jack did not sit down because Mat did not. Sometimes there were things to do, and they were busy. Space for the coffin had to be made in the living room. Furniture had to be moved. When the time came, the laden coffin had to be moved into place. But, busy or not, Mat was almost constantly moving, as if seeking his place in a world newly made that day, a world still shaking and doubtful underfoot. And Jack both moved with him and stayed apart from him, watching. When they spoke again, they would speak on different terms.

There was a newness in the house, a solemnity, a sort of wariness, a restlessness as of a dog uneasy on the scent of some creature undeniably present but unknown. In its quiet, the house seemed to be straining to accommodate Ben's absence, made undeniable and insistent by the presence of his body lying still under his folded hands.

Jack would come later to his own reckoning with that loss, the horror and the pity of it, and the grief, the awe and gratitude and love and sorrow and regret, when Ben, newly dead and renewing sorrow for others dead before, would wholly occupy his mind in the night, and could give no comfort, and would not leave. But now Jack stayed by Mat and helped as he could.

In the latter part of the afternoon came Della Budge, Miss Della, bearing an iced cake on a stand like a lighted lamp. As she left the kitchen and started for the front door, she laid her eyes on Jack, who was standing in the door between the living room and the hall. She was a large woman, far gone in years. It was a labor for her to walk. She advanced each foot ahead of the other with care, panting, her hand on her hip, rocking from side to side. She wore many clothes, for her blood was thin and she was easily chilled, and she carried a fan, for sometimes she got too warm. Her little dustcap struggled to stay on top of her head. A tiny pair of spectacles perched awry on her nose. She had a face like a shriveled apple, and the creases at the corners of her mouth were stained with snuff. Once she had been Jack's teacher. For years they had waged a contest in which she had endeavored to teach him the begats from Abraham to Jesus and he had refused to learn them. He was one of her failures, but she maintained a proprietary interest in him nonetheless. She was the only one left alive who called him "Jackie."

As she came up to him he said, "Hello, Miss Della."

"Well, Jackie," she said, lifting and canting her nose to bring her spectacles to bear upon him, "poor Ben has met his time."

"Yes, ma'am," Jack said. "One of them things."

"When your time comes you must go, by the hand of man or the stroke of God."

"Yes, ma'am," Jack said. He was standing with his hands behind him, leaning back against the doorjamb.

"It'll come by surprise," she said. "It's a time appointed, but we'll not be notified."

Jack said he knew it. He did know it.

"So we must always be ready," she said. "Pray without ceasing."

"Yes, ma'am."

"Well, God bless Ben Feltner. He was a good man. God rest his soul."

Jack stepped ahead of her to help her out the door and down the porch steps.

"Why, thank you, Jackie," she said as she set foot at last on the walk.

He stood and watched her going away, walking, it seemed to him, a tottering edge between eternity and time.

Toward evening Margaret laid the table, and the family and several of the neighbor women gathered in the kitchen. Only two or three men had come, and they were sitting in the living room by the coffin. The table was spread with the abundance of food that had been brought in. They were just preparing to sit down when the murmur of voices they had been hearing from the road down in front of the stores seemed to converge and to move in their direction. Those in the kitchen stood and listened a moment, and then Mat started for the front of the house. The others followed him through the hall and out onto the porch.

The sun was down, the light cool and directionless, so that the colors of the foliage and of the houses and storefronts of the town seemed to glow. Chattering swifts circled and swerved above the chimneys. Nothing else moved except the crowd that made its way at an almost formal pace into the yard. The people standing on the porch were as still as everything else, except for Jack Beechum, who quietly made his way forward until he stood behind and a little to the left of Mat, who was standing at the top of the steps.

The crowd moved up near the porch and stopped. There was a moment of hesitation while it murmured and jostled inside itself.

"Be quiet, boys," somebody said. "Let Doc do the talking."

They became still, and then Doctor Starns, who stood in the front rank, took a step forward.

"Mat," he said, "we're here as your daddy's friends. We've got word that Thad Coulter's locked up in the jail at Hargrave. We want you to know that we don't like what he did."

Several voices said, "No!" and "Nosir!"

"We know it was a thing done out of meanness. We don't think we can stand for it, or that we ought to, or that we ought to wait on somebody else's opinion about it. He was seen by a large number of witnesses to do what he did."

Somebody said, "That's right!"

"We think it's our business, and we propose to make it our business."

"That's right!" said several voices.

"It's only up to you to say the word, and we'll ride down there tonight and put justice beyond question. We have a rope."

And in the now silent crowd someone held up a coil of rope, a noose already tied.

The doctor gave a slight bow of his head to Mat and then tipped his hat to Nancy who now stood behind Mat and to his right. And again the crowd murmured and slightly stirred within itself.

For what seemed to Jack a long time, Mat did not speak or move. The crowd grew quiet again, and again they could hear the swifts chittering in the air. Jack's right hand ached to reach out to Mat. It seemed to him again that he felt the earth shaking under his feet, as Mat felt it. But though it shook and though they felt it, Mat now stood resolved and calm upon it. Looking at the back of his head, Jack could still see the boy in him, but the head was up. The voice, when it came, was steady:

"No, gentlemen. I appreciate it. We all do. But I ask you not to do it."

And Jack, who had not sat down since morning, stepped back and sat down.

Nancy, under whose feet the earth was not shaking, if it ever had, stepped up beside her son and took his arm.

She said to the crowd, "I know you are my husband's friends. I thank you. I, too, must ask you not to do as you propose. Mat has asked you; I have asked you; if Ben could, he would ask you. Let us make what peace is left for us to make."

"If you want to," Mat said, "come and be with us. We have food, and you all are welcome."

He had said, in all, six brief sentences. He was not a forward man. This, I think, was the only public speech of his life.

"I can see him yet," my grandmother said, her eyes, full of sudden moisture, again turned to the window. "I wish you could have seen him."

And now, after so many years, perhaps I have. I have sought that moment out, or it has sought me, and I see him standing without prop in the deepening twilight, asking his father's friends to renounce the vengeance that a few hours before he himself had been furious to exact.

This is the man who will be my grandfather — the man who will be the man who was my grandfather. The tenses slur and slide under pressure of collapsed time. For that moment on the porch is not a now that was, but a now that is and will be, inhabiting all the history of Port William that followed and will follow. I know that in the days after his father's death — and after Thad Coulter, concurring in the verdict of his would-be jury in Port William, hung himself in the Hargrave jail and so released Martha Elizabeth from her watch — my grandfather renewed and carried on his friendship with the Coulters: with Thad's widow and daughters, with Dave Coulter and his family, and with another first cousin of Thad's, Marce Catlett, my grandfather on my father's side. And when my father asked leave of the Feltners to marry their daughter Bess, my mother, he was made welcome.

Mat Feltner dealt with Ben's murder by not talking about it, and thus keeping it in the past. In his last years, I liked to get him to tell me about the violent old times of the town, the hard drinking and the fighting. And he would oblige me up to a point, enjoying the outrageous old stories himself, I think. But always there would come a time in the midst of the telling when he would become silent, shake his head, lift one hand and let it fall; and I would know — I know better now than I did then — that he had remembered his father's death.

Though Coulters still abound in Port William, no Feltner of the name is left. But the Feltner line continues, joined to the Coulter line, in me, and I am here. I am blood kin to both sides of that moment when Ben Feltner turned to face Thad Coulter in the road and Thad pulled the trigger. The two families, sundered in the ruin of a friendship, were united again first in new friendship and then in marriage. My grandfather made a peace here that has joined many who would otherwise have been divided. I am the child of his forgiveness.

After Mat spoke the second time, inviting them in, the crowd loosened and came apart. Some straggled back down into the town; others, as Mat had asked, came into the house, where their wives already were.

But Jack did not stay with them. As soon as he knew he was free, his thoughts went to other things. His horse had stood a long time, saddled, without water or feed. The evening chores were not yet done. Ruth would be wondering what had happened. In the morning they would come back together, to be of use if they could. And there would be, for Jack as for the others, the long wearing out of grief. But now he could stay no longer.

As soon as the porch was cleared, he retrieved his hat from the hall tree and walked quietly out across the yard under the maples and the descending night. So as not to be waylaid by talk, he walked rapidly down the middle of the road to where he had tied his horse. Lamps had now been lighted in the stores and the houses.

As he approached, his horse nickered to him.

"I know it," Jack said.

As soon as the horse felt his rider's weight on the stirrup, he started. Soon the lights and noises of the town were behind them, and there were only a few stars, a low red streak in the west, and the horse's eager footfalls on the road.

KIM EDWARDS

Gold

FROM ANTAEUS

ON THE DAY THAT GOLD WAS DISCOVERED near his village, Mohammed Muda Nor had worked all morning tapping rubber. At one o'clock he walked out from the airy rows of trees, waved to Abdullah, the entry guard, who was already eating his lunch, and started down the dusty road home. The call to prayer wavered from the village mosque, and it seemed to Muda that he could see it, waves of sound shimmering concurrently with the midday heat. It was the end of the fruit season, one of the last hot weeks before the rains began, and the weather was a fiery hand against his back. Muda walked with his straw hat pulled down low over his forehead, so he didn't see the children running toward him until they were quite near. They circled around him and pulled in close, like the petals on a closing flower.

"Pachik Muda." It was his oldest nephew, a boy named Amin. He was wearing shorts and holding the hand of his youngest sister, Maimunah, who stood brown and naked beside him. "Uncle, our mother says for you to come quickly to the river."

Muda stopped to consider. He was hungry, and the river was in the opposite direction of his home. He had risen before dawn and had worked hard all morning. Each tree required a narrow cut in the bark and a cup, precisely set, to collect the rubbery white sap. There were hundreds of trees in his area. He had worked hard, and he was hungry.

"Tell your mother," he said, "that I will come later. Right now I am going for my lunch." He expected them to run off then. They were the children of his sister, Norliza, and they were rarely naughty. But instead Amin released his sister's hand. He reached out and tugged at Muda's sarong.

"My mother says to come," he repeated. "Please, Pachik Muda, she says it is important."

Muda sighed then, but he turned and followed the children back along the road. Red rambutans and smooth green mangoes hung from the trees. He plucked some of these and ate them as he walked, wondering what he would find on the riverbank. Norliza had worked the rubber too, before she married, and she would not take him lightly from his rest and prayers.

When he reached the river he saw a cluster of women standing on the grassy bank. Norliza was in the center, her sarong wet to the knees, holding something out for the others to see.

"Norliza," he called. He was going to scold her for consuming his time with her bit of woman's nonsense, but before he could speak she ran to him and uncurled her fist. The lines in her palm were creased with dirt, so that the skin around them looked very pale. The words he had planned stopped in his mouth. For on her palm lay a piece of gold as large as a knuckle. It was wet with river water, and it caught the noon light like fire in her hand.

"The children found it," she said. "I was digging for roots." Norliza was a midwife, known in the village for her skill with herbs and massage. She came into the jungle every week to search for the healing roots and bark. "I was digging there, near the trees by the river. The children were playing next to me, sorting out the rocks for a game. This one they liked because of its shine. At first I did not realize. It was only when Amin washed it in the river that I understood." Her dark eyes gleamed with an unfamiliar excitement. "To think," she said. "To think he might have dropped it, and I would never have known."

Muda reached out and took the knot of gold. It was smooth, almost soft, against his fingers. He ran his thumb against it again and again. Some of the women drew close to stare. Others, he noticed, were already moving away with the news.

"It's not real," he said loudly, and dropped the lump of gold back into his sister's hand.

"Muda!" she said. She looked up at him from dark eyes. Once she had been the most beautiful girl in the village. Now the dark eyes were connected by a finely etched skin, and the expression on her face was reproachful. He took a deep breath and spoke again.

"I've worked all day in the rubber, and you waste my lunch-time with this foolishness. You are a silly woman," he added, though it gave him great pain to see how she flinched under the eyes of the other women. A ripple of murmuring voices moved through the crowd. They had lived in the village all their lives, and he had never spoken sharply to his sister. Even the women who had reached the road paused and turned back to watch. "You are a foolish woman," he repeated. "Foolish. And I am going home."

He turned and walked away with slow dignity. He didn't look back, but when he was certain he was out of sight he began to run with a speed he had not summoned since he was a boy.

Khamina was washing dishes when he burst inside. His lunch was set out on the floor — a plate of fish stuffed with coconut, a vegetable curry, several small bananas — but he paid no attention to it. Instead he ran to the wooden porch, where his wife was squatting amid a pile of soapy dishes.

"Khamina," he said. "Give me your cooking pot."

She stood up in surprise and gestured to the soapy wok soaking in the water. Then her eyes narrowed, and she looked him up and down.

"Muda," she said. "Why are you running through my house with your shoes on? Where is your mind? Today I scrubbed these floors, and here you are dragging the rubber field across them."

"Khamina," he said. He had scrubbed the pot and was now pouring water over it, clearing away the soap. "Let me tell you something. It is no time to complain about a little mud. This is an important day. My sister Norliza may be here soon. If she comes I want you to tell her that I have gone back to the river. Tell her to come there at once. She is not to speak to anyone. Do you hear me? Not to anyone! Tell her to come alone."

Muda splashed water on his face. Then he picked up Khamina's cooking pot and left the house. She followed him, stepping over the food he had ignored, standing in the doorway to watch him running through the heat of the day, her black pot swinging from his hand.

The sun was so hot that day that it consumed the sky and filled the air with a harsh metallic glare that had driven all the animals — chickens, cats, and mangy dogs — underneath the houses for shade. Nonetheless, Muda ran the entire way back to the river, not even pausing at the fork which led to the rubber plantation. When he reached the river he saw that Norliza and her children were still there, crouching by a shallow hole they had dug. The knuckle of gold was resting on a flat gray rock. When Norliza saw him she jumped up at once, wiping her damp hands against her sarong. She snatched the gold from the rock and ran to him.

"Muda, you fool," Norliza said, planting herself before him. He had run so hard that he could not answer and stood before her gasping for breath. "How could you speak to me so in front of the women from the village when I have made the greatest discovery in the memory of any person alive? Muda, you are my brother, but you are also a fool."

To her surprise Muda smiled at her, then broke out in laughter. No one had spoken to him this way since he had become a man.

"Norliza," he said, when he could speak, "take care of what you say. I am not one of your children, and I am no fool. You might as well say so of a crocodile, sitting still and thoughtless as a log in the river."

"This is gold," she insisted, but in a softer voice. Strands of hair had fallen against her face and she brushed at them with the back of her hand.

Muda reached out and once again held the nugget in his hand. He could not get enough of the soft feel of it on his skin, and he worked it between his fingers.

"Yes," he said. "It is gold. Now show me exactly where you found it before all the women in this village return, with their husbands and their neighbors, to dig."

Once Norliza understood, she worked as Muda had known she would — quietly, quickly, and with the fierce determination of a woman who had always been poor. Together they drove stakes into the ground, marking off a plot that stretched along the river and reached to the edge of the jungle. When the stakes were secure he tied ropes between them. Then he climbed inside the area they had claimed and began to dig. Norliza sent the two oldest boys into the shallows of the river, where they washed the stones she and Muda took from the red earth. The younger children ferried dirt and rocks back and forth in the cooking pot. The older boys sorted the stones into two piles for their mother to examine: those that shone, and those that did not.

On the long run from his house Muda had lost his straw hat, and now his hair was like lit kindling against his neck and ears. From time to time he went to the river and splashed water over his head, but he did not stop to rest. In the rubber trees he had learned how to work efficiently in the midday heat. There he knew how much work had to be finished and how long it would take, and so he rested often in the hot afternoons, sometimes curling up in the old caretaker's huts, other times leaning against the slender trunk of a tree. Here the heat was greater, the work harder, but there was also no limit to what he might find. He worked surely and swiftly and without a single break in the movements of his hands.

Muda was a poor man. As a child this had never bothered him. Everyone in the village was poor, after all, and in the next village it was just the same. He had not thought of it as a lack. There was always fruit to eat, the river was full of fish, and water buffaloes were killed for wedding feasts. As a child, running in the murky water of the rice fields, or shimmying up the young coconut trees to shake down the fruit, he had been happy.

At sixteen all of this changed. He was offered a job at the rubber plantation. That first day, he had walked the six miles from his house to arrive, scared and shy, before daybreak. In those early months he worked as he was working now in the earth, all his attention focused on the rows of graceful rubber trees, on the thin streams of white that flowed into the cups he placed. Due to his industry he won a bonus, which he used to buy a motorbike, the first in his village. He was the envy of the men and he knew he could have any of the young girls, swaying in their tight sarongs as he sped past them, for his wife.

It was then that he began to notice the new cars and expensive suits of the plantation owners. They came once a month to inspect their investments and Muda watched them with awe — their shiny leather shoes, the odd flap of their ties — as they disappeared beneath the trees. When they were out of sight he crept up to one of the cars, a gold Mercedes, and ran his fingers across the smooth, hot metal. Inside, the seats were upholstered in a leather as soft as a monkey's palm. He thought of his own small motorbike, how it sent sparks through the girls and put envy in the eyes of his former schoolmates, and tried to imagine how it would feel to own this gleaming car. Then the men were coming back; he moved silently into the trees and watched them drive away, the golden car disappearing in a cloud of fine red dust. Later, deep in the forest, making the thin cuts in the bark, his fingertips still held the various textures of the car. He worked at the rubber harder than ever, determined that one day such a car would be his.

The next year he married. Khamina was not the prettiest girl in the village, but she was famous for her pandan weaving, for deft fingers that could shape the fragrant leaves. She made a mat for his bike to rest on, and when they were married she covered the whole of their little house with woven mats. At night they lay on these. He was surrounded by the smell of cut grass, by the warm, fleshy scent that rose like smoke from Khamina. In that year his plans for the rubber trees diminished. He thought: Next week I will get to the plantation early, I will tap another dozen trees, I will earn another bonus, and another, and someday I will be rich. But he had not done that, preferring to linger near the smooth, tempting body of his new wife, and within a year the first baby came. He was working just as hard but suddenly there was less money, not more, and as his other children came he was working more and more hours just to earn enough to feed them. Now, as he dug, he did not think of the endless rows of rubber trees. He did not regret the white sap falling silently, spilling over in the cups and wasting on the earth. What he remembered was the buttery car of the plantation boss, trimmed with brilliant gold.

In the late afternoon the other villagers began to arrive. When they saw what Muda and Norliza had done, excitement spread among them like a swift river wind. Muda heard their sighs, their gasps and exclamations, he heard the stakes driven into land, the sound of digging and excited voices. But he did not look up, and he did not change his pace.

He did not look up until a shadow fell across his back like the brush of a cool hand. It was Khamina standing over him. She had been a delicate girl, lithe and nimble. Now her sarong found no indentation at the waist and the fabric of her blouse pulled tightly against her breasts and arms. Even the skin on her face was drawn tightly over her cheekbones. Her lips were thin and they trembled with anger.

"Muda!" she called out sternly. All the heads turned at once to look at her. They were familiar faces, each one known to her for as many years as she had lived on earth, but she ignored them and looked directly at her husband. "Muda," she said. "What has possessed you?"

"Khamina," he said, standing up. "This is a great day in the village, Khamina. We have discovered gold."

"Gold?" she repeated. Behind him Norliza came up with the nugget displayed in her palm.

"It is true, Khamina. Gold."

"One piece," she scoffed.

"There must be more," Muda said. "To find only one nugget would be like finding only a single leaf on a tree."

For a moment it seemed she would be pacified by these words and by the bright irregular lump in Norliza's dirty palm. Then her eyes, following the trenches Muda had been digging, fell upon her cooking pot. With a cry she reached down and swept it up, shaking out the red dust and rocks he had carefully assembled.

"I have one cooking pot," she said. "It is not for carrying dirt. And I have one husband, whose job is in the rubber trees. What are you doing here, Muda? Abdullah has been to the house twice looking for you. Your trees have spread their sap all over the ground. Muda, I did not marry a ditch digger."

She turned then toward home, holding the dirty pot out to her side. She walked quickly and Muda knew that she was hurrying because the dusk was coming. Khamina was religious, but she also believed in spirits, and she did not want to be alone on the road at the hour when they came out.

Khamina was not alone in her fears, and before the sun set many people went home. Muda watched them leave, wondering which among them would seek his job in the rubber trees. Still, despite Khamina's words, he did not leave. Like others, he lit torches along the riverbank and kept digging long past the time he could see clearly. Finally Norliza put her hand on his shoulder and told him to stop. She handed him some rice she had brought from home. He rinsed his hands in the river and began to eat, sucking the sticky grains off his fingers. He had missed his lunch, and in the cool night air from the river he was suddenly very hungry.

"What will you do?" Norliza asked finally. Only a few people were left, quietly digging. "Will you come back tomorrow?" Muda shaped some pebbles into a small hill. Then he dug his hands into the center of it and let the smooth stones rain across the ground. As they fell an idea came to him.

"I will spend tonight at the mosque praying about this matter."

She nodded. It had been their father's habit to sleep in the mosque when faced with a severe problem, waiting for guidance. They sat quietly for several minutes. Muda continued sifting through the stones. He liked their smooth feel, the warmth they still retained from the heat of the day. It was Norliza who noticed that one stone caught the moonlight in a different way, and Muda who picked it up and rinsed it in the river. It was another nugget, much smaller than Norliza's piece. But it was gold, all the same.

"Your fate," she said, wonder in her voice.

"Yes," Muda said. He felt the wonder too.

Khamina could not answer him when he handed her the gold and the story of the sign he had received, but she was not happy. She closed her lips and refused to make him food to take to the riverside, and after a few days he realized that she had sent the children to her mother's house and had taken over his job in the rubber trees. This shamed him. However, his days were full of hard work, and the excitement that had possessed him on the first day did not die. Even when a day passed, or sometimes two or three days, in which no gold was found, Muda maintained his hope. Some people gave up; others began to grumble and speak of quitting. The mood of the group would grow dark and futile, and the pace of the work would slow. Then, suddenly, there would come a shout. No find was as big as the first one Norliza had made, but each one was enough to revive the spirits of the gold diggers. For every person who quit, two others came to dig, and soon the area was a swamp of mud and deep holes that filled with water when they were left overnight.

Muda dug. Even at night he dreamed that he was digging, and in his dreams his shovel touched vast boulders of gold, or caches of gold nuggets that he lifted up and let spill from his fingers. Once, in his dream, he unearthed a big car made purely of gold, and another time it was hermit crabs that came running to him, discarding their stolen shells, their soft bodies and scuttling legs all made, miraculously, from gold. He often woke from these dreams with a start, into the deep night, the soft breathing of his wife and children all around him. At these times he looked at Khamina's face, soft with sleep. She would no longer speak to him, and put his evening rice down with a tired thump. Even the children avoided him now; when he came in, late and muddy, they retreated to the edges of the room, staring, as if he were a river spirit that had come to carry them off. Once awake, Muda often could not return to sleep. Instead, he went to the river, where he worked the rest of the night in the dark, as if by blurring the state between waking and dreaming he could bring the plenty of his dreams into the vivid light of day.

Yet he found no more gold. Many others had success; even Norliza had a small bag around her waist, heavy with nuggets she had sifted from the mud and water. It seemed to be a gift in her hands, that they knew where to seek, felt the shine that Muda could only see. Muda worked hard, sometimes digging far into the night, until the hole he had made reached up above his shoulders. Because Khamina had taken over his job, he worked with a great and ongoing guilt. Some nights he was afraid that if he went home he would not have the courage to return to the gold fields the next day. On those nights he went instead to the mosque. There, lying on the cool stone floor, he held his single piece of gold in his palm and prayed. For if this was truly a message from his god, why now was he being ignored, while all around him others profited?

One day the rains began, first as a light mist and then harder, so that a small pool formed in the bottom of his newest hole, and mud ran down his arms with each shovel he lifted from the earth. Late that afternoon, as Muda squatted on his heels by the side of the river, soaking wet and empty-handed, he thought that

Khamina was right. He should give it up, this foolishness. He could not continue to live on hope. The night before, he had been forced to ask for a loan of rice from one of his friends. Walking home, the rice had been an enormous weight in his hands. He remembered the joy of his wedding, and how that joy had dwindled into something much smaller, smaller with each child and responsibility until it no longer buoyed him up, but hung from him like a weight.

He knew he should quit the gold fields. The thought of this relieved the weight, but to such a degree that he felt riddled with an emptiness, as if his emotions reflected the spoiled, hacked landscape of the riverbank. For he saw now that working in the rubber trees was a hopeless life. Many went there with dreams, but no rubber tapper would ever own a car the color of the sun. People tried hard, he himself had tried, but there was no evidence of their effort in the village, where the houses were still lit by kerosene and the only running water flowed in the river. With gold they might drive themselves to ruin, but at least the hope was always there.

The rain was warm. It swept across the river like prayer veils in the wind and fell so heavily that he could not see the opposite shore. He was wet, and the dirt between his fingers was a warm, gritty mud. He rubbed it mechanically, feeling it melt away into nothing. Then he came upon something hard and sharp. Curious, thinking it was a piece of glass or tin, he rinsed the object in the river. To his surprise it was a tiny gold kris, a wavering Malay sword about ten centimeters long, inscribed with a verse from the Koran. Its tiny point was still sharp, but Muda could tell that it was very old.

"Norliza," he called through the veil of rain to where his sister was kneeling in the mud. "Norliza, come look at what I have found."

Muda was not devout, and so he was astonished by the reaction of the village to his discovery. The news spread quickly, until Muda could not go anywhere without people asking to see the kris. Even Ainon, the vegetable seller, held a newspaper over her head against the rain in order to have a glimpse, turning the kris in her brown fingers. She handed it back to him and quickly pressed her palms together in a prayer.

"You are blessed," she said. Then she chose the largest melon from the pile and handed it to him. "Take this one, please. Take it as a gift, and remember this old woman in your prayers."

No longer did people joke about his bad luck with the gold. Even Khamina was somewhat appeased. She served his rice more gently in the evening, and took to covering her hair when she went outside to shop. In the gold fields he felt the reverence of people like a circle of quietness around him.

One morning Muda arrived at the gold fields to find a dozen men in khaki uniforms handing out sheets of damp paper, announcing their news through a megaphone that cut through the mist and echoed back from the river's opposite shore.

"What is this?" he asked the nearest official, who turned toward him and thrust a paper in his hand.

"There's been a complaint," he said. He was a very young man, as young as Muda had been when he first went to the rubber plantation. "About illegal digging. Didn't you know? You must have a paper before you dig this land."

"Who complained?" Muda asked. He was not surprised to learn that it was a group from another village, latecomers who had found no gold on their faraway plots. Now these strangers stood around the fringes of the gold field, smiling because they already held the required papers in their hands. They looked greedily at the careful stakes and cordoned areas which, with a single government decree, had become ownerless.

"This isn't right," Muda said. "It isn't fair. When we go to the capital for our papers, these others will take our claims." His hand went to the kris around his neck. He'd started to wear it on a piece of string, and took some inexplicable comfort from the feel of its inscription.

The young man noticed his action. "Uncle," he said, "what's that you've got there?" Muda pressed the kris once before he opened his hand to display it for the officer. Its sharp point pricked his skin with an illuminating pain.

"This is my divine guidance," he began, and he told the young man how he had found the kris. "So, you see, this decree of yours goes beyond unfairness. It works against the directive of the heavens, as well."

The young man looked uncomfortable. He pushed the cap back on his dark hair and shook his head.

"But what can I do?" he said.

"You can give us one day. Let one person go from each family for a paper. Let the others stay and dig. If there is someone without a permit tomorrow, that person must give up the claim. But we deserve this day of grace."

The young man went to talk with his superior, and then the two of them went to see still another man. Muda watched them talking, shifting their feet uneasily in the muddy ground. Soon the chief officer came over to hear Muda's story. He also examined the kris and held it in his palm. Then he picked up the megaphone and announced that the villagers would be given one day to file their claims.

It was Norliza who went from their family, running home for money and to change her clothes, giving Muda the small sack of nuggets she carried on her waist. She kissed each of her children twice on the forehead, and told Amin, her oldest, to watch after them carefully. Then she, along with the others, was gone.

All morning Muda felt the unspoken animosity of the people from the other villages. He tried to work, but sometimes had a sense of foreboding so strong that the back of his neck felt cold and damp, as if suddenly beneath the shadow that would precede a blow. Several times he jerked swiftly around, but there was nothing. People worked stodgily at their claims, and when he looked at them the sense of danger disappeared like mist. Still, he would remember the feeling later, the drifting unease that became manifest early in the afternoon.

Muda was up to his waist in a new hole when he heard the shouts. He jumped out of the earth and saw Amin screaming, pointing frantically at the head of his sister as she surfaced from where she had fallen in the river. Briefly, Muda saw her head and shoulders turn in the slow current near the riverbank. It had been a calm river when the gold was discovered, but the rains had fattened it. Water surged with force near the center, making frothy, churning patterns that had fascinated Maimunah and drawn her to the river's edge. Now she drifted from the shore, and entered the chaos. Muda, who could not swim well himself, did not think twice. The faces of his own children were in his mind as he leaped after her into the swirling waters.

The current was a thousand hands, pulling him in different directions. He fought it at first, but each time he thrust his head above water he was pulled down again, rushed against the riverbed, whose stones, he thought, feeling them rub against his face and stomach, might well have been made of gold. Gold. In the churning water death, he understood the emptiness of gold. His lungs ached, and he was thrust out of the water long enough to gulp a deep breath, long enough to catch a glimpse of Maimunah's terrified face, inches away from him. He dove forward, grasping water, and wished he had the power of his sister's hands, hands that could sift out gold from stones, hands that coaxed life into the world. Hands that would know how to fend off these river spirits who were dragging him below again.

Somewhere at the bottom of the river, rushed along so that his pockets filled with stones and water, he gave up. By some miracle the kris was still around his neck; he closed his hand around it and stopped fighting. He was a log, heavy, a log burning inside but motionless, bounced along with the current, tossed this way, then that. He was smashed into an underwater boulder with such force that he thought his arm must have broken, but even then he did not resist. And suddenly, as if he were a mouse in the mouth of the river spirits, they tired of their game and tossed him up into a calm place, a buckle in the river where the water was still and quiet.

This calmer water was full of debris. Broken branches floated near him, and he pushed past the carcasses of dead cats and lizards as he made his way to the shore. Maimunah was there. Her shorts had been torn away but her shirt was still on and was tangled in some branches. He feared she was dead, because she did not answer when he called to her. She was alive — when he touched her, she turned her head to look at him — but he was filled with a deep fear because her gaze was still and blank, like calm water, and he thought that one of the river spirits had entered her while they held her underneath the water. He hooked his broken arm around a branch, wedging his elbow tightly into the mud. He was so exhausted, suddenly, that he thought he might slip back into the calm water and sink like a stone. It was only Maimunah who caused him to hold on. He collected her in his good arm, where she clung to him like a sea creature. He put his mouth very close to her ear, and he began to sing. The old songs, first of all, songs about the land, the trees, the tall grass that waved around the river. When his voice began to fade he turned to prayers that he remembered, interspersed with the verses from his lucky kris. In the end, he was reduced to only a phrase, muttering it over and over. His arms had gone numb from the weight of the child and of the tree. That was how the villagers found them.

The people of the village had not discussed the river spirits in years, but after Muda became so sick, they began to remember the stories. There were spirits of the water who could drag you underneath to live on air and algae; there were spirits of the currents who could enter your mind and set it spinning for the rest of your life. This was the one they feared had entered Muda. For ten days he was overtaken by a fever so strong that he twisted and mumbled on the floor of his home, and he flailed at Khamina when she tried to bring him water. The imam came, and the local healer, who lit candles in all four corners of the room and changed verses from the Koran, and cried out in the voices of the river spirits, trying to lure them out, to lure them home. In the end even he left, shaking his head, saying that these spirits were strong — there was nothing to be done but to wait, and pray.

On the eleventh day the fever broke by itself. Khamina had fallen into an uneasy sleep, propped against the wall across from Muda. She woke to a silence, a certain strangeness in the air. For an instant she thought he had died, but when she opened her eyes she saw him staring at her from across the room. He blinked, and asked quite clearly for a glass of water. Yet even after the fever had broken, he remained weak. People who came to visit him noticed that he hardly spoke, that his eyes wandered into the dark corners of the house, and that he was constantly touching the kris hanging from his neck. Often he was heard murmuring the verses that were inscribed there by a hand long dead.

In this time, when the villagers feared for his mind but not for his life, Muda himself was afraid of dying. During the fever he had dreamed recurring dreams of light, as strong as midday sun but without the heat. When the fever broke, these dreams did not vanish. It seemed to him that he was walking between two worlds, the familiar world of his home and one that he had dreamed, warm and unfamiliar and full of a white, soothing light. He did not wish to see anyone, not because he felt weak but because their voices seemed to come to him from so far away, through a sound like water rushing, that it cost him a great effort to listen to them. For several weeks he sat on the porch of his home, looking out into the white light that surrounded him day and night, and waited for some signal. He had it one day when the call to prayer came to him clearly, a low, sweet, peaceful voice that was not marred by the rush and static of other sounds. He listened to it, moved by its clarity, by the familiar rhythm of the words. He touched the gold kris on his bony chest. It took several days, but from that moment the world began to come back to him, until everything around him shone with a vividness, a clarity, that he did not remember from before.

When he was well enough, Muda went back to his job in the rubber trees. Khamina rejoiced at first, thinking he had returned to his senses. She reestablished her place on the porch with her stacks of fragrant leaves, and for a few days she watched Muda carefully, hardly daring to believe again in the normal pattern of her life. Yet even when the village leaders came to explain how they had saved his plot at the gold fields, Muda was not tempted. He waved them away, saying only that the claim was Norliza's now; she could do what she wanted with it.

It was only as the days passed into weeks that Khamina began to understand that the madness of the gold had not disappeared, but had only been transformed. In the evenings, after the last call to prayer, she set Muda's rice out carefully on the leaves and waited for him to come home. But as in the worst days of gold, he did not appear. She discovered that he was stopping at the mosque on his way home, and that sometimes he stayed there far into the night, his forehead pressed to the cool stone floor in prayer. At home he often retreated to the porch with a lamp and his new copy of the holy book, and she sometimes woke in the middle of the night to see him there, the light flickering across his face as he murmured in the language of the imams. He grew thin and the fever-light in his eyes did not fade. He moved through his days with a terrible strange energy. She was afraid, but she could not complain, not about the Koran, or about his hard work, or anything.

He took his new devotion even into the rubber trees with him.

No longer did he nap throughout the long afternoons; instead, he prayed, a murmur that mingled with the rustling sounds of the trees. That was how the boys found him when the plantation owners came one day to his house. They followed the sound of his voice at prayer. He was resting in the rubber trees, drinking tea and turning the pages of his holy book. Muda heard the boys coming, and put the cup down slowly on the ground. When they burst into the small clearing, he saw the excitement and fear on their faces, and his hand moved without thought to cover the kris on his chest. He said one last prayer, then followed the children back to his house, where the men were waiting.

It was the kris they wanted. That much he understood even before they spoke. The village chief was there, drinking the expensive Coca-Cola that Khamina had poured for all the visitors. The plantation owner did all the talking. He explained to Muda that he had heard about the kris from a government official. Did Muda know that his kris had probably belonged to a sultan's wife, over one hundred years before? She was a devout woman, and she wore it on a thin gold chain around her neck. According to the family story, she had lost it one day while crossing the river in a boat. It was a miracle, really, that it was found. Now, the kris belonged in a museum. It wasn't as though Muda was giving it away, really. He could go to see it any time. But this way others could see it too. They were sure he would want to share this kris. And it was, after all, a decree of the sultan.

Muda listened carefully, the kris resting in the palm of his hand as the man spoke. This kris was his, only his; that was something he knew. He thought about the way he had found it, how it had saved the gold fields for his village, how it had saved his life. The thought that someone could come and take it made him burn inside, go breathless. He started to speak, but the words died in his mouth. It would do no good. A decree of the sultan was not something with which one could argue. The kris would be taken regardless of what he said. And so, when they finally finished speaking, he did not say a word. He put the kris into the rich man's hand, a hand that was soft and damp with sweat. Then he stood up gracefully and walked out of his house, but Khamina noted that for all his dignity the wild light had gone completely out of his eyes.

They had come in the gold car and Muda followed them as it

left, walking steadily after the glimmering gold as it receded on the horizon. Even after it was long out of sight, the dust it had stirred up settling on the fruit trees, he walked. Finally all trace of the car was gone, and he squatted down on the side of the road in the shade. He tried to tell himself it was the divine will, but all the holy verses, even the one on the kris, which he had known in his fingertips, had fled from his mind. He sat like that, quite silent, in a vast emptiness. Across from him the golden dome of the mosque glinted in the midday sun, brightly, like a jewel.

DIANE JOHNSON

Great Barrier Reef

FROM THE NEW YORKER

THE MOTEL had smelled of cinder block and cement floor, and was full of Australian senior citizens off a motor coach, but when we woke up in the morning a little less jet-lagged, and from the balcony could see the bed of a tidal river, with ibis and herons poking along the shallows, and giant ravens and parrots in the trees — trees strangling with Monstera vines, all luridly beautiful — we felt it would be all right. But then, when we went along to the quay, I felt it wouldn't. The ship, the *Dolphin,* was smaller than one could have imagined. Where could sixteen passengers possibly sleep? Brown stains from rusted drain spouts spoiled the hull. Gray deck paint splattered the ropes and ladders, orange primer showed through the chips. Wooden crates of lettuce and cabbages and a case of peas in giant tin cans were stacked on the deck. This cruise had been J.'s idea, so I tried not to seem reproachful, or shocked, at the tiny, shabby vessel. But I am not fond of travel in the best of circumstances — inconvenient displacements punctuated by painful longings to be home. For J., travel is natural opium.

J. was on his way to a meeting in Singapore of the International Infectious Disease Council, a body of eminent medical specialists from different lands who are charged with making decisions about diseases. Should the last remaining smallpox virus be destroyed? What was the significance of a pocket of polio in Sri Lanka? Could leprosy be finished off with a full-bore campaign in the spring? Was tuberculosis on the way back now via AIDS? What about measles in the Third World? I had not realized until

I took up with J. that these remote afflictions were still around, let alone that they killed people in the millions. A professor of medicine, J. did research on things that infected the lungs.

He had always longed to visit the Great Barrier Reef, and afterward would give some lectures in Sydney and Wellington, and we planned to indulge another whim en route — skiing in New Zealand in the middle of summer, just to say we'd skied in August and as a bribe to me to come along, for I will go anywhere to ski, it is the one thing. For me the voyage was one of escape from California after some difficult times, and was to be — this was unspoken by either of us — a sort of trial honeymoon (though we were not married) on which we would discover whether we were suited to live together by subjecting ourselves to that most serious of tests, traveling together.

A crewman named Murray, a short, hardy man with a narrow Scots face and thick Aussie accent, showed us our stateroom. It had been called a stateroom in the brochure. Unimaginably small. J. couldn't stand up all the way in it. Two foam mattresses on pallets suspended from the wall, and a smell. The porthole was seamed with salt and rust. Across the passage, the door of another stateroom was open, but that one was a large, pretty room, with mahogany and nautical brass fittings and a desk, and the portholes shone. It was the one, certainly, that had been pictured in the brochure.

"This one here, the Royal, was fitted for Prince Charles, Prince of Wales, when he come on this voyage in 1974," Murray said.

"How do you book the Royal?" I asked.

"First come, first served," Murray said. Australian, egalitarian, opposed to privilege.

Up on deck, thinking of spending five days on the *Dolphin,* I began to be seized by feelings of panic and pain I couldn't explain. They racketed about in my chest, my heart beat fast, I felt as if a balloon were inflating inside me, squeezing up tears and pressing them out of my eyes and thrusting painful words up into my throat, where they lodged. What was the matter with me? Usually I am a calm person (I think); five days is not a lifetime; the aesthetics of a mattress — or its comfort — is not a matter for serious protests. A smell of rotten water sloshing somewhere inside the hull could be gotten used to. Anyone could eat tinned peas five days and survive, plenty of people in the world were glad to get tinned peas. I knew all that. I knew I wasn't reacting appropriately, and was sorry for this querulous fit of passion. Maybe it was only jet lag.

All the same, I said to J., "I just can't," and stared tragically at the moorings. He knew, of course, that I could and probably would, but he maintained an attitude of calm sympathy.

"You've been through a rough time," he said. "It's the court thing you're really upset about." Maybe so. The court thing, a draining and frightening custody suit, had been only a week ago, and now here we were a hemisphere away.

The other passengers came on board, one by one or two by two. Cases clattered on the metal gangs. To me, only one person looked possible — a tall, handsome, youngish man with scholarly spectacles and a weathered yachting cap. The rest were aged and fat, plain, wore shapeless brown or navy blue coat-sweaters buttoned over paunches, had gray perms and bald spots, and they all spoke in this accent I disliked, as if their vowels had been slammed in doors. They spoke like cats, I thought: *eeeoooow*. Fat Australians, not looking fond of nature, why were they all here?

"Why are these people here?" I complained to J. "What do they care about the Great Barrier Reef?"

"It's a wonder of the world, anyone would want to see it," J. said, assuming the same dreamy expression he always wore when talking or thinking about the Great Barrier Reef, so long the object of his heart.

I hated all the other passengers. On a second inspection, besides the youngish man, only a youngish couple, Dave and Rita, looked promising, but then I was infuriated to learn that Dave and Rita were Americans — we hadn't come all this way to be cooped up for five days in a prison of an old Coast Guard cutter with other Americans — and, what was worse, Rita and Dave had drawn the Prince Charles cabin, and occupied it as if by natural right, Americans expecting and getting luxury.

Of course, I kept these overwrought feelings to myself. No Australian complained. None appeared unhappy with the ship; no satirical remark, no questioning comment, marred their apparent delight with the whole shipshape of things — the cabins, even the appalling lunch, which was under way as soon as the little craft set out, pointing itself east, toward the open sea, from Mackay Harbor.

After we lost sight of land, my mood of desperate resentment did not disappear, as J. had predicted, but deepened. It was more than the irritability of a shallow, difficult person demanding comfort, it was a failure of spirit, inexplicable and unwarranted on this bright afternoon. How did these obese Australian women, these stiff old men, clamber so uncomplainingly belowdecks to their tiny cells, careen along the railings, laughing crazily as they tripped on ropes? Doubtless one would fall and the voyage would be turned back. When I thought of the ugliness of the things I had just escaped from — the unpleasant divorce, the custody battle, the hounding of lawyers and strangers — only to find myself in such a place as this, really unmanageable emotions made me turn my face away from the others.

Dinner was tinned peas, and minted lamb overdone to a gray rag, and potatoes. J. bought a bottle of wine from the little bar, which the deckhand Murray nimbly leaped behind, transforming himself into waiter or bartender as required. We sat with the promising young man, Mark, and offered him some wine, but he said he didn't drink wine. He was no use; he was very, very prim, a bachelor civil servant from Canberra, with a slight stammer, only handsome and young by some accident, and would someday be old without changing, would still be taking lonely cruises, eating minted lamb, would still be unmarried and reticent. He had no conversation, had never been anywhere, did not even know what we wanted from him. Imagining his life, I thought about how sad it was to be him, hoping for whatever he hoped for but not hoping for the right things, content to eat these awful peas, doomed by being Australian, and even while I pitied him I found him hopeless. Even J., who could talk to anyone, gave up trying to talk to him, and, feeling embarrassed to talk only to each other as if he weren't there, we fell silent and stared out the windows at the rising moon along the black horizon of the sea.

There didn't seem a way, in the tiny cabin, for two normal-sized people to exist, let alone to make love; there was no space that could accommodate two bodies in any position. Our suitcases filled half the room. With our summer clothing, our proper suits to wear in Wellington and Sydney, and bulky ski clothes of quilted down, we were ridiculously encumbered with baggage. It seemed stupid now. We were obliged to stow our bags and coats precariously on racks overhead, our duffel bags sleeping at the feet of our bunks like lumpy interloper dogs. J. took my hand comfortingly in the dark, across the space between the two bunks, before he dropped off to sleep; I lay awake, seized with a terrible fit of traveler's panic, suffocating with fearful visions of fire, of people in prison cells or confined in army tanks, their blazing bodies emerging screaming from the holds of ships to writhe doomed on the ground, their stick limbs ringed in flame, people burned in oil splashed on them from the holds of rusted ships, and smells of underground, smells of sewers, the slosh of engine fuel from the hell beneath.

As is so often the traveler's fate, nothing on the cruise was as promised or as we had expected. The seedy crew of six had tourist-baked smiles and warmed-over jokes. There was a little faded captain who climbed out of his tower to greet us now and then, and a sort of Irish barmaid, Maureen, who helped Murray serve the drinks. The main business of the passage seemed not to be the life of the sea or the paradise of tropical birds on Pacific shores or the balmy water but putting in at innumerable islands to look at souvenir shops. J., his mind on the Great Barrier Reef, which we were expected to reach on the fourth day, sweetly bore it all, the boredom and the endless stops at each little island, but I somehow couldn't conquer my petulant dislike.

It fastened, especially, on our shipmates. Reluctantly, I learned their names, in order to detest them with more precision: Don and Donna from New Zealand, Priscilla from Adelaide — portly, harmless old creatures, as J. pointed out. Knowing that the derisive remarks that sprang to my lips revealed me only as petty and complaining to good-natured J., I didn't speak them aloud. But it seemed to me that these Australians wanted to travel only to rummage in the souvenir shops, though these were all alike from island to island: Daydream Island, Hook Island — was this a cultural or a generation gap? I brooded on the subject of souvenirs: why they should exist, why people should want them, by what law they were made ugly — shells shaped like toilets, a row of swizzlesticks in the shapes of women's silhouetted bodies, thin, fatter, fat, with bellies and breasts increasingly sagging as they graduated from "Sweet Sixteen" to "Sixty." I was unsettled to notice that the one depicting a woman of my age had a noticeably thickened middle. I watched a man buy a fat one and hand it to his wife. "Here, Mother, this one's you," he said. Laughter a form of hate. It was not a man from our ship, luckily, or I would have pushed him overboard. I brooded on my own complicity in the industry of souvenirs, for didn't I buy them myself? The things I bought — the tasteful (I liked to think) baskets and elegant textiles I was always carting home — were these not just a refined form of souvenir for a more citified sort of traveler?

Statuettes of drunken sailors, velvet pictures of island maidens, plastic seashell lamps made in Taiwan. What contempt the people who think up souvenirs have for other people! Yet our fellow passengers plunked down money with no feeling of shame. They never walked on the sand or looked at the colors of the bright patchwork birds rioting in the palm trees. Besides us, only the other Americans, Rita and Dave, did this. It was Dave who found the perfect helmet shell, a regular treasure, the crew assured them, increasingly rare, protected even — you weren't supposed to carry them away, but who was looking? I wanted it to have been J. who got it.

Each morning, each afternoon, we stopped at another island. This one was Daydream Island. "It's lovely, isn't it, dear?" Priscilla said to me. "People like to see a bit of a new place, the shopping, they have different things to make it interesting." But it wasn't different, it was the same each day: the crew hands the heavy, sacklike people, grunting, down into rowboats, and hauls them out onto a sandy slope of beach. Up they trudge toward a souvenir shop. This one had large shells perched on legs, and small shells pasted in designs on picture frames, and earrings made of shells, and plastic buckets, and plastic straw hats surrounded with fringe, and pictures of hula dancers.

"I don't care, I do hate them," I ranted passionately to J. "I'm right to hate them. They're what's the matter with the world, they're ugly consumers, they can't look at a shell unless it's coated in plastic, they never look at the sea — why are they here? Why don't they stay in Perth and Adelaide — you can buy shells there, and swizzlesticks in the shape of hula girls." Of course J. hadn't any answer for this, of course I was right.

I wandered onto a stretch of beach and took off my shoes, planning to wade. Whenever I was left alone I found myself harking back to the court hearing, my recollections just as sharp and painful as a week ago. I couldn't keep from going over and over my ordeal, and thinking of my hated former husband, or not really him so much as his lawyer, Waxman, a man in high-heeled boots and aviator glasses. I imagined him here in these waters. He has fallen overboard off the back of the ship. I am the only one to notice, and I have the power to cry out for his rescue but I don't. Our eyes meet; he is down in the water, still wearing the glasses. I imagine his expression of surprise when he realizes that I'm not going to call for help. What for him had been a mere legal game, a job, would cost him his life. He had misjudged me. The ship speeds along. We are too far away to hear his cries.

It was the third day, and we had set down at Happy Island. Here we had to wade across a sandbar. This island had goats grazing. "This is the first we've gotten wet," I bitterly complained. We stood in ankle-deep water amid queer gelatinous seaweed. I had wanted to swim, to dive, to sluice away the court and the memories, but hadn't been permitted to, because these waters, so innocently beautiful, so seductively warm, were riddled with poisonous creatures, deadly toxins, and sharks.

"Be careful not to pick up anything that looks like this," Murray warned, showing us a harmless-looking little shell. "The deadly cone shell. And the coral, be careful a' that, it scratches like hell. One scratch can take over a year to heal. We have some ointment on board, be sure to tell one of the crew if you scratch yourself."

From here, I looked back at the ship, and, seeing the crew watching us, I suddenly saw ourselves, the passengers, with the crew's eyes: we were a collection of thick bodies, mere cargo to be freighted around, slightly volatile, likely to ferment, like damp grain, and to give trouble — difficult cargo that boozed, sent you scurrying unreasonably on tasks, got itself cut on coral, made you laugh at its jokes. I could see that the crew must hate us.

Yet, a little later, I came upon Murray tying on a fishhook for old George, whose fingers were arthritic. Murray was chatting to him with a natural smile. I studied them. Perhaps Murray by himself was a man of simple good nature, but the rest, surely, hated us. The captain, staring coolly out from his absurd quarterdeck, made no pretense of liking us, seemed always to be thinking of something else, not of this strange Pacific civilization of Quonset huts and rotting landing barges and odd South Sea denizens strangely toothless, beyond dentistry, beyond fashion, playing old records over and over on P.A. systems strung through the palms. You felt the forlornness of these tacky little islands that should have been beautiful and serene. I even wondered if we would ever get back to America. Not that I wanted to. America was smeared with horrible memories, scenes of litigation. Why shouldn't J. and I simply stay here? Why, more important, was I not someone who was able, like the lovely goat that grazed on the slope near here, to gaze at the turquoise sea and enjoy the sight of little rose-colored parrots wheeling in the air? Why was I not, like a nice person, simply content to *be,* to enjoy beauty and inner peace? Instead I must suffer, review, quiver with fears and rages — the fault, I saw, was in myself, I was a restless, peevish, flawed person. How would I be able to struggle out of this frame of mind? Slipping on the sandy bank, I frightened the little goat.

By the third day I began to notice a sea change in our shipmates, who had begun in sensible gabardines and print dresses, but now wore violently floral shirts and dresses, and were studded with shells — wreaths of shells about their necks and at their ears, hats embroidered with crabs and gulls. By now I knew a bit more about them. They were all travelers. George and Nettie, Fred and Polly, had been friends for forty years, and spent a part of each year, now that they were all retired, traveling in Europe in their caravans. Dave and Rita were both schoolteachers, and Rita raised Great Danes. Priscilla was going along on this cruise with her brother Albert, because Albert had just lost his wife. Mark was taking his annual vacation. Don and Donna were thinking of selling their Auckland real-estate business, buying a sailboat to live on, and circumnavigating the globe. J. told me that George was a sensitive and sweet man who had lived his whole life in Australia, and only now in his retirement had begun to see something of the world. "And he says that the most beautiful place on earth is some place near Split, in Yugoslavia, and if I take you there, my darling, will you for God's sake cheer up now?" But I couldn't.

Tonight we were dining ashore, in a big shed on Frenchie's Island, a shabby tin building. Music was already playing on loudspeakers. Groups of people from other ships, or hotels, strolled around carrying drinks. A smell of roasted sausages, someone singing "Waltzing Matilda" in the kitchen at the back. The *Dolphin* passengers were lined up at the bar and in the souvenir shop. In the big hangar of a room little tables encircled a dance floor, and at one end a microphone stood against a photo mural of the South Seas, as if the real scene outdoors were not sufficiently evocative. The sun lowered across the pink water, setting in the east, and the water in the gentle lagoon was as warm as our blood. "I wish a hurricane would come and blow it all away," I said to J.

When the diners had tipped their paper plates into a bin, they began to sing old American songs. Sitting outside, I could hear Maureen singing "And Let Her Sleep Under the Bar." Then came canned music from a phonograph, and people began to dance — the ones who were not too decrepit. I tried to hear only the chatter of the monkeys or parrots in the palm trees, innocent creatures disturbed by the raucous humans. J. was strangely cheerful and shot some pool with a New Zealander, causing me all of a sudden to think, with a chill of disapproval, that J. possibly was an Australian at heart and that I ought not to marry him or I would end up in a caravan in Split. His good looks and professional standing were only a mask that concealed . . . simplicity.

It didn't surprise me that people liked the handsome and amiable J.; it didn't even surprise me that they seemed to like me. I had concealed my tumult of feelings, and I was used to being treated by other people with protective affection, if only because I am small. This in part explained why the courtroom, and its formal process of accusation, its focus on me as a stipulated bad person, had been such a shock. It was as if a furious mob had come to smash with sticks the porcelain figure of my self. I had a brief intimation that the Australians, with their simple friendliness, could put me back together if I would let them, but I would rather lie in pieces for a while.

The moon was full and golden. "What a beautiful, beautiful night," said Nettie from Perth, the wife of George, coming out onto the beach. Who could disagree? Not even I. The ship on the moonlit water lapped at anchor, resting, awaiting them, looking luxurious and serene. J. came out and showed us the Southern Cross. At first I couldn't see it, all constellations look alike to me — I have never been able to see the bears or belts or any of it. But now, when J. turned my chin, I did see it, and it did look like a cross.

In the night I had another dream, in which the lawyer had said, "Isn't it true that you have often left your children while you travel?" He had been looking not at me but at a laughing audience. He was speaking over a microphone. The audience wore fringed hats of plastic straw.

"Not willingly, no," I had said. "Not often."

"How many times did you go on trips last year and leave them at home?"

"Oh, six, I don't know."

"That's not often?"

"Just a day or two each time. A man takes a business trip, you don't call it 'leaving,' or 'often.' " But I was not allowed to speak or explain.

"We're looking at how often you are in fact away from your children."

Here I had awakened, realizing that it was all true, it wasn't just a dream, it was what had happened — not, of course, the audience in plastic hats. Even though in the end I had been vindicated in the matter of the children, I still felt sticky with the encumbrance of their father's hate. All I had wanted was to be free, and now I was so soiled with words spoken at me, about me, by strangers, by lawyers I had never seen before, who had never seen me. It didn't seem fair that you could not prevent being the object of other people's emotions, you were not safe anywhere from their hate — or from their love, for that matter. You were never safe from being invaded by their feelings when you wanted only to be rid of them, free, off, away.

*

In the morning I had wanted to swim, to bathe in the sea, to wash all this stuff off, splash; my longing must have been clear, because Cawley, the other deckhand, laughed at me. "Not here you don't, love," he said. "There's sharks here as long as a boat."

The captain, Captain Clarke, made one of his few visits. He had kept aloof in the pilot cabin above, though he must have slipped down to the galley to eat, or maybe the crew took him his food up there. Now he invited his passengers two by two to the bridge. When people were tapped, they hauled themselves up the metal ladder, steadied by Cawley or Murray, then would come down looking gratified. Albert, who went up alone, suggested that he had helped avoid a navigational accident.

J. and I were invited on the morning of the fourth day, the day we were to arrive at the reef itself in the late afternoon. I went up despite myself. Captain Clarke was a thin, red-haired man sitting amid pipes and instruments. He let us take the wheel, and showed us the red line that marked our route through the labyrinth of islands on the chart. His manner was grave, polite, resigned. No doubt these visits were dictated by the cruise company.

"But there are thousands of islands between here and the Great Barrier Reef!" said J., studying the charts.

"Souvenir shops on every one," I couldn't help saying. J. fastened me with a steady look in which I read terminal exasperation.

"These islands are not all charted," said the captain. "The ones that are were almost all charted by Captain Cook himself, after he ran aground on one in 1770. He was a remarkable navigator. He even gave names to them all. But new ones are always being found. I've always hoped to find one myself."

"What would you name it?" J. asked.

"I would give it my name, or, actually, since there is already a Clarke Island, I would name it for my wife, Laura — Laura Clarke Island — or else for Alison, my daughter."

"Do you keep your eyes open for one?"

"I mean to get one," he said.

When we went down to the deck again, Maureen was gazing at the waves. "It's getting choppy," she observed, unnecessarily, for the boat had begun to rear up like a prancing horse.

"Right, we probably won't make it," Murray agreed.

"What do you mean?" I asked, alarmed by the tinge of satisfaction that underlay their sorry looks.

"To the reef. No point in going if the sea's up, like it's coming up — washed right up, no use going out there. If it's like this, we put in at Hook Island instead."

Astonished, I looked around to see if J., or anyone else, was listening. No, or not worried — would just as soon have Hook Island. They continued to knit and read along the deck, which now began to heave more forcefully, as if responding to the desire of the crew to return to port without seeing the great sight.

"How often does it happen that you don't go to the reef?" I asked Murray, heart thundering. The point of all this, and J.'s dream, was to go to the reef, and now they were casually dismissing the possibility.

"Oh, it happens more often than not. This time of year, you know. Chancy, the nautical business is."

"Come out all this way and not see it?" I insisted, voice rising.

"Well, you can't see it if the waves are covering it up, can you? You can bump your craft into it, but you can't see it. Can you?"

"I don't know," I cried. "I don't even know what it is." But the shape of things was awfully clear; given the slightest excuse, the merest breeze or ripple, the *Dolphin* would not take us to the Great Barrier Reef, and perhaps had never meant to. I thought in panic of not alerting J., but then I rushed to tell him. He put down his book, his expression aghast, and studied the waves.

The midday sky began to take on a blush of deeper blue, and now that our attention was called to it, the sea seemed to grow dark and rough before our eyes. Where moments before it had been smooth enough to row, we now began to pitch. The report of the prow smacking the waves made me think of cannons, of Trafalgar. In defiance of the rocking motion, the Australian passengers began to move around the cabin and along the deck, gripping the railings, looking trustfully at the sky and smiling. Their dentures were white as teacups.

"Christ," said Murray, "one of these bloody old fools will break a hip. Folks, why don't you sit down?" Obediently, like children, the Australians went inside the main cabin and sat in facing rows of chairs. Despite the abrupt change in the weather, the ship continued its course out to sea. J. and I anchored ourselves in the prow, leaning against the tool chest, resolutely watching the horizon, not the bounding deck beneath our feet — a recommended way to avoid seasickness. In twenty minutes the sea had changed altogether, from calm to a thing that threw the little ship in the air. We felt as if we were slithering along the back of a sea monster that was toiling beneath us.

Soon the dread specter of seasickness was among us. The captain, rusty-haired, pale-eyed, as if his eyes had been bleached with sea wind, climbed off the bridge and glanced inside the cabin at his passengers.

"Oh, please, they want to go, they'll be all right," I called to him, but the words were swept off by the wind. The others were so occupied with the likelihood of nausea that they hadn't grasped that the ship might turn back, and they seemed rather to be enjoying the drama of getting seasick. Every few minutes someone would get up, totter out to the rail, retch over it, and return to the laughter and commiseration of the others. The friendly thing was to be sick, so I was contrarily determined not to be, and J. was strong by nature. One of the Australians, Albert, gave us a matey grin as he lurched over our feet toward a bucket. I looked disgustedly away, but J. wondered aloud if he should be helping these old folks.

"Of course, they'll use this as an excuse for not going," I was saying bitterly. These barfing Australian senior citizens would keep us from getting to the Great Barrier Reef. My unruly emotions, which had been milder today, now plumped around in my bosom like the boat smacking on the waves. J. watched the Australians screaming with laughter and telling each other, "That's right, barf in the bin."

"This is a rough one," Albert said, and pitched sharply against the cabin, so that J. leaped up to catch him. Murray, tightening ropes, called for him to go back inside.

"Tossed a cookie meself." He grinned at J. and me.

"We don't think it's so rough," I said.

"I've seen plenty rougher," Murray agreed. "Bloody hangover is my problem."

When the captain leaned out to look down at the deck below him, I cried, "Oh, we just have to go to the reef, we have to! Oh, please!"

"What's the likelihood this sea will die down?" J. shouted to the captain. The captain shrugged. I felt angry at J. for the first time, as if he were a magnet. It was unfair, I knew, to say it was J.'s fault — the storm, the tossing sea, the *Dolphin,* and, of course, the rest. J., who had signed us up for this terrible voyage, during which we would be lost at sea, before reaching the Great Barrier Reef, whatever it was, and who had caused the sea to come up like this. All J.'s fault. If I ever saw the children again it would be a miracle — or else they would be saying in after years, Our mother perished on the high seas somewhere off Australia. What would they remember of me? The sight of the boiling waves, now spilling over the bow, now below us, made me think of throwing myself in — just an unbidden impulse trailing into my mind, the way I half thought, always, of throwing my keys or my sunglasses off bridges. Of course I wouldn't do it.

The ship pitched, thrust, dove through the waters. Yet we had not turned back. "Whoooeee," the Aussies were screaming inside the lounge. Life was like this, getting tossed around, and then, right before the real goal is reached, something, someone, impedes you.

"J., don't let them turn back," I said again, for the tenth time, putting all the imperative passion I could into my voice. Without hearing me, J. was already climbing the ladder to the bridge. I looked at my fingers whitely gripping the rope handle on the end of the tool chest. A bait locker slid across the deck, back, across, back, and once, upon the impact of a giant wave, a dead fish stowed in it sloshed out onto the deck. Then, in the wind, I heard Murray's thin voice call out, "It's all right, love, we're going to the reef! The captain says we're going to the reef!"

As abruptly as the storm had started, it subsided meekly, the sky once more changed color, now to metallic gray, lighter at the horizon, as if it were dawn. Ahead of us an indistinguishable shape lay in the water like the back of a submerged crocodile, a vast bulk under the surface. The captain had stopped the engines, and we drifted in the water. "The reef, the reef!" cried the Australians, coming out on deck. I shouted, too. The crew began to busy themselves with readying the small boats, and the other passengers came boisterously out of the cabin, as if nothing had been wrong. "Ow," they said, "that was a bit of a toss."

"You'll have two hours on the reef, not more," the captain told us before we climbed again into the rowboats. "Because of the tide. If you get left there at high tide, if we can't find you, well, we don't come back. Because you wouldn't be there." The Australians laughed at this merry joke.

J. handed me out of the boat and onto the reef. My first step on it shocked me. For I had had the idea of coral, hard and red, a great lump of coral sticking out of the ocean, a jagged thing that would scratch you if you fell on it, that you could carve into formations dictated by your own mind. We had heard it was endangered, and I had imagined its destruction by divers with chisels, carrying off lumps at a time.

Instead it was like a sponge. It sank underfoot, it sighed and sucked. Looking down, I could see that it was entirely alive, made of eyeless formations of cabbagey creatures sucking and opening and closing, yearning toward tiny ponds of water lying on the pitted surface, pink, green, gray, viscous, silent. I moved, I put my foot here, then hurriedly there, stumbled, and gashed my palm against something rough.

"Where should you step? I don't want to step on the things," I gasped.

"You have to. Just step as lightly as you can," J. said.

"It's alive, it's all alive!"

"Of course. It's coral, it's alive, of course," J. said. He had told me there were three hundred and fifty species of living coral here, along with the calcareous remains of tiny polyzoan and hydrozoan creatures that helped to form a home for others. Anemones, worms, gastropods, lobsters, crayfish, prawns, crown of thorns, other starfish, hydrocorals, the red Lithothamnion algae, the green Halimeda.

"Go on, J., leave me," I said, seeing that he wanted to be alone to have his own thoughts about all this marine life, whatever it meant to him. It meant something. His expression was one of rapture. He smiled at me and wandered off.

I had my Minox, but I found the things beneath my feet too fascinating to photograph. Through the viewer of my camera they seemed pale and far away. At my feet, in astonishing abundance, they went on with their strange life. I hated to tread on them, so stood like a stork and aimed the camera at the other passengers.

These were proceeding cautiously, according to their fashion, over the delicate surface — Mark in his yachting cap, with his camera, alone; the Kiwis in red tropical shirts more brilliant than the most bright-hued creatures underfoot; even the crew, with insouciant expressions, protectively there to save their passengers from falls or from strange sea poisons that darted into the inky ponds from the wounded life beneath our feet. For the first time, I felt, seeing each behaving characteristically, that I knew them all, and even that I liked them, or at least that I liked it that I understood what they would wear and do. Travelers like myself.

I watched J. kneeling in the water to peer into the centers of the mysterious forms. Almost as wonderful as this various life was J.'s delight. He was as dazzled as if we had walked on stars, and, indeed, the sun shining on the tentacles, wet petals, filling the spongy holes, made things sparkle like a strange underfoot galaxy. He appeared as a long, sandy-haired, handsome stranger, separate, unknowable. I, losing myself once more in the patterns and colors, thought of nothing, was myself as formless and uncaring as the coral, all my unruly, bad-natured passions leaching harmlessly into the sea, leaving a warm sensation of blankness and ease. I thought of the Hindu doctrine of *ahimsa,* of not harming living things, and I was not harming them, I saw — neither by stepping on them nor by leaving my anger and fears and the encumbrances of real life with them. For me, the equivalent of J.'s happiness was this sense of being cured of a poisoned spirit.

At sunset we headed landward into the sun, a strange direction to a Californian, for whom all sunsets are out at sea. We would arrive at Mackay at midnight — it also seemed strange that a voyage that had taken four days out would take only six hours back, something to do with the curve of the continental shelf. A spirit of triumph imbued our little party — we had lived through storms and reached a destination. People sat in the lounge labeling their film.

Maureen came along and reminded us that as this was our last night on board, there would be a fancy-dress party. When we had read this in the brochure, I had laughed. It had seemed absurd that such a little ship would give itself great liner airs. J. and

I had not brought costumes. In our cabin, I asked him what he meant to wear. Since my attitude had been so resolutely one of noncompliance, he seemed surprised that I was going to participate in the dressing up. "I know it's stupid, but how can we not?" I said. "It would be so churlish, with only sixteen of us aboard."

J. wore his ski pants, which were blue and tight, with a towel cape, and called himself Batman. I wore his ski parka, a huge, orange, down-filled garment. The others were elaborately got up, must have brought their masks and spangles with them. Rita wore a black leotard and had painted cat whiskers on her face, and Dave had a Neptune beard. Nettie wore a golden crown, and Don a harlequin suit, half purple, half green. I drew to one side and sat on the table with my feet drawn up inside J.'s parka, chin on my knees, watching the capers that now began. "Me? I am a pumpkin," I explained, when they noticed the green ribbon in my hair, my stem. It wasn't much of a costume, but it was all I could think of, and they laughed forgivingly and said that it looked cute.

J. won a prize, a bottle of beer, for the best paper cutout of a cow. I was surprised, watching him making meticulous little snips with the scissors, to see how a cow shape emerged under his hands, with a beautiful, delicate udder and teats, and knobs of horn. I had not thought that J. would notice a cow.

"I have an announcement," Mark said, in a strangely loud and shaky voice, one hand held up, his other hand nervously twisting his knotted cravat. The theme of his costume was not obvious.

"Excuse me, an announcement." The others smiled and shushed. "I've had word from my friend — a few months ago I had the honor to assist a friend with his astronomical observations, and I've just had word that he — we — that the comet we discovered has been accepted by the international commission. It will bear his name, and, as I had the honor to assist, I'll be mentioned, too. Only a little comet, of course, barely a flash in the sky. There are millions of them, of course. There are millions of them, but —"

A cheer, toasts. Mark bought drinks for everybody. The crew bought drinks for the guests, dishing up from behind the little bar with the slick expertise of landside bartenders. They seemed respectful at Mark's news. I raised my glass with the rest and felt ashamed at the way I had despised Mark's life — indeed, a nice life, spent exploring the heavens with a friend. How had I thought him friendless, this nice-looking young man?

"Split, Yugoslavia, is the most beautiful place on earth," George was telling me. "Like a travel poster. I've been almost everywhere by now, except China, but there, at Split, my heart stopped." My attention was reclaimed from my own repentant thoughts; for a second I had been thinking that he was describing a medical calamity, and I had been about to say "How terrible!"

But no, he was describing a moment, an epiphany, the experience of beauty. He had the long, bald head of a statesman, but he was a farmer, now retired, from Perth. I was ashamed that it had taken me so long to see that the difference between Americans and Australians was that Americans were tired and bored, while for Australians, stuck off at the edge of the world, all was new, and they had the energy and spirit to go off looking for abstractions like beauty, and comets.

"Let me get you another one of those," George said, taking my wineglass, for a pumpkin cannot move.

"How long have you been married?" asked Nettie, smiling at me. I considered, not knowing whether I wanted to shock them by admitting that we were not married at all. "Two years," I said.

"Really?" Nettie laughed. "We all thought you was newlyweds." Her smile was sly.

I felt myself flush inside the hot parka. The others had thought all my withdrawn unfriendliness was newlywed shyness and the preoccupations of love. They were giving me another chance.

"It seems like it." I laughed. I would never marry J., I thought. He was too good-natured to be saddled with a cross person like me. And yet now I wasn't cross, was at ease and warm with affection for the whole company. Don and Donna were buying champagne all around, and the crew, now that they were about to be rid of this lot of passengers, seemed sentimental and sorry, as if we had been the nicest, most amusing passengers ever. The prize for the best costume was to be awarded by vote. People wrote on bits of paper and passed them to Maureen, who sat on the bar and sorted them. There was even a little mood of tension, people wanting to win.

"And the prize for the best costume" — she paused portentously — "goes to the pumpkin!" My shipmates beamed and applauded. In the hot parka I felt myself grow even warmer with shame and affection. People of good will and good sense, and I had allowed a snobbish mood of acedia to blind me to it. Their white, untroubled smiles.

In a paper parcel was a key ring with a plastic-covered picture of the *Dolphin,* and the words "Great Barrier Reef" around the edge of it. I was seized by a love for it, would always carry it, I decided, if only as a reminder of various moral lessons I thought myself to have learned, and as a reminder of certain bad things about my own character.

"Thank you very much," I said. "I'll always keep it. And I'll always remember the *Dolphin* and all of you" — for I thought, of course, that I would. J. was looking at me with a considering air, as if to inspect my sincerity. But I was sincere.

"I know I've been a pig," I apologized to him later, as we gathered our things in the stateroom. "These people are really very sweet."

"I wonder if you'd feel like that if you hadn't gotten the prize," he said, peevishly. I was surprised at his tone. Of course, it wasn't the prize — only a little key chain, after all — that had cured me, but the process of the voyage, and the mysterious power of distant places to dissolve the problems the traveler has brought along. Looking at J., I could see that, for his part, he was happy but let down, as if the excitement and happiness of seeing the reef at last, and no doubt the nuisance of my complaining, had worn him out for the moment, and serious thoughts of his coming confrontations with malaria and leprosy and pain and sadness were returning, and what he needed was a good night's sleep.

LORRIE MOORE

Terrific Mother

FROM THE PARIS REVIEW

ALTHOUGH she had been around them her whole life, it was when she reached thirty-five that holding babies seemed to make her nervous — just at the beginning, a twinge of stage fright swinging up from the gut. "Adrienne, would you like to hold the baby? Would you mind?" Always these words from a woman her age looking kind and beseeching — a former friend, she was losing her friends to babble and beseech — and Adrienne would force herself to breathe deep. Holding a baby was no longer natural — she was no longer natural — but a test of womanliness and earthly skills. She was being observed. People looked to see how she would do it. She had entered a puritanical decade, a demographic moment — whatever it was — when the best compliment you could get was: You would make a terrific mother. The wolf whistle of the nineties.

So when she was at the Spearsons' Labor Day picnic, and when Sally Spearson had handed her the baby, Adrienne had burbled at it as she would a pet, had jostled the child gently, made clicking noises with her tongue, affectionately cooing, "Hello punkinhead, hello my little punkinhead," had reached to shoo a fly away and, amidst the smells of old grass and the fatty crackle of the barbecue, lost her balance when the picnic bench, dowels rotting in the joints, wobbled and began to topple her — the bench! The wobbly picnic bench was toppling her! And when she fell backward, spraining her spine — in the slowed quickness of this flipping world she saw the clayey clouds, some frozen faces, one lone star like the nose of a jet — and when the baby's head hit the stone retaining wall of the Spearsons' newly terraced yard and bled fatally into the brain, Adrienne went home shortly thereafter, after the hospital and the police reports, and did not leave her attic apartment for seven months, and there were fears, deep fears for her, on the part of Martin Porter, the man she had been dating, and on the part of almost everyone, including Sally Spearson who phoned tearfully to say that she forgave her, that Adrienne might never come out.

Those months were dark and cavernous with mourning. Martin Porter usually visited her bringing a pepper cheese or a Casbah couscous cup; he had become her only friend. He was divorced and worked as a research economist, though he looked more like a Scottish lumberjack — graying hair, red-flecked beard, a favorite flannel shirt in green and gold. He was getting ready to take a trip abroad. "We could get married," he suggested. That way, he said, Adrienne could accompany him to northern Italy, to a villa in the Alps set up for scholars and academic conferences. She could be a spouse. They gave spouses studios to work in. Some studios had pianos. Some had desks or potter's wheels. "You can do whatever you want." He was finishing the second draft of a study of first world imperialism's impact on third world monetary systems. "You could paint. Or not. You could not paint."

She looked at him closely, hungrily, then turned away. She still felt clumsy and big, a beefy killer in a cage, in need of the thinning prison food. "You love me, don't you," she said. She had spent the better part of seven months napping in a leotard, an electric fan blowing at her, her left ear catching the wind, capturing it there in her head, like the sad sea in a shell. She felt clammy and doomed. "Or do you just feel sorry for me?" She swatted at a small swarm of gnats that had appeared suddenly out of an abandoned can of Coke.

"I don't feel sorry for you."

"You don't?"

"I *feel* for you. I've grown to love you. We're grown-ups here. One grows to do things." He was a practical man. He often referred to the annual departmental cocktail party as "standing around getting paid."

"I don't think, Martin, that we can get married."

"Of course we can get married." He unbuttoned his cuffs as if to roll up his sleeves.

"You don't understand. Normal life is no longer possible for me. I've stepped off all the normal paths and am living in the bushes. I'm a bushwoman now. I don't feel that I can have the normal things. Marriage is a normal thing. You need the normal courtship, the normal proposal." She couldn't think what else. Water burned her eyes. She waved a hand dismissively, and it passed through her field of vision like something murderous and huge.

"Normal courtship, normal proposal," Martin said. He took off his shirt and pants and shoes. He lay on the bed in just his socks and underwear and pressed the length of his body against her. "I'm going to marry you, whether you like it or not." He took her face into his hands and looked longingly at her mouth. "I'm going to marry you 'til you puke."

They were met at Malpensa by a driver who spoke little English but who held up a sign that said VILLA HIRSCHBORN, and when Adrienne and Martin approached him, he nodded and said, "Hello, *buon giorno.* Signor Porter?" The drive to the villa took two hours, uphill and down, through the countryside and several small villages, but it wasn't until the driver pulled up to the precipitous hill he called La Madre Vertiginoso, and the villa's iron gates somehow opened automatically, then closed behind them, it wasn't until then, winding up the drive past the spectacular gardens and the sunny vineyard and the terraces of the stucco outbuildings, that it occurred to Adrienne that Martin's being invited here was a great honor. He had won this *thing,* and he got to live here for a month.

"Does this feel like a honeymoon?" she asked him.

"A what? Oh, a honeymoon. Yes." He turned and patted her thigh indifferently.

He was jet-lagged. That was it. She smoothed her skirt, which was wrinkled and damp. "Yes, I can see us growing old together," she said, squeezing his hand. "In the next few weeks, in fact." If she ever got married again, she would do it properly. The awkward ceremony, the embarrassing relatives, the cumbersome, ecologically unsound gifts. She and Martin had simply gone to

City Hall, and then asked their family and friends not to send presents but to donate money to Greenpeace. Now, however, as they slowed before the squashed-nosed stone lions at the entrance of the villa, its perfect border of forget-me-nots and yews, its sparkling glass door, Adrienne gasped. *Whales,* she thought quickly. *Whales* got my crystal.

The upstairs "Principessa" room, which they were ushered into by a graceful, bilingual butler named Carlo, was elegant and huge — a piano, a large bed, dressers stenciled with festoons of fruit. There was maid service twice a day, said Carlo. There were sugar wafers, towels, mineral water and mints. There was dinner at eight, breakfast until nine. When Carlo bowed and departed, Martin kicked off his shoes and sank into the ancient, tapestried chaise. "I've heard these 'fake' quattrocento paintings on the wall are fake for tax purposes only," he whispered. "If you know what I mean."

"Really," said Adrienne. She felt like one of the workers taking over the Winter Palace. Her own voice sounded booming. "You know, Mussolini was captured around here. Think about it."

Martin looked puzzled. "What do you mean?"

"That he was around here. That they captured him. I don't know. I was reading the little book on it. Leave me alone." She flopped down on the bed. Martin was changing already. He'd been better when they were just dating, with the pepper cheese. She let her face fall deep into the pillow, her mouth hanging open like a dog's, and then she slept until six, dreaming that a baby was in her arms but that it turned into a stack of plates, which she had to juggle, tossing them into the air.

A loud sound awoke her. A falling suitcase. Everyone had to dress for dinner, and Martin was yanking things out, groaning his way into a jacket and tie. Adrienne got up, bathed and put on pantyhose, which, because it had been months since she had done so, twisted around her leg like the stripe on a barber pole.

"You're walking as if you'd torn a ligament," said Martin, locking the door to their room, as they were leaving.

Adrienne pulled at the knees of the hose, but couldn't make them work. "Tell me you like my skirt, Martin, or I'm going to have to go back in and never come out again."

"I like your skirt. It's great. You're great. I'm great," he said, like a conjugation. He took her arm and they limped their way down the curved staircase (Was it sweeping? Yes! It was sweeping!) to the dining room, where Carlo ushered them in to find their places at the table. The seating arrangement at the tables would change nightly, Carlo said in a clipped Italian accent, "to assist the cross-pollination of ideas."

"Excuse me?" said Adrienne.

There were about thirty-five people, all of them middle-aged, with the academic's strange, mixed expression of merriment and weariness. "A cross between flirtation and a fender bender," Martin had described it once. Adrienne's place was at the opposite side of the room from him, between a historian writing a book on a monk named Jaocim de Flore and a musicologist who had devoted his life to a quest for "the earnest andante." Everyone sat in elaborate wooden chairs, the backs of which were carved with gargoylish heads that poked up from behind either shoulder of the sitter, like a warning.

"De Flore," said Adrienne, at a loss, turning from her carpaccio to the monk man. "Doesn't that mean 'of the flower'?" She had recently learned that *disaster* meant "bad star" and she was looking for an opportunity to brandish and bronze this tidbit in conversation.

The monk man looked at her. "Are you one of the spouses?"

"Yes," she said. She looked down, then back up. "But then so is my husband."

"You're not a screenwriter, are you?"

"No," she said. "I'm a painter. Actually more of a printmaker. Actually, more of a — right now I'm in transition."

He nodded and dug back into his food. "I'm always afraid they're going to start letting *screenwriters* in here."

There was an arugula salad, and osso bucco for the main course. She turned now to the musicologist. "So you usually find them insincere? The andantes?" She looked quickly out over the other heads to give Martin a fake and girlish wave.

"It's the use of the minor seventh," sniffed the musicologist. "So fraudulent and replete."

"If the food wasn't so good, I'd leave now," she said to Martin. They were lying in bed, in their carpeted skating rink of a room.

It could be weeks, she knew, before they'd have sex here. "*So fraudulent and replete,*" she said in a high nasal voice the likes of which Martin had heard only once before, in a departmental meeting chaired by an embittered, interim chair who did imitations of colleagues not in the room. "Can you even use the word *replete* like that?"

"As soon as you get settled in your studio, you'll feel better," said Martin, beginning to fade. He groped under the covers to find her hand and clasp it.

"I want a divorce," whispered Adrienne.

"I'm not giving you one," he said, bringing her hand up to his chest and placing it there, like a medallion, like a necklace of sleep, and then he began softly to snore, the quietest of radiators.

They were given bagged lunches and told to work well. Martin's studio was a modern glass cube in the middle of one of the gardens. Adrienne's was a musty stone hut twenty minutes farther up the hill and out onto the wooded headland, along a dirt path where small darting lizards sunned. She unlocked the door with the key she had been given, went in, and immediately sat down and ate the entire bagged lunch — quickly, compulsively, though it was only nine-thirty in the morning. Two apples, some cheese, and a jam sandwich. "A jelly bread," she said aloud, holding up the sandwich, scrutinizing it under the light.

She set her sketchpad on the worktable and began a morning full of killing spiders and drawing their squashed and tragic bodies. The spiders were star shaped, hairy, and scuttling like crabs. They were fallen stars. Bad stars. They were earth's animal-try at heaven. Often she had to step on them twice — they were large and ran fast. Stepping on them once usually just made them run faster.

It was the careless universe's work she was performing, death itchy, and about like a cop. Her personal fund of mercy for the living was going to get used up in dinner conversation at the villa. She had no compassion to spare, only a pencil and a shoe.

"Art *trouvé?*" said Martin, toweling himself dry from his shower, as they dressed for the evening cocktail hour.

"Spider *trouvé,*" she said. "A delicate, aboriginal dish." Martin let out a howling laugh that alarmed her. She looked at him, then looked down at her shoes. He needed her. Tomorrow she would have to go down into town and find a pair of sexy Italian sandals that showed the cleavage of her toes. She would have to take him dancing. They would have to hold each other and lead each other back to love or they'd go nuts here. They'd grow mocking and arch and violent. One of them would stick a foot out, and the other would trip. That sort of thing.

At dinner she sat next to a medievalist who had just finished his sixth book on *The Canterbury Tales*.

"Sixth," repeated Adrienne.

"There's a lot there," he said defensively.

"I'm sure," she said.

"I read deep," he added. "I read hard."

"How nice for you."

He looked at her narrowly. "Of course, *you* probably think I should write a book about Cat Stevens." She nodded neutrally. "I see," he said.

For dessert Carlo was bringing in a white chocolate torte, and she decided to spend most of the coffee and dessert time talking about it. Desserts like these are born, not made, she would say. She was already practicing, rehearsing for courses. "I mean," she said to the Swedish physicist on her left, "until today, my feeling about white chocolate, was: Why? What was the point? You might as well have been eating goddamn *wax*." She had her elbow on the table, her hand up near her face, and she looked anxiously past the physicist to smile at Martin at the other end of the long table. She waved her fingers in the air like bug legs.

"Yes, of course," said the physicist, frowning. "You must be — well, are you one of the *spouses?*"

She began in the mornings to gather with some of the other spouses — they were going to have little tank tops printed up — in the music room for exercise. This way she could avoid hearing words like *Heideggerian* and *ideological* at breakfast; it always felt too early in the morning for those words. The women pushed back the damask sofas, and cleared a space on the rug where all of them could do little hip and thigh exercises, led by the wife of the Swedish physicist. Up, down, up down.

"I guess this relaxes you," said the white-haired woman next to her.

"Bourbon relaxes you," said Adrienne. "This carves you."

"Bourbon carves you," said a redhead from Brazil.

"You have to go visit this person down in the village," whispered the white-haired woman. She wore a Spalding sporting goods T-shirt.

"What person?"

"Yes, what person?" asked the blonde.

The white-haired woman stopped and handed both of them a card from the pocket of her shorts. "She's an American masseuse. A couple of us have started going. She takes lire or dollars, doesn't matter. You have to phone a couple days ahead."

Adrienne stuck the card in her waistband. "Thanks," she said, and resumed moving her leg up and down like a toll gate.

For dinner there was *tachino a la scala*. "I wonder how you make this?" Adrienne said aloud.

"My dear," said the French historian on her left. "You must never ask. Only wonder." He then went on to disparage sub-altered intellectualism and dormant tropes.

"Yes," said Adrienne, "dishes like these do have about them a kind of *omnihistorical reality*. At least it seems like that to me." She turned quickly.

To her right sat a cultural anthropologist who had just come back from China, where she had studied the infanticide.

"Yes," said Adrienne. "The infanticide."

"They are on the edge of something horrific there. It is the whole future, our future as well, and something terrible is going to happen to them. One feels it."

"How awful," said Adrienne. She could not do the mechanical work of eating, of knife and fork, up and down. She let her knife and fork rest against each other on the plate.

"A woman has to apply for a license to have a baby. Everything is bribes and rations. We went for hikes up into the mountains, and we didn't see a single bird, a single animal. Everything, over the years, has been eaten."

Adrienne felt a light weight on the inside of her arm vanish and return, vanish and return, like the history of something, like the story of all things. "Where are you from ordinarily?" asked Adrienne. She couldn't place the accent.

"Munich," said the woman. "Land of Oktoberfest." She dug

into her food in an exasperated way, then turned back toward Adrienne to smile a little formally. "I grew up watching all these grown people in green felt throwing up in the street."

Adrienne smiled back. This was how she would learn about the world, in sentences at meals; other people's distillations amidst her own vague pain, dumb with itself. This, for her, would be knowledge — a shifting to hear, an emptying of her arms, other people's experiences walking through the bare rooms of her brain, looking for a place to sit.

"Me?" she too often said, "I'm just a dropout from Sue Bennet College." And people would nod politely and only sometimes ask, "Where's that?"

The next morning in her room she sat by the phone and stared. Martin had gone to his studio; his book was going fantastically well, he said, which gave Adrienne a sick, abandoned feeling — of being unhappy and unsupportive — which made her think she was not even one of the spouses. Who was she? The opposite of a mother. The opposite of a spouse.

She was Spider Woman.

She picked up the phone, got an outside line, dialed the number of the masseuse on the card.

"Pronto," said the voice on the other end.

"Yes, hello, *per favore, parle anglese?*"

"Oh, yes," said the voice. "I'm from Minnesota."

"No kidding," said Adrienne. She lay back and searched the ceiling for talk. "I once subscribed to a haunted-house newsletter published in Minnesota," she said.

"Yes," said the voice a little impatiently. "Minnesota is full of haunted-house newsletters."

"I once lived in a haunted house," said Adrienne. "In college. Me and five roommates."

The masseuse cleared her throat confidentially. "Yes. I was once called on to cast the demons from a haunted house. But how can I help you today?"

Adrienne said, "You were?"

"Were? Oh, the house, yes. When I got there, all the place needed was to be cleaned. So I cleaned it. Washed the dishes and dusted."

"Yup," said Adrienne. "Our house was haunted that way, too."

There was a strange silence in which Adrienne, feeling something tense and moist in the room, began to fiddle with the bagged lunch on the bed, nervously pulling open the sandwiches, sensing that, if she turned just then, the phone cradled in her neck, the baby would be there, behind her, a little older now, a toddler, walked toward her in a ghostly way by her own dead parents, a nativity scene corrupted by error and dream.

"How can I help you today?" the masseuse asked again, firmly.

Help? Adrienne wondered abstractly, and remembered how in certain countries, instead of a tooth fairy, there were such things as tooth spiders. How the tooth spider could steal your children, mix them up, bring you a changeling child, a child that was changed.

"I'd like to make an appointment for Thursday," she said. "If possible. Please."

For dinner there was *vongole in umido,* the rubbery, wine-steamed meat prompting commentary about mollusk versus crustacean anatomy. Adrienne sighed and chewed. Over cocktails there had been a long discussion of peptides and rabbit tests.

"Now lobsters, you know, have what is called a hemi-penis," said the man next to her. He was a marine biologist, an epidemiologist, or an anthropologist. She'd forgotten which.

"Hemi-penis." Adrienne scanned the room a little frantically.

"Yes." He grinned. "Not a term one particularly wants to hear in an intimate moment, of course."

"No," said Adrienne, smiling back. She paused. "Are you one of the spouses?"

Someone on his right grabbed his arm, and he now turned in that direction to say why yes he did know Professor so-and-so . . . and wasn't she in Brussels last year giving a paper at the hermeneutics conference?

There came *castagne al porto* and coffee. The woman to Adrienne's left finally turned to her, placing the cup down on the saucer with a sharp clink.

"You know, the chef has AIDS," said the woman.

Adrienne froze a little in her chair. "No, I didn't know." Who was this woman?

"How does that make you feel?"

"Pardon me?"

"How does that make you feel?" She enunciated slowly, like a reading teacher.

"I'm not sure," said Adrienne, scowling at her chestnuts. "Certainly worried for us if we should lose him."

The woman smiled. "Very interesting." She reached underneath the table for her purse and said, "Actually, the chef doesn't have AIDS — at least not that I'm aware of. I'm just taking a kind of survey to test people's reactions to AIDS, homosexuality and general notions of contagion. I'm a sociologist. It's part of my research. I just arrived this afternoon. My name is Marie-Claire."

Adrienne turned back to the hemi-penis man. "Do you think the people here are mean?" she asked.

He smiled at her in a fatherly way. "Of course," he said. There was a long silence with some chewing in it. "But the place *is* pretty as a postcard."

"Yeah, well," said Adrienne, "I never send those kinds of postcards. No matter where I am I always send the kind with the little cat jokes on them."

He placed his hand briefly on her shoulder. "We'll find you some cat jokes." He scanned the room in a bemused way and then looked at his watch.

She had bonded in a state of emergency, like an infant bird. But perhaps it would be soothing, this marriage. Perhaps it would be like a nice warm bath. A nice warm bath in a tub flying off a roof.

At night she and Martin seemed almost like husband and wife, spooned against each other in a forgetful sort of love — a cold, still heaven through which a word or touch might explode like a moon, then disappear, unremembered. She moved her arms to place them around him, and he felt so big there, huge, filling her arms.

The white-haired woman who had given her the masseuse card was named Kate Spalding, the wife of the monk man, and in the morning she asked Adrienne to go jogging. They met by the lions, Kate once more sporting a Spalding T-shirt, and then they headed out over the gravel, toward the gardens. "It's pretty as a postcard here, isn't it?" said Kate. Out across the lake the mountains seemed to preside over the minutiae of the terra cotta villages nestled below. It was May and the Alps were losing their snowy caps, nurses letting their hair down. The air was warming. Anything could happen.

Adrienne sighed. "But do you think people have *sex* here?"

Kate smiled. "You mean casual sex? Among the guests?"

Adrienne felt annoyed. "*Casual* sex? No, I don't mean *casual* sex. I'm talking about difficult, randomly profound, Sears and Roebuck sex. I'm talking marital."

Kate laughed in a sharp, barking sort of way, which for some reason hurt Adrienne's feelings.

Adrienne tugged on her socks. "I don't believe in casual sex." She paused. "I believe in casual marriage."

"Don't look at me," said Kate. "I married my husband because I was deeply in love with him."

"Yeah, well," said Adrienne. "I married my husband because I thought it would be a great way to meet guys."

Kate smiled now in a real way. Her white hair was grandmotherly, but her face was youthful and tan, and her teeth shone generous and wet, the creamy incisors curved as cashews.

"I'd tried the whole single thing but it just wasn't working," Adrienne added, running in place.

Kate stepped close and massaged Adrienne's neck. Her skin was lined and papery. "You haven't been to see Ilke from Minnesota yet, have you?"

Adrienne feigned perturbance. "Do I seem that tense, that lost, that . . ." and here she let her arms splay spastically. "I'm going tomorrow."

"He was a beautiful child, didn't you think?" In bed Martin held her until he rolled away, clasped her hand and fell asleep. At least there was that: a husband sleeping next to a wife, a nice husband sleeping close. It meant something to her. She could see how through the years it would gather power, its socially sanctioned animal comfort, its night life a dreamy dance about love. She lay awake and remembered when her father had at last grown so senile and ill that her mother could no longer sleep in the same bed with him — the mess, the smell — and had had to move him, diapered and rank, to the guest room next door. Her mother had cried, to say this farewell to a husband. To at last lose him like this, banished and set aside like a dead man, never to sleep with him again: she had wept like a baby. His actual death she took less hard. At the funeral she was grim and dry and invited everyone over for a quiet, elegant tea. By the time two years had passed, and she herself was diagnosed with cancer, her sense of humor had returned a little. "The silent killer," she would say, with a wink. "The *silent killer.*" She got a kick out of repeating it, though no one knew what to say in response, and at the very end she kept clutching the nurses' hems to ask, "Why is no one visiting me?" No one lived that close, explained Adrienne. No one lived that close to anyone.

Adrienne set her spoon down. "Isn't this soup *interesting?*" she said to no one in particular. *"Zup-pa mari-ta-ta!"* Marriage soup. She decided it was perhaps a little like marriage itself: a good idea that, like all ideas, lived awkwardly on earth.

"You're not a poetess, I hope," said the English geologist next to her. "We had a poetess here last month, and things got a bit dodgy here for the rest of us."

"Really." After the soup there was risotto with squid ink.

"Yes. She kept referring to insects as 'God's typos' and then she kept us all after dinner one evening so she could read from her poems, which seemed to consist primarily of the repeating line, 'The hairy kiwi of his balls.' "

"Hairy kiwi," repeated Adrienne, searching the phrase for a sincere andante. She had written a poem once herself. It had been called "Garbage Night in the Fog" and was about a long sad walk she'd taken once on garbage night.

The geologist smirked a little at the risotto, waiting for Adrienne to say something more, but she was now watching Martin at the other table. He was sitting next to the sociologist she'd sat next to the previous night, and as Adrienne watched she saw Martin glance, in a sickened way, from the sociologist, back to his plate, then back to the sociologist. "The *cook?*" he said loudly, then dropped his fork and pushed his chair from the table.

The sociologist was frowning. "You flunk," she said.

*

"I'm going to see this masseuse tomorrow." Martin was on his back on the bed, and Adrienne was straddling his hips, usually one of their favorite ways to converse. One of the Mandy Patinkin tapes she'd brought was playing on the cassette player.

"The masseuse. Yes, I've heard," said Martin.

"You have?"

"Sure, they were talking about it at dinner last night."

"Who was?" She was already feeling possessive, alone.

"Oh, one of them," said Martin, smiling and waving his hand dismissively.

"Them," said Adrienne coldly. "You mean one of the spouses, don't you. Why are all the spouses here women? Why don't the women scholars have spouses?"

"Some of them do, I think. They're just not here."

"Where are they?"

"Could you move," he said irritably, "you're sitting on my groin."

"Fine," she said, and climbed off.

The next morning she made her way down past the conical evergreens of the terraced hill — so like the grounds of a palace, the palace of a moody princess named Sophia or Giovanna — ten minutes down the winding path to the locked gate to the village. It had rained in the night, and snails, golden and mauve, decorated the stone steps, sometimes dead center, causing Adrienne an occasional quick turn of the ankle. A dance step, she thought. Modern and bent-kneed. Very Martha Graham. *Don't kill us. We'll kill you.* At the top of the final stairs to the gate she pressed the buzzer that opened it electronically, and then dashed down to get out in time. YOU HAVE THIRTY SECONDS, said the sign. TRENTA MINUTI SECONDI USCIRE. PRESTO! One needed a key to get back in from the village, and she clutched it like a charm.

She had to follow the Via San Carlo to Corso Magenta, past a hazelnut gelato shop and a bakery with wreaths of braided bread and muffins cut like birds. She pressed herself up against the buildings to let the cars pass. She looked at her card. The masseuse was above a *farmacia,* she'd been told, and she saw it now, a little sign that said, MASSAGGIO DELLA VITA. She pushed on the outer door and went up.

Upstairs through an open doorway, she entered a room lined with books: books on vegetarianism, books on healing, books on juice. A cockatiel, white with a red dot like a Hindu wife's, was perched atop a picture frame. The picture was of Lake Como or Garda, though when you blinked it could also be a skull, a fissure through the center like a reef.

"Adrienne," said a smiling woman in a purple peasant dress. She had big, frosted hair and a wide, happy face that contained many shades of pink. She stepped forward and shook Adrienne's hand. "I'm Ilke."

"Yes," said Adrienne.

The cockatiel suddenly flew from its perch to land on Ilke's shoulder. It pecked at her big hair, then stared at Adrienne, accusingly.

Ilke's eyes moved quickly between Adrienne's own, a quick read, a radar scan. She then looked at her watch. "You can go into the back room now, and I'll be with you shortly. You can take off all your clothes, also any jewelry — watches, or rings. But if you want you can leave your underwear on. Whatever you prefer."

"What do most people do?" Adrienne swallowed in a difficult, conspicuous way.

Ilke smiled. "Some do it one way; some the other."

"All right," Adrienne said and clutched her pocketbook. She stared at the cockatiel. "I just wouldn't want to rock the boat."

She stepped carefully toward the back room Ilke had indicated, and pushed past the heavy curtain. Inside was a large alcove, windowless and dark, with one small bluish light coming from the corner. In the center was a table with a newly creased flannel sheet. Speakers were built into the bottom of the table, and out of them came the sound of eerie choral music, wordless *oohs* and *aahs* in minor tones, with a percussive sibilant chant beneath it that sounded to Adrienne like, "Jesus is best, Jesus is best," though perhaps it was "Cheese, I suspect." Overhead hung a mobile of white stars, crescent moons and doves. On the blue walls were more clouds and snowflakes. It was a child's room, a baby's room, everything trying hard to be harmless and sweet.

Adrienne removed all her clothes, her earrings, her watch, her rings. She had already grown used to the ring Martin had given her, and so it saddened and exhilarated her to take it off, a quick glimpse into the landscape of adultery. Her other ring was a smoky quartz, which a palm reader in Milwaukee — a man dressed like a gym teacher and set up at a card table in a German restaurant — had told her to buy and wear on her right index finger for power.

"What kind of power?" she had asked.

"The kind that's real," he said. "What you've got here," he said, waving around her left hand, pointing at the thin silver and turquoise she was wearing, "is squat."

"I like a palm reader who dresses you," she said later to Martin in the car on their way home. This was before the incident at the Spearson picnic, and things seemed not impossible then; she had wanted Martin to fall in love with her. "A guy who looks like Mike Ditka, but who picks out jewelry for you."

"A guy who tells you you're sensitive, and that you will soon receive cash from someone wearing glasses. Where does he come up with this stuff?"

"You don't think I'm sensitive."

"I mean the money and glasses thing," he said. "And that gloomy bit about how they'll think you're a goner, but you're going to come through and live to see the world go through a radical physical change."

"That was gloomy," she agreed. There was a lot of silence and looking at the night-lit highway lines, the fireflies hitting the windshield and smearing, all phosphorescent gold, as if the car were flying through stars. "It must be hard," she said, "for someone like you to go out on a date with someone like me."

"Why do you say that?" he'd asked.

She climbed up on the table, stripped of ornament and the power of ornament, and slipped between the flannel sheets. For a second she felt numb and scared, naked in a strange room, more naked even than in a doctor's office, where you kept your jewelry on, like an odalisque. But it felt new to do this, to lead the body to this, the body with its dog's obedience, its dog's desire to please. She lay there waiting, watching the mobile moons turn slowly, half revolutions, while from the speakers beneath the table came a new sound, an electronic, synthesized version of Brahms's lullaby. An infant. She was to become an infant again. Perhaps she would become the Spearsons' boy. He had been a beautiful baby.

Ilke came in quietly and appeared so suddenly behind Adrienne's head, it gave her a start.

"Move back toward me," whispered Ilke, "move back toward me," and Adrienne shifted until she could feel the crown of her head grazing Ilke's belly. The cockatiel whooshed in and perched on a nearby chair.

"Are you a little tense?" she said. She pressed both her thumbs at the center of Adrienne's forehead. Ilke's hands were strong, small, bony. Leathered claws. The harder she pressed the better it felt to Adrienne, all of her difficult thoughts unknotting and traveling out, up into Ilke's thumbs.

"Breathe deeply," said Ilke. "You cannot breathe deeply without it relaxing you."

Adrienne pushed her stomach in and out.

"You are from the Villa Hirschborn, aren't you?" Ilke's voice was a knowing smile.

"Ehuh."

"I thought so," said Ilke. "People are very tense up there. Rigid as boards." Ilke's hands moved down off Adrienne's forehead, along her eyebrows to her cheeks, which she squeezed repeatedly, in little circles, as if to break the weaker capillaries. She took hold of Adrienne's head and pulled. There was a dull, cracking sound. Then she pressed her knuckles along Adrienne's neck. "Do you know why?"

Adrienne grunted.

"It is because they are overeducated and can no longer converse with their own mothers. It makes them a little crazy. They have literally lost their mother tongue. So they come to me. I am their mother, and they don't have to speak at all."

"Of course they *pay* you."

"Of course."

Adrienne suddenly fell into a long falling — of pleasure, of surrender, of glazed-eyed dying, a piece of heat set free in a room. Ilke rubbed Adrienne's earlobes, knuckled her scalp like a hairdresser, pulled at her neck and fingers and arms, as if they were jammed things. Adrienne would become a baby, join all the babies, in heaven where they lived.

Ilke began to massage sandalwood oil into Adrienne's arms, pressing down, polishing, ironing, looking, at a quick glimpse, like one of Degas's laundresses. Adrienne shut her eyes again and listened to the music, which had switched from synthetic lullabies to the contrapuntal sounds of a flute and a thunderstorm. With these hands upon her, she felt a little forgiven and began to think generally of forgiveness, how much of it was required in life: to forgive everyone, yourself, the people you loved, and then wait to be forgiven by them. Where was all this forgiveness supposed to come from? Where was this great inexhaustible supply?

"Where are you?" whispered Ilke. "You are somewhere very far."

Adrienne wasn't sure. Where was she? In her own head, like a dream; in the bellows of her lungs. What was she? Perhaps a child. Perhaps a corpse. Perhaps a fern in the forest in the storm; a singing bird. The sheets were folded back. The hands were all over her now. Perhaps she was under the table with the music, or in a musty corner of her own hip. She felt Ilke rub oil onto her chest, between her breasts, out along the ribs, and circularly on the abdomen. "There is something stuck here," Ilke said. "Something not working." Then she pulled the covers back up. "Are you cold?" she asked, and though Adrienne didn't answer, Ilke brought another blanket, mysteriously heated, and laid it across Adrienne. "There," said Ilke. She lifted the blanket so that only her feet were exposed. She rubbed oil into her soles, the toes, something squeezed out of Adrienne, like an olive. She felt as if she would cry. She felt like the baby Jesus. The grown Jesus. *The poor will always be with us.* The dead Jesus. Cheese is the best. Cheese is the best.

At her desk in the outer room, Ilke wanted money. Thirty-five thousand lire. "I can give it to you for thirty thousand, if you decide to come on a regular basis. Would you like to come on a regular basis?" asked Ilke.

Adrienne was fumbling with her wallet. She sat down in the wicker rocker near the desk. "Yes," she said. "Of course."

Ilke had put on reading glasses and now opened up her appointment book to survey the upcoming weeks. She flipped a page, then flipped it back. She looked out over her glasses at Adrienne. "How often would you like to come?"

"Every day," said Adrienne.

"Every day?"

Ilke's hoot worried Adrienne. "Every *other* day?" Adrienne peeped hopefully. Perhaps the massage had bewitched her, ruined her. Perhaps she had fallen in love.

Ilke looked back at her book and shrugged. "Every other day," she repeated slowly as a way of holding the conversation still while she checked her schedule. "How about at two o'clock?"

"Monday, Wednesday and Friday?"

"Perhaps we can occasionally arrange a Saturday."

"Okay. Fine." Adrienne placed the money on the desk and stood up. Ilke walked her to the door and thrust her hand out formally. Her face had changed from its earlier pinks to a strange and shiny orange.

"Thank you," said Adrienne. She shook Ilke's hand, but then leaned forward and kissed her cheek; she would kiss the business out of this. "Good-bye," she said. She stepped gingerly down the stairs; she had not entirely returned to her body yet. She had to go slow. She felt a little like she had just seen God, but also a little like she had just seen a hooker. Outside she walked carefully back toward the villa, but first stopped at the gelato shop for a small dish of hazelnut ice cream. It was smooth, toasty, buttery, like a beautiful liqueur, and she thought how different it was from America, where so much of the ice cream now looked like babies had attacked it with their cookies.

"Well, Martin, it's been nice knowing you," Adrienne said smiling. She reached out to shake his hand with one of hers and pat him on the back with the other. "You've been a good sport. I hope there will be no hard feelings."

"You've just come back from your massage," he said a little numbly. "How was it?"

"As you would say, 'Relaxing.' As I would say — well, I wouldn't say."

Martin led her to the bed. "Kiss and tell," he said.

"I'll just kiss," she said, kissing.

"I'll settle," he said. But then she stopped and went into the bathroom to shower for dinner.

At dinner there was *zuppa alla paesana* and then *salsicce alla griglia con spinaci.* For the first time since they'd arrived, she was seated near Martin, who was catercorner to her left. He was seated next to another economist and was speaking heatedly with him about a book on labor division and economic policy. "But Wilkander ripped that theory off from Boyer!" Martin let his spoon splash violently into his *zuppa* before a waiter came and removed the bowl.

"Let us just say," said the other man calmly, "that it was a sort of homage."

"If that's 'homage,' " said Martin, fidgeting with his fork, "I'd like to do a little 'homage' on the Chase Manhattan Bank."

"I think it was felt that there was sufficient looseness there to warrant further explication."

"Right. And one's twin sibling is simply an explication of the text."

"Why not," smiled the other economist, who was calm, probably a supply-sider.

Poor Martin, thought Adrienne. Poor Keynesian Martin, poor Marxist Martin, perspiring and red. "Left of Lenin?!" she had heard him exclaiming the other day to an agriculturalist. "Left of *Lenin?!* Left of the Lennon Sisters, you mean!" Poor godless, raised-an-atheist-in-Ohio Martin. "On Christmas," he'd said to her once, "we used to go down to The Science Store and worship the Bunsen burners."

She would have to find just the right blouse, just the right perfume, greet him on the chaise lounge with a bare shoulder and a purring "Hello, Mister Man." Take him down by the lake near the Sfondrata chapel and get him laid. Hire somebody. She turned to the scholar next to her, who had just arrived this morning.

"Did you have a good flight?" she asked. Her own small talk at dinner no longer shamed her.

"Flight is the word," he said. "I needed to flee my department, my bills, my ailing car. Come to a place that would take care of me."

"This is it, I guess. Though they won't fix your car. Won't even discuss it, I've found."

"I'm on a Guggenheim," he said.

"How nice!" She thought of the museum in New York, and of a pair of earrings she had bought in the gift shop there but had never worn because they always looked broken, even though that was the way they were supposed to look.

". . . but I neglected to ask the foundation for enough money. I didn't realize what you could ask for. I didn't ask for the same amount everyone else did, and so I received substantially less."

Adrienne was sympathetic. "So instead of a regular Guggenheim, you got a little Guggenheim."

"Yes," he said.

"A Guggenheimy," she said.

He smiled in a troubled sort of way. "Right."

"So now you have to live in Guggenheimy town."

He stopped pushing at a sausage with his fork. "Yes. I heard there would be wit here."

She tried to make her lips curl, like his.

"Sorry," he said. "I was just kidding."

"Jet lag," she said.

"Yes."

"Jetty laggy." She smiled at him. "Baby talk. We love it." She paused. "Last week of course we weren't like this. You've arrived a little late."

He was a beautiful baby. In the dark there was thumping, like tom-toms, and a piccolo high above it. She couldn't look, because when she looked, it shocked her, another woman's hands all over her. She just kept her eyes closed, and concentrated on surrender, on the restful invalidity of it. Sometimes she concentrated on being where Ilke's hands were — at her feet, at the small of her back.

"Your parents are no longer living, are they?" Ilke said in the dark.

"No."

"Did they die young?"

"Medium. They died medium. I was a menopausal, after-thought child."

"Do you want to know what I feel in you?"

"All right."

"I feel a great and deep gentleness. But I also feel that you have been dishonored."

"Dishonored?" So Japanese. Adrienne liked the sound of it.

"Yes. You have a deeply held fear. Right here." Ilke's hand went just under Adrienne's rib cage.

Adrienne breathed deeply, in and out. "I killed a baby," she whispered.

"Yes, we have all killed a baby — there is a baby in all of us. That is why people come to me, to be reunited with it."

"No, I've killed a real one."

Ilke was very quiet and then she said, "You can do the side-lying now. You can put this pillow under your head; this other one between your knees." Adrienne rolled awkwardly onto her side. Finally Ilke said, "This country, its pope, its church, makes murderers of women. You must not let it do that to you. Move back toward me. That's it."

That's not *it,* thought Adrienne, in this temporary dissolve, seeing death and birth, seeing the beginning and then the end, how they were the same quiet black, same nothing ever after: everyone's life appeared in the world like a movie in a room. First dark, then light, then dark again. But it was all staggered so that somewhere there was always light.

That's not it. That's not it, she thought. But thank you.

When Adrienne left that afternoon, seeking sugar in one of the shops, she moved slowly, blinded by the angle of the afternoon light but also believing she saw Martin coming toward her in the narrow street, approaching like the lumbering logger he sometimes seemed to be. Her squinted gaze, however, failed to catch his, and he veered suddenly left into a *calle.* By the time she reached the corner, he had disappeared entirely. How strange, she thought. She had felt close to something, to him, and then suddenly not. She climbed the path back up toward the villa and went and knocked on the door of his studio, but he wasn't there.

*

"You smell good," she greeted Martin. It was some time later and she had just returned to the room to find him there. "Did you just take a bath?"

"A little while ago," he said.

She curled up to him, teasingly. "Not a shower? A bath? Did you put some scented bath salts in it?"

"I took a very masculine bath," said Martin.

She sniffed him again. "What scent did you use?"

"A manly scent," he said. "Rock. I took a rock-scented bath."

"Did you take a bubble bath?" She cocked her head to one side.

He smiled. "Yes, but I, uh, made my own bubbles."

"You did?" She squeezed his biceps.

"Yeah. I hammered the water with my fist."

She walked over to the cassette player and put a cassette in. She looked over at Martin, who looked suddenly unhappy. "This music annoys you, doesn't it?"

Martin squirmed. "It's just — why can't he sing any one song all the way through?"

She thought about this. "Because he's Mr. Medley-head?"

"You didn't bring anything else?"

"No."

She went back and sat next to Martin, in silence, smelling the scent of him, as if it were odd.

For dinner there was *vitello alla salvia,* baby peas and a pasta made with caviar. "Nipping it in the bud," sighed Adrienne. "An early frost." A fat, elderly man arriving late pulled his chair out onto her foot, then sat down on it. She shrieked.

"Oh, dear, I'm sorry," said the man, lifting himself up as best he could.

"It's okay," said Adrienne. "I'm sure it's okay."

But the next morning, at exercises, Adrienne studied it closely during the leg lifts. The big toe was swollen and blue, and the nail had been loosened and set back at an odd and unhinged angle. "You're going to lose your toenail," said Kate.

"Great," said Adrienne.

"That happened to me once, during my first marriage. My husband dropped a dictionary on my foot. One of those subconscious things."

"You were married before?"

"Oh, yes," she sighed. "I had one of those rehearsal marriages, you know, where you're a feminist and train a guy, and then some *other* feminist comes along and *gets* the guy."

"I don't know." Adrienne scowled. "I think there's something wrong with the words *feminist* and *gets the guy* being in the same sentence."

"Yes, well —"

"Were you upset?"

"Of course. But then, I'd been doing everything. I'd insisted on separate finances, on being totally self-supporting. I was working. I was doing the child care. I paid for the house, I cooked it, I cleaned it. I found myself shouting, "This is feminism? Thank you, Betty!"

"But now you're with someone else."

"Pre-taught. Self-cleaning. Batteries included."

"Someone else trained him, and you stole him."

Kate smiled. "Of course. What, am I crazy?"

"What happened to the toe?"

"The nail came off. And the one that grew back was wavy and dark and used to scare the children."

"Oh," said Adrienne.

"Why would someone publish six books on Chaucer?" Adrienne was watching Martin dress. She was also smoking a cigarette. One of the strange things about the villa was that the smokers had all quit smoking, and the nonsmokers had taken it up. People were getting in touch with their alternative centers. Bequeathed cigarettes abounded. Cartons were appearing outside people's doors.

"You have to understand academic publishing," said Martin. "No one reads these books. Everyone just agrees to publish everyone else's. It's one big circle jerk. It's a giant economic agreement. When you think about it, it probably violates the Sherman Act."

"A circle jerk?" she said uncertainly. The cigarette was making her dizzy.

"Yeah," said Martin, reknotting his tie.

"But six books on Chaucer? Why not, say, a Cat Stevens book?"

"Don't look at me," he said. "I'm in the circle."

She sighed. "Then I shall sing to you. Mood music." She made up a romantic, Asian-sounding tune and danced around the room with her cigarette, in a floating, wing-limbed way. "This is my Hopi dance," she said. "So full of hope."

Then it was time to go to dinner.

The cockatiel now seemed used to Adrienne and would whistle twice, then fly into the back room, perch quickly on the picture frame and wait with her for Ilke. Adrienne closed her eyes and breathed deeply, the flannel sheet pulled up under her arms, tightly, like a sarong.

Ilke's face appeared overhead in the dark, as if she were a mother just checking, peering into a crib. "How are you today?"

Adrienne opened her eyes to see that Ilke was wearing a pin that said: Say a Prayer. Pet a Rock.

Say a Prayer. "Good," said Adrienne. "I'm good." Pet a Rock.

Ilke ran her fingers through Adrienne's hair, humming faintly.

"What is this music today?" Adrienne asked. Like Martin, she too had grown weary of the Mandy Patinkin tapes, all that unshackled exuberance.

"Crickets and elk," Ilke whispered.

"Crickets and elk."

"Crickets and elk and a little harp."

Ilke began to move around the table, pulling on Adrienne's limbs and pressing deep into her tendons. "I'm doing choreographed massage today," Ilke said. "That's why I'm wearing this dress."

Adrienne hadn't noticed the dress. Instead, with the lights now low, except for the illuminated clouds on the side wall, she felt herself sinking into the pools of death deep in her bones, the dark wells of loneliness, failure, blame. "You may turn over now," she heard Ilke say. And she struggled a little in the flannel sheets to do so, twisting in them, until Ilke helped her, as if she were a nurse and Adrienne someone old and sick — a stroke victim, that's what it was. She had become a stroke victim. Then lowering her face into the toweled cheek plates the brace on the table offered up to her (the cradle, Ilke called it), Adrienne began quietly to cry, the deep touching of her body, melting her down to some equation of animal sadness, shoe leather and brine. She began to understand why people would want to live in these dusky nether zones, the meltdown brought on by sleep or drink or this. It seemed truer, more familiar to the soul than was the busy complicated flash that was normal life. Ilke's arms leaned into her, her breasts brushing softly against Adrienne's head, which now felt connected to the rest of her only by filaments and strands. The body suddenly seemed a tumor on the brain, a mere means of conveyance, a wagon; the mind's go-cart taken apart, laid in pieces on this table. "You have a knot here in your trapezius," Ilke said, kneading Adrienne's shoulder. "I can feel the belly of the knot right here," she said, pressing hard, bruising her shoulder a little, and then easing up. "Let go," she said. "Let go all the way, of everything."

"I might die," said Adrienne. Something surged in the music and she missed what Ilke said in reply, though it sounded a little like, "Changes are good." Though perhaps it was "Chances aren't good." Ilke pulled Adrienne's toes, milking even the injured one, with its loose nail and leaky underskin, and then she left Adrienne there in the dark, in the music, though Adrienne felt it was she who was leaving, like a person dying, like a train pulling away. She felt the rage loosened from her back, floating aimlessly around in her, the rage that did not know at what or whom to rage though it continued to rage.

She awoke to Ilke's rocking her gently. "Adrienne, get up. I have another client soon."

"I must have fallen asleep," said Adrienne. "I'm sorry."

She got up slowly, got dressed, and went out into the outer room; the cockatiel whooshed out with her, grazing her head.

"I feel like I've just been strafed," she said, clutching her hair.

Ilke frowned.

"Your bird. I mean, by your bird. In there" — she pointed back toward the massage room — "*that* was great." She reached into her purse to pay. Ilke had moved the wicker chair to the other side of the room so that there was no longer any place to sit down or linger. "You want lire or dollars?" she asked and was a little taken aback when Ilke said rather firmly, "I'd prefer lire."

Ilke was bored with her. That was it. Adrienne was having a

religious experience, but Ilke — Ilke was just being social. Adrienne held out the money and Ilke plucked it from her hand, then opened the outside door and leaned to give Adrienne the rushed bum's kiss — left, right — and then closed the door behind her.

Adrienne was in a fog, her legs noodly, her eyes unaccustomed to the light. Outside, in front of the *farmacia,* if she wasn't careful, she was going to get hit by a car. How could Ilke just send people out into the busy street like that, ducks for the kill, fatted calves, a farewell to arms? Her body felt doughy, muddy. This was good, she supposed. Decomposition. She stepped slowly, carefully, her Martha Graham step, along the narrow walk between the street and the stores. And when she turned the corner to head back up toward the path to the Villa Hirschborn, there stood Martin, her husband, rounding a corner and heading her way.

"Hi!" she said, so pleased suddenly to meet him like this, away from what she now referred to as "the compound." "Are you going to the *farmacia?*" she asked.

"Uh, yes," said Martin. He leaned to kiss her cheek.

"Want some company?"

He looked a little blank, as if he needed to be alone. Perhaps he was going to buy condoms.

"Oh, never mind," she said gaily. "I'll see you later, up at the compound, before dinner."

"Great," he said, and took her hand, took two steps away, and then let her hand go, gently, midair.

She walked away, toward a small park — il Giardino Leonardo — out past the station for the vaporetti. Near a particularly exuberant rhododendron sat a short, dark woman with a bright turquoise bandanna knotted around her neck. She had set up a table with a sign: CHIROMANTE: TAROT E FACCIA. Adrienne sat down opposite her in the empty chair. "Americano," she said.

"I do faces, palms or cards," the woman with the blue scarf said.

Adrienne looked at her own hands. She didn't want to have her face read. She lived like that already. It happened all the time at the villa, people trying to read your face — freezing your brain with stony looks and remarks made malicious with obscurity, so that you couldn't read *their* faces, while they were busy reading yours. It all made her feel creepy, like a lonely head on a poster somewhere.

"The cards are the best," said the woman. "Ten thousand lire."

"Okay," said Adrienne. She was still looking at the netting of her open hands, the dried riverbed of life just sitting there. "The cards."

The woman swept up the cards, and dealt half of them out, every which way in a kind of swastika. Then without glancing at them, she leaned forward boldly and said to Adrienne, "You are sexually unsatisfied. Am I right?"

"Is that what the cards say?"

"In a general way. You have to take the whole deck and interpret."

"What does this card say?" asked Adrienne, pointing to one with some naked corpses leaping from coffins.

"Any one card doesn't say anything. It's the whole feeling of them." She quickly dealt out the remainder of the deck on top of the other cards. "You are looking for a guide, some kind of guide, because the man you are with does not make you happy. Am I right?"

"Maybe," said Adrienne, who was already reaching for her purse to pay the ten thousand lire so that she could leave.

"I am right," said the woman, taking the money and handing Adrienne a small, smudged business card. "Stop by tomorrow. Come to my shop. I have a powder."

Adrienne wandered back out of the park, past a group of tourists climbing out of a bus, back toward the Villa Hirschborn — through the gate, which she opened with her key, and up the long stone staircase to the top of the promontory. Instead of going back to the villa, she headed out through the woods toward her studio, toward the dead tufts of spiders she had memorialized in her grief. She decided to take a different path, not the one toward the studio, but one that led farther up the hill, a steeper grade, toward an open meadow at the top, with a small Roman ruin at its edge — a corner of the hill's original fortress still stood there. But in the middle of the meadow, something came over her — a balmy wind, or the heat from the uphill hike, and she took off all her clothes, lay down in the grass and stared around at the dusky sky. To either side of her the spokes of tree branches crisscrossed upward in a kind of cat's cradle. More directly overhead she studied the silver speck of a jet, the metallic head of its white stream like the tip of a thermometer. There were a hundred people inside this head of a pin, thought Adrienne. Or was it, perhaps, just the head of a pin? When was something truly small, and when was it a matter of distance? The branches of the trees seemed to encroach inward and rotate a little to the left, a little to the right, like something mechanical, and as she began to drift off, she saw the beautiful Spearson baby, cooing in a clown hat, she saw Martin furiously swimming in a pool, she saw the strewn beads of her own fertility, all the eggs within her, leap away like a box of tapioca off a cliff. It seemed to her that everything she had ever needed to know in her life she had known at one time or another, but she just hadn't known all those things at once, at the same time, at a single moment. They were scattered through, and she had had to leave and forget one in order to get to another. A shadow fell across her, inside her, and she could feel herself retreat to that place in her bones where death was and you greeted it like an acquaintance in a room; you said hello and were then ready for whatever was next — which might be a guide, the guide that might be sent to you, the guide to lead you back out into your life again.

Someone was shaking her gently. She flickered slightly awake to see the pale, ethereal face of a strange older woman leaning over, peering down at her as if Adrienne were something odd in the bottom of a teacup. The woman was dressed all in white — white shorts, white cardigan, white scarf around her head. The guide.

"Are you — the guide?" whispered Adrienne.

"Yes, my dear," the woman said in a faintly English voice that sounded like the good witch of the north.

"You are?" Adrienne asked.

"Yes," said the woman. "And I've brought the group up here to view the old fort, but I was a little worried that you might not like all of us traipsing past here while you were, well — are you all right?"

Adrienne was more awake now and sat up to see at the end of the meadow the group of tourists she'd previously seen below in the town, getting off the bus.

"Yes, thank you," mumbled Adrienne. She lay back down to think about this, hiding herself in the walls of grass, like a child hoping to trick the facts. "Oh, my god," she finally said, and groped about to her left to find her clothes and clutch them, panicked, to her belly. She breathed deeply, then put them on, lying as flat to the ground as she could, hard to glimpse, a snake getting back inside its skin, a change, perhaps, of reptilian heart. Then she stood, zipped her pants, secured her belt buckle and, squaring her shoulders, walked bravely past the bus and the tourists who, though they tried not to stare at her, did stare.

By this time everyone in the villa was privately doing imitations of everyone else. "Martin, you should announce who you're doing before you do it," said Adrienne, dressing for dinner. "I can't really tell."

"Cube-steak yuppies!" Martin ranted at the ceiling. "Legends in their own mind! Rumors in their own room!"

"Yourself. You're doing yourself." She straightened his collar and tried to be wifely.

For dinner there was *cioppino* and *insalata mista* and *pesce con pignoli,* a thin piece of fish like a leaf. From everywhere around the dining room scraps of dialogue — rhetorical barbed wire, indignant and arcane — floated over toward her: "As an aesthetician, you can't not be interested in the sublime!" or "Why, that's the most facile thing I've ever heard!" or "Good grief, tell him about the Peasants' Revolt, would you?" But no one spoke to her directly. She had no subject, not really, not one she liked, except perhaps movies and movie stars. Martin was at a far table, his back toward her, listening to the monk man. At times like these, she thought, it was probably a good idea to carry a small hand puppet.

She made her fingers flap in her lap.

Finally, one of the people next to her turned and introduced himself. His face was poppy-seeded with whiskers, and he seemed to be looking down, watching his own mouth move. When she asked him how he liked it here so far, she received a fairly brief history of the Ottoman Empire. She nodded and smiled, and at the end he rubbed his dark beard, looked at her compassionately, and said, "We are not good advertisements for this life. Are we?"

"There *are* a lot of dingdongs here," she admitted. He looked a little hurt, so she added, "But I like that about a place. I do."

When after dinner she went for an evening walk with Martin, she tried to strike up a conversation about celebrities and movie stars. "I keep thinking about Princess Caroline's husband being killed," she said.

Martin was silent.

"That poor family," said Adrienne. "There's been so much tragedy."

Martin glared at her. "Yes," he said facetiously. "That poor, cursed family. I keep thinking, what can I do to help? What can I do? And I think, and I think, and I think so much I'm helpless. I throw up my hands and end up doing nothing. I'm helpless!" He began to walk faster, ahead of her, down into the village. Adrienne began to run to keep up. Marriage, she thought, it's an institution, all right.

Near the main piazza, under a streetlamp, the CHIROMANTE: TAROT E FACCIA had set up her table again. When she saw Adrienne, she called out, "Give me your birthday, signora, and your husband's birthday, and I will do your charts to tell you whether the two of you are compatible! Or —" She paused to study Martin skeptically as he rushed past. "Or, I can just tell you right now."

"Have you been to this woman before?" he asked, slowing down. Adrienne grabbed Martin's arm and started to lead him away.

"I needed a change of scenery."

Now he stopped. "Well," he said sympathetically, calmer after some exercise, "who could blame you." Adrienne took his hand, feeling a grateful, marital love — alone, in Italy, at night, in May. Was there any love that wasn't at bottom a grateful one? The moonlight glittered off the lake like electric fish, like a school of ice.

"What are you doing?" Adrienne asked Ilke the next afternoon. The lamps were particularly low, though there was a spotlight directed onto a picture of Ilke's mother, which she had placed on an end table, for the month, in honor of Mother's Day. The mother looked ghostly, like a sacrifice. What if Ilke were truly a witch? What if fluids and hairs and nails were being collected as offerings in memory of her mother?

"I'm fluffing your aura," she said. "It is very dark today, burned down to a shadowy rim." She was manipulating Adrienne's toes and Adrienne suddenly had a horror-movie vision of Ilke with jars of collected toe juice in a closet for Satan, who, it would be revealed, *was* Ilke's mother. Perhaps Ilke would lean over suddenly and bite Adrienne's shoulder, drink her blood. How could Adrienne control these thoughts? She felt her aura fluff like the fur of a screeching cat. She imagined herself, for the first time, never coming here again. Good-bye. Farewell. It would be a brief affair, a little nothing; a chat on the porch at a party.

Fortunately, there were other things to keep Adrienne busy.

She had begun spray-painting the spiders and the results were interesting. She could see herself explaining to a dealer back home that the work represented the spider web of solitude — a vibration at the periphery reverberates inward (experiential, deafening) and the spider rushes out from the center to devour the gong, the gonger and the gong. Gone. She could see the dealer taking her phone number and writing it down on an extremely loose scrap of paper.

And there was the occasional after-dinner sing-song, scholars and spouses gathered around the piano in various states of inebriation and forgetfulness. "Okay, that may be how you learned it, Harold, but that's *not* how it goes."

There was also the Asparagus Festival, which, at Carlo's suggestion, she and Kate Spalding in one of her T-shirts — *all right already with the T-shirts, Kate* — decided to attend. They took a hydrofoil across the lake and climbed a steep road up toward a church square. The road was long and tiring and Adrienne began to refer to it as the Asparagus Death Walk.

"Maybe there isn't really a festival," she suggested, gasping for breath, but Kate kept walking, ahead of her.

Adrienne sighed. Off in the trees were the ratchety cheeping of birds and the competing, hourly chimes of two churches, followed later by the single off-tone of the half hour. When she and Kate finally reached the asparagus festival, it turned out to be only a little ceremony where a few people bid very high prices for clutches of asparagus described as "bello, bello," the proceeds from which went to the local church.

"I used to grow asparagus," said Kate on their walk back down. They were taking a different route this time, and the lake and its ocher villages spread out before them, peaceful and far away. Along the road wildflowers grew in a pallet of pastels, like soaps.

"I could never grow asparagus," said Adrienne. As a child her favorite food had been "asparagus with holiday sauce." "I did grow a carrot once, though. But it was so small I just put it in a scrapbook."

"Are you still seeing Ilke?"

"This week, at any rate. How about you?"

"She's booked solid. I couldn't get another appointment. All the scholars, you know, are paying her regular visits."

"Really?"

"Oh, yes," said Kate very knowingly. "They're tense as dimes." Already Adrienne could smell the fumes of the Fiats and the ferries and delivery vans, the asparagus festival far away.

"Tense as dimes?"

Back at the villa, Adrienne waited for Martin, and when he came in, smelling of sandalwood, all the little deaths in her bones told her this: he was seeing the masseuse.

She sniffed the sweet parabola of his neck and stepped back. "I want to know how long have you've been getting massages. Don't lie to me," she said slowly, her voice hard as a spike. Anxiety shrank his face: his mouth caved in, his eyes grew beady and scared.

"What makes you think I've been getting —" he started to say. "Well, just once or twice."

She leaped away from him and began pacing furiously about the room, touching the furniture, not looking at him. "How could you?" she asked. "You know what my going there has meant to me! How could you not tell me?" She picked up a book on the dressing table — *Industrial Relations Systems* — and slammed it back down. "How could you horn in on this experience? How could you be so furtive and untruthful?"

"I am terribly sorry," he said.

"Yeah, well, so am I," said Adrienne. "And when we get home,

I want a divorce." She could see it now, the empty apartment, the bad eggplant parmigiana, all the Halloweens she would answer the doorbell, a boozy divorcée frightening the little children with too much enthusiasm for their costumes. "I feel so fucking *dishonored!*" Nothing around her seemed able to hold steady; nothing held.

Martin was silent and she was silent and then he began to speak, in a beseeching way, there it was the beseech again, rumbling at the edge of her life like a truck. "We are both so lonely here," he said. "But I have only been waiting for you. That is all I have done for the last eight months. To try not to let things intrude, to let you take your time, to make sure you ate something, to buy the goddamn Spearsons a new picnic bench, to bring you to a place where anything at all might happen, where you might even leave me, but at least come back into life at last —"

"You did?"

"Did what?"

"You bought the Spearsons a new *picnic bench?*"

"Yes, I did."

She thought about this. "Didn't they think you were being hostile?"

"Oh . . . I think, yes, they probably thought it was hostile."

And the more Adrienne thought about it, about the poor bereaved Spearsons, and about Martin and all the ways he tried to show her he was on her side, whatever that meant, how it was both the hope and shame of him that he was always doing his best, the more she felt foolish, deprived of reasons. Her rage flapped awkwardly away like a duck. She felt as she had when her cold, fierce parents had at last grown sick and old, stick-boned and saggy, protected by infirmity the way cuteness protected a baby, or should, it should protect a baby, and she had been left with her rage — vestigial girlhood rage — inappropriate and intact. She would hug her parents good-bye, the gentle, emptied sacks of them, and think, where did you go?

Time, Adrienne thought. What a racket.

Martin had suddenly begun to cry. He sat at the bed's edge and curled inward, his soft, furry face in his great hard hands, his head falling downward into the bright plaid of his shirt.

She felt dizzy and turned away, toward the window. A fog had drifted in, and in the evening light the sky and the lake seemed a singular blue, like a Monet. "I've never seen you cry," she said.

"Well, I cry," he said. "I can even cry at the sports page if the games are too close. Look at me, Adrienne. You never really look at me."

But she could only continue to stare out the window, touching her fingers to the shutters and frame. She felt far away, as if she were back home, walking through the neighborhood at dinner-time: when the cats sounded like babies and the babies sounded like birds, and the fathers were home from work, their children in their arms gumming the language, air shaping their flowery throats into a park of singing. Through the windows wafted the smell of cooking food.

"We are with each other now," Martin was saying. "And in the different ways it means, we must try to make a life."

Out over the Sfondrata chapel tower, where the fog had broken, she thought she saw a single star, like the distant nose of a jet; there were people in the clayey clouds. She turned, and for a moment it seemed they were all there in Martin's eyes, all the absolving dead in residence in his face, the angel of the dead baby shining like a blazing creature, and she went to him, to protect and encircle him, seeking the heart's best trick, *oh, terrific heart.* "Please, forgive me," she said.

And he whispered, "Of course. It is the only thing. Of course."

MARY GORDON

The Important Houses

FROM THE NEW YORKER

SOME DAYS, I would be left at my grandmother's house. I never knew why. Usually, I could ask my father anything, but I couldn't ask him either of these things: Why are you leaving me here? Why won't you take me with you? I knew that it was considered a privilege to be in that house; I knew that even my father wouldn't understand my reluctance. It was only a partial reluctance anyway, and I believed then that I had no business communicating anything I only partially understood. I knew I must keep silent. At least I knew that.

Entering that house, I was plunged into an atmosphere of bafflement. The words, the manners, all the *things* were foreign to me. The foreignness often seemed literal: often I didn't understand what the people in my grandmother's house were saying, and often what I said was not understood. My father always understood me. "You speak the same language," my mother would remark from the position to which my father and I had banished her: the admiring outsider, the foreign servant. She thought of my grandmother's house — her mother's house — as home. I don't know what she thought of the apartment where we lived — what my father and I called home but which was to her something else. Something unserious and temporary. Something there was no need to have a name for. In her mother's house, everything had been named long ago, once and for all.

I had trouble placing my grandmother's house. I knew it had nothing to do with America. Or postwar life. And yet it stood at the center of the lives of all her children and her children's children. It expressed an era — ahistorical, perhaps wholly imaginary — that we grandchildren only vaguely understood. We knew that it had ended long before we were born: it seemed to have touched upon our parents' early childhood, but we weren't sure. There were twenty-one grandchildren who visited my grandmother's house regularly. Of her nine children, only two had settled more than ten miles from her. We all lived on Long Island, in towns that bordered Queens and took their identity more from "the city" than "the Island." My grandmother had lived in the same house since 1920, when the area was farmland; she despised the people who had moved there from Brooklyn or the Bronx after the war. She condemned new houses and the objects in them.

Each object in her house belonged to the Old World. Nothing was easy; everything required maintenance of a complicated and specialized sort. Nothing was disposable, replaceable. There were no errors of taste because there were no imaginable other choices. I was not unhappy there: each object's rightness of placement made me feel honored to be among them. Yet I was always guilty among these things, as if they knew I preferred what was in my glamorous aunt's house. She lived in the next town from my grandmother; her husband owned a liquor store and made more money than anyone we knew. My aunt and uncle bought things easily, unlike the rest of the family, and so the house was full of new or newish objects: the plastic holders for playing cards, like shells or fans, the nut dishes in the shape of peanuts, the corn dishes in the shape of ears of corn, the hair dryer like a rocket, the makeup mirror framed by light bulbs, the bottles of nail polish, the ice bucket, the cocktail shaker, the deep freeze. And the house was stocked with pleasurable things to eat, drink, sit on, listen to, lean against, watch, sleep in, ride, or wear. I knew these pleasures to be inferior, but I sank into them each time, stealing their luxury and fearing for my soul, as I half feared for my aunt's, which I couldn't imagine to be safe, interested as she was in having a good time.

My grandmother had no interest in having a good time — that is, in doing anything that would result only in pleasure — and her house proclaimed this, as it proclaimed everything about her. Her house was her body and, like her body, was honorable, daunting, reassuring, defended, castigating, harsh, embellished, dark. I can't imagine how she lived: that is to say, how she didn't die of the endless labor her life entailed. Nine children. It's easy either to romanticize her or utterly to push her aside. She casts a light in which my life can only look remiss. I can conjure no Heaven from which she would speak the slightest word of non-condemnation to me. I would never even dream of praise.

Yet I did, somehow, like her house. Old-fashioned flowers, bright-colored, a little wild: marigold, cosmos, foxglove, phlox. Older varieties of roses, whose petals seemed thinner than those of more recent types, more susceptible, like my soft flesh, to insect bites that made them horrible to the eye. I liked her garden even better than my aunt's, where the greens were deeper than the greens of any leaves or grass I'd seen anywhere else. I linked this dark-greenness to prosperity, as if my uncle had invested in that greenness so that we would all be more secure. My grandmother's house had no connection to prosperity: it had righteousness instead.

There were three ways you could enter the house: through the front porch, the side porch, or the kitchen. The kitchen was the most common way. Tacked on, it hadn't originally been part of the house. It floated on nothing, it had no foundation, it was a ship that sailed on air. And yet it was a serious place. Difficult and steady work went on there; the kitchen was productive, rigorous. And yet so light! Its lightness was a particular pleasure in summer. The screen door opened with a leisurely, indulgent creak. It bent back on a steel hasp, and even a child could hook it open easily. All the things that kitchen contained: marjoram, nutmeg, green peppercorns, sage from the garden, mason jars of preserved fruit. Some hints of the Italian from my Italian grandfather: ricotta mixed with cinnamon and sugar, almond *biscotti,* fresh figs purple at the top, fading to a tender green. Irish soda bread my grandmother had learned to make as a girl at home. Inexplicably: *hamantaschen* — a way of using the jars and jars of preserved figs. She would save a little dough, a little bit of fig for me to make my own. She'd put mine in the oven along with hers, but mine were much, much smaller and they always burned. Beside her rows of golden pastry hats were my two burnt offerings, charred and solid black. I would eat them anyway, pretending they were good. I felt I had to, out of loyalty. "Don't eat those things, eat one of my nice ones here," she'd always say, and, guiltily, I would.

What was this all about? She was an expert baker. Why didn't she put my pastries in first and take them out before she put hers in? Or put mine in later, so they'd be ready at the same time as hers? What was she trying to show me? That I could try and try but would never be as good as she? That I should not have trusted her? That I should always keep an eye out, because whatever I did in life would be my own affair? It never occurred to me that the situation could be any different. My grandmother's implacable posture made the idea of alternatives impossible. What was, was. Because it had to be.

That kitchen was a monument to her refusal to accept the modern world. The sink was deep and had two narrow spigots, made of brass, that let out only thin, slow streams of water, unlike the jubilant spurts from the stainless-steel faucets of ordinary fifties sinks. The table was white deal, with a seam down the middle where it could be made to fold, but it was never folded. My grandmother would run a knife blade through that seam and the ones along the sides, to dislodge crumbs or dried food. This was the sort of thing she was doing when people perceived her as being still. The linoleum was dull gray with spattered dots of red, yellow, and black. Her dishes were white with gentle floral patterns, pink and blue. I don't know where they might have come from.

There were a lot of things around the house that, like those dishes, suggested a half-glimpsed gentility. If you went into the side porch, for example, which you rarely did, there were objects of mimed opulence: black jardinieres with Oriental scenes painted on them, holding palms or tall, full philodendrons. The side porch had been my grandfather's workroom; he'd been a jeweler. He died when I was one year old. The room was kept purposely useless, in memory of him. I often stayed there, lonely, feeling I'd stolen grace.

In my grandmother's house I was often alone, left to myself because my grandmother was always busy. Sometimes she'd include me in her tasks: I would hold open the trapdoor so she could carry the wash up from the basement. She'd ask me to hold the funnel steady so she could pour antifreeze into the car. Sometimes I'd help her find a thimble or a pin while she was sewing at her machine: her thick foot in its black, low-heeled oxford pushing her treadle. The words she spoke when at her sewing machine seemed ancient to me, since she was the only one I'd ever heard using them: "rickrack," "grosgrain," "dotted swiss." Nothing she sewed was for me, nothing was for anyone I knew. I never understood what happened to all that sewing; it disappeared magically, like sewing for the dead, her black foot steady on the treadle like the hoof of fate.

She rarely talked. She lifted pots and tools and basketfuls of earth and bowls of vegetables. She tore meat off bones and carcasses and made it into soup; she beat eggs into silky custards. I believe she very much enjoyed her life. But she had no time to play with children. And so I wandered the dark house alone, from room to room, beginning with the front porch, where my bachelor uncle, who still lived with her, slept winter and summer. There was a piano on the porch, and bound music books nobody opened, full of songs no one I knew had ever sung: "Believe Me, If All Those Endearing Young Charms," "Columbia, the Gem of the Ocean," "High Above Cayuga's Waters," "Eli Yale!" And odd pieces of sheet music: "My Buddy," "I'll Take You Home Again, Kathleen."

Why did they make my uncle sleep there? It was cold in winter, hot in summer. He slept on a couch that was only the semblance of a bed, camouflaged each morning with a gray-and-red spotted cover. There was almost no place for his things; I don't know where he put his clothes. But I have no understanding of how my uncle lived. I've never come across anybody like him, anyone who would even give me a clue to why he was the way he was. He conformed to no type.

He served the family, especially his mother, with the devotion of a pilgrim to a sacred shrine. He surprised them all by marrying at forty-three — one of the happiest marriages I have known, but that was later. Throughout his twenties and thirties, the family thought of him as at their beck and call. He was a tall, strong, handsome man, a champion athlete, head at one time of all the lifeguards at Jones Beach. Yet they expected him to do their bidding, to be at their service when they needed him. There were nine brothers and sisters; all but two of them had mates and children. Someone was always sick or weak or broke or down on his luck. They called and he arrived.

Just this year, seven years after his death, at seventy-four, his wife told me that he had decided when he was fourteen that he would dedicate himself to making his mother's life easier. He made the decision when he saw her fixing the roof during a storm. She was six months pregnant, nailing down tarpaper while the wind blew and the rain fell in torrents. He told her to go inside, that he'd take care of everything. From that time on, for nearly thirty years, that was his job: taking care of everything. When he married, it was his only defiance of my grandmother. She fainted at the wedding, which wasn't a Mass: he was marrying a non-Catholic. He moved seven miles away. He moved his things off the porch, his few things with their male smells: *Popular Mechanics* magazines, turpentine, neat's-foot oil. Things I always stood far away from if I ever wandered onto his part of the porch, averting my eyes and fixing them instead on the garlands, green and pink, around the words of the sheet music on the piano — "I'll Take You Home Again, Kathleen."

One of my mother's younger sisters, the only one who hadn't married, had taken over the upstairs of the house. The upstairs didn't seem quite connected to the rest, but, unlike the innocent detachment of the kitchen, this disconnection seemed sinister. There was an awkward step down after you reached the top of the staircase leading from the living room. After you stepped down, there were two rooms on the right side of the corridor; a bathroom (the only one in the house) was on the left. In this bathroom, there was blue-black linoleum on the floor, an old bathtub with claw feet, a small sink, a white wooden bureau, a white wooden washstand, a basin and pitcher, from which protruded more overripe philodendron. I had a vague but powerful distaste for what I imagined the water in the pitcher might be like: the slimy stems in the unclear yellow liquid. The old-fashionedness of the bathroom made me feel it wasn't quite hygienic, not like the sky blue tiles, the chrome fittings of my glamorous aunt's bathroom, or the light apple green of the bathroom in our apartment. Only my aunt who lived upstairs used the bathroom regularly; my grandmother had what she called a "commode" in her bedroom downstairs. She emptied it sometime, no one knew when, in the upstairs toilet. She never took a bath. Yet it would never have occurred to me to call her dirty. In some way we didn't know, sponging herself at the kitchen sink, perhaps, or dipping rags in a large bowl she concealed somewhere, she kept herself exceptionally clean.

My aunt's bedroom was large, industrial, and cold. There was gray linoleum on the floor; her bed and dresser were gray deal. The walls and trim were painted the same shade of gray. No rugs softened or warmed the room. Each footfall, even your own, sounded ominous in your ears.

My aunt kept some small boxes of jewelry on her oversized dresser. I remember one pin: a cluster of false-looking purple grapes. She had many more dresses in her closet than my mother did, but none of them had the cool freshness of my mother's summer cottons or the urbane, theatrical fragrance of her winter suits. My aunt didn't keep a bottle of perfume on her dresser like that vessel of transparent amber I so loved to approach among my mother's things. My mother's perfume had a name I also loved: Command Performance.

All these lacks on my aunt's part made me pity her. I felt she'd missed the point of it all: adulthood, womanhood. She'd thrown away her chance, and that seemed connected to her childlessness, her cruelty, her bitter tongue, the dark circles below her eyes, the deep imprint of her vaccination scar, her miserliness, her law-abidingness, the way she would dream aloud about the new appliances and modern furniture she'd seen on TV. Her instinct to cut people down. I pitied her and yet I feared her; no one else could make me feel so bad. My wrongs were so abundant: talking too much, not being quick enough to help clear the table, reading too much, dreaming, dreaming. Her hair was thick and black; her eyes light brown and surveillant. She was thought a beauty; I could not understand why.

The room next to my aunt's was another place in the house, like the front porch, that I couldn't comprehend. It had four iron cots and a gray iron bunk bed. It was nearly always empty. When I asked why my uncle couldn't use that room instead of sleeping on the porch, or half the porch, my mother said, "It has to be like that. In case people need to stay over." But who needed to stay over? Everyone in the family had less than half an hour's drive to get to my grandmother's house. Twice a year, perhaps, the two families who lived far away — in Baltimore, in Philadelphia — might or might not arrive. Meanwhile, my uncle slept outside.

I'd walk around this empty room, set up like a dormitory, remembering that this was where my mother had slept as a child. The oldest, she always had to share a bed with the next youngest baby. I'd heard all this, but I didn't believe any of it. The child who was my mother, who lived not with me but in this house, was no one I could have known.

It's impossible to believe in one's parents' childhood. My father had no pictures of himself as a child, so I dismissed out of hand the possibility of his having been alive without me. He seemed to take in my being as a kind of necessary sustenance: how could I believe in a life for him anterior to mine? With my mother it was different. I had material proof that she had been a child without me: photographs of a girl whose features I could discern in the living woman, artifacts — here was her bed — but none of it really mattered. The girl who slept in this room was not my mother. That girl had died at the moment of my birth. My mother was someone I had given birth to; whatever had gone before had sunk, like a stone in dark water, into the oblivion of life before me. She was dead, the girl my mother was: this empty room, with the blank iron beds and the walls that echoed when I shouted out my mother's name, was only a shrine kept for the veneration of the dead.

I didn't like staying upstairs for long, so I'd walk down to the living room, which was a place where no one ordinarily spent time. Both the living room and the dining room, where meals were had only on holidays, were about display. There was a sad, apologetic falseness to them. They were rooms that had to appear to be inhabited; occasional actual habitation was a by-product, a necessary and regretted step that had to be got through to reach the true and desired end: display. The motif of the living room was pastoral. Fragonard's aristocrats gamboled in high-heeled boots and feathered hats on the front faces of the maroon table lamps. Curlicued gilt mirrors, inexplicable bibelots: a Venetian glass lady's slipper, a floral cup and saucer, stood on a shelf beside life-size heads of the Mater Dolorosa and of Jesus suffering beneath the Crown of Thorns. The tears congealed on her cheeks; sweat made bumps on his brow, which I liked to run my fingers over, fearing I'd sinned by taking pleasure in the Savior's represented anguish. It was the texture in itself that captured my attention, not the living memory of the Sorrows of the Lord. On this shelf there was also a thin black stork riding on a turtle's back. I'd been told that it was originally bronze, but I had no reason to believe that. No one ever touched it: it stood for my grandmother's astonishing fecundity. Nine children, all born healthy, all still alive. Beside the stork there was a clump of peat, wedge-shaped and porous, that she'd brought from Ireland. She arrived in 1897, alone, at seventeen, to be met by strangers and to take up a domestic's life.

There were no pictures in the living room or in the dining room or in the halls or on the stairways or on the front or side porches. The pictures, all religious, were clustered together in my grandmother's small bedroom. Her bedroom had no door, only a doorway. Anyone could go inside it at any time; we imagined she could always see out of that room, see whatever we were doing. All her grandchildren made several ostensibly aimless trips into her room during each visit. We did it to frighten ourselves. The room was particularly frightening at night.

Her smells: lavender, ammonia, Pine-Sol (always at the bottom of the commode) — a green pool reminding you inevitably of the corruption that you, as a human, had no right pretending you could rise above. Old lace, smelling of dust — hair oil, liniment. Unmodern smells that seemed to us Indian or pagan, rising from darkness, punitive or curing: we could not tell which.

The pictures on her walls were not about pleasing the eye. There was a brown picture with an imprint of Jesus' head: the Shroud of Turin. Then the words to "Now I Lay Me Down to Sleep" on a blue background, framed with an ivory border. A picture of Christ, with long, smooth, girlish hair, pointing to his Sacred Heart, the size and shape of a pimiento or a tongue. Most mysterious: a picture made of slats. You turned your head one way: it was the Scourging at the Pillar. Another turn of the head produced Jesus Crowned with Thorns. If you looked absolutely straight ahead, you saw the Agony in the Garden. I spent hours looking at that picture, frightened, uncomprehending. It was part of my grandmother's hidden and supernal path into the mystery of things — a hard road, unforgiving, made of beaten flesh.

The floor of her bedroom was always undependable. I knew you could push the iron bed against the wall and lift a large part of the floor right up if you grabbed hold of an iron ring and pulled. This was the trapdoor to the basement. I was always afraid that I'd walk into her room one day, heedless, dreaming or reading (which I'd been accused of doing far too much), and hurtle down to the dark basement. I didn't think it would mean my death. I thought my bones would break and then I would be punished by the family. For what they believed was my chief offense: not paying attention.

How could I tell them how much, and with what life-and-death intensity, I paid attention? They wouldn't want to know, and anyway they'd say I paid attention to the wrong things, the wrong things for a child: that was the problem with me. I thought about the wrong things, which was why I never would be happy and why I would never prosper. They were just trying to help me to a good and happy life.

There was some story about a cousin of my mother's falling through the trapdoor, landing on his head, then sitting up in my grandmother's bed, his head swaddled in bandages, and being fed soft-boiled eggs and tea. All the family despised him. I thought about him — his shame, his fear. Perhaps he read magazines in the bed or looked all day at the pictures on the walls while his head reeled and his vision clouded and he fell in and out of fitful sleep. He knew they laughed at him behind the kitchen door. This invalid, whom I felt to be my brother, was old enough to be my father. They all despised my father, as they'd despised the bandaged boy.

*

Unlike the people of my grandmother's house, my father lived in the world. But then he was a Jew. He had converted, he was more devout than they, but it didn't matter: he was still a Jew. They hated Jews. But, no, that wasn't it, it wasn't a full-blown hatred; it was a contempt for the bad values they believed Jews lived by: their interest in pleasure and success. My grandmother's family believed that, unlike the Jews, they stood on a high, unapproachable plateau. This was, of course, her body life: the children born, the endless work, and all against such odds. They stood on the remorseless history of her body, which could never be reproached. And there they judged. They judged the false against the true, they distinguished the important from the trivial. They thought it was the Church that was their buckler and their shield, but they were wrong: it was that large, unyielding, unapproachable maternal body that had undergone so much.

My father's body had no chance against it. My father's body was in charge of nothing they considered real. It could not make money. It was neither strong nor swift nor dexterous. For them, he had no body: by which they meant hands, arms, a back, and legs. He couldn't fix a thing. He couldn't lift anything heavy. He could read books, speak languages. Sometimes he talked to priests, but the family was doing all the work — the real work of the world.

He was in the world, and they were only in the shadow of their mother's body. For his part, he claimed to adore her. He would bring her Irish books, illuminated cards with Celtic sacred symbols. She pretended to be grateful. She was better to him than her children were. As if she sensed that he, too, had some connection with the dark pictures in her room and the wedge of peat and the black stork that rode on the back of the black turtle.

We always arrived at my grandmother's house for family gatherings late, unhelpful, overdressed, but somehow daunting to the others. Six other households were represented — only the upstairs aunt wasn't living somewhere else. But except for my glamorous aunt, her generous, prosperous husband, and her fashionably dressed children — all exceptional because they lived so modernly, so differently from everything my grandmother stood for — the rest were minor characters, undistinguished background figures. Nevertheless, each family but ours had some function: the women cooked and served food; the men carried things, moved furniture. We were simply there, representing something they despised: the outside world.

We were coming from where we lived — not a house but the top half of a house; we called it our apartment, liking the urban sound. It was just three blocks away, but traveling there meant some border had to be crossed. The transition made me fretful and fatigued. Often, going to my grandmother's house made me physically ill, as if we were making a journey over difficult mountains and had experienced a change of air.

My father wore a suit to family parties; my uncles wore dark trousers and plaid shirts. He would often sit in a corner and read; the festivities went on around him. Sometimes I would have to get him to rescue me from my brutal uncle, not one of us by blood. He was in love with my glamorous aunt, who was, of course, married to someone else, and so he came to family parties to be near her. Later, he married my aunt who lived upstairs. He liked to give children the feeling of entrapment: this was his idea of fun. He would pin little girls to the floor and tickle us. It felt to me that I was being smothered; I thought I would lose my breath and die in the middle of the party, right on the floor, in front of everyone. It didn't matter if you said to him, as I did, "Please don't do that to me. I don't like being tickled." He'd say, "Ah, c'mon, whassa matter with you, you afraid of a little fun?" The beery slur of the abuser. The glimpse of chest hair above the neck of his corduroy shirt. His pushing us onto the floor and into corners. Telling us we had to laugh.

When he was around, I wouldn't leave my father's side. He wouldn't touch me if I stayed near my father. I can't imagine what held him back.

Arriving at my grandmother's house from our apartment was like walking from a movie set onto a stage where some slow-moving, slightly out-of-date play was in the middle of the second act. Some operetta: girls in curls, men in mustaches. Flowers, horses, women with their hands in muffs, women in dresses with elaborate trains. But this makes the atmosphere sound too pleasant, as if the brocade couches and gilt mirrors were the whole of the house. Underneath the floral playfulness of the décor, there was always that implacable judgment emanating from the body of my grandmother. She never had to say a word or do a thing: her daughters with their cruel tongues, her sons with their strong backs, took care of everything.

At these family parties, everything seemed to take too long: the games, the songs, the meals, the stories. There were no wisecracks, no abbreviations, no slang, no snacks. Everything seemed the same unvarying texture: thick and heavy, serious, unchangeable, forbidding. In our apartment, there were bold patches of vividness, alterations of texture: glass and chrome, striped wallpapers, lamps of a color known as bisque, whose bases looked like ice cream. I would touch them with my tongue: they were delicious, carved and polished, cool. Their satin shades, pinkish and smooth as dresses, gave the living room an amorous shadowiness when you lit them at dusk.

I don't know where my mother got our furniture. Or if my parents bought it together, an engaged couple, before the wedding. But that's impossible. My father would never have shopped for furniture. He took pride in ignoring his surroundings. To care about things like furniture would have been for him the proof of an inferior nature. To shop for it with his bride-to-be would have made him feel both emasculated and declassed.

So she must, my mother, have gone shopping by herself. To buy the maple bedroom set, the dresser shellacked on top, the lamps, the carpets, the soft chairs. Was she lonely in this, or exhilarated? She was leaving her mother's house for the first time, at the age of thirty-nine. She'd been the major support of her family. Every month from June of 1928, when she graduated from business college (she married in October 1947), she'd paid the mortgage on the house. And who would pay it now? The brothers and sisters never forgave her for saying "Not me. Not anymore. I'm getting married." They divided the mortgage payment nine ways, resenting my parents, and each of them contributed eight dollars a month. My parents contributed the same amount.

My grandfather had always needed his older children's help to support the family. Yet no one ever saw this as shameful. My father's enterprises (he wasn't idle, only unable to make his enterprises pay) were seen as a blot, a cross for my efficient mother. Leaving her parents' house for the wedding, my mother was handed a slip of paper by her father, who wouldn't be attending the ceremony. My parents were driving to the western part of New York State, a trip of ten hours, to be married by the priest they both considered their best friend. My grandfather thought the drive wasn't worth it. In the car, my mother read her father's note. In his formal, European script, the words "You will work till the day you die."

She did work. She came home from the lawyer's office in her navy blue suit, putting down her leather purse with its built-in compact, changing into a housedress — crisp, printed, fresh-colored — and then she cooked for us. She washed our clothes on a washboard. Originally, she'd used the washing machine in her mother's house, but my upstairs aunt insisted she stop. She said the water bill was sky-high. Hadn't my mother thought of that? My mother cried all night. I don't know what my father did. Perhaps he told her to keep her mind on higher things. Or perhaps he cuddled her or bought her candy. Any of these things is imaginable, as much as I can imagine them, without me, in their new apartment, after their wedding, settling down among their new light furniture, using their brightly colored dishes, towels, cups and saucers, salt-and-pepper sets.

Perhaps he took her to the movies. All three of us loved the movies. It was the only thing that we could share. I think my mother got the idea for her marriage from the movies, or at least the courage to defy her parents and move away from home with a strange, unsuitable man. Which is why the colors of our house seemed to me the colors of the movies: the Pyrex dishes in Technicolor shades, with clear glass lids so you could see the food you'd stored (no frightening surprises, no secret rot). So enlivening in the refrigerator, these colors: strawberry red, sun yellow, peacock blue. My mother's wedding china with its playful patterning of unnaturally colored fruit: sapphire apples, pears made of red-and-white checks. We weren't happy in the apartment, but we had it in us to be playful. We sang songs from musicals; we danced to the radio. We did imitations and told jokes. We made fun of stuck-up people. We went out to eat.

Our familial ideal, taken from the movies, never included midwestern families around the dinner table; our treasured models were connected not to small towns or farmlands but to show business or crime. Our particular favorites were childless couples who lived in penthouses; food prepared and consumed inside the house was of no importance in our lives, as it wasn't for them. My parents took pride in this. "Why do you have concern for what you put in your mouth?" Jesus had said. "It goes into the belly and ends up in the drain." My parents thought they were living by these words of Jesus, but it wasn't eating that displeased them — it was cooking and setting and clearing the table they didn't like. We were happy eating in luncheonettes or bar-and-grills where we were served by waiters and waitresses my mother had known for years. They praised her for her husband and her child. Childless themselves, or long past bearing children, they would look at me and say, "God bless her," awed that at the age of forty-one my mother had reproduced. I don't know what they said to my father. They may have slapped him on the back.

When we came back home after our meals or movies, my parents would immediately begin fighting. They fought a lot, and always about money. I would go up to the attic. Upstairs, away from them, I felt free. What had money to do with me, or I with money? I stood beneath the bare beams, in the emptiness, watching the gold light strike the bare wood floor in straight vertical bars. I would sing loudly so I couldn't hear what they were saying. "I won't give you one red cent for carfare." "You ought to have your head examined." I twirled around and around, pretending my skirts were long and billowing. I thought the dust motes traveling down the shafts of light were a blessed substance, like manna. I was privileged to be in proximity to it, but I would never dream of following the light upward to its source, for who has looked upon the face of God and lived?

The attic was meant to be our storage place, but we had nothing to store. My mother had taken nothing from her mother's house, and my father had lived nowhere: in spare rooms of other people's houses, in hotels. I believed that the people who owned the house before us had stored treasures in the attic for years. Their name was Chamberlain. "English," my father said, meaning "Protestant. Nothing to do with us." I associated those bare beams, that clear light, and all that space with Protestants. Chamberlain — the clean sound, the clipped-off consonants, the relaxed polysyllable. No need to rush or argue for the Chamberlains. They'd left a beer stein on one of the attic windowsills — a black background, green figures in salmon-colored pantaloons and black tricornered hats. I never touched it. I believed that if I touched it the Chamberlains would never come back. I longed for them to come back and give me retroactive permission to inhabit their attic. Perhaps they would move in there with me: I could imagine the sun striking their blond hair. Sometimes I'd look out the window and imagine I could see them walking up the street. I'd never met them, but I knew I'd recognize them the moment they appeared.

From the attic, I could hear my father and the radio. WQXR: the Radio Station of the New York *Times.* I'd sneak up on him and tease him for conducting a phantom orchestra. He said that his mother had been a concert pianist, but he lied so much about his family, who knows if this was true. He ripped a picture of Beethoven out of the encyclopedia and hung it near my toy box, at a level where I could see that imposing head when I was trying to play my games. The only other picture in the house was his print of Holbein's Thomas More. No landscapes, no still lifes, no pretty children in ornate hats. There were photographs of ourselves, as if we were movie stars that we admired. But photos of no one else.

My mother listened to radio serials while she ironed. I remember the name of one of them: "Yours Truly, Johnny Dollar." In my memories of my mother ironing, it's always a summer evening. She sips cool drinks, which she leaves on the end of the ironing board. Her arms are lovely in her sleeveless dress: buoyant and fragrant, freckled like an early apple. The iron hisses on the damp fabric, and the joyous smell of cleanliness enters the air of the living room. Then there is the sound of gunshots from the radio and low, conspiratorial, no-nonsense voices. I was happy just to sit and watch my mother; she seemed happy, for once not angry, not fighting with my father. I don't know where my father was.

I didn't miss him those nights, though I felt his absence. I never felt my mother's absence when I was alone in the apartment with my father. How could I? There was nothing that I lacked.

We were as happy as a couple in a movie musical. We didn't

sing our words to each other, but we could have. It was impossible for me to perform even the slightest wrong gesture; every turn of my head, each step from one room to another was delightful, as if its perfection had been choreographed, rehearsed, then filmed. You could say that this self-consciousness was the death of spontaneity, but that was a small loss: in exchange, each act took on the sheen of permanence. It existed without danger of being forgotten. I believed that everything I did was of the greatest importance to my father, and would be till the end of time, and then beyond that, in eternity.

We moved without hesitation from the world of romance to the cool, high world of spirit. We became Europeans. The same Europe that had sent my grandmother. But we weren't servants: we commanded, and the world was ours. The work of maintenance and its inevitable partner, judgment, was nothing to us. We walked in the green lights of our demesne, the noble father and his noble daughter. In and out our breaths came, natural and without strain. Silently, my father and I prayed in Latin. I was made to understand that men would die for me, but there was no need for me to think of, to go near, a man. I was with my father. We were alone in our apartment; we were in Hollywood, in feudal Europe. What could there be on earth that I would need? Particularly from another man.

When my father and I were alone, all the objects that we touched became transformed. They existed for their representative, not their practical, value. They stood for something — something about ourselves. We ate and drank only from unusual plates, glasses, cups. We had orange juice from the chrome Manhattan set: we drank from chalices, goblets, or the kind of stemware that sophisticated playwrights drank from, toasting each other on their balconies that looked down at the river and the Fifty-ninth Street Bridge. My father put my sandwiches on clear glass plates with the print of an iris etched onto their surfaces, like the print of a skeleton in sand. We kept them for serving cake on when priests came; we didn't tell my mother that we'd used them for ourselves. He made real tea for me, sweet with honey, enlivened with lemon, and poured it into my doll's blue and white china cups. Nothing was itself, everything was a prop. The drama we were in was being filmed; I didn't know by whom. I believed that one day we would go into an ornate theater —

Radio City Music Hall, perhaps — and see ourselves, larger than life but recognizable: the projection of everything the family would not allow us to acknowledge that we were.

Our scale was grand, my father's and mine. Perhaps that was why he refused to have a television: it would be too small for us. That wasn't what he said, of course: he said it was an invention by fools for fools. But it was worse than that: Madison Avenue would control the people's hearts and minds. He wanted the people's hearts and minds to be controlled by Rome — how quick he was to sense the competition.

To watch television, we went either to my grandmother's or to my glamorous aunt's. My aunt's TV was in the middle of a room they called the TV room, but my grandmother's was hidden in a piece of furniture. Perhaps that way she could pretend to herself most of the time that she hadn't capitulated to modern life, that she hadn't bought anything *new*.

To get to the TV, you approached a mahogany console. You opened the doors slowly to see the treasure, hidden like pornography: the turquoise screen with its tiny central moon, the size of a fingernail, that appeared when you turned the dial and disappeared after you turned it off.

On Tuesdays, we went to her house to watch Bishop Sheen. Those nights, after the moon vanished and the screen filled in its image, what you saw first was an empty chair. His. The bishop's. And then himself, in his beautifully fitted cassock with its purple sash. (We knew it was purple — all bishops had purple sashes — although we saw only black and white.)

I had never seen a bishop, but priests were familiar in the three important houses: my grandmother's, ours, my aunt's. The priests were there, always, because my mother had made the initial connection — she was good at befriending priests, who, after all, must have been rather lonely. The family resented her for this; her brothers and sisters suspected that it made her think she was better than they were. They were partly right.

The priests who came to the three houses were very different. Usually, missionaries came to my grandmother's house, grateful for the spaghetti dinners she regularly held to earn money for their outposts in Africa, in China. The priests who went to my aunt's house were interested in having a good time; sometimes she tempted them to sleep in in the morning, not to say Mass, if they'd had a late and raucous night before. But the priests who came to our apartment came to argue with my father — to be insulted by him, it seemed to me. He would take the priests into his study (it was where he really slept: I slept in the bedroom with my mother, but none of us admitted that). He would close the door and shout. The priests would sheepishly mumble responses. I sat on the threshold listening through the door, to my father crying out "Orthodoxy," "Heresy," and "Canon law." I folded my hands in prayer and squeezed them together, as if the small pain would be a further proof of the seriousness of my intention. I was praying that we wouldn't have to pay for my father's bad behavior to the priests. A priest was a sacred vessel, and my father was shouting at the sacred vessel. Shouting *into* it. The words would be contained — they wouldn't evaporate, like ordinary words, into the air. I feared for us all. Retribution certainly would come down on our heads; as a family, we would be punished, marked with a tribal sign.

After they were through with their arguing, my father and the priest would come out into the hall. And what happened then would alarm me more than anything. My father would fall to his knees and ask the priest for his blessing. The priest would place his hands on my father's head, whisper some Latin words, and make the sign of the cross above him.

I knew everything this was supposed to mean: that it didn't matter that my father had insulted the priest *as a man* — the office of the priesthood was infinitely respectable and humbling to him. My father had no hesitation about falling to his knees. But I hated it. I didn't believe in the possibility of this division of identity — the object of scorn / the sacred vessel; the persecutor / the humble penitent — although it was part of my faith to do so. I didn't like seeing my father on his knees. In resisting this tableau, I knew that I transgressed, but this transgression didn't torment me like the others of which I was guilty. I was quite sure that I was right, and my rightness was a window letting in a disturbing light that fell straight onto the white stone of ancient practice.

*

The TV bishop had nothing to do with my kneeling father and the priests raising their hands in blessing near his head. We drove to my grandmother's house to watch the bishop. We sat with her and my aunt until just the right moment to turn the set on. We watched as the Bishop sat in silence a few seconds before he spoke. His eyes seemed transparent. They knew everything. They looked into your sinful soul. There was a blackboard on which he drew diagrams and wrote key words. He said that during the station break his guardian angel erased the blackboard. I believed this, and was thrilled by the conjunction of the supernatural and the technological. When the upstairs aunt told me it was just a joke, I wept against my father's jacket. Then I had to endure her contempt. "Why does she cry so much? She cries for nothing," my aunt said to my mother. I don't know what my mother said.

We sat in a circle, rapt and proud. We understood that all over the country people were sitting in their living rooms in circles like ours, in a similar silence. Even non-Catholics. We had heard that this was true. For once, *they* were looking enviously at us. We had the truth, and they wondered if our truth could make them free. They might even act on their surmises. Dreams swelled our breasts: ourselves in the majority.

I have no memory of what the bishop said, but I know I was convinced of its importance. Here was someone talking about the Faith, just as Edward R. Murrow talked about Russia. I didn't know how this could be, but I believed in its rightness. My father did not believe. He hated Bishop Sheen for his watered-down message. I assumed he didn't like him because the bishop didn't shout, as my father did behind the closed door with the priests, or use words like "heresy" and "orthodoxy." "Compromiser," my father called the bishop. I had no idea what the word meant. It sounded to me as if my father believed the bishop was infecting us all with disease. "Keep the American people happy. *Make them feel good.* Make them feel they're fine as long as they're sincere." "Sincere" was another word whose meaning I couldn't comprehend. Sincerity seemed to be something everyone but my father thought was a good thing. Yet I knew only my father was right.

Could he be right about the bishop? Didn't those eyes mean anything to him? Did he come along with my mother and me only because he liked kneeling for the Rosary, which my grandmother led after we turned off the set when the bishop's show was done? After the Rosary, we drove home, and my parents would argue about Bishop Sheen while I longed for the attic. But it was too late for the attic: I had to listen to them from my bed, my mother saying, "If it's so terrible, for Christ's sake don't go next time." But I knew he would always go and that afterward, in the car and in the house, the same words would always be spoken.

On Friday nights, my mother and I went without my father to my glamorous aunt's house to watch television. Nothing pious happened there. We watched silly, crackbrained girls: "My Little Margie," "My Friend Irma." Then the prizefights went on. The women and children disappeared. We played and talked somewhere else: we could hear the bell signaling the end of a round, but it seemed terribly far away, in some country that had nothing to do with us. We children played dress-up with my aunt's old clothes. My uncles drank beer out of glasses that I believed had come from Germany. The glasses frightened me. The war had been over less than ten years, and those years existed for me like a long, unenterable tunnel, having nothing — utterly nothing — to do with the way we lived now and yet shedding from its depths a brownish, toxic light on everything we did. I had visions of the war: women with their heads shaved, made to stand naked in town squares, shot by Nazis. Or children starving, heroic, with one chocolate coin between them, which they ran a wet finger over each day, licking their fingers, making the chocolate coin last a month. The first idea, the idea of the woman with the shaved head, I actually got from television. A show called "Playhouse 90," a show my aunt and my mother were watching one night while the uncles were out at a basketball game. It was a show I wasn't supposed to watch. All the children were meant to be asleep, and my cousins were, but I crept in and watched the television from the stairwell, where the women didn't see me. I'd stolen a box of chocolate stars, and shoved them hypnotically into my mouth as the television spoke about the woman with her shaved head. Listening, I was sick with guilt and an excess of sugar, my mouth sore and dry, as if I were tasting ash.

I was always sick and guilty when I went to my aunt's house. We were always allowed to eat too much, too many things that were bad for us. We ate potato chips and cheap sweets, foods my grandmother condemned and vilified. We drank all the Cokes in the refrigerator; we laughed too much and were warned that that kind of laughing always ended up in tears. Sometimes it did, but not always, and it made us distrust our mothers, because we knew they believed it *always would.* My cousins and I fought, because we all wanted to be the mother in the games we played — except occasionally one cousin would agree to be the child if she could be spanked on her bare bottom, hard. After those nights, I lay in my bed, feeling I'd just escaped something modern and dangerous, something that could take me away from my parents' house. Our place was so fragile and so tentative; we didn't have any margin for mistakes. I lay awake, waiting for my punishment.

One night it came. We'd been at my aunt's all evening. Soon after I was back home and in bed, the phone rang. It was Bellevue Hospital. My father had had a heart attack in the Forty-second Street Library.

There is a sound of disaster, and a quiet after it, when the universe becomes still from shock; the wind stops, the light is colorless, and humans have no words, because no words fit the enormity. Then a hum enters the air; normal activity begins again, but slowly, as if everyone were under water. People move, pick things up in their hands, walk from place to place, but the hum supports each action; you can mark the time when the disaster is completed and something else — the rest of life — begins. You know this because the hum no longer supports each act. I have never been in an earthquake, or the aftermath of battle, but I know their sound. The shocked sound of proximity to death. I heard it when my mother hung up the phone and said, "Your father's had a heart attack." There were a few seconds of silence, a few beats of inactivity, before she went to the phone again and called my glamorous aunt, asking that she send my uncle over to drive her to the hospital. Those few seconds of hushed paralysis ate a hole into the center of the earth, and what had been my life disappeared, like fool's gold cast away without a thought.

That was a Monday night. I remembered that, on the Friday before, I woke to hear my father moaning in the kitchen. I walked down the hall to see him sitting at the table, across from my mother, drinking a glass of whiskey. "My heart is killing me," I heard him say. When he saw me at the door, he tried to sit up and speak brightly.

"You said your heart was killing you," I said.

"It's just an expression," he said. "I'm fine." I knew that it wasn't an expression — he wasn't playing with language, he was describing his own death. That night, his death entered the room, the air was saturated with it; with each breath I took his death into my body, and I was not free of it again.

My prosperous uncle arrived, along with my uncle who'd lived on the front porch. I don't know how he found out, but he was there, as always, because one of the family was in trouble. The two uncles drove my mother to the hospital. They packed some things for me and took me to my grandmother's. I never saw our apartment again.

For thirty days, my mother drove in to the hospital and spent the evenings with my father. I wasn't allowed to go. I stayed with my grandmother. I slept in her dark room, with the frightening pictures, next to her large, bitter-smelling body. One night, I woke for no reason. It was nearly midnight. I went into the living room. My mother let me sit on the couch beside her and watch television. We watched Jack Paar. Ten minutes later, the phone rang. It was the hospital. My father had just died.

I don't know what they did with all the things in our apartment. The furniture, the lamps, the cheerful dishes. Or my toys: my windup Cinderella, my tin dollhouse, the Alice in Wonderland rug. They were banished. Were they burned, sold, put upstairs in the Chamberlain attic? I was afraid to ask. My aunt who lived with my grandmother, with whom I would now live, said I had to remember there was very little room in the house. I understood. But I wished someone would say something to me about what had happened to my things. Everything was simply gone, no longer on earth — it had all disappeared, as my father's body, for no better reason, had disappeared.

My mother bought twin beds and flowered cardboard

dressers. We moved into the room in my grandmother's house where my mother had slept as a child. My mother impressed upon me that my aunt and grandmother were doing us a big favor by letting us live with them, that we mustn't seem to be in the way. I hid and I was quiet. I lived nowhere. I took up no space. I was invisible. I was the dead child of a dead father. I knew better than to think I had a home.

For a while, I thought he would come back. I climbed up the dark stairs, stepped down the large, dangerous step, walked past my aunt's room to my own. I thought he would be waiting. His hands, his rings, his sweaters would be available to me again. His voice, singing, telling jokes, saying there was a real place for me and he would take me there — some place that he owned, his property.

This was how I lived until I gave up hope. Until I understood he wasn't coming back. After that, the years were a dark corridor, illumined only by the lightning of my grandmother's last illness, her death, when her house would fall to ruin and there wasn't a thing I could do to stop it, even if I'd wanted to.

But that was later. At the time of my father's death, when we moved into my grandmother's house, I saw that my mother was happy. She had come back home. She didn't have to work so hard. My grandmother did everything. My mother no longer ironed in the evenings, listening to the radio, sipping iced drinks. Nobody played the radio. We never went to the movies. After supper, the grownups watched television. I stayed upstairs alone, waiting for my father, although I no longer believed he would come. But I had to have a place for mourning. Mourning was my business: the room I slept in wasn't a habitation but a place of work. The work was crucial; there was no one else to do it. Nobody else mourned him. My mother seemed to have forgotten that he'd lived, that he'd lived, that he'd lived *anyplace,* that there were places he had walked that would no longer know his step. Only I remembered that he had lived among us once and now was somewhere else, somewhere I couldn't go, among the dead. Among the light dead, rootless, homeless, with no place to rest or lay his head.

Contributors' Notes

WENDELL BERRY was born in 1934 and is still living. He is a native of Henry County, Kentucky, where, with his wife, Tanya, he inhabits a small farm on the west bank of the Kentucky River.

▪ Though I make no such requirement, I am always comforted to know that a story I have imagined is validated by a real story somewhere behind it. "Pray Without Ceasing" has a real story behind it. And so the story I have written is an inherited story, one that I have both known and imagined for many years but could not write until I understood pretty fully what I had been entrusted with.

No real story, as known, is whole. Nobody knows the whole of any real story. For a story, even a real one, to become whole, it has to be imagined. Though I am not a proper judge of the story I have written, I have tried to make it whole; the real story, that I knew only in part, has had to become imaginary. Nothing exactly like this ever happened to people exactly like these. And yet my imagined story, if it is whole, speaks of something that is potential — really there — in the world. Both the real and the imagined story say to me, among other things, that forgiveness is possible and that it works.

The community, composed of inevitably flawed human beings, is itself inevitably flawed. If it is to hold together, it must hold together by forgiveness. That "things fall apart" is undoubtedly the dominant truth of our time. The story we are most familiar with is probably the story of the disintegration of cultures and ecosystems, of communities, families, marriages, and even the characters of individual people. But in the face of this general falling apart, some things also hold together. It has taken me a long time to see that the way things hold together is as much a story as the way things fall apart. Forgiveness too is a story that can be told.

STEPHEN DIXON was born, raised, and educated in New York City, and he has a B.A. from City College in International Relations. For about twenty years he held various jobs, including newsman, public school teacher, tour leader, artist's model, waiter, bartender, busboy, technical writer, and department store salesman. Since 1980 he has been teaching in the Writing Seminars at Johns Hopkins University. He has published about 350 short stories, 9 story collections, and 5 novels. His last novel, *Frog* (British American Publishing, 1991) was a PEN/Faulkner finalist in 1992 as well as a National Book Award finalist in 1991. His most recent story collection, *Long Made Short,* in which "Man, Woman and Boy" appears, was published in 1993 by Johns Hopkins University Press. In 1994, Henry Holt will bring out a selected collection of 65 of his stories and his new novel, *Interstate.* Stephen Dixon lives in Baltimore with his wife, Anne Frydman, who is a translator of Russian and a teacher, and his two daughters, Sophia and Antonia.

▪ I know how some of my stories originate, but not "Man, Woman and Boy." Some come from anecdotes told to me, or they start from something I've heard on the radio or read in the newspaper that day. Or, I have a dream and when I awake I feel it could be a story, with a little fiddling so it won't seem like a dream. Or, I might write a story loosely based on a writing exercise I've heard an instructor give to his class as the opening for a story: "A man in a red raincoat gave a small package to a woman in a pink parka. Now do something with it."

Or, a story may come from a series of events that happen to me on a street: A dog bites me, and when I ask, "Whose dog is this?" two transvestites sitting on a public bench raise their hands, and when I roll up my trouser leg to show them the dog bites, they whistle and say I have nice legs, and one thing leads to another — the A.S.P.C.A. is on strike so I can't test the dog for rabies — and all I have to do when I get home is start it off simply, tell it chronologically, and come up with an ending.

But this story came like ninety percent of the stories I write. I'd finished a story the previous day, I wanted to write a story today, so I sat in front of my manual typewriter and typed the first line that came to my head. That line led to another and suddenly the characters were running around on the page and saying things I didn't know they would and the story took on a momentum of its own. I was in a trance, almost, being my own secretary taking dictation, writing whatever came to me. If I went off in the wrong direction, I would take control for a moment and bring the story back, and then continue in a different direction, till the story seemed finished and I felt anything more would be excessive.

This story, like the first draft of most of my stories, took about an hour to an hour and a half to write. The next day I started, page by page, rewriting the story, and that took a month.

"Man, Woman and Boy" is totally imagined. The man isn't I, the woman isn't my wife, the boy isn't ours, and the events that take place aren't like anything that has happened to me or anyone else I know. They weren't dreamed up, nor did they come from some other teacher's creative writing exercise or from anything I heard on the radio or read in a newspaper. But the home where the story takes place is where my wife, two daughters, and I lived for six years, till we moved a few months ago.

TONY EARLEY is a native of Rutherfordton, North Carolina. He is a graduate of Warren Wilson College and the University of Alabama, where in 1992 he received an M.F.A. in Creative Writing. His work has appeared in *Harper's Magazine* and *TriQuarterly,* and has been anthologized in *New Stories from the South.* His collection of stories, *Here We Are in Paradise,* will be published in January 1994 by Little, Brown and Company.

▪ "Charlotte" is a story that I wrote in a week after trying unsuccessfully to write it for over a year. It started with the voice of a guy who was unhappy with the superficiality of his life in Charlotte and distraught over his relationship with his girlfriend. I also knew that he had something to say about professional wrestling and about the Hornets, Charlotte's new N.B.A. basketball team, but for a long time I didn't know what. All the early attempts at the story didn't deal with wrestling at all, but with Starla's tragic past, and they were all bad. I was finally able to write the story when I figured out the relationship between Charlotte's departing professional wrestlers and its struggling professional basketball players. Then I knew what was going on between the narrator and Starla. I didn't like the story much at first because I thought it was *slick,* and metaphorically *one-dimensional* — exactly the kind of story I had always sworn I would never write. Later I decided it wasn't as bad as I'd thought because the metaphor the narrator used to describe his relationship with Starla — the professional wrestling bout between Lord Poetry and Bob Noxious — was itself an illusion, which made his every declaration suspect. And being paid for the story didn't hurt. Over time my own allegiances have switched from the narrator to Starla, whom I've come to realize is a woman without delusions, the kind of person Charlotte, or any other place, could use more of. She still has her tragic past, but only a few patient people at the University of Alabama and I know what it is. As I write this, the Hornets are headed to the playoffs for the first time, and I hope that Starla will be at the Coliseum watching.

KIM EDWARDS grew up in Skaneateles, New York, and studied at Colgate University and the University of Iowa. She spent the past five years living in Asia, first on Malaysia's rural east coast, later in a small city in Japan, and finally in Phnom Penh, Cambodia. In 1990 she won the Nelson Algren Award for short fiction. Her stories have appeared in numerous magazines, including *Antaeus, The Paris Review, American Short Fiction, The North American Review, The Threepenny Review,* and *Ploughshares.* She lives in Pittsburgh, Pennsylvania, with her husband, Thomas Clayton.

▪ The rural east coast of Malaysia is a place that seemed to me, the longer I lived there, to be in many times at once. As in a palimpsest, the various pasts of the country were always rising to the surface and mingling with the present. There were shopping malls and rickety river houses standing side by side. New highways traveled through ancient jungles, and at night elephants came to sleep on the warm asphalt, leaving huge declivities. This conflation of time happened in the spiritual realm as well. Despite the increasingly strict presence of Islam, many of my friends still maintained their beliefs in the animist world of spirits. It wasn't uncommon to hear of people being possessed and in need of a *bomoh,* a traditional doctor, to cure them, and I was often warned not to go out at dusk, a dangerous time when it was possible to lose one's soul. I was interested in this secret spiritual life, which seemed to well up, like a persistent spring, despite the contrary injunctions of scientific and Islamic law. And I learned, in Malaysia, to release the limits on my imagination, because things I would have thought unlikely happened all the time there.

This particular story began when I read a newspaper article about the discovery of gold in the state just north of where I lived. I didn't initially think of it as a short story, but the image of people growing discontented with their lives, and sacrificing everything for the elusive promise of wealth, stayed with me. It seemed to encompass many of the things I witnessed in Malaysia, especially the lingering effects of British colonial rule. I don't usually write outlines for stories, but I wrote a three-page summary of this one just before I left Malaysia. I must have wanted to get it down in some form while my life was somewhat stable, and it's a good thing I did. I moved to Japan; my computer broke; the story, unwritten, simmered away for months. When I finally got back to it, Pachik Muda was walking out of the rubber plantation, thinking about his lunch, and the story grew from there.

At first it seemed easy to trace this story's origin — I remembered the article, and the rich texture of life in Malaysia — but the more I think about it, the more I'm reminded that writing is always a bit mysterious, more alchemy than logic. My stories all have many sources, small but significant moments and insights which gather over time, and mingle, and finally transmute into something else entirely.

HARLAN ELLISON has written or edited more than 1300 stories, essays, articles, newspaper columns, and teleplays. Among his many awards and honors, he has won the Mystery Writers of America Edgar Allan Poe award twice, the Horror Writers of America Bram Stoker Award twice, the Nebula three times, the Hugo 8½ times, the Writers Guild of America Most Outstanding Teleplay Award for solo work an unprecedented four times, the Silver Pen for Journalism from PEN, and the universal opinion that he is the most contentious person now walking the Earth. He is now completing a new collection of short stories, *Slippage,* which will be his sixtieth published book.

▪ On the day I sit down to write this note, ruminations meant to add a grace note to an event, a publication, a fervent wish, a vain hope I've harbored for thirty-eight years (since I sold my first story at the end of 1955) — I have just hung up the phone, having been informed that my pal, the most excellent and virtually unremembered master talent, the great Avram Davidson, has died.

And I am suddenly more concerned with stealing a moment here to honor him, than I am with blowing my own horn about how clever I was to have written "The Man Who Rowed Christopher Columbus Ashore." Because, you see, for all the hot air and Monday-morning-quarterback deconstructionist horse puckey that writers and academics like to slather on the subject, there are only a couple of genuine Secrets about writing.

The first has to do with the *why.* And most of what is said and written is sententious claptrap, intended to buy us a shot at posterity by providing untenured educationists drivel for their treatises. Quentin Crisp once observed that "Artists in any medium are nothing more than a bunch of hooligans who cannot live within their income of admiration." Oh, how we want that assurance that once we're gone, no matter that we were as specialized a savory as Nathanael West or as common a confection as Clarence Budington Kelland, that we will be read fifty years hence. Because the *why* is as simply put as this: "I write only because I cannot stop." Don't credit that one to me, I'm not that smart. It was Heinrich Von Kleist. And he nailed it; what he suggests, in literary terms, is the equivalent of the answer to *most* of the stuff that we do: "It seemed like a good idea at the time."

But West is barely read today, not to mention Shirley Jackson (who was the inspiration for "The Man Who Rowed—"), or James Agee, or William March, or Jim Tully, or even John O'Hara or Zoë Oldenbourg. Or Avram Davidson, who was one of the most stylish, witty, erudite, and wildly imaginative writers of our time. Author of more than twenty-five books. None of them in print.

He died in a VA hospital's liaison "recuperation facility" called Resthaven; in Bremerton, Washington; all alone save for a compassionate nurse who knew his name as a superior fantasist; penniless, unknown to a nation of readers though he was working right up to the end; seventy years old and cranky as a screw being turned against its threads; a man who wrote like a wonky, puckish, amusing Henry James, sans the stick up his butt.

Avram dies, and like Kelland, who was as commercially successful in his time as Stephen King is in his, or Jackson, who was never higher than "mid-list," gone is gone, and Posterity is busy figuring out who among today's Flavors-of-the-Month will bring in the most money by going "interactive."

On this day that I sit down to write my note to accompany (finally, after thirty-eight years of dreaming about it, lusting after it) my inclusion in *The Best American Short Stories,* all I can think about is Avram, and how he deserved many times to have been included here over the years, how he never got that notice, how posterity may have escaped him entirely, and I keep returning to this damned question of why we miss going to the movies, or attending a concert, or spending a quiet evening with a loved one, or taking that trip to the Great Barrier Reef . . . because we've got yet another deadline, yet another story to write, yet another idea burning to be slammed onto paper. It's far far less, I think, of Mario Vargas Llosa's "The writer is an exorcist of his own demons," than it is what Von Kleist and Quentin Crisp said.

I have a T-shirt that bears the message NOT TONIGHT, DEAR, I HAVE A DEADLINE.

Funny, till the last deadline comes, as it did for Avram. And then, like West or Tully or F. Van Wyck Mason, you're no-price. So what was it all about?

The secret is this: *anyone* can become a writer. If you look at the actual work of many of the creatures appearing on the bestseller lists, you know that things that flourish in petri dishes can become writers. The trick, the secret, is to *stay* a writer. To produce a body of work that you hope improves and changes with time and the accumulation of skill. To stay a writer day after year after story, till at last you get smart enough, or work long enough pulling the plow, to write something that gets included in *The Best American Short Stories,* a dream you know (in those cold moments when you can't lie to yourself) will always elude you, because there is no great bearded sentience in the universe, and "it ain't fair . . . I deserve it" doesn't mean shit, as David Webb Peoples said in his screenplay for *Unforgiven* (which should've won the Oscar for Best Original Screenplay). There is no god, or even upper-case God, wasting his, her, or its time mucking about in our daily affairs. There is only random chance and the cupidity of the uncaring cosmos.

Which is *exactly* what "The Man Who Rowed Christopher Columbus

Ashore" is about. There is no pattern; no pantheon of busybody entities up there in the clouds ordaining our lives; no Grand Scheme. You can be walking down the street, slip and tear your Achilles tendon, and walk with a limp for the rest of your life, thereby killing your career as a ballet dancer, but forcing you to make a living at brain surgery, during which career you discover the cure for brain cancer. *That's* what the story is about. Don't listen to the bonehead deconstructionists when they start all that "basic Appolonian-Dionysian Conflict" hooey. The story is about nothing more difficult or loftier than the admonition that *you* are responsible, that posterity is a snare, that memory is short, and that life is an absolutely unriggable crap shoot, with the stickman a civil servant who works for some department as inept as you are. Some days he does something swell, some days he does something creepy, some days he does something crummy, and some days, well, he don't do nothin' at all.

Even if you're standing all alone in the middle of the Gobi Desert at high noon, and a Mosler safe falls out of the baggage compartment of a Concorde zipping by overhead at 33,000 feet, and the great heavy thing falls right on top of you and squashes you to guava jelly . . . it was your fault. You're responsible. It was, after all, *you* who chose to stand in that spot, at that moment.

And it only took me fourteen years, from conception and the writing down of the first few lines of the story, to get smart enough to write the *complete* story, and do it properly. And I cannot tell you how goofily pleased I am to be here. It only took thirty-eight years, and I'm nuts with pleasure. I'm one of the lucky ones. Avram never made it.

Rest in peace, old pal.

ALICE FULTON is the author of three books of poems, including *Powers of Congress* (David R. Godine), *Palladium* (University of Illinois Press), and *Dance Script with Electric Ballerina* (University of Pennsylvania Press). Currently a fellow of the John D. and Catherine T. MacArthur Foundation, she teaches at the University of Michigan at Ann Arbor.

▪ Several years before writing "Queen Wintergreen," I looked up the death notice of my great-grandmother, Margaret Kane, at the library. Since she died in 1919, the smalltown newspaper account of her death was longer than such a report would be today. The sentences were archaic in tone and rather complex in construction. I made a photocopy from the microfilm, which came out as a negative print: white type on a black background. The visual darkness of this reverse image coupled with the musty journalistic style gave the newspaper page a grim patina that felt all the more convincing and authoritative. (The hydroairplane and the Irish Freedom Meeting happened to be mentioned on the same page.)

As I read of my great-grandmother's death, I was chilled by the recurrence of certain extraordinary events across the generations; the facts formed deep structural repetitions. This patterned quality led me, years later, to retrieve the darkly faded photocopy from a notebook and use it as the catalyst for "Queen Wintergreen." It is the first of a projected series of fictions suggested by the women on my mother's side of the family. They were Catholic stoics of extremely modest means, from an Irish-American culture that has vanished — along with its values and mild heroics. In creating the characters, voices, and physical world of the story, I drew upon the memories of my mother, Mary Callahan, as well as what I could recall of the elderly Irish couple who lived next door to us when I was a child.

I thought there would be no point to setting a story in 1919 unless it could explore some area of experience that had not received quite the same emphasis in the literature of its day. I worried that I might create another Mother Ireland figure. Yet by concentrating on the constraints of gender, class, and language for a woman of Peg's generation, I hoped to avoid such literary typecasting. It seemed to me that the private life — including sexuality and childbirth experiences — of a woman such as Peg Merns could stand more attention from a female writer. This encouraged me to try.

MARY GAITSKILL is thirty-eight years old. She is the author of *Bad Behavior,* a collection of short stories, and *Two Girls, Fat and Thin,* a novel.

▪ When "The Girl on the Plane" appeared in *Mirabella,* a handful of readers wrote to the magazine to complain that the story, in their view, endorsed gang rape. This really pained me. I don't know why they responded that way; maybe the subject was (understandably) so emotionally loaded for them, that just to see it described seemed like an endorsement. They might be interested to know that a male friend of mine criticized the story for being, as he read it, an aggressively moralistic antirape statement. Yet another man said to my editor, "I mean, what am I supposed to *feel*?" All these responses are probably complexly nuanced and, as emotional viewpoints, I can respect them. What interests me is that they seem to be part of an attitudinal continuum. The first and third comments presuppose that a story should function as an edification manual, that is, to reinforce what the reader already thinks, or, in case he doesn't know, to tell him what to think. The second response seems to arise from a hypervigilant wariness about being told what to think — a sense that if the writer overtly expresses an opinion, then there is no room for the reader to have an opinion, too; the poor bastard has to just lie there and get steamrollered. All three make me think of the various magazine essays I've read during the last two years about taking responsibility for yourself as opposed to being a victim. I don't see how people can be responsible for their behavior if they are not responsible for their own thoughts and feelings. In my opinion, most of us have not been taught how to be responsible for our thoughts and feelings. I see this strongly in the widespread tendency to read books and stories as if they exist to confirm how we are supposed to be, think, and feel. I'm not talking wacky political correctness, I'm talking mainstream. And not just written stories either; I was flabbergasted by the public debate over the film *Thelma and Louise,* in which grown people discussed a Hollywood movie as if its purpose was to instruct us on how to live our lives, condemning or praising it based on whether they thought the instructions were valid. (I would not be surprised if some of these same people also wrote essays bemoaning "victimism.") Ladies and gentlemen, please. Stop asking "What am I supposed to feel?" Why would an adult look to me or to any other writer to tell him or her what to feel? You're not *supposed* to feel anything. You feel what you feel. Where you go with it is your responsibility. If a writer chooses to aggressively let you know what he or she feels, where you go with it is still your responsibility.

MARY GORDON was born on Long Island, grew up in Queens, and was educated at Barnard College, where she is now the McIntosh Professor of English. She has published four novels — *Final Payments, The Company of Women, Men and Angels,* and *The Other Side* — and a collection of stories, *Temporary Shelter,* as well as numerous essays and articles. She lives with her husband and two children in New Paltz, New York.

▪ The story of this "story" is that it is not a story. It is part of a project I am working on, a sort of biography, a sort of memoir — a history of my father. He was such a fantastical character, with so many, often conflicting sides, that I knew I couldn't render anything like a recognizable portrait of him by looking at him head-on. I have to suppose that this read like "fiction" because I am primarily a fiction writer, and I create a character using the techniques of fiction: an accretion of detail, a penetration to the inner life, a series of scenes. This of course brings up the question of whether there is a different method for fiction and nonfiction, which is the kind of thing that makes me want to take to my bed with the vapors.

DIANE JOHNSON is a novelist, critic, biographer, and screenwriter. She was born in Moline, Illinois, and lives in San Francisco. She has received Guggenheim and Woodrow Wilson fellowships, the Rosenthal Award, and the Mildred and Harold Strauss Living from the American Academy and Institute of Arts and Letters, and numerous other honors. Her most recent novel is *Health and Happiness*. Her articles and reviews appear in the *New York Review of Books* and other periodicals. She is coauthor of the Stanley Kubrick film *The Shining* and is currently at work on a film for Francis Ford Coppola.

▪ My story "Great Barrier Reef," is, like most fiction, mostly true, and was written about a trip I took with my husband, John, on a little ship much like the *Dolphin,* rusty and slow, with Australian companions and endless stops at souvenir shops. I took notes after the voyage and put them aside for some years, until a time when, having done much more traveling, I decided to make stories of all my travel experiences.

What is odd is that I can no longer remember which details are utterly true and which are the fictional embellishments. Was I myself so unpleasant a travel companion? Or have I made the protagonist of the story a little worse, for dramatic purposes, so that her reformation would be more striking and needed? I know that it is true that I won the prize for my pumpkin costume.

In the story, the protagonist is involved in a custody fight with her former husband. This is an example of how fiction can work to reorder the world into a more bearable form. In real life, the custody arrangements had included, at the insistence of my former husband, the stipulation that he was not obliged to take the children at all, for any vacation or weekend. This was designed, I suppose, to blight my hopes of having a little vacation myself from time to time. Today, paternal fashions have changed considerably, and I thought that reality would not be believable in this fiction.

Beyond all this, it seemed to me that the Great Barrier Reef was a good metaphor for the condition of every traveler, barred from understanding the mind and customs of other peoples and places by the ideas and emotions she brings with her. And that, perhaps, became the theme of the entire collection of travel stories, *Natural Opium.* The title refers to a remark by Baudelaire, to the effect that each man carries within himself his dose of natural opium, and to my idea that for some, traveling is that drug.

THOM JONES's story collection, *The Pugilist at Rest: Stories,* was published by Little, Brown in June. The title story of that collection appeared in *The Best American Short Stories 1992* and was the first-prize winner in the *1993 O. Henry Prize Stories.* Mr. Jones lives in Olympia, Washington, where he is at work on a novel.

▪ The particulars of "I Want to Live!" are basically true. I wrote the story shortly after the death of my mother-in-law, a woman I loved and admired very much. I'm a baby boomer and as my family went through the experience of her illness, it seemed to me that a lot of my friends had had a parent, sometimes even a sibling, with cancer, and few of the ultimate outcomes were pleasant. Moreover, it seemed that every time I picked up a magazine or newspaper, I was confronted with an array of newly identified environmental culprits that were responsible for cancer, so that the very word, after years of accumulation, became charged with such fear, and so many horrible implications, that I found myself casting my eyes away from it lest it sink too deeply, too many times, in my own brain, and start some trouble there — genesis.

Cancer is just a word, but I don't like hearing it since it has become loaded with a kind of dreadful, crazy power. Because of that, I wrote "I Want to Live!" using a voice that a friend has described as "in your face." It seemed that the enemy had such an overwhelming advantage over the victim that it was unreasonable and disrespectful. Also, the official medical proclamation, "terminal," seemed to cast the condemned into a hell of isolation and terror from which there was no escape, no hope, no ally — only pain, suffering, and futility. While I felt considerable empathy for my mother-in-law, like most bystanders in these situations I was frustrated since there was little I could do except befriend her on her last journey.

I wrote "I Want to Live!" for one of the quiet heroes of life, a wonderful human being who faced her death as she lived her life — with courage, dignity, and love. My heart and prayers go out to all those people who have personally experienced some version of this story in their own lives, or who may in the future.

ANDREA LEE was born in Philadelphia, attended The Baldwin School, and received B.A. and M.A. degrees from Harvard University. She is the author of the nonfiction *Russian Journal,* which was nominated for a National Book Award, and the novel *Sarah Phillips.* She is a staff writer for *The New Yorker* and lives in Turin, Italy.

▪ "Winter Barley" was inspired by a passage from *King Lear,* the brief speech made by Lear to Cordelia which begins, "Come, let's away to prison / We two alone will sing like birds i' the cage." Spoken in the midst of the most desperate possible situation, when Lear and Cordelia are both captives facing death, these few lines suddenly sketch out the image of an improbable idyll — a short-lived perfect moment between two people which holds not only mutual love, but also absolute comprehension. I wanted to develop a story from this small glimpse, to write about such an evanescent paradise. The idea of the father and daughter who are all in all to each other I found romantic and curiously erotic — so I created a pair of lovers who are father and daughter on another level.

LORRIE MOORE is the author of a novel, a children's book, and two collections of stories, *Self-Help* and *Like Life.* She teaches at the University of Wisconsin in Madison.

▪ In this story I was interested in the improvised convalescence of a mourner, as well as in grief and its incongruous settings, including a setting that might ordinarily be the stuff of satire — life often has the strange bad taste to follow catastrophe with farce.

I worked very hard on this story — for months and months — trying to make it work, to bring about the tonal weave of it. When it was rejected by two different magazines, my reaction was typical of so many writers: I wasn't so much surprised as I was hurt (part annoyance, part shame) and then quickly worried about money and hard luck in that dark and looming way familiar to most short story writers.

But George Plimpton saw something in the story; he was familiar with the Como region of Italy, trusted the voice, liked a couple of the jokes. He wisely suggested I cut a scene from the beginning (I did) and kindly allowed me to keep almost everything else, including such phrases as "garbage night," despite his mild protest.

I'm very grateful to him.

Alice Munro's most recent collection of stories is *Friend of My Youth* (Knopf, 1990). Born in Wingham, Ontario, Ms. Munro now lives in Clinton, Ontario. She has received Canada's Governor General's Award for two of her books.

▪ When I was finding out all sorts of things, a few years ago, about Albania in the early years of the twentieth century, I discovered the tradition of the Albanian Virgin. This was a woman who was allowed to own property, carry weapons, smoke and carouse with the men, and be waited on by women at table, all provided she gave up on one thing — sex — forever and ever. It wasn't, then, inherent weakness of mind or body that made women unfit for lives of independence, unfit for companionship or conversation, it was sex pure and simple. I thought about how this had been true to some degree in my own society, which did contain the idea and the reality of the somewhat absurd, somewhat ridiculed, but often heroic and not unenvied, apparently not unhappy, sexless woman. So I made one of these the heroine of a romance. Then I had to have Millicent give her the final push, because Millicent believes that people should never be allowed to get out of happy endings.

I got three stories out of that Albanian obsession and only one of them even mentions Albania.

Antonya Nelson's stories have appeared in *The New Yorker, Esquire, Redbook, TriQuarterly, Story,* and elsewhere, and are collected in *The Expendables* (winner of the Flannery O'Connor Award for Short Fiction), *In the Land of Men* (William Morrow), and the forthcoming *Family Terrorists* (Houghton Mifflin), in which "Naked Ladies" will appear. She teaches creative writing and English literature at New Mexico State University in Las Cruces, where she lives with her husband, the writer Robert Boswell, and their two children.

▪ "Naked Ladies" began as a title, a provocative pair of words, like two breasts. I wrote a whole series of stories with two-word titles ("Loaded Gun," "Dirty Words," "Loose Cannon," "Family Terrorists," "Ugly Dog") because that was the trick that worked, for a while.

Children are endlessly interested in the workings of their parents' marriage — the friction and sex and unhappiness — and Laura Laughlin is no exception. What makes her interesting to me, her author, is her stated desire to keep peace, yet her real inclination to make war. That contradiction is what seems to me to drive the story. I am indebted to Daniel Menaker, the story's editor, who asked me to turn down the heat of the Easter Frolic so that the more subtle elements could generate their own odd glow.

Writing a story is a lot like having a nightmare: we recognize the settings, the characters, the icons, the trouble, the truth, the possibility, the fears, the hidden desires, but they've all lined themselves up askew. I think we like our nightmares better than we admit. Their elements are all ours, but scrambled out of time and context. Why and how they should all be together is where *story* comes in.

JANET PEERY's fiction has appeared in *New Virginia Review, Shenandoah, American Short Fiction, Black Warrior Review, Quarterly West, Kansas Quarterly, Chattahoochee Review, Southwest Review,* and other magazines. She received the Jeanne Charpiot Goodheart Prize from Washington and Lee University in 1990 and 1991 and has held Fiction Fellowships from Wichita State University and Writers at Work in Park City, Utah. In 1992 she was awarded a Literature Fellowship from the National Endowment for the Arts. Her stories have received the KQ/KAC and Seaton Awards, awards from the Hemingway Short Story Competition, and two Pushcart Prizes. She was recently the visiting writer at Sweet Briar College. "What the Thunder Said" will appear in Janet Peery's first collection of stories, *Alligator Dance,* to be published in the fall of 1993 by Southern Methodist University Press.

▪ Perhaps it's because I come from a place where people take their maxims to heart that I'm reminded now, as I think about how I came to write this story, of the one about looking a gift horse in the mouth.

I know it sounds vague and mysterious to say that "What the Thunder Said" came to me, but that's essentially how it happened. The first draft was written during three summer days at a time when I was letting go of a part of my life that had been both terrible and sweet. The story's circumstances are imagined, but its heart comes out of that release. I remember typing, but I recall little else about the three days but the good, strong heat, the smell of sun on dust, and my astonishment at how easily and whole the story appeared. Only after I no longer heard it, after it had left me to work alone through the many versions the story went through, did I realize that there had been a voice — urgent and determined — delivering itself of the story. The voice was my own, no doubt, but from a deeper, truer source now lost to my recall.

So, rather than try to sort out what remains to me the mystery of the story's making, I'll talk about its setting, the Arkansas River bottomland country where I spent many summers among the quiet-spoken people of my mother's family, their friends and neighbors — people who surely thought and felt, I imagined, a great deal more than they said — and about something I once saw in this place and that returned to me when I was ready to know what it meant.

When I was ten my grandparents took me to see a fire on a neighboring farm, abandoned during the Depression. I had seen the place only from a distance, from the road: a ramshackle barn collapsed beneath the weight of trumpet brambles, sheds weathered gray as ghosts, a house no one had occupied for thirty years. As we turned into the lane, the truck headlights illuminated a scene that was the very vision of midwestern Baptist Sunday School apocalypse. Flames licked at blistered barn walls and outbuildings smoldered. The house was a mound of char and cinder. I don't remember that anyone spoke beyond my grandfather's terse "Heat lightning."

Though the spectacle of flames should have taken my attention, it was the burned-out house that held me. It looked nothing like a house, and the only object I could put a name to was a teapot, the old cast-iron kind, its spiral handle a small, black arc against the smoke-white air. It seemed the emblem of domestic ruin, loss, and want, of gone things, and though it was perhaps the smallest thing I could have noticed, this teapot seemed to contain largeness, tragedy, to stand for some act of scarifying moment, and I was terrified. Then, in the way that often happens with those sights we promise ourselves we'll fasten into memory, I forgot it.

Thirty years later when I was writing this story and the narrative drew near the time when the beliefs Mackie Spoon had made of will revealed themselves for the hollow things they were, the teapot reappeared, and it was this vessel that she seized.

As the throwing of my teapot was for Mackie Spoon, the writing of her story was for me. Both acts hold in common the notion from *Remembrance of Things Past* that the souls of those whom we have lost are held captive in "some inferior being, in an animal, in a plant, in some inanimate object" and so lost to us until we "pass by the tree" or obtain possession of the object that has formed their prison. Then, Proust writes,

"They start and tremble, they call us by our name, and as soon as we have recognized their voice the spell is broken. We have delivered them: they have overcome death and return to share our lives." When this happens, regardless of how long it has taken, it is nothing less than a gift, especially miraculous when the souls we have lost, or have come close to losing, have been our own.

SUSAN POWER is an enrolled member of the Standing Rock Sioux tribe (Yanktonnai Dakota) and a native Chicagoan. She received her B.A. from Harvard/Radcliffe, J.D. from Harvard Law School, and M.F.A. from the University of Iowa Writers' Workshop, where she was the first recipient of an Iowa Arts Fellowship. She has also been granted a James Michener Fellowship and a Bunting Institute Fellowship at Radcliffe College. Her short fiction has appeared in several literary journals, including *High Plains Literary Review, Ploughshares,* and *Story,* and is forthcoming in the anthology *Reinventing the Enemy's Language* (edited by Joy Harjo). Her first novel, *The Grass Dancer,* will be published by Putnam in 1994.

▪ I grew up listening to my mother's stories about her childhood on the Standing Rock Sioux Reservation. She was a child during the Depression and vividly remembers the dust bowl years; years when thousands of our people were stricken with tuberculosis and sent to the "Sioux San" never to return. I have frequently been asked why death is such a pervasive theme in my writing — why do so many of my characters have to die? I explain that in our community — whether it be reservation or urban Indian area — death is a familiar companion who steals away too many of our young people. I cannot ignore his presence, pretend I do not recognize his face.

Dancing is a very important activity in our culture, and since the time I could walk I danced at powwows. I was also fascinated by classical ballet and believed for a time that I would follow in the footsteps of our great Osage ballerina, Maria Tall Chief. One of my favorite ballets was a production of "The Red Shoes," the story based on a tale by Hans Christian Andersen. The story intrigued me as it combined death and dancing: two of the most powerful forces in my life.

In writing "Red Moccasins" I had two images in mind: the beguiling red slippers and a little towheaded boy who was dying. He was rocked by a full-blooded Sioux woman — his mother — who was unable to keep him in this world. I knew the images belonged together, but it became my mission to discover the connection.

JOANNA SCOTT is the author of the novels *Fading, My Parmacheene Belle, The Closest Possible Union,* and *Arrogance,* which received the Rosenthal

Award from the American Academy and Institute of Arts and Letters and was nominated for the 1991 PEN/Faulkner Award. "Concerning Mold upon the Skin, Etc.," will be in her collection of short fiction, *Various Antidotes,* forthcoming from Henry Holt. She received a MacArthur Fellowship in 1992. She teaches in the English Department at the University of Rochester.

▪ In some ways, the story behind "Concerning Mold upon the Skin, Etc." is quite straightforward. I had an organizing idea for a collection of short fiction before I began this piece — I intended to refer, plainly or indirectly, to the history of medicine in each of my stories. So I went looking for fifteenth- and sixteenth-century scientists in such quirky and unreliable books as Howard Haggard's *Devils, Drugs, and Doctors,* and *Rats, Lice, and Men.* I found the Dutch naturalist Antonie van Leeuwenhoek and his microscope almost everywhere I looked.

I found other possibilities as well. But Leeuwenhoek's fierce secrecy caught my attention. He worked outside the mainstream scientific circles of his day and for many years jealously guarded his invention. Still, I might have let Leeuwenhoek slip by if it hadn't been for the excerpts of his letters quoted by Haggard. These letters reveal an endearing sensibility, enthusiastic, territorial, and passionate. Haggard's translation is partly at fault — in other translations, Leeuwenhoek sounds much more scholarly. But authenticity didn't matter to me at that stage. I preferred the passionate, childish inventor.

One thing I might note about the character of the daughter: as a fiction writer, I'm interested in the vast silences of history, and like many women, Marie floats silently in the background of her father's biography. So she became the center of the narrative, the presence that enabled me to reshape history into fiction.

I should confess a more personal inspiration behind this story as well. A few years ago I came down with a strep infection. I didn't know that at some time in my adult life I had developed an allergy to penicillin, so I took my doses dutifully for three days and ended up with a terrible reaction that lasted for months. That such an elixir should suddenly become a poison to my system seemed a great betrayal. When I read about Leeuwenhoek scraping off the skin on his arm to look at it under his microscope, I implicated him in my misery. I delved deeper into his life. I though about the correlation between fanaticism and curiosity. I suppose I played out my anxieties about my allergy in this fiction — exactly how, I'm not sure. Maybe it's accurate enough to say that I wrote this story because one morning I woke up covered with spots.

JANE SHAPIRO's first novel, *After Moondog,* was published in 1992 and nominated for a Los Angeles Times Book Prize. Her journalism and short stories have appeared in *The New Yorker,* the *Village Voice,* the *New York Times, Mirabella, Ms.,* and elsewhere. She is at work on a collection of stories. She grew up on Long Beach Island, in New Jersey, and lives in Princeton.

▪ I was staying at the home of a friend, and in the night the clinking of the dog's chain woke me up, and as I was waking I realized that Zack, a character I'd been writing about for years, would at age sixteen get in a car with his friends and try to drive down to Washington to see the Vietnam Memorial. I got up and found some small index cards next to the kitchen phone and wrote, on ten or twelve of them, the story of Zack's long night out. The rest of "Poltergeists" built itself up around that recounting of the nighttime ride, which is now lodged in the middle.

The section about parties and Shooting the Boot and slang expressions for vomiting came from my writing students at Rutgers. I asked them to tell me about their high school evenings; they were galvanized and talked on and on. What they said appears in pretty much the order they said it.

I got up my nerve and sent the story to Chip McGrath at *The New Yorker.* He called and told me some things I could do to fix the writing and I tried to follow his advice; this happened three or four times. Chip McGrath is an extremely skillful and generous editor (famous for it), and he improved this story immeasurably. I think his bio should be listed in the Contributors' Notes.

JOHN UPDIKE was born in 1932, in Shillington, Pennsylvania, and graduated from Harvard College in 1954. After a year at an English art school and a two-year stint as a Talk of the Town reporter for *The New Yorker,* he moved to Massachusetts in 1957, and has lived there ever since. His most recent novel is *Memories of the Ford Administration;* his most recent book is *Collected Poems 1953–93*.

▪ This is the only story, as best I can remember, that I wrote on request — the new editor of *The New Yorker* relayed word to me that she would be happy to have a story of mine in her first issue. Flattered silly, I pawed through the slips of paper on which I jot down story ideas, often just the titles, and came upon this title. One thing led to another, as I sat at the word processor, most of them having to do with the sensations and hallucinations of late middle age. I have written about aging, doddery, nostalgic American men whose names begin with "F" before, and let loosely related incidents weave their way around a central theme, or bitter fact, before; but the recipe seemed to produce a warmer, richer dish than usual here — at least its presence in this collection encourages me to think so. Life is an adventure, all right, from beginning to end, but life after sixty is a part of the tale that perhaps is more eagerly told than heard. It is the young we love, in print as on the silver screen, as they play with the dynamite of mating. For some time, I have noticed, my heroes seem older than I feel to myself, as if, lacking sex appeal to make them dramatic, they are cozying up to death.

The many little mysteries and gaps that Fanshawe observes in his stream of experience were added to, after the story appeared in print, by a writer in the *Wall Street Journal* who opined, with an indignation itself mysterious, that the bird whose nest the Fanshawes disturb could not have been a warbler but must have been a phoebe. At the risk of reviving the obsolete convention of the omniscient author, I can assure you, gentle *BASS* reader, that that was no phoebe.

LARRY WOIWODE was born in North Dakota in 1941, grew up in Illinois and New York City, and over a decade ago returned to North Dakota, where he lives with his family. His novels include *Beyond the Bedroom Wall, Born Brothers,* and *Indian Affairs,* and his second collection of short fiction, *Silent Passengers,* takes its title from this year's selection — his fourth appearance in *The Best American Short Stories.*

▪ I used to say (and so used to think, I would hope), that if fiction had a salubrious effect, that was secondary. Art, you know, *art.* But after living through many different sorts of responses over the years to my work, and especially to this particular story, I'm not so sure about that. Isn't it important for fiction to bring about moments of stasis, of restoration — of healing, if you will? It was largely people who underwent some such experience who responded to "Silent Passengers" by writing to me.

The story, triggered by an accident a fourteen-year-old son had with a lawn mower, was an attempt to free myself of another incident, of years' duration, that I was finding it difficult to live with. *The New Yorker* turned down the story with an unusual rider: two editors recommending changes I might attempt, including purging the story of a theme never resolved, and of a Japanese computer expert one editor in particular found distracting, and trying again.

I did, and the purging helped me toward precision and a sentence devoted to another character's computer chips — a way of balancing such mechanics against the infinitely organized makeup of the mind — and for some reason, in the way these metaphorical matters work, the scene of the nurse and father speaking over the boy expanded. When the story was accepted, I felt as convicts must, once freed. So isn't it important when a reader, in response, feels "a cycle of healing turn," or comes awake to the world, or senses an angel's presence, or gets out of bed ready to forgive that enemy, feeling there's a reason now to live?

100 Other Distinguished Stories of 1992

SELECTED BY KATRINA KENISON

ABBOTT, LEE K.
A Man Bearing Snow. *Epoch,* Vol. 41, No. 2.

ADAMS, ALICE
Love and Work. *Southwest Review,* Autumn.

ANSAY, A. MANETTE
Lullabye. *Quarterly West,* No. 34, Winter/Spring.

BAKER, ALISON
The Heaven of Animals. *Alaska Quarterly Review,* Vol. 10, Nos. 3 & 4.

BASS, RICK
Platte River. *The Paris Review,* No. 125.

BAUSCH, RICHARD
Evening. *The Southern Review,* Vol. 28, No. 4.

BAXTER, CHARLES
Created Things. *Harper's Magazine,* November.

BERLIN, LUCIA
So Long. *ZYZZYVA,* Fall.

BERRY, WENDELL
A Jonquil for Mary Penn. *The Atlantic Monthly,* February.

BINGGELI, ELIZABETH
The Backyard. *Ploughshares,* Vol. 18, No. 4.

BLAINE, MICHAEL
The Linoleum Sea. *New Letters,* Vol. 58, No. 2.

BOSWELL, ROBERT
Glissando. *The Iowa Review,* Vol. 22, No. 1.

BRAVERMAN, KATE
The Woman after Rain. *The American Voice,* No. 28.

BRONER, E. M.
Camp. *Kalliope,* Vol. 14, No. 1.

BROWN, LARRY
A Birthday Party. *The Southern Review,* Vol. 28, No. 4.

BUCHBINDER, JANE
Angel in the Snow. *Ploughshares,* Vol. 18, No. 4.

BUSH, MARY
Rex the King. *Ploughshares,* Vol. 18, Nos. 2 & 3.

BUTLÉR, ROBERT OLEN
Preparation. *The Sewanee Review,* Vol. C, No. 10.

CADY, JACK
Tinker. *Glimmer Train,* Spring.
CARLSON, RON
The Summer of Vintage Clothing. *Harper's Magazine,* June.
CHABON, MICHAEL
Mrs. Box. *The New Yorker,* May 18.
CHAMBERS, CAROLE
The Making of a Naturalist. *Room of One's Own,* Vol. 14, No. 3.
CHAON, DAN
Spirit Voices. *American Short Fiction,* No. 7.
CHRISTOPHER, PETER
Son of Man. *Alaska Quarterly Review,* Vol. 10, Nos. 3 & 4.
COFER, JUDITH ORTIZ
Not for Sale. *The Kenyon Review,* Vol. 14, No. 4.
COONEY, ELLEN
Nurses. *The New Yorker,* June 8.

DEMARINIS, RICK
The Mortician's Apprentice. *GQ,* June.
DOERR, HARRIET
Goya and the Widow Bowles. *Epoch,* Vol. 41, No. 3.

EARLEY, TONY
My Father's Heart. *TriQuarterly,* 84.
ELY, SCOTT
The Lady of the Lake. *The Southern Review,* Vol. 28, No. 1.

FITZGERALD, EILEEN
Zoo Bus. *The Iowa Review,* Vol. 22, No. 2.
FORD, RICHARD
Jealous. *The New Yorker,* November 30.

GAITSKILL, MARY
The Crazy Person. *Open City,* No. 1.
GALLANT, MAVIS
Mlle. Dias de Corta. *The New Yorker,* December 28–January 4.
GARDINER, JOHN ROLFE
Morse Operator. *American Short Fiction,* No. 8.
GILES, RICHARD
Crawford and Luster's Story. *Ploughshares,* Vol. 18, No. 4.
GOODMAN, ALLEGRA
Fantasy Rose. *The New Yorker,* November 16.
GOODMAN, MATTHEW
Men of Limited Motion. *The Georgia Review,* Vol. 46, No. 4.
GOVER, PAULA K.
Chances with Johnson. *Crosscurrents,* Vol. 10, No. 2.
White Boys and River Girls. *The Virginia Quarterly Review,* Vol. 68, No. 2.
GOWDY, BARBARA
Body and Soul. *Descant 75,* Vol. 22.
GRINER, PAUL
Grass. *Ploughshares,* Vol. 18, Nos. 2 & 3.

HANNAH, BARRY
The Tyranny of the Visual. *The Southern Review,* Vol. 28, No. 4.
HOOD, JACOBA
Send Me Meat. *Crazyhorse,* No. 42.
HULL, JEFF
Ninepipe. *Ploughshares,* Vol. 18, No. 4.
HUSTON, PAULA
Mercy. *American Short Fiction,* No. 8.

JOHNSON, DENIS
Beverly Home. *The Paris Review,* No. 124.
Rescuing Ed. *The New England Review,* Vol. 14, No. 3.
JOHNSON, DENNIS
Forrest in the Trees. *Ploughshares,* Vol. 18, No. 1.
JOHNSON, WAYNE
On the Observation Car. *Glimmer Train,* Winter.

JONES, EDWARD
Marie. *The Paris Review,* No. 122.
JONES, THOM
The Black Lights. *The New Yorker,* October 12.

KAPLAN, KATE
Baby. *Folio,* Winter.
KEEBLE, JOHN
The Fishers. *American Short Fiction,* No. 8.
KERR, BAINE
Light Sweet Crude. *The Missouri Review,* Vol. 15, No. 1.

LE GUIN, URSULA K.
Standing Ground. *Ms.,* Vol. 3, No. 1.
LOUDON, ELIZABETH
The Guardian. *The Gettysburg Review,* Winter.

MACDONALD, D. R.
Green Grow the Grasses O. *TriQuarterly,* 83.
MAHER, BLAKE
Safe Places. *The Greensboro Review,* No. 52.
MASON, BOBBIE ANN
Shooting the Dog. *The Southern Review,* Vol. 28, No. 4.
MCCAFFERTY, JANE
An Evocation. *Seattle Review,* Vol. 15, No. 2.
MCCAULEY, STEPHEN
The Whole Truth. *Harper's Magazine,* July.
MCCORKLE, JILL
Gold Mine. *The Greensboro Review,* No. 51.
MILLER, HEATHER ROSS
The Other Side of the World. *Shenandoah,* Vol. 42, No. 3.
MORRIS, MARY MCGARRY
The Perfect Tenant. *Glimmer Train,* No. 8.
MORRIS, WILLIE
Asphalt. *The Oxford American,* Vol. 2.
MUNRO, ALICE
A Wilderness Station. *The New Yorker,* April 27.
MYERS, JILL
The Man in the Bathtub. *New Letters,* Vol. 58, No. 2.

NELSON, ANTONYA
Loaded Gun. *The New Yorker,* November 9.
NORRIS, HELEN
The Cracker Man. *The Gettysburg Review,* Vol. 5, No. 3.
NUGENT, BETH
Another Country. *Grand Street,* No. 40.

OATES, JOYCE CAROL
Depot. *American Short Fiction,* No. 7.
O'BRIEN, TIM
The People We Marry. *The Atlantic Monthly,* January.

PASSARO, VINCE
My Mother's Lover. *Esquire,* July.
Cathedral Parkway. *Open City,* No. 1.
PEARLMAN, EDITH
The Non-Combatant. *Alaska Quarterly Review,* Vol. 10, Nos. 3 & 4.
PEERY, JANET
Daughter of the Moon, *American Short Fiction,* No. 8.
South Padre, *American Short Fiction,* No. 5.
POVERMAN, C. E.
Cutter. *Ontario Review,* No. 37.
POWER, SUSAN
Moonwalk. *Ploughshares,* Vol. 18, Nos. 1 & 2.
PROSE, FRANCINE
Talking to the Dog. *The Yale Review,* Vol. 80, Nos. 1 & 2.

RENSBERGER, SUSAN
Communion. *Prairie Schooner,* Spring.

ROOKE, LEON
The Woman from Red Deer Who Went to Johannesburg, Set Herself Afire, and Leapt Four Floors to Her Apparent Death. *The Malahat,* No. 100.

RYAN, PATRICK
The Lake. *Denver Quarterly,* Vol. 27, No. 2.

SCHWARTZ, LYNNE SHARON
Francesca. *American Short Fiction,* No. 7.

SEARLE, ELIZABETH
My Body to You. *The Kenyon Review,* Vol. 14, No. 4.

SEGAL, LORE
The Talk in Eliza's Kitchen. *The New Yorker,* April 6.

SHARENOV, EVELYN
Magic Affinities. *Glimmer Train,* Summer.

SHEARER, CYNTHIA
Flight Patterns. *The Oxford American,* Vol. 2.

SMITH, SCOTT B.
The Empty House. *The New Yorker,* June 15.

SPATZ, GREGORY
My Mother, Jolene, and Me. *New England Review,* Vol. 14, No. 2.

TAYLOR, PETER
The Waiting Room. *The Southern Review,* Vol. 28, No. 4.

THOMAS, ABIGAIL
Buddy's Best Work. *The Missouri Review,* Vol. 15, No. 1.

TOMA, T. L.
Citadel. *Black Warrior Review,* Vol. 18, No. 2.

WALKER, CHARLOTTE ZOE
Goat's Milk. *Ms.,* May/June.

WETHERELL, W. D.
The Road to the City. *American Short Fiction,* No. 6.

WIDEMAN, JOHN EDGAR
All Stories Are True. *Harper's Magazine,* January.

WILSON, ROBERT SPENCER
Safe at Home. *American Short Fiction,* No. 8.

WINDLEY, CAROL
The Etruscans. *Descant 75,* Vol. 22.

WOLFF, TOBIAS
Lady's Dream. *Harper's Magazine,* December.

Editorial Addresses of American and Canadian Magazines Publishing Short Stories

When available, the annual subscription rate, the average number of stories published per year, and the name of the editor follow the address.

Agni Review
Creative Writing Department
Boston University
236 Bay State Road
Boston, MA 02115
$12, 10, Askold Melnyczuk

Alabama Literary Review
Smith 253
Troy State University
Troy, AL 36082
$9, Theron E. Montgomery

Alaska Quarterly Review
Department of English
University of Alaska
3221 Providence Drive
Anchorage, AK 99508
$8, 28, Ronald Spatz

Alfred Hitchcock's Mystery Magazine
Davis Publications, Inc.
380 Lexington Avenue
New York, NY 10017
$25.97, 130, Cathleen Jordan

Amelia
329 East Street
Bakersfield, CA 93304
$27, 9, Frederick A. Raborg, Jr.

American Literary Review
University of North Texas
P.O. Box 13615
Denton, TX 76203
$10, 7, James Ward Lee

American Short Fiction
Parlin 108
Department of English
University of Texas at Austin
Austin, TX 78712-1164
$24, 32, Laura Furman

American Voice
332 West Broadway
Louisville, KY 40202
$15, 20, Sallie Bingham, Frederick Smock

Analog Science Fiction/Science Fact
380 Lexington Avenue

New York, NY 10017
$34.95, 70, Stanley Schmidt

Antaeus
100 West Broad Street
Hopewell, NJ 08525
$30, 6, Daniel Halpern

Antietam Review
82 West Washington Street
Hagerstown, MD 21740
$5, 8, Suzanne Kass

Antioch Review
P.O. Box 148
Yellow Springs, OH 45387
$25, 11, Robert S. Fogarty

Apalachee Quarterly
P.O. Box 20106
Tallahassee, FL 32316
$12, 10, Barbara Hardy et al.

Appalachian Heritage
Besea College
Besea, KY 40404
$18, 6, Sidney Saylor Farr

Ascent
P.O. Box 967
Urbana, IL 61801
$6, 8, group editorship

Atlantic Monthly
745 Boylston Street
Boston, MA 02116
$15.94, 13, C. Michael Curtis

Belles Lettres
11151 Captain's Walk Court
North Potomac, MD 20878
$20, 2, Janet Mullaney

Bellowing Ark
P.O. Box 45637
Seattle, WA 98145
$15, 7, Robert R. Ward

Beloit Fiction Journal
P.O. Box 11, Beloit College
Beloit, WI 53511
$9, 14, Clint McCown

Black Warrior Review
P.O. Box 2936
Tuscaloosa, AL 35487-2936
$7.50, 13, Alicia Griswold

Blood & Aphorisms
Suite 711
456 College Street
Toronto, Ontario
MGG 4A3 Canada
$18, 20, Hilary Clark

BOMB
New Art Publications
594 Broadway, 10th floor
New York, NY 10012
$16, 4, Betsy Sussler

Border Crossings
Y300-393 Portage Avenue
Winnipeg, Manitoba
R3B 3H6 Canada
$18, 12, Robert Enright

Boston Review
33 Harrison Avenue
Boston, MA 02111
$15, 6, editorial board

Boulevard
P.O. Box 30386
Philadelphia, PA 19103
$12, 17, Richard Burgin

Briar Cliff Review
3303 Rebecca Street
P.O. Box 2100
Sioux City, IA 51104-2100
$3, 4, Tricia Currans-Sheehan

Bridge
14050 Vernon Street
Oak Park, MI 48237
$8, 10, Helen Zucker

Brooklyn Free Press
268 14th Street
Brooklyn, NY 11215
$1, 10, Raphael Martinez Alequin

Buffalo Spree
4511 Harlem Road, P.O. Box 38
Buffalo, NY 14226
$8, 16, Johanna Shotell

BUZZ
11835 West Olympic Blvd.
Suite 450
Los Angeles, CA 90064
$12, 5, Renee Vogel

California Quarterly
100 Sproul Hall
University of California
Davis, CA 95616
$14, 4, Elliott L. Gilbert

Callaloo
Johns Hopkins University Press
701 West 40th Street, Suite 275
Baltimore, MD 21211
$21, 6, Charles H. Rowell

Calyx
P.O. Box B
Corvallis, OR 97339
$18, 11, Margarita Donnelly

Canadian Fiction
Box 946, Station F
Toronto, Ontario
M4Y 2N9 Canada
$32.10, 23, Geoffrey Hancock

Capilano Review
Capilano College
2055 Purcell Way
North Vancouver,
British Columbia
V7J 3H5 Canada
$25, 12, Robert Sherrin

Carolina Quarterly
Greenlaw Hall 066A
University of North Carolina
Chapel Hill, NC 27514
$10, 13, Marielle Blais

Changing Men
306 North Brooks Street
Madison, WI 53715
$24, 2, Jeff Kirsch

Chariton Review
Division of Language & Literature
Northeast Missouri State University
Kirksville, MO 63501
$9, 6, Jim Barnes

Chattahoochee Review
DeKalb Community College
2101 Womack Road
Dunwoody, GA 30338-4497
$15, 21, Lamar York

Chelsea
P.O. Box 5880
Grand Central Station
New York, NY 10163
$11, 6, Sonia Raiziss

Chicago Review
5801 South Kenwood
University of Chicago
Chicago, IL 60637
$20, 20, Elizabeth Arnold

Christopher Street
P.O. Box 1475
Church Street Station
New York, NY 10008
$27, 50, Tom Steele

Cimarron Review
205 Morrill Hall
Oklahoma State University
Stillwater, OK 74078-0135
$12, 15, Gordon Weaver

Clockwatch Review
Department of English
Illinois Wesleyan University
Bloomington, IL 61702
$8, 6, James Plath

Colorado Review
Department of English
Colorado State University
Fort Collins, CO 80523
$15, 8, David Milofsky

Columbia
404 Dodge
Columbia University
New York, NY 10027
$11, 14, rotating editorship

Commentary
165 East 56th Street
New York, NY 10022
$39, 5, Norman Podhoretz

Concho River Review
English Department
Angelo State University
San Angelo, TX 76909
$12, 7, Terence A. Dalrymple

Confrontation
English Department
C. W. Post College of Long Island University
Greenvale, NY 11548
$8, 25, Martin Tucker

Crab Creek Review
4462 Whitman Avenue North
Seattle, WA 98103
$8, 3, Linda Clifton

Crazyhorse
Department of English
University of Arkansas
Little Rock, AR 72204
$10, 13, Judy Troy

Cream City Review
University of Wisconsin, Milwaukee
P.O. Box 413
Milwaukee, WI 53201
$10, 30, Cathleen Lester, Patricia Montalbano

Crescent Review
P.O. Box 15065
Winston-Salem, NC 27113
$10, 23, Guy Nancekeville

Critic
205 West Monroe Street, 6th floor
Chicago, IL 60606-5097
$17, 4, John Sprague

Crosscurrents
2200 Glastonbury Road
Westlake Village, CA 91361
$18, 38, Linda Brown Michelson

Crucible
Barton College
College Station
Wilson, NC 27893
Terence L. Grimes

Cut Bank
Department of English
University of Montana
Missoula, MT 59812
$12, 20, Mary Vanek

Delos
P.O. Box 2800
College Park, MD 20741
$20, Reed Whittemore

Denver Quarterly
University of Denver
Denver, CO 80208
$15, 5, Donald Revell

Descant
P.O. Box 314, Station P
Toronto, Ontario
M5S 2S8 Canada
$28.47, 20, Karen Mulhallen

Descant
Department of English
Texas Christian University
Box 32872
Fort Worth, TX 76129
$12, 16, Stanley Trachtenberg, Betsy Colquitt, Harry Opperman

Dialogue
University Station
UMC-7805
Logan, UT 84332
$25, F. Ross Peterson, Mary Kay Peterson

Eagle's Flight
2501 Hunter's Hill Drive, No. 822

Enid, OK 73703
Rekha Kulkarni

Elle
1633 Broadway
New York, NY 10019
$24, 2, John Howell

Epoch
251 Goldwin Smith Hall
Cornell University
Ithaca, NY 14853-3201
$11, 23, Michael Koch

Esquire
1790 Broadway
New York, NY 10019
$17.94, 6, Rust Hills

Essence
1500 Broadway
New York, NY 10036
$12.96, 6, Stephanie Stokes Oliver

event
c/o Douglas College
P.O. Box 2503
New Westminster, British Columbia
V3L 5B2 Canada
$15, 18, Maurice Hodgson

Fantasy & Science Fiction
P.O. Box 56
Cornwall, CT 06753
$21, 75, Edward L. Ferman

Farmer's Market
P.O. Box 1272
Galesburg, IL 61402
$8, 10, Jean C. Lee

Fiction
Fiction, Inc.
Department of English
The City College of New York
New York, NY 10031
$7, 15, Mark Mirsky

Fiction International
Department of English and
Comparative Literature
San Diego State University
San Diego, CA 92182
$14, Harold Jaffe, Larry McCaffery

Fiction Network
P.O. Box 5651
San Francisco, CA 94101
$8, 25, Jay Schaefer

Fiddlehead
Room 317, Old Arts Building
University of New Brunswick
Fredericton, New Brunswick
E3B 5A3 Canada
$16, 20, Don McKay

Florida Review
Department of English
University of Central Florida
P.O. Box 25000
Orlando, FL 32816
$7, 14, Pat Rushin

Folio
Department of Literature
The American University
Washington, D.C. 20016
$10, 12, Elisabeth Poliner

Four Quarters
LaSalle University
20th and Olney Avenues
Philadelphia, PA 19141
$8, 10, John J. Keenan

Free Press
P.O. Box 581
Bronx, NY 10463
$25, 10, Michael Broder

Gamut
1218 Fen Tower
Cleveland State University
Cleveland, OH 44115
$15, 4, Louis T. Milic

Georgia Review
University of Georgia
Athens, GA 30602
$18, 10, Stanley W. Lindberg

Gettysburg Review
Gettysburg College
Gettysburg, PA 17325
$15, 10, Peter Stitt

Glamour
350 Madison Avenue
New York, NY 10017
$20.50, 3, Laura Mathews

GlimmerTrain Stories
812 SW Washington Street
Suite 1205
Portland, OR 97205
$29, 40, Susan Burmeister, Linda Davies

Good Housekeeping
959 Eighth Avenue
New York, NY 10019
$17.97, 7, Arleen L. Quarfoot

GQ
350 Madison Avenue
New York, NY 10017
$19.97, 12, Thomas Mallon

Grain
Box 1154
Regina, Saskatchewan
S4P 3B4 Canada
$15, 21, Geoffrey Ursell

Grand Street
131 Varick Street
New York, NY 10013
$30, 20, Jean Stein

Granta
250 West 57th Street, Suite 1316
New York, NY 10107
$28, Anne Kinard

Gray's Sporting Journal
205 Willow Street
South Hamilton, MA 01982
$34.95, 4, Edward E. Gray

Great River Review
211 West 7th
Winona, MN 55987
$10, 6, Ruth Forsythe et al.

Green Mountain Review
Box A 58
Johnson State College
Johnson, VT 05656
$4, 8, Tony Whedon

Greensboro Review
Department of English
University of North Carolina
Greensboro, NC 27412
$8, 16, Jim Clark

Gulf Coast
Department of English
University of Houston
4800 Calhoun Road
Houston, TX 77204-3012
$22, 10, Alexis Quinn, Amy Storrow

Gulf Stream
English Department
Florida International University
North Miami Campus
North Miami, FL 33181
$4, 6, Lynne Barrett

Habersham Review
Piedmont College
Demorest, GA 30535-0010
$8, David L. Greene, Lisa Hodgens Lumkin

Hadassah
50 West 58th Street
New York, NY 10019
$4, 2, Zelda Shluker

Harper's Magazine
666 Broadway
New York, NY 10012
$18, 9, Lewis H. Lapham

Hawaii Review
University of Hawaii
Department of English
1733 Donaghho Road
Honolulu, HI 96822

$15, 18, Carrie Hoshino, Michael McGinnis

Hayden's Ferry Review
Matthews Center
Arizona State University
Tempe, AZ 85287-1502
$10, 8, Deborah Partington, Linda Faber Swenson

High Plains Literary Review
180 Adams Street, Suite 250
Denver, CO 80206
$20, 7, Robert O. Greer, Jr.

Hudson Review
684 Park Avenue
New York, NY 10021
$24, 8, Paula Deitz, Frederick Morgan

Hyphen
3458 W. Devon Ave., No. 6
Lincolnwood, IL 60659
$12, 8, Margaret Lewis, Dave Mead

Idler
255 Davenport Road
Toronto, Ontario
M5R 1J9 Canada
$28.50, 3, David Warren

Indiana Review
316 North Jordan Avenue
Bloomington, IN 47405
$12, 13, Dorian Gossy

Innisfree
P.O. Box 277
Manhattan Beach, CA 90266
$22, 100, Rex Winn

Interim
Department of English
University of Nevada
4505 Maryland Parkway
Las Vegas, NV 89154
$8, A. Wilber Stevens

Iowa Review
Department of English
University of Iowa
308 EPB
Iowa City, IA 52242
$18, 10, David Hamilton

Iowa Woman
P.O. Box 680
Iowa City, IA 52244
$15, 15, Marianne Abel

Isaac Asimov's Science Fiction
Davis Publications, Inc.
380 Lexington Avenue
New York, NY 10017
$25.97, 27, Gardner Dozois

Italian Americana
University of Rhode Island
College of Continuing Education
199 Promenade Street
Providence, RI 02908
$25, 6, Carol BonoMo Ahearn

Jewish Currents
22 East 17th Street, Suite 601
New York, NY 10003-3272
$20, 8, editorial board

Journal
Department of English
Ohio State University
164 West 17th Avenue
Columbus, OH 43210
$8, 5, Michelle Herman

Kalliope
Florida Community College
3939 Roosevelt Blvd.
Jacksonville, FL 32205
$10.50, 12, Mary Sue Koeppel

Kansas Quarterly
Department of English
Denison Hall
Kansas State University
Manhattan, KS 66506
$20, 18, Ben Nyberg, John Rees, C. W. Clift

Karamu
English Department
Eastern Illinois University

Charleston, IL 61920
Peggy L. Brayfield

Kenyon Review
Kenyon College
Gambier, OH 43022
$22, 15, Marilyn Hacker

Kinesis
P.O. Box 4007
Whitefish, MT 59937-4007
$18, 6, David Hipschman

Konch
Ishmael Reed Publishing Co.
P.O. Box 3288
Berkeley, CA 94703
$14.95, 6, Ishmael Reed

Laurel Review
Department of English
Northwest Missouri State University
Maryville, MO 64468
$8, 20, Craig Goad, David Slater

Left Bank
Blue Heron Publishing, Inc.
24450 N.W. Hansen Road
Hillsboro, OR 97124
$14, 6, Linny Stoval

Lilith
The Jewish Women's Magazine
250 West 57th Street
New York, NY 10107
$16, 5, Susan Weidman

Literary Review
Fairleigh Dickinson University
285 Madison Avenue
Madison, NJ 07940
$18, 10, Walter Cummins

The Little Magazine
English Department
SUNY
Albany, NY 12222
$6, 7, John Sandman

Lost Creek Letters
Box 373A
Rushville, MO 64484
$15, 10, Pamela Montgomery

Louisiana Literature
Box 792
Southeastern Louisiana University
Hammond, LA 70402
$10, 8, David Hanson

Louisville Review
Bingham Humanities 315
University of Louisville
Louisville, KY 40292
$10, 5, Sena Jeter Naslund

McCall's
110 Fifth Avenue
New York, NY 10011
$15.94, 6, Laura Manske

Mademoiselle
350 Madison Avenue
New York, NY 10017
$28, 10, Ellen Welty

Madison Review
University of Wisconsin
Department of English
H. C. White Hall
600 North Park Street
Madison, WI 53706
$7, 8, Sara Goldberg

Malahat Review
University of Victoria
P.O. Box 1700
Victoria, British Columbia
V8W 2Y2 Canada
$15, 20, Derk Wynand

Manoa
English Department
University of Hawaii
Honolulu, HI 96822
$18, 12, Robert Shapard, Frank Stewart

Maryland Review
Department of English and
Languages

University of Maryland, Eastern Shore
Princess Anne, MD 21853
$6, 7, Chester M. Hedgepeth, Jr., Cary C. Holladay

Massachusetts Review
Memorial Hall
University of Massachusetts
Amherst, MA 01003
$15, 3, Mary Heath, Jules Chametzky, Paul Jenkins

Matrix
c.p. 100 Ste.-Anne-de-Bellevue
Quebec
H9X 3L4 Canada
$15, 8, Linda Leith

Metropolitan
6307 North 31st Street
Arlington, VA 22207
$7, 13, Jacqueline Bergsohn

Michigan Quarterly Review
3032 Rackham Building
University of Michigan
Ann Arbor, MI 48109
$18, 10, Laurence Goldstein

Mid-American Review
106 Hanna Hall
Department of English
Bowling Green State University
Bowling Green, OH 43403
$8, 11, Ellen Behrens

Minnesota Review
Department of English
State University of New York
Stony Brook, NY 11794-5350
$8, 10, Fred Pfeil

Mirabella
200 Madison Avenue
New York, NY 10016
$17.98, 6, Pat Towers

Mississippi Review
University of Southern Mississippi
Southern Station, P.O. Box 5144
Hattiesburg, MS 39406-5144
$10, 25, Frederick Barthelme

Missouri Review
Department of English
231 Arts and Sciences
University of Missouri
Columbia, MO 65211
$15, 23, Speer Morgan

Mother Jones
1663 Mission Street
2nd floor
San Francisco, CA 94103
$18, 3, Jeffrey Klein

Ms.
230 Park Avenue
New York, NY 10169
$45, 7, Robin Morgan

Nassau Review
English Department
Nassau Community College
One Education Drive
Garden City, NY 11530-6793
Paul A. Doyle

Nebraska Review
Writers' Workshop
ASH 212
University of Nebraska
Omaha, NE 68182-0324
$6, 10, Art Homer, Richard Duggin

Negative Capability
62 Ridgelawn Drive East
Mobile, AL 36605
$12, 15, Sue Walker

New Delta Review
Creative Writing Program
English Department
Louisiana State University
Baton Rouge, LA 70803
$7, 9, David Tilley

New England Review
Middlebury College
Middlebury, VT 05753
$18, 9, T. R. Hummer

New Letters
University of Missouri
4216 Rockhill Road
Kansas City, MO 64110
$17, 10, James McKinley

New Mexico Humanities Review
P.O. Box A
New Mexico Tech
Socorro, NM 87801
$8, 15, John Rothfork

New Orleans Review
P.O. Box 195
Loyola University
New Orleans, LA 70118
$25, 4, John Biguenet, John Mosier

New Quarterly
English Language Proficiency Programme
University of Waterloo
Waterloo, Ontario
N2L 3G1 Canada
$14, 15, Peter Hinchcliffe

New Renaissance
9 Heath Road
Arlington, MA 02174
$11.50, 5, Louise T. Reynolds

New Yorker
25 West 43rd Street
New York, NY 10036
$32, 50, Tina Brown

Nimrod
Arts and Humanities Council of Tulsa
2210 South Main Street
Tulsa, OK 74114
$10, 10, Francine Ringold

North American Review
University of Northern Iowa
1222 West 27th Street
Cedar Falls, IA 50614
$18, 13, Robley Wilson, Jr.

North Atlantic Review
15 Arbutus Lane
Stony Brook, NY 11790-1408
$10, 9, John Gill

North Dakota Quarterly
University of North Dakota
P.O. Box 8237
Grand Forks, ND 58202
$15, 13, Robert W. Lewis

North Stone Review
Box 14098, D Station
Minneapolis, MN 55414
$15, 4, James Naiden

Northwest Review
369 PLC
University of Oregon
Eugene, OR 97403
$14, 10, Hannah Wilson

Ohio Review
Ellis Hall
Ohio University
Athens, OH 45701-2979
$16, 10, Wayne Dodd

Old Hickory Review
P.O. Box 1178
Jackson, TN 38301
$4, 6, Dorothy Starfill

Omni
1965 Broadway
New York, NY 10023-5965
$24, 20, Ellen Datlow

Ontario Review
9 Honey Brook Drive
Princeton, NJ 08540
$10, 8, Raymond J. Smith

Open City
118 Riverside Drive, Suite 14A
New York, NY 10024
$20, 12, Thomas Beller

Other Voices
University of Illinois at Chicago
Department of English
(M/C 162) Box 4348

Chicago, IL 60680
$16, 30, Sharon Fiffer, Lois Hauselman

Oxalis
Stone Ridge Poetry Society
P.O. Box 3993
Kingston, NY 12401
$18, 12, Shirley Powell

Oxford American
115½ South Lamar
Oxford, MS 38655
$16, 12, Marc Smirnoff

Paris Review
541 East 72nd Street
New York, NY 10021
$24, 10, George Plimpton

Parting Gifts
3006 Stonecutter Terrace
Greensboro, NC 27405
Robert Bixby

Partisan Review
236 Bay State Road
Boston, MA 02215
$18, 4, William Phillips

Passages North
Kalamazoo College
1200 Academy Street
Kalamazoo, MI 49007
$5, 8, Mary LaChapelle

Pikeville Review
Humanities Division
Pikeville College
Pikeville, KY 41501
$4, 6, James Alan Riley

Playboy
Playboy Building
919 North Michigan Avenue
Chicago, IL 60611
$24, 10, Alice K. Turner

Ploughshares
Emerson College
100 Beacon Street
Boston, MA 02116
$19, 15, Don Lee

Potpourri
P.O. Box 8278
Prairie Village, KS 66208
$12, 48, Polly W. Swafford

Prairie Schooner
201 Andrews Hall
University of Nebraska
Lincoln, NE 68588-0334
$20, 20, Hilda Raz

Prism International
Department of Creative Writing
University of British Columbia
Vancouver, British Columbia
V6T 1W5 Canada
$16, 20, Zsuzsi Gartner

Provincetown Arts
650 Commercial Street
Provincetown, MA 02657
$9, 4, Christopher Busa

Puerto del Sol
P.O. Box 3E
Department of English
New Mexico State University
Las Cruces, NM 88003
$10, 12, Kevin McIlvoy, Antonya Nelson

Quarry Magazine
P.O. Box 1061
Kingston, Ontario
K7L 4Y5 Canada
$20.33, 20, Steven Heighton

Quarterly
Vintage Books
201 East 50th Street
New York, NY 10022
$36, 81, Gordon Lish

Quarterly West
317 Olpin Uniòn
University of Utah
Salt Lake City, UT 84112
$11, 10, Darin Cain, Jeffrey Vasseur

RE:AL
School of Liberal Arts
Stephen F. Austin State University
P.O. Box 13007, SFA Station
Nacogdoches, TX 75962
$8, 5, Lee Schultz

Redbook
959 Eighth Avenue
New York, NY 10017
$11.97, 10, Dawn Raffel

River Styx
Big River Association
14 South Euclid
St. Louis, MO 63108
$20, 30, Lee Schreiner

Room of One's Own
P.O. Box 46160, Station G
Vancouver, British Columbia
V6R 4G5 Canada
$20, 12, rotating editorship

Salmagundi
Skidmore College
Saratoga Springs, NY 12866
$15, 4, Robert Boyers

San Jose Studies
c/o English Department
San Jose State University
One Washington Square
San Jose, CA 95192
$12, 5, Fauneil J. Rinn

Santa Monica Review
Center for the Humanities
Santa Monica College
1900 Pico Boulevard
Santa Monica, CA 90405
$12, 16, Jim Krusoe

Saturday Night
511 King Street West, Suite 100
Toronto, Ontario
M5V 2Z4 Canada
$26.45, 7, Anne Collins, Dianna Simmons

Seattle Review
Padelford Hall, GN-30
University of Washington
Seattle, WA 98195
$8, 12, Charles Johnson

Seventeen
850 Third Avenue
New York, NY 10022
$13.95, 8, Sarah Patton Duncan

Sewanee Review
University of the South
Sewanee, TN 37375-4009
$16, 10, George Core

Shenandoah
Washington and Lee University
P.O. Box 722
Lexington, VA 24450
$11, 17, Dabney Stuart

Short Fiction by Women
Box 1276 Stuyvesant Station
New York, NY 10009
$18, 20, Rachel Whalen

Sinister Wisdom
P.O. Box 3252
Berkeley, CA 94703
$17, 25, Elana Dykewoman

Snake Nation Review
2920 North Oak
Valdosta, GA 31602
$12, 16, Roberta George

Sonora Review
Department of English
University of Arizona
Tucson, AZ 85721
$10, 12, Jane Martin

So to Speak
4400 University Drive
George Mason University
Fairfax, VA 22030-444
$7, 10, Colleen Kearney

South Carolina Review
Department of English

Clemson University
Clemson, SC 29634-1503
$7, 8, Richard C. Calhoun

South Dakota Review
University of South Dakota
P.O. Box 111 University Exchange
Vermillion, SD 57069
$15, 15, John R. Milton

Southern California Anthology
Master of Professional Writing
Program WPH 404
University of Southern California
Los Angeles, CA 90089–4034
$7.95, 10, Richard P. Aloia, Jr.

Southern Exposure
P.O. Box 531
Durham, NC 27702
$24, 12, Susan Ketchin

Southern Humanities Review
9088 Haley Center
Auburn University
Auburn, AL 36849
$15, 5, Dan R. Latimer, Thomas L. Wright

Southern Review
43 Allen Hall
Louisiana State University
Baton Rouge, LA 70803
$18, 17, James Olney, Dave Smith

Southwest Review
Southern Methodist University
P.O. Box 4374
Dallas, TX 75275
$20, 15, Willard Spiegelman

Sou'wester
School of Humanities
Department of English
Southern Illinois University
Edwardsville, IL 62026-1438
$10, 10, Roger Ridenour

Stories
14 Beacon Street
Boston, MA 02108
$18, 12, Amy R. Kaufman

Story
1507 Dana Avenue
Cincinnati, OH 45207
$17, 52, Lois Rosenthal

Story Quarterly
P.O. Box 1416
Northbrook, IL 60065
$12, 20, Margaret Barrett, Anne Brashler, Diane Williams

Strange Plasma
Edgewood Press
P.O. Box 264
Cambridge, MA 02238
$10, Steve Pasechnick

Sun
107 North Roberson Street
Chapel Hill, NC 27516
$30, 30, Sy Safransky

Tampa Review
P.O. Box 19F
University of Tampa
401 West Kennedy Boulevard
Tampa, FL 33606-1490
$10, 2, Andy Solomon

Thema
Box 74109
Metairie, LA 70053-4109
$16, Virginia Howard

Threepenny Review
P.O. Box 9131
Berkeley, CA 94709
$12, 10, Wendy Lesser

Tikkun
5100 Leona Street
Oakland, CA 94619
$36, 10, Michael Lerner

Touchstone
Tennessee Humanities Council
P.O. Box 24767

Nashville, TN 37202
Robert Cheatham

TriQuarterly
2020 Ridge Avenue
Northwestern University
Evanston, IL 60208
$20, 15, Reginald Gibbons

Turnstile
175 Fifth Avenue, Suite 2348
New York, NY 10010
$24, 12, group editorship

University of Windsor Review
Department of English
University of Windsor
Windsor, Ontario
N9B 3P4 Canada
$10, 6, Joseph A. Quinn

Urbanus
P.O. Box 192561
San Francisco, CA 94119
$8, 4, Peter Drizhal

Vincent Brothers Review
4566 Northern Circle
Mad River Township
Dayton, OH 45424
$4.50, 12, Kimberly A. Willardson

Virginia Quarterly Review
One West Range
Charlottesville, VA 22903
$15, 14, Staige D. Blackford

Voice Literary Supplement
842 Broadway
New York, NY 10003
$17, 8, M. Mark

Wascana Review
English Department
University of Regina
Regina, Saskatchewan
S4S 0A2 Canada
$7, 8, J. Shami

Weber Studies
Weber State College
Ogden, UT 84408
$10, 2, Neila Seshachari

Webster Review
Webster University
470 East Lockwood
Webster Groves, MO 63119
$5, 2, Nancy Schapiro

Wellspring
770 Tonkawa Road
Long Lake, MN 55356
$8, 10, Maureen LaJoy

West Branch
Department of English
Bucknell University
Lewisburg, PA 17837
$7, 10, Robert Love Taylor

West Wind Review
Stevenson Union, Room 321
Southern Oregon State College
1250 Siskiyou Boulevard
Ashland, OR 97520
$6, 11, Dale Vidmar, Catherine Ordal

Western Humanities Review
University of Utah
Salt Lake City, UT 84112
$18, 10, Barry Weller

Whetstone
Barrington Area Arts Council
P.O. Box 1266
Barrington, IL 60011
$6.25, 11, Sandra Berris

William and Mary Review
College of William and Mary
P.O. Box 8795
Williamsburg, VA 23187
$5, 4, Collin Heffern, Thom Zadra

Willow Springs
MS-1
Eastern Washington University
Cheney, WA 99004
$8, 8, Paul Leathers

Wind
RFD Route 1
P.O. Box 809K
Pikeville, KY 41501
$7, 20, Quentin R. Howard

Witness
31000 Northwestern Highway, Suite 200
Farmington Hills, MI 48018
$16, 15, Peter Stine

Worcester Review
6 Chatham Street
Worcester, MA 01690
$10, 8, Rodger Martin

Writ
Innis College
University of Toronto
2 Sussex Avenue
Toronto, Ontario
M5S 1J5 Canada
$15, 7, Roger Greenwald

Writers Forum
University of Colorado
P.O. Box 7150
Colorado Springs, CO 80933-7150
$8.95, 15, Alexander Blackburn

Xavier Review
Xavier University
Box 110C
New Orleans, LA 70125
6, Thomas Bonner, Jr.

Yale Review
1902A Yale Station
New Haven, CT 06520
$20, 12, J. D. McClatchy

Yankee
Yankee Publishing, Inc.
Dublin, NH 03444
$22, 4, Judson D. Hale, Sr.

Yellow Silk
P.O. Box 6374
Albany, CA 94706
$30, 10, Lily Pond

Yokoi
415 E. Olive
Bozeman, MT 59715
$16, 5, Marjorie Smith

ZYZZYVA
41 Sutter Street, Suite 1400
San Francisco, CA 94104
$28, 12, Howard Junker